The Girls In The Basement

ALSO BY STEENA HOLMES

BERVIE SPRINGS SERIES
Book 1: Engaged To A Serial Killer
Book 2: The Twin

STANDALONES
The Sister Under The Stairs
The Girls In The Basement

THE GIRLS IN THE BASEMENT

STEENA HOLMES

JOFFE BOOKS

Joffe Books, London
www.joffebooks.com

First published in Great Britain in 2025

Cover art by Nick Castle

ISBN: 978-1-80573-057-6

TRIGGER WARNING

Dear thriller reader . . .

In case you thought you were picking up a different book to read — this is a psychological thriller novel.

As psychological thriller readers, you and I both know that these books often delve into 'controversial' plot lines. It's part of the thrill, isn't it?

For those looking for a trigger warning — consider this it.

Overall — I hope you enjoy the read!

I dedicate this book to my youngest daughter, Judah.
She complained I've never dedicated a book only to her, so here it is.
I wonder how long it will take her to realize
I've done this . . . any guesses?
(for the record — I know she'll see this eventually . . .)

CHAPTER ONE

Lola

The echo of a slamming door shatters the silence, jolting Lola into action. The rising chaotic symphony of voices has her closing the oven door with a quick flick of her wrist. She snatches her sweater and slips out the side door, her movements swift and silent like a shadow.

She makes it just in time.

Dropping into a crouch, Lola sneaks around the corner to her regular hiding spot behind a tall bush. With her fingers crossed, she whispers a silent prayer that no one will notice her absence.

As long as no one notices she's not there, she's safe.

Staying safe is the only way she's managed to survive so far, and survival is key if she ever hopes to escape this place.

"You couldn't have given me a heads-up?" Mother's voice, coming through the open window, is rough, harsh, and sharper than the knives she keeps locked in the drawer.

"Maybe check your messages. I called from the road." The gruff snarl grows louder. That voice belongs to Jerold, a man Lola has learned to stay away from as much as possible.

There is a sound from above, and she knows that if she only looked up, she'd see him standing over her.

She doesn't look up.

"It's been a little busy here. We don't have room for all of them. I told you that last time."

"And like I told you, I don't get no say. I do as I'm told, just like you. If you've got an issue with it, the Oil Man is at the house. I saw him pull in."

Nothing is said for a long time, and Lola wonders if they've left the room until she hears the slamming of a cupboard door and the tap turning on.

"He's not the one I deal with, and you know it." Lola recognizes the weariness in Mother's voice. "What am I supposed to do with them down there?" Mother sounds exasperated and stressed. She doesn't like it when there are too many girls in the house. She says it's not safe and that mistakes tend to happen when people become sloppy.

"If all you're going to do is bitch about it, I'm leaving." Jerold's feet thud on the floor as he walks away. "Any I can take with me?"

Lola freezes.

"You're kidding me, right?"

"Never stopped you from giving me one before."

Mother sighs. "The one you wanted is already gone. If I'd known you were coming . . ." Mother lets the sentence fall, insinuating this is all on him.

"How about next time you just answer the damn phone. I'm supposed to get one to take with me, and you know it. It's part of my deal."

"You've already had your girl this month. Don't be greedy."

"It gets lonely out there."

"Not my problem. I thought you said you were leaving. I don't have time to chit-chat, not with all them rats downstairs."

A rush of air releases from Lola's chest; it sounds loud to her ears. She looks up toward the window and can barely make out Mother's hair, which she's tied into a braid. She feels something brush up against her ankles and glances down to see Mabel, a black cat with white paws, weaving her way around Lola's legs. Without thinking, Lola reaches down to pet the purring cat.

"Some days you're an effin—"

"Don't bother finishing that sentence," Mother interrupts him, "unless you're ready to handle the consequences." The threat in Mother's voice is real, and a tiny smile grows on Lola's face. The only person Lola's ever seen stand up to Jerold is Mother, and she often leaves him quaking in his boots.

The thud of footsteps trails off, followed by a slam of a door and then the rev of an engine. Jerold is leaving.

"All right, you." Mother's voice comes from above her. "You can come out now, he's gone, and we've got work to do."

Slowly, Lola climbs to her feet and turns to look through the window. Mother frowns and waves her inside.

The first thing Lola does is head to the oven and open the door. Using a kitchen towel, she pulls out the casserole dish and sets it on top of the stove. Thankfully, it didn't burn.

"Well, that's not going to be enough," Mother complains. "I'm sure you heard, but we've got more girls downstairs. What else can you whip up?"

Lola opens the pantry door and heaves out a big Tupperware container of dehydrated mashed potato mix.

Mother nods. "That will do. We've got a dozen mouths to feed now." Her lips withdraw into a solid straight line while her hands land on her hips. "What are they thinking, sending us more girls like that at the last minute?"

Lola pulls a large pot from the bottom cupboard, fills it with water, and sets it on the stove.

Mother's phone rings, and she heaves a long sigh. "Yes, ma'am," she says as she answers. "Yes indeed, he just brought them." Mother pauses as she listens. "All of them?" Her forehead puckers as she listens. "The other girls are ready, but this new batch . . ." Lola watches as a flash of anger rushes across

3

Mother's face. "If you insist," she says, her voice tight. "Yes, I'll have them ready first thing." She slams her phone down on the table with a thud. "Who the hell does she think she is talking to me like that . . . ?" Mother's voice trails off.

"That woman will be here first thing for her inspection, so make sure this place is cleaned up nice, and then stay out of the way unless you want to be added to the lineup," Mother warns. "I can only protect you for so long, but eventually, it won't matter. All it takes is for one person to notice you; you realize that, don't you? Don't you forget I'm the reason you're still alive."

"Yes, Mother," Lola whispers, her voice full of anything but thankfulness. "I can help with the new ones tonight," she offers. "I know how important tomorrow is."

"What do you know about tomorrow, huh?" Mother's hand lifts, ready to strike, then drops.

Lola bows her head and wishes she could hide.

"Like it or not, those girls need to be ready. What the hell am I going to do about everything now? I can't make diamonds out of shit within a few hours." Mother runs her hands over her long braid, over and over, as she stares about the room.

Lola focuses on the pot, hoping it will hurry and boil. Mother may forget she's even here if she stands still long enough.

The squeak of a chair as it is pulled from the table sends shivers up Lola's spine, but she remains still.

"Tomorrow is going to be a long day." Mother rubs her face, and Lola takes that time to spoon dry flakes of dehydrated potatoes into the pot. "You know the plan."

Lola nods. Once a month, she climbs into her hiding spot and stays there all day. It's the same routine she's had for longer than she can remember. Out of sight, off the auction line. She hates that space, though. It's cramped and hot, and sometimes the auction takes forever. A few times, she was almost caught because she had to sneak out to use the washroom.

"Maybe we should start thinking about alternative arrangements," Mother says, her head cocked to the side as she studies

Lola. "It might be best to get you out of the house completely. One of these days, a girl will slip up and mention you."

Lola's breath hitches in her chest, and a cascading waterfall of chills runs over her body. Nothing good ever happens to anyone who leaves the house, even for a short period. Alternative arrangements mean being given to someone as a reward, and Lola doesn't like being someone's reward.

Those given as a reward are never brought back. Lola doesn't know exactly what happens to them, but she knows they end up dead and left in some field to rot, forgotten.

"I'll need to think about it," Mother tells her, pushing her chair back. "Finish with that food and bring it downstairs. It's going to be a long night."

Lola turns and gives Mother a slight nod. She'll do anything and everything she can not to be on that block. That's all she's done for the past ten years or more, doing whatever is needed to protect herself.

Tomorrow night is the monthly auction party, where the twelve girls from downstairs will be sold like cattle to whoever is willing to pay the highest price for a sex slave.

If it weren't for her disfigurement, Lola herself would have been sold on that block. It's what she'd been born for, after all.

CHAPTER TWO

Jillian

Speeding through the ribbon of country roads that slice through northern Montana, Jillian Harper's heart pounds like a drumbeat against her ribs.

"Damn it. Damnit, damnit, damnit, damnit." She grips the steering wheel a little tighter as she wills time to stop moving.

Ethan's school bus is due to leave in exactly two minutes. Douglas, the driver, doesn't wait for anyone, not even if he sees the dust cloud of her truck in his rearview mirror. She's learned that the hard way.

"Mom, it's 7:43. We're not going to make it." Ethan's worry-laced voice cuts through the diesel truck's loud hum.

"We'll make it, bud," Jillian reassures him, more to convince herself than her son. Her knuckles on the steering wheel whiten, the leather creaking beneath her grip. They round the final bend, and there it is — the yellow school bus idling by a lone signpost that serves as the bus stop, its red lights flashing a lazy warning in the crisp morning air.

Jillian brings the truck to a halt right in front of the bus, gravel crunching beneath her tires. She throws a quick glance in the rearview mirror and waves at Douglas, who only shakes his head when he taps the watch on his wrist.

"Have a great day, kiddo," Jillian says as her son unbuckles his seatbelt and hops out of the truck with the energy only an eleven-year-old can possess. She, on the other hand, struggles to contain a yawn.

Jillian watches her son climb the stairs, then leans her head back against her seat with a sigh.

She calls her husband and waits for him to pick up, like she has all morning, except, just like what's happened all morning, it goes to voicemail.

"Seriously, Tuck? Where the hell are you?" She hangs up and pounds the steering wheel. She hit the ground running this morning from sleeping in, the coffee machine going on the fritz, and then the stupid washing machine overflowing and flooding her floor. She gave Ethan both a banana and a granola bar for breakfast while she raced toward the bus, and now she can only pray there are no police cars hanging around on the backroads since she's going to be late for work. Again.

She sends Trina, her co-worker, a quick text asking her to cover her desk, just in case. She watches the speedometer inch higher and higher as she races toward town. If she can just beat the clock, hopefully, her tardiness won't be noticed by too many. Specifically, her boss. Jake Walkin is one of the worst people she's ever met, and yet job opportunities in Shelby, Montana, are sparse unless she wants to work at one of the hotel chains.

When the door swings open, she feels every eye on her. As the head office for Supply & Co, a local supply chain within Montana, Jillian's role is the front desk, where she covers the phones, deals with customers, and handles anything else thrown on her desk. Lately, it's been a lot of invoicing. Behind her desk is an open space with four cubicles and then five offices for the higher-ups.

Sitting at Jillian's desk, Trina looks up from the computer, her lips pursed in silent disapproval. She knows Trina hates covering for her, not just that she hates the desk, but she hates her sense of order being disrupted by the unexpected.

"Sorry, Trina, this morning has just been . . . hellish," Jillian says as she pulls out her bottom desk drawer and drops her purse in it.

"Clearly," Trina replies, her words clipped. She stands and gathers the papers she's been working on, her motions precise and deliberate.

"Anything urgent come up?" Jillian asks, hoping her attempt at normalcy will smooth the tension. She knew Trina would be prickly, but not like this.

"Wouldn't know, would I? Not my desk, not my job," Trina retorts, handing over a stack of messages with an air of measured detachment.

Jillian accepts the silent rebuke and the messages, offering a nod of thanks masked in humility. Trina's heels click a steady rhythm against the linoleum floor as she walks toward her own office. Trina once sat at this desk but was then promoted to head some of their client list. Her promotion meant she'd never have to cover the desk again, so Jillian does her best to make sure it doesn't happen too often.

Unfortunately, that's not always easy.

The hours pass by in a blur as Jillian puts out one fire after another, answering emails and taking messages. Her *tap-tap-tap* on the keyboard adds to the muted conversations within the office.

"I'm in a better mood now." Trina leans against the edge of her desk, her hands clasped in front of her. "Spill it." Her eyes hold a flicker of concern beneath her stern facade.

Jillian pauses midsentence and pushes her keyboard away. "This morning was crazy, and everything just piled up." She stops briefly to collect her scattered thoughts. "I forgot to set my alarm, the coffee machine decided to quit working, then when I threw a load into the washer, it decided to spring a leak at the worst possible time, and I couldn't find Tucker to help."

"Again, with the vanishing act?" Trina raises an eyebrow, skepticism etched into her expression.

Jillian's first instinct is to defend her husband, but Trina's words hit a nerve. "Yeah, again. Almost missed the bus this morning, too."

"Kid stuff, house chaos, husbands . . . It never ends, does it?" Trina's voice softens, the edge giving way to empathy.

"Feels like some days are cursed, you know?" Jillian shakes her head as she pushes aside the stack of messages she needs to take care of.

"You should have Tucker take Ethan to the game tonight and enjoy some quiet time at the house," Trina suggests. "Have a bath, drink some wine, you know, me time. And call Miller Jones — he's the best in town and can take care of whatever is wrong with your washer."

"Already taken care of," Jillian says. "He was my first call after Tucker didn't pick up."

"Where do you think he goes?"

Jillian shrugs. "Checking out the property, I think. There's so much to do . . ."

"I think everyone in town was surprised when it sold. Old Man Cummings swore he'd hold on to that land till his dying breath, and then he upped and moved to what . . . Florida? Craziest thing any of us ever heard."

Jillian has no words to say. Since they moved to Montana, all they've heard is how strange it is that the old owner just upped and left. Seems no one really knows the whole truth.

And everyone calls him Old Man Cummings, which in itself is weird.

She glances out the window, noting the sun's arc is high in the sky. Shelby's quaint charm feels like a facade, hiding some obscure truth just beyond her reach. Even though she's used to small-town life, moving to this small country town has been a hard adjustment. With the local population only hitting slightly above three thousand residents, everyone

9

knows everyone, all their secrets are old news, and the idea of new blood has all the old townie folks hungry for new gossip. That's all she and Tucker are to them, even though it's been three months now — just new gossip.

The wail of sirens pierces the air, drawing Jillian's gaze to where she can see the flurry of activity on Main Street from the main window. Police cruisers with their lights flashing speed by, one after another, heading toward the outskirts of Shelby. She counts three . . . no, four cars blurring past, their urgency sending a shiver down her spine.

"Another one?" Trina murmurs as she stands by the window, craning her neck to catch a glimpse. "What in the world is going on?" She pulls up the blinds for a better view just as the sheriff's vehicle rushes by. "Unless it's something big." Trina's eyes are wide with speculation. "You know Sheriff Landry's been cracking down on all that drug mess. Maybe they found another stash — or worse."

Almost everyone leaves the office and stands out on the sidewalk, Jillian included. Her old town was never like this — so intrigued by anything new. Most people have left the storefronts and businesses to stand on the sidewalk and watch the cruisers speed by. A few minutes drag on until the sound of the sirens is lost in the wind, and one by one, everyone returns to what they were doing before all the commotion.

"All right, folks." Jake, Jillian's boss, stands at the door and claps his hands. "The excitement is over, and I need everyone back to work. We've got a mountain to climb before day's end," he says, "and if it doesn't get done, we're all staying late."

A grumble of groans fills the small space. Jillian puts her head down and refocuses her attention on the files she's been given. Although her official title is office manager, she does everything, from data entry to ordering supplies and, of course, being the face of the office — aka the receptionist.

By the time she glances at her phone again, it's almost three o'clock and there's still been no word from Tucker.

The door to the office jingles, and Jillian glances up with a smile.

"Hey, did you hear about all the cops flying through town?" Martha Jenkins, Shelby's self-appointed informant/gossiper, stands at Jillian's desk, breathless — whether due to her trek from wherever she came from, or excitement, Jillian can't tell.

"Hard not to notice." Jillian keeps her tone neutral. "Any idea why?"

Martha leans in, lowering her voice to a conspiratorial whisper. "I heard from Janie, who heard from Pete at the diner, that they're headed toward the old mill. Says it looks like they're prepping for a raid of some sort." Her eyes gleam with the thrill of the rumor.

Jillian's brows rise while she tries to keep her voice calm. "A raid? In Shelby? I thought this was a town where absolutely nothing happens?"

"Oh, honey, if you believe that, you still don't understand what country life is like. There's more going on round these parts than anyone will ever let on. It's northern Montana, after all." Martha's conspiratorial smile grows wide.

"So you tend to get a lot of raids?" Jillian finds this hard to believe.

"Oh, our sheriff is a busy woman. She's part of that big task force we have; don't tell me you haven't heard of it. There's been articles in the bulletin that goes out on the community board, you surely read that?"

Jillian barely has time to respond before Martha barrels on, leaning close.

"Big Sky Safe Trails Taskforce. You'd be surprised at the level of drug and other kinds of smuggling that happens here," Martha says softly. "A lot of serious crime in these parts. Our last sheriff got shot trying to stop stuff like that."

Jillian's eyes widen at the news. Stuff like this isn't supposed to happen in this part of Montana. What happened to it being one of the safest places they could live?

"Well, I'll be off. Chat later." Martha waves before pushing the door open and letting it slam behind her.

"All that woman likes to do is gossip." Jake emerges from his office and eyes the door with disdain. "Next time she comes in, tell her you have work to do. Gossip on your time, not mine." He stands there, arms crossed. "I need you to stay late to finish up the latest round of invoicing. We're nowhere close to being done, and you coming in late didn't help, either."

"Of course," Jillian automatically agrees, the muscle memory of responsibility kicking in.

Moving to Montana was meant to make their lives easier, and in a way it has. Tucker works as a transportation agent within the trucking industry. He started out working for his parents' transport company and, over the years, expanded his expertise so that he works remotely now for a variety of clients. Working remotely has been essential for them over the past few years, and he's in high enough demand that they were able to purchase their home debt-free. While she doesn't need to work, she wants and likes to. There's nothing wrong with being a stay-at-home parent, but with Ethan now in school, getting out of the house has been important to her mental health.

Besides, as much as she loves her husband, being with him all day, every day . . . some couples can do it, but not them. She thought moving here would help save their relationship, but all it's done is put more distance between them, and she doesn't know how to fix that.

An alarm sounds on her phone. Ethan is out of school and should be on the school bus by now. She checks his location, and sure enough, the bus is headed out of town. She checks Tucker's location, and it's still turned off. He hasn't responded to her messages.

Where is he? This has been happening way too often lately.

Forty-five minutes pass, and she gets a text alert from Ethan. *Dad isn't here. Mrs. Allan is going to drop me off at home.*

Jillian sends Stacey Allan a quick text thanking her. She glances at the time and hopes Tucker is home.

Hey — I have to work late, so you're good to take Ethan to his game, right? What could he be doing that has him out of service for so long?

Trina comes out of her office with her purse slung over her shoulder. "I'm on a coffee run since we're all going to need it. Jake says he'll order dinner from next door. So, just your regular vanilla cold brew?"

"That's great, thank you," Jillian says, wondering if she should mention something about being unable to stay. Before she can decide, Trina has left. Biting her lip, Jillian glances behind her to Jake's office. He's on the phone, but he's watching her. Something in his gaze has always unnerved her, so she turns around and opens up the next file on her desk.

When her phone rings and Ethan's photo pops up on the display, her stomach curdles. "Hey, buddy, what's up? How was school?"

"Dad's not here." Three words that contain so much emotion. Jillian winces at Ethan's quiet voice.

"That's okay. I'm on my way."

"But we have that game . . ."

Jillian forces a bright smile into her voice. She can picture her son sitting at the kitchen table, doing his best not to be disappointed. "And we'll get there. How about you get ready and get everything packed? We'll leave as soon as I get to the house, okay?"

"But we have to bring the ice cream treat for after . . . Is there time?"

"Absolutely. Don't you worry, okay? I'll see you soon." Without even thinking, Jillian saves the files she's been working on, closes the computer screen, and pushes the stack of files she still needs to work on to the side. She grabs her purse and heads to Jake's office, knocking lightly on the door.

"Jillian, is there a problem?" Jake's impatience strains through his polite veneer.

"Actually, I need to leave," she confesses, her voice firmer than she feels. "Ethan has a baseball game in Havre. I can't miss it."

"You did hear me earlier? Correct? Everyone needs to stay late."

"I know, and honestly, I thought I could, but my husband is unavailable, so I need to leave." She glances at her watch. "I'll make up for it tomorrow, I promise."

Jake Walkin might scare her, but when it comes to her son, he doesn't stand a chance. Having one parental figure at Ethan's games is important to Jillian — and since Tucker isn't around, it's on her. If she loses her job for placing her family first, so be it.

Although, she doesn't want to lose this job.

"Fine," Jake concedes with a sigh. "I see you've done quite a bit, so thank you. But I'll expect the rest of what's on your desk to be completed tomorrow, regardless of what comes up."

Jillian offers a tight nod, her mind already racing down the highway toward home, to a son who needs stability in his life, and to a husband, who, for whatever reason, seems to have disappeared. Again. Despite the pit in her stomach, Jillian knows her husband well enough to realize something is going on, and they need to have a chat that has been a long time coming.

14

CHAPTER THREE

Agent Meri Amber

Some days are nightmares. Some are horror shows. Others are full of pure evil that scar a person beyond recognition.

Today is that day.

Meri Amber's soul will never be clean again.

"Well done." A hand rests on her shoulder. She swivels in her chair and glances up to see Agent Lindsay standing there, his proverbial frown etched on his face. "You did what no one has been able to do."

She searches his eyes but only sees the horror mirrored from her own. There are days she hates this job. Days she loves it. Then there are days she wishes she'd chosen a different career.

She looks away from him and nudges her head toward the rest of the team. "We did it."

Lindsay scoffs. "This team would never have been able to find them, not in time, at least. Once again, I'm glad you joined the team on an official basis, Special Agent Meri." He wipes at his face with the palm of his hand. "What a fine fucking mess that was, but we'll let them have it."

The mood in the room is jovial and exhaustive at the same time. Weary smiles and back slaps. Hidden yawns and glances at the time.

Today is a day for celebration, and yet all Meri Amber wants to do is head home, pull on her comfiest pajamas, and sleep. She just hopes she won't be plagued by nightmares after today.

Since leaving her police unit and joining the FBI special task force run by Lindsay, they'd been searching for a cell within Idaho, a cell that kidnapped and sold human beings for sex trafficking, and after a year of hot and cold trails, of near misses and long shots, of trailing after a pipeline always a day too late, Meri stumbled upon a group on the dark web that led her directly to the base of operations.

Today, over forty women and men were found within a dozen cathouses, and many more involved in the ring were arrested. The living conditions, the ages of those held hostage. . . those memories can never be wiped clean, and she will always remember their names. Their road to healing is long, but she knows that Lindsay will ensure a team and strategy are in place to help every single person they saved today.

Their whole team, including countless other agencies, have done an excellent job today.

"I, for one, cannot wait to head home and take that vacation you said I deserve." She leans back in her seat and gives an exhaustive sigh. "I'm thinking sandy beach, all-inclusive, hammocks over the water . . ."

Lindsay laughs. "You in a hammock? Over water? In all the time I've known you, you've never stopped long enough to relax."

She gives him a weak smile before closing her eyes briefly. "All I can think about right now is relaxing." She doesn't bother to hide her yawn.

"Go. Get some sleep. I'll arrange flights back for tomorrow." He gives her chair a slight kick. His phone rings, and with a sigh, he walks away to answer it.

Meri pops a sugar-free Halls into her mouth, watching Lindsay. The call could go either way: it's a call of congratulations or a call for another case. She could really use some sleep, so rather than wait to find out, she grabs her bag and leaves without saying a word to anyone.

Once inside her rented SUV, she leans back against the headrest. She's so ready to leave Idaho and return home. In the two years since she joined the FBI to work with Lindsay and his team, she's crossed one end of the country to the other, from east to west, south to north. Every cell she's been a part of taking down has been worth it; every man and woman rescued from hell has been a balm to her soul. But the reason she joined the task force isn't because she needed her soul healed, but because she needs to find her missing sister, River. It's been over twenty years now since Andrew Rawlings, a cross-country truck driver, took her. Dead or alive, she is determined to find her sister and bring her home.

Knock-knock.

"What the . . ." Meri jumps at the intrusive noise. Lindsay stands outside her door, knuckles to the glass.

She rolls down the window and groans. "Let me guess . . . I'm not headed home?"

"There's been a body dump discovery in Montana. I'd send someone else, but there's something there you'll want to see."

CHAPTER FOUR

Jillian

Today is a day that needs to end, and it needs to end fast.

Standing in the middle of the grocery store, Jillian glances at her phone for the millionth time, her teeth grinding at the lack of communication from her husband. So far, he's zero for seven. Zero replies to her seven messages, and he knows how irritated she gets when he leaves her on read. She smiles as Ethan returns to her with his necessary bag of sunflower seeds and hopes her frustration isn't too obvious.

"They don't have the dill pickle flavor," he says, his face scrunching into a frown. "Taco Supreme should be okay, right?" There's a look of hope on his face, a need to hear that their game won't be ruined because he doesn't have the right flavor.

She reaches out and lightly pinches his chin. "It's a new flavor, right? I bet that will mean even more home runs. Remember when you first tried the dill pickle? It was a new-to-you flavor then, right? And you hit three home runs that game."

He shrugs. "Yeah, but it wasn't a new-new flavor, Mom. What if we lose? It'll be all my fault."

18

"Or, what if you win?" It amazes her that she has a son who is a glass-half-empty personality, whereas she has always been the opposite. He must get it from his father.

"Is that all we're bringing? What about ice cream sandwiches, too?" Ethan glances in the cart and shakes his head at her.

"What else were you hoping to have? We've got flavored water, strawberry licorice, cheese crackers, and" — she moves aside some of the groceries to find Ethan's number one favorite snack — "celery sticks with peanut butter for the ride home."

Normally, she'd have his celery all ready, along with all the snacks she brings, but today has been a day when nothing has gone right. The fact that they even made it with time to rush in to buy snacks is a miracle in itself.

"Hello, earth to Mom?" Ethan pulls at the cart so that it slips from her grasp. "Ice cream, remember? We're going to be late."

Glancing at the time, she follows Ethan toward the freezer section. "You run ahead and grab the same ice cream sandwiches as last time, okay? Make sure to get the club pack." She glances at her watch and mentally calculates the time — if they rush, they should make it in time. If there's one thing she hates, it's being late.

Ethan grabs the box of treats and then races off around the corner, leaving her behind. She picks up her pace, frustrated at his disappearing act. As she rounds the corner, her cart collides with someone before jolting to the side and hitting the corner display. A few boxes of waffle cones tumble to the floor, their cardboard corners denting from the impact.

"Whoops, I'm so sorry," Jillian says, reaching out to the young boy she ran into. The boy, who looks about Ethan's age, in a baseball uniform, stands there, his glove still in one hand while the other rubs his arm where the cart hit him. His face is a mirror of surprise, his eyes wide beneath the brim of his cap.

"Are you okay?" Jillian bends to retrieve the scattered snacks while keeping an eye on him.

"Y-yeah, I'm fine," the boy stammers, his youthful voice cracking as he looks around.

Jillian follows his gaze, looking for his parental figure, but there's no one around. "Are you in a rush to get to the game, too? Or is yours over?" She glances over her shoulder and sees Ethan in the distance, one arm lifted in a hurry-up kind of wave.

The boy nods, a grin breaking through his shyness. "Just on our way. Mom needed to grab some snacks."

Jillian smiles and gestures to her cart. "Me too."

"Jamie, where are you?" A woman rounds the corner, her features cast in a soft shadow beneath the brim of a well-worn baseball cap. "We need to get a move on, bug." The woman barely gives her a look before she reaches for her son's hand and walks away.

Jillian doesn't move. Her hand hovers midair as time compresses, the store's fluorescent lights dimming as if the universe has narrowed its focus to this singular encounter, shouting at Jillian to pay attention. The circular birthmark at the corner of the woman's right eye is like a punch to the gut for Jillian.

She knows that face. Despite the goosebumps pricking across her skin, and her son calling her name, she stands there in shock. Twenty years ago, her best friend went missing. Her best friend with the same mark on the same side of her face. Except that can't be Becky, right? Because *her* Becky, her best friend from twenty years ago, would have recognized her too and said something. She knows she would have. It's not like Jillian has changed much. Sure, she's older, with a few wrinkles and more rolls than she likes to admit around her midsection. Still, according to everyone she's known since childhood, she looks the same as she did twenty years ago, or so everyone said the last time they'd been home.

"Mom!" Ethan runs toward her, hand gripping the cart, tugging it hard. "We're going to be late, and you know how Coach Neil gets." He's wearing a fierce frown and jumps on the spot.

"Argh, sorry," Jillian says, her words an automatic reflex. "Focus, Jillian." She scolds herself under her breath, steering

20

the cart toward the self-checkouts. She rushes through, scanning each item, the routine beep of items mind-numbing as she finds herself looking around for the woman who looks so much like her long-lost friend.

"Mooooommmmm . . ." Ethan grabs some bags as she pays, then races ahead toward the store doors.

"Wait up there, kiddo," Jillian calls out. She grinds her teeth, unsure of who she's more frustrated with — herself for not finding her footing today, Ethan for racing ahead of her, or her husband, who could have answered at least one simple text message.

At the truck, Ethan helps put the snacks in the bin in the back and fills the cooler with the ice cream treats. Beside her, in an SUV, she hears voices raised in an obvious argument. She tries not to look, knowing whatever is happening is none of her business, but when she hears the forced calmness in the mother's tone, she immediately turns and gives a small wave.

"I don't care how long you cry. Until you put that seatbelt on, we're not moving." Marly, one of their neighbors, leans forward and gives Jillian a small wave while also rolling her eyes.

Jillian knocks on the bottom half of the back window to grab Marly's son, Micah's, attention. "Hey, slugger, we need you at the game, so put that seatbelt on, okay? Besides, you don't want to miss out on the ice cream sandwiches Ethan grabbed." She smiles as she points toward the seatbelt, and it only takes a few moments of hesitation before Micah puts it on. She's not surprised. Micah is at her house often for playdates, and he's a sweet kid.

"Oh sure, you listen to Jillian, but not me. Figures." Marly turns on the ignition and rolls down the passenger window. "See you there?"

Jillian climbs into the truck and checks to make sure Ethan has his own seatbelt on. His arms are crossed over his chest, and the frown on his face hasn't disappeared. "All right, all right, we're going."

Pulling into the crowded parking lot, Jillian scans the sea of families unloading lawn chairs and coolers. "See, bud, we're not that late." She points toward another family from their team who pulls in a few spaces from them. This doesn't seem to help. Ethan grabs the wagon from the back and fills it with bags of snacks and water. Jillian rearranges things so the cooler of ice cream sandwiches can fit, then hands Ethan one of the collapsible chairs she always keeps in the back of the truck.

With a clipboard in hand, Coach Neil gives her a slight nod before he glances down at his watch. He has a rule that if you're late for more than three games, you have to sit out for one.

"We've still got five minutes," Jillian tells him as she stands at his side. "I had to grab the after-game treat."

"Excuses, excuses. Where's that husband of yours? I thought he'd be here today. Shouldn't you still be at work?" Neil gives Ethan a high five and then points to a spot on the bench for him to sit.

"I should be, except I've no idea where Tucker is. He hasn't returned any of my calls or messages today."

Neil frowns. "Same. Trina isn't too happy you aren't there, by the way. She'd like to be here too." He gives her a pointed look, one that she ignores. "Any one of us would have brought Ethan tonight, you know that."

Jillian shrugs, pushing down the guilt of disappearing from work while Trina, Neil's wife, was getting the coffee. "And you, of all people, know how important it is to us that at least one parent is always here to watch Ethan."

"Which is why I told Trina you'll probably bring in coffee or something tomorrow to make up for it." There's an expectation in Neil's gaze, like he's expecting an apology or something.

"Of course I will. Jake will probably make me stay late tomorrow, too, just to make a point." She leaves him to go set up her chair as the game is about to begin. Her gaze rolls over the crowd of parents on both sides of the field, and she thinks she sees that woman from before, but she can't tell. The baseball cap is pulled down really low, and her face is angled away. From this distance, she really can't see anything. Her mind is playing tricks, that's all. Her heart wants it to be Becky, but her mind knows it probably isn't.

After all these years, the likelihood of her childhood best friend still being alive is almost nil. And yet, the chance of a doppelganger is just as unlikely.

Her thoughts return to that day, twenty years ago, when her friend disappeared after they walked home from a party. Nightmares of that night often plague her, with memories of her standing at her front door, waving to Becky, as she continued walking down the road. Despite Becky's house only being a few doors down, she never made it. She just vanished. The police believed someone was waiting for her.

She's always hoped her friend is still alive, but after all these years, how realistic is that?

And she feels guilty for that lack of faith.

The crowd erupts in cheers as the game begins, and Jillian turns her focus from her memories to the present. Ethan loves playing baseball, and while he'd prefer to cover one of the bags, specifically third base, he's out in the left field today. She waves as he secures his position, feet shoulder length apart, his stance shouting, 'I'm ready.'

As the game progresses, Jillian settles in her seat among the other parents, chatting and bragging about each hit, catch, and run made by their team. She keeps an eye on Ethan, and when it's his turn to bat, she leaps to her feet, cheering loudly as he swings and makes contact. The ball soars off into the field, and as Ethan runs, his legs pumping as fast as they can go, she yells herself hoarse.

He makes the first home run, and she is so proud of him. She's glad she's here and not Tucker, that she didn't miss this moment with her son. Tucker is going to be jealous, and it's going to eat at him that he wasn't here to cheer Ethan on, and it should.

When the game ends with Ethan's team winning, Jillian waits by the cooler she's brought and hands each child an ice cream treat after giving them all high fives. As she packs up the wagon, she keeps an eye on Ethan, standing off to the side with a few of his friends. Off in the distance, she catches a glimpse of the boy from earlier at the store, holding hands with his mother. The woman is probably only a reflection of the past, yet her heart weighs heavy as she watches them walk away.

CHAPTER FIVE

Her truck tires hum a steady rhythm on the asphalt while Jillian taps her fingers to the music on the local radio station. The road stretches out in front of her, endless fields the only sight. She's barely listening to the radio until a bell dings, alerting listeners to a special news bulletin. The anchor's voice is heavy.

"Authorities are reporting the site of a body dump northwest of Shelby. Good evening, Shelby. This is Emma Johnson with your six o'clock news update." The anchor's tone carries an edge that catches Jillian's attention. She pictures Emma sitting in the small booth with a large mug of coffee beside her on the desk. Normally, her voice is full of brightness, laughter, teasing, and inspiration. Rarely, in the short time that they've been here, has she heard this tone.

"In a shocking discovery earlier this afternoon," Emma continues, "a body dump was found on a farm northwest of Shelby. According to an anonymous source, authorities have uncovered a large quantity of human remains in two trailers located on the property. This gruesome find will no doubt promote an extensive investigation, and we will provide updates as more information becomes available. If you have any information, please contact the Shelby Police Department's tip line. Stay tuned for more updates. This is Emma Johnson for Shelby Radio News."

Jillian's fingers tighten around the leather of the steering wheel, her knuckles whitening with the grip. The gravity of the story sinks its hook into her chest. A body dump. Here, in the middle of all the sprawling farms and rugged ranches where community means familiarity and safety. Tucker promised her things would be better here, safer, more stable. This is the exact opposite of what he promised her life would be like.

Stealing a glance in the rearview mirror, Ethan is absorbed in his own world, headphones cupped over his ears and eyes fixed on the glow of his iPad. He'll eventually hear about this — something like this will spread like wildfire throughout town — but the longer she can keep his innocence intact, the better.

Jillian jabs at the power button, turning it off. For a moment, she focuses on her breathing, how the air fills her lungs and escapes in controlled puffs. She doesn't want to hear of any updates. Not right now. Not with Ethan here.

"Mom?" Ethan's voice pierces the quiet, muffled slightly by his headphones now dangling around his neck. "Everything okay?"

She swallows hard. "Fine, honey," she says, her voice betraying none of the turmoil that twists inside her. "Just focusing on the road." But as the miles toward home peel away beneath them, the news anchor's dire report echoes in her head, each word a lead weight in her stomach.

"Keep your eyes open for deer," she tells Ethan, forcing a lightness into her tone. "It's still early, but we might see some out in the fields."

What else is hidden out there? What other secrets are just waiting to be found? The news said a body dump was located in some trailers on a farmer's property. That could be anywhere and any farm. They even have some on a section of land they own. All along the county roads are old trailers, rusted-out vehicles, and even some army trucks put to pasture. Who would do such a thing?

"Hey, Mom." Ethan's bright blue eyes meet Jillian's in the rearview mirror. "What's for dinner? I'm starving."

She chuckles as she glances at the clock — right on time. Her son is growing and needs food every hour, on the hour, or so it seems.

"Have some of those crackers first," Jillian suggests, pointing to the grocery bag at his feet. Her fingers twitch on the steering wheel, still clammy from the news update. "Any ideas on what you'd like after that?"

"Can we get pizza?" Ethan's voice is hopeful, a lightness that contrasts sharply with the weight of Jillian's thoughts.

Considering she didn't have time to take anything out for dinner, she has no problem with this plan. "Sure, pizza sounds good." She manages a smile for him through the mirror. "Why don't we call Dad and see if he's in the mood, too? Then you can tell him about your home runs."

She brings up Tucker's number on the phone and waits for it to ring. Considering her husband hasn't answered any of her calls or texts today, she'd be surprised if he does now. But she's also starting to get worried. He's often out and about introducing himself to new possible clients and checking out their expansive new property in his downtime, at times being without cell service, but considering her husband's career is online based, he's never unavailable for this length of time.

She doesn't want to think the worst, though. She can't. She won't go there, not again. Out here is different. He promised.

The phone rings once, twice, and then her husband's familiar voice breaks through the line, startlingly clear and immediate.

"Jill, I—"

"Tucker, finally," she says, her body deflating from the stress she's been holding in. "Where have you been? I've been texting you all day." She works hard to keep the frustration out of her voice since she's on speaker and doesn't want Ethan to pick up on it. "Didn't you get any of my messages? We're on our way, but Ethan suggested pizza. Can you call to order it, and I'll pick it up on my way home?"

There's silence on the other end for longer than Jillian likes. "Listen, I uh . . . I need you to come straight home, okay?" The urgency lacing his words sends a shiver down her spine.

"Tucker? What's going on? Is everything okay?" Her heart quickens, every possibility flashing like the red and blue lights she sees in the distance. She leans forward and realizes they are at the turn toward Shelby. If she's going to get pizza, she needs to turn left. Otherwise, the quickest route is straight ahead.

"Just come home, okay?" Tucker's voice is hushed and muffled, as if he doesn't want to be overheard. The line goes dead, leaving a void filled only by the sound of Ethan munching crackers.

Jillian's grip on the steering wheel tightens, mirroring the constriction in her chest. Whatever awaits them at home, it's enough to make Tucker's steady voice waver. She slows as she approaches the stop sign and waves at the officer standing in front of the barricade.

She turns and checks the rearview mirror, finding Ethan wide-eyed and staring out at the vehicles. "What's going on?" he asks.

She thinks about that news report, her stomach twisting at what's happening. It's like a scene right out of her favorite television show, *Criminal Minds*. Police vehicles would be blocking the entrance to whatever property the body dump was found on, and she can only imagine the people searching those grounds. She doesn't even want to think about what was found.

An officer approaches as Jillian rolls to a stop. With her window down, the crisp air carries the scent of dust and an undercurrent of something else — fear, perhaps, or anticipation.

"Excuse me, officer! What's going on?" she calls out, her voice steadier than she feels.

"Ma'am, you'll need to take a detour. Road's closed." His reply and stance are cold and curt.

"Detour," she repeats, more to herself than to Ethan, whose face presses against the window, his curiosity piqued by the flurry of activity outside. "But our farm is just up ahead."

"Apologies for the inconvenience." The officer steps back.

With a heavy heart, Jillian turns right, away from the barricade and further away from home.

"Are we lost?" Ethan's voice is tinged with concern.

"No, honey. Just a little detour." Her reassurance sounds hollow, even to her own ears, as she navigates the back roads. She turns on the map app on her phone and glances at it to ensure the road she's turning on is an actual road, not a driveway. She sends a voice message through text to Tucker, letting him know she's being detoured. He only sends a thumbs-up as a reply.

"Why were the police there?" Ethan asks.

Jillian shrugs.

"Maybe an accident?" Ethan continues, giving Jillian the out she needs. Eventually, he'll hear the truth, and it should come from her and Tucker, not from classmates on the bus tomorrow.

"Maybe." She smiles at him from the rearview mirror.

"What about the pizza?"

She'd all but forgotten dinner. "I think we have some in the freezer, bud. Remember you picked out a few last time we went shopping?" She lifts her voice like she's smiling when, really, her insides are all a mess.

Ethan returns the headphones to his ears, and Jillian forces herself to let go of her tight grip on the steering wheel. She follows the detour, evading the potholes and patches of loose gravel as best she can before finally turning onto the road that will take them home.

Except there's another blockade with a police car. Rolling down her window, she recognizes the officer walking toward her. His son plays on Ethan's baseball team.

"Hey, slugger." Officer Charlie Green leans in close and waves toward Ethan. "How was the game?"

"We won." Pride rings through Ethan's voice.

"Of course you did." The smile on Officer Green's face is forced.

"Charlie, what's going on?" Jillian keeps her voice hushed, not liking the shadow crossing Charlie's eyes.

"You headed home?"

She nods.

"It's not good, Jillian. I know you aren't involved, but . . ." He sighs before he turns and listens to someone speaking in his ear. "I'll let them know you're on your way."

CHAPTER SIX

Agent Meri Amber

There are fifteen boxes of horror, and so far, Meri Amber has only located five of them. Two years to find five boxes.

When Andrew Jeremiah Rawlings Junior told her the location of the boxes he'd buried during her one and only visit to the FCI Sandstone Institution five years ago, she should have known he was sending her on a wild goose chase.

She has a lot of regrets in her life, and not going back to see Junior is one of them. Unfortunately, he died last year during a prison riot.

It is her personal mission to find the boxes, not just the five that Rawlings told her about, but all of them. Deep in her bones, she knows one of those boxes belongs to her sister. There are only ten more to find.

For twenty-one years, Meri has been searching for her missing sister. She almost thought she'd found her when she arrived in Paisley Valley on the trail of Andrew Rawlings, the truck driver she's always believed kidnapped her sister. But all she found was his son, a monster disguised as a minister.

Instead of heading home, Agent Lindsay sent her here, to nowhere Montana, to face another nightmare. She tried to sleep on the plane, but after reading the reports, sleep eluded her.

Now, standing in the middle of a field where wind-whipped grasses bow and dance to the somber tune of the wind, she can't seem to move her body. The air is heavy with tension, a tension she can see on the faces of the officers around her.

She's been here before — not this field, not this state, but this scenario — too many times to count. Agent Meri Amber stands rigid amid the surrounding chaos, her eyes fixed on the two weathered trailers that stand like sentinels guarding the secrets of monsters.

She hates monsters.

The grounds are busy with local police enforcement, everyone glancing her way out of curiosity. One hand in her pocket, she fingers the pack of cough drops she grabbed from her bag earlier. She has a feeling she's going to need them.

"Sheriff Mato asked for you to wait until she gets back. She's on a call with the Montana Medical Office." An officer stands at her side, arms crossed, as he stares out at the scene with her. He's been her constant escort since she flew in, and she still doesn't remember his name. She's been so focused on the reports and preparing herself for what's to come — though, that's not an excuse.

"Understood, Officer . . ." Meri says, glancing at his badge, "O'Brian." She clears her throat at the way he looks at her like he knows she has no idea who he is. "Sorry." She takes ownership of her oversight and breathes in. He smells like hay, mold, and dirt. In fact, a lot of the people she's met since flying in smell like that. She has a thing about smells — she's able to associate a smell with a memory and vice versa, but she has a feeling that's not going to work out here.

"Actually, my first name is Barry. That might be easier for you to remember since it rhymes with yours and all." The corner of his lips twerks into a smile.

Meri — Barry. Yeah, that will be easier for her.

"So, Barry, you've worked in Shelby long?" Her tone betrays none of the turmoil churning inside her. Her hands, clad in gloves meant to protect and serve, are now clasped tightly behind her back — a physical manifestation of her restraint and discipline, or she hopes that's the appearance she's giving.

"Born and raised." Barry O'Brian is proud of that fact, something she doesn't understand. The minute she could leave her hometown, she did. But she nods her head as if the distinction is an important one.

"Is this . . . common out here?" She nudges her head toward the trailers.

"No, ma'am. Not this." He glances around and then leans in closer. "We've had our fair share of things to deal with being so close to the border and all, but this many bodies in one place? It's a first for me, and I've been with the department for almost five years now."

"These trailers, though . . . you've got a lot of them out here in the fields." It was like northern Montana was the vacation trailer graveyard capital.

"Yes, ma'am, that we do." The sigh in his voice suggests he's thinking the same thing as her. They'll need to search all of them to see if there are any more bodies.

The trailers themselves aren't special. Average, run-of-the-mill type of trailer you'd pull with a pickup truck. The kind you'd place in a camping ground by a river, the kind you see on the highways during the summertime.

From the peeling paint and boarded windows, you'd think they'd be full of garbage or critters, not bodies. The trailers, relics now corrupted by the shadows of untold stories, hold the key to a puzzle that has consumed her for the last two years. Each trailer apparently contains a metal box, the same style of box that haunts her waking thoughts and sleepless nights.

From behind her, she hears the rustle of someone moving through the long grass and her name being called. She turns.

The sheriff gestures to Meri. "Sorry about that. I had to confirm a few things with the team heading our way. This is a . . . mess, and I want to make sure it's handled properly."

Sheriff Nakomi Mato is nothing like Meri expected. She's a tall woman with straight black hair that reaches past midway on her back, piercing green eyes, and she walks with a wolf at her side.

A freaking wolf. Meri instinctively steps back.

Sheriff Mato snaps her finger, and the wolf sits. "Don't mind Tala. She's harmless unless I tell her otherwise."

"You walk around with a wolf and say it's harmless?" Meri finds that hard to believe.

"Wolf-dog, legal in Montana, and I've raised her as a pup. She rarely leaves my side, so if you plan on sticking around, you might want to get used to her." Sheriff Mato gives Tala a scratch on the head. "Again, sorry about the wait, but I trust O'Brian has kept you company?"

"I appreciate the pickup from the airport, and trust me, I don't mind the wait," Meri says. "Regarding this mess, if there's anything I can do to help, let me know. This isn't my first body dump site."

Sheriff Mato eyes her with interest. "Lindsay said you would be an asset. Good to know."

"You know Lindsay?" She can't hide her intrigue. The man is still a closed book to her, even after two years of working together. He doesn't let many get in close. Especially after the whole facade with Andrew Rawlings Junior, aka Pastor Jeremy. Lindsay had called the man friend, and the idea he'd never seen the man for the monster he really was has always bothered him.

"Better than you, from the sound of it."

"He's a bit closed off."

"Do you blame him?" Sheriff Mato gives her a look and then gestures toward the trailers. "This way, then." Her low voice carries the weight of the grim scene they're about to enter.

Meri steps carefully, following the path trampled by previous officers, her heart rate ticking up with each step nearer to the trailer. The sheriff lifts the yellow tape for her, and she ducks beneath it, a shiver crawling up her spine despite the determination set in her jaw. She pulls out a Halls from her pocket and pops it in her mouth.

"Ready?" the sheriff asks, pausing at the dilapidated door hanging off its hinges.

"Let's see what we're dealing with," Meri says, her tone even but her insides coiling tight.

The door creaks ominously as they push it open, the sound slicing through the quiet. Sheriff Mato flicks a switch, and a single bulb buzzes to life, casting an eerie glow over the scene within.

Meri's breath catches. Skeletal remains litter the floor, each one a silent scream echoing through the years. The air is stale, heavy with the weight of death, the scent of decay, and secrets long buried. She steps closer, her gaze sweeping over the bones laid out like macabre breadcrumbs.

"God . . ." The word escapes her in a whisper, barely audible over the thrumming in her ears.

"God has nothing to do with this," Sheriff Mato murmurs, her own discomfort palpable. "This is all man. Time and weather did a number on the place, but not enough to hide everything."

Meri kneels beside a cluster of ribs, the bones yellow with age. Her fingers hover above them, resisting the urge to touch, to feel the reality of what's happened here.

"Do you have an official count yet?" Meri glances over her shoulder.

Sheriff Mato shakes her head.

Meri stands, swallowing hard. "There's got to be at least twenty that I can see, maybe more." Her voice is steady despite the chaos swirling inside her. "All these lives . . ." She trails off, her mind racing with the implications.

"You've seen this before?" The sheriff's reply is terse, her eyes scanning the perimeter of the room.

She nods. "Idaho. South Dakota. Wisconsin. All linked to sex trafficking rings. No place is immune, not even here."

"Never said it was. I'm not blind to what happens in the corner of my world." The sheriff sounds annoyed. "Lindsay told me not to touch the boxes, that they were to be in your custody."

The boxes. She's not sure if she's ready for them yet. This horror in front of her is enough.

The skeletal remains lie scattered, each telling a story without words — a story she's read too many times to count. The stories are all the same, with threads of loss, pain, and a truth someone desperately wants to stay buried.

"I'm surprised the media isn't out there yet."

"We're a tight-knit county, Special Agent Amber. Unlike what you're used to in the big cities, we all work together. Details of the location haven't been leaked yet, but there are enough people out on these roads; they'll see the vehicles and know something's up."

"So that anonymous source . . ."

"Not so anonymous."

Meri dips her head in acknowledgment. From what she can tell, the sheriff has a tight grip on what's going on. She's not here to tell her how to run things, just to help as needed. She's also here for the boxes. The boxes most of all.

"Let's get started then," she says, her resolve hardening. This isn't just a crime scene; it's a testament to human cruelty.

Meri's gaze snaps to the table, an island in a sea of decay. The metal box sits there, its surface dulled by time yet reflecting the feeble light that fights through the trailer's grime-coated windows. Her breath catches in her throat, the chill of recognition seeping into her bones. This is it — the object that has haunted too many of her waking hours and darkened too many of her nightly dreams.

The question, though, is who left it here? She believes she knows, but life has a way of throwing curve balls, so she's always ready for the unexpected.

"Is that . . ." The sheriff's voice trails off, her question hanging in the air like mist.

"Exactly what we've been looking for?" Meri asks, her tone low, laced with gravity. "I take it Lindsay told you about them?"

"That Rawlings was one messed up sonofabitch, wasn't he?"

"Which one? The son or the father?"

Sheriff Mato gives her a look of disbelief. "I heard about the son. That messed up Lindsay good. You actually believe the father is still alive?"

"Until proven otherwise." Meri approaches the box with a reverence that belies the grotesque setting. Everything about her life lately has led to this moment, this container of secrets and silent testimonies. A shiver runs up her spine as her fingertips brush against the cold metal.

"Be careful now. I don't like it, but Lindsay says you get the first look." The sheriff's warning is unnecessary. Every move she makes is measured, every breath controlled.

"If it's what I think it is, I won't touch anything inside — not until it's properly processed," Meri murmurs, her eyes never leaving the box.

On the top of the steel box is a name written in black permanent marker. Birdie Sherling. A female. With a firm touch, she flips the latch. The click echoes through the trailer, a sound far too loud in the cramped space.

The lid swings open, revealing exactly what she thought she'd find. Her heart clenches painfully, and the sting of tears threatens to shake her professional composure.

"I'm so sorry," she whispers, not to the sheriff or any potential eavesdroppers, but to the lost soul whose belongings were left here to be forgotten. "I'll help you get back to your family," she promises. The pledge is as much for her as the victim. It's a vow to chase the shadows, to pull at the threads until she can unravel the tapestry of madness.

"Meri?" The sheriff's hand on her shoulder brings her back from the brink, grounding her in the present.

"Let's seal it up until forensics arrives," Meri says, clearing her throat. "We've got a long road ahead." She closes the lid with a sense of finality, the metallic sound marking both an end and a beginning.

Nothing is said for a long time, and when Meri glances at the sheriff, her eyes are closed as if silently praying. Meri gives her a moment of privacy.

"So," Sheriff Mato finally utters, "this is what you were expecting, or at least, hoping for. That box. And Birdie, that was her name?" Her face reflects the weight of their grim discovery.

"I believe so. That's been the pattern so far. Andy Rawlings Senior kidnapped teenage girls, tortured them for a year, then killed them, and these boxes are his trophies. His son found them in his childhood home's basement and hid them around the country. We've located five. Now" — she points to the box — "six out of fifteen."

"Fifteen? I almost didn't want to believe him." The heavy words sink between them. "Well, damn, if the next box is the same, that will be number seven."

Seven boxes. Seven boxes in two years. The knot in her stomach only tightens at the thought.

CHAPTER SEVEN

Jillian

The gravel beneath Jillian's truck crunches as she pulls up to the farmhouse she's always dreamed of owning. Until today, every time she'd pulled up in front of her house, she couldn't help but smile, knowing this place was hers. It's everything she's ever dreamed of, other than being in the middle of nowhere, away from family and friends. From the wraparound porch, to the white-and-black farmhouse look, to the rustic barn set off to the side, to the weaving pathway through her flower beds . . . it's ninety percent perfect.

If they were back in New York State, it would be one hundred percent perfection, everything her heart ever dreamed of, the very pictures of life she's kept on her dream board for the past ten years. Unfortunately, that's no longer a possibility.

Life is what you make it. Happiness isn't based on where you live, but on who you live it with, her mother had told her a long time ago. One day, she'll believe it.

Her heart beats a staccato against the stillness of Shelby's sprawling pastures. This is their new home. A home that's meant to be safe. A home that's supposed to be forever. So why does all of that feel threatened now?

Tucker, what did you do?

The flashing lights of the Sheriff's truck paint the rustic barn Tucker uses as storage in urgent strokes of red and blue.

Her gaze flickers from the lights to the vehicle to the knot of figures huddled on the wraparound porch of Jillian's house — a porch she's recently finished repainting. Tucker is there, running his hands through the front of his hair, where a bold silver streak stands out from the rest of the dark hair. His movement is a tell-tale sign of his distress. He's standing beside two people, one being the town sheriff.

This can't be good.

Jillian has only met Sheriff Nakomi Mato once, and it was only because Ethan had seen her walking through the downtown park with her wolf-dog and wanted to pet it. Never having seen a wolf-dog before, Jillian was apprehensive, but the dog was so gentle with Ethan that it erased all of Jillian's fears. The sheriff wasn't what she'd expected either. She was welcoming and calm, but at the same time, her straight stance and direct gaze told Jillian she didn't miss much.

Considering their past, Jillian isn't sure if that's a good thing or not.

"Tucker?" She steps out of her truck, hand resting on the back handle, unsure if she should let Ethan out. Her voice is steady despite the tremor of unease that ripples through her.

He turns, his expression taut as if every muscle in his face is fighting to maintain composure. "Jill . . . they found something."

Ethan knocks on the glass, a soft reminder that he's waiting. She opens the door, and he makes a beeline for the sheriff's dog, who is sniffling the grass off to the side. She glances over at Sheriff Mato, who gives a nod.

"Ma'am, I'll watch them while you all chat." An officer approaches from the side. He is skinny, has short hair, and is softly spoken. He looks like he's fresh out of school.

Her heart sinks another level at his words. She makes her way toward the group. The tension between them is thick, but her attention is only for her husband.

"Tucker, what did they find?" Her question slices the air, each word heavy with dread.

He shakes his head, but does that mean he doesn't want to tell her he doesn't know, or is that his way of telling her it's not like last time?

Please let it not be like last time. She can't live through that again.

"Mrs. Harper, I'm Special Agent Meri Amber. Perhaps we can move this inside?" Agent Meri's voice brokers no argument, and Jillian opens the door for them.

Tucker hesitates and then follows. "Where have you been?" Jillian hisses, stopping him as he goes to walk past. He looks different. Older. A man with a shadowed past that's finally caught up to him. She can't do this again. She won't. "Tucker, please tell me this isn't—"

"It's not." His voice breaks, but as he looks her in the eyes, Jillian's heart calms a beat, and the panic doesn't rush as fast as before. She believes him.

Her house isn't a disaster, but she still feels a little shame at the untidiness. She rushes ahead of the women as they enter the living room. "Please excuse the mess," she says, picking up a throw and folding it. "I was running late this morning, and then with Ethan's ball game . . ."

"Jillian, it's all good. I've always wanted to step inside this house, and it's more than I've ever imagined." Sheriff Mato places one hand on Jillian's arm, calming her. "As a child, this was the dream. Growing up on the reserve, sharing a room with my twin sisters. Whenever we'd drive by this place, I used to daydream about what it would be like to live in something so big. And the porch looks great." Sheriff Mato and the agent take a seat on the couch. Jillian sits in one of the armchairs.

"It's amazing what a fresh coat of paint will do," she says, regretting the moment she looks the agent in the eyes. A gravity in her gaze will haunt Jillian for the rest of her life.

"There's no easy way to say this, so forgive the bluntness, but we don't have time for small talk." Agent Meri sits at the edge of the couch, hands clasped together. "We found some trailers," Meri says, her voice strong and tethered, "full of dead bodies. They were hidden behind a copse of trees on your property out back."

Jillian reaches a hand across the seats and grabs hold of her husband's, her grip strong. She's not hearing what she's hearing. That woman didn't say what she just said. It's not possible.

"They've been there for quite some time," Sheriff Mato interjects.

"Dead bodies?" Jillian's voice cracks around the edges, a visceral image seizing her thoughts. "I don't . . . in those trailers?" She swallows hard.

"Yes ma'am," Sheriff Mato says, her words clipped.

"On our land? But we just bought . . ." Jillian turns to her husband. "Tucker, how could this happen? How . . . why . . . I don't . . . I don't understand." Jillian's eyes seek out his, searching for something — anything — that might make sense of the chaos. But he won't meet her gaze.

"I don't know." His voice is a low rumble.

She wants to believe him. She needs to believe him.

"Tucker . . ." There is an imploring note in her voice now, a wife's plea for honesty in the face of horror. She knows the others hear it, hears her desperation, but she doesn't care.

"Jill, I swear—" he starts, but Agent Meri cuts him off.

"Mr. Harper, I realize that you only recently purchased this property, but it's important that we know everything — any visitors, unusual activities, anything you might have overlooked." Agent Meri is all business. Her eyes cut across the room and demand honesty, and her voice showcases just how serious this is.

"Overlooked?" Tucker repeats, a shadow of defensiveness creeping into his posture. "I already told you we don't know anything. We bought this property sight unseen, trusting the real estate agent with the images he showed us. Since we've moved here, I've little by little been exploring our land, but haven't really looked into the trailers yet. On my list of things to take care of, they were at the bottom."

"So you've never been out to those trailers then? Is that what you're saying?"

"That's what I said, isn't it? You do realize how many acres we own, right? It's crazy how much space you all have out here. I do what I can when I can." Tucker's legs jitter as he sits in the chair. His fingers clench and unclench as he struggles to remain calm. If Jillian sees it, she knows the others do as well.

"I just want to be clear," the agent reiterates. "I wouldn't want us to find any of your DNA out there, like on the door handles or even inside the trailers."

That's all it takes for Tucker to push himself up off the chair and go to stand behind it, his hands gripping the edge with tension even Jillian can feel.

"We didn't even know about them," Jillian says, hoping to move the attention from her husband to herself. "They weren't in any of the photos or the description, were they?" She glances toward Tucker and then looks at Sheriff Mato. "You probably know the area better than us. Have you ever seen them before?"

The look on Sheriff Mato's face says it all, from the way her eyes narrow just enough to tell Jillian she's walking on thin ice.

"Do you still have the paperwork?"

Jillian nods. "It's in Tucker's office." She glances at him, but he's already left the room. She swallows hard, uncomfortable to be left alone with the two women.

"Jillian." Meri addresses her directly. "Tucker mentioned he works from home. Has he mentioned anything unusual recently? Have there been any unexpected visitors?"

She shakes her head, but doubt anchors her tongue. They haven't been here long. "Honestly, I wouldn't know. Tucker is the one here all day while I work in town."

"Your husband is in the transportation business, correct? What does he do exactly?" Sheriff Mato asks.

43

"He's a transportation agent or consultant, I guess you could say. He sets up new clients for his parents' business back east and also works with a team that handles the logistics of moving freight and cargo for these companies."

"Freight and cargo, such as?"

Jillian shrugs. "Whatever the companies need moving? They have contracts with a wide variety of industries. They've worked with NASA, Nascar, Walmart and . . . others. I generally stay out of it, so if you need particulars, you'll have to ask him."

Meri writes this down in her notebook. "But when you've been home, you haven't noticed anything?"

"Like I said, we're still new here. I wouldn't know what was normal or unusual." There's no lie in her words or her tone, and yet there's a trailer full of dead bodies on her land . . .

"I can't find them." Tucker returns, his hands clasped behind his back. "No idea where they were put. Sorry. Maybe . . . maybe the realtor still has copies?"

Jillian tries to meet his gaze, but he won't look at her. In fact, he won't look at any of them. Instead he stares at the table in the middle of the room. She wants to argue with him because she knows they are in the pull-out cabinet in his office, but she's never gone against her husband before in the presence of others, and she won't start now.

She knows he's lying. She just doesn't know why.

CHAPTER EIGHT

Jillian's fingers curl around the edge of the kitchen counter, her knuckles blanching as she listens to Ethan's faint laughter fade into silence upstairs. Tucker's heavy tread on the stairs as he heads her way fills her with tension that has only been growing since she drove up to the house and saw the police. She fills up a glass of water, like she does every night when he comes downstairs after reading to Ethan, complaining he's parched.

When he walks into the kitchen, he has a tiredness on his face, in his eyes, and weighing down his shoulders that she hasn't seen in a long time.

"Tucker," she begins, her voice steady despite the storm brewing within her chest. "We need to talk."

He reaches for the glass of water and guzzles it down. When he plants the glass on the counter and turns his back on her, her shoulders deflate.

"Tucker, I'm serious."

His only reply is a head shake as he leaves the kitchen and heads into the living room. He stands by the fireplace, his posture rigid.

"Please tell me this isn't happening again, at least." Despite the defeat in her voice, she's on fire for a fight, but she

45

knows her husband, knows what makes him tick and what sets him off. She also knows she can't live through the nightmare that they left behind in New York — she can't. She believed him when he promised her that things had changed and that he wasn't that same person.

He turns slowly, his eyes searching hers with an intensity that borders on desperation. It's that desperation that scares her the most. "Do you really think I would go back on my promise?"

She doesn't answer. Not because she doesn't want to but because she can't. She's afraid to voice what she truly thinks he would or would not do.

They ran from a life that she thought had been perfect. A life that was full of promise for a future they'd figure out together. Home in Parishville, New York, was idyllic, everything you'd assume small-town living to be. But even there, in a town of less than a thousand people, a current of mistrust and evil flowed beneath the surface. Tucker had gotten involved with the wrong sort of people to fix a problem she didn't even know they had, and the outcome was a prison sentence that would tear their family apart unless Tucker turned in the people he worked with. Those people landed in jail for sexual exploitation of minors, and, after deciding to leave the WITSEC program, they moved, intent to start a new life first in Iowa and then here.

Jillian never understood why they left the protective custody of the US Marshals. She still doesn't.

"That's not answering my question, and you know it." She drops her hand, giving him the space to answer or walk away. She shouldn't have to demand answers from him.

"Jill, now isn't the time," he says, his words far too calm for the tension between them.

"Not the time? Are you kidding me? There are trailers full of dead bodies on our property, Tucker. I think now is exactly the time." Jillian presses, stepping closer. "Did you know when you agreed to buy this place?" She always thought the offer was too good to be true. This new life here in Montana had been handed to them on a silver platter. Someone is being played for a fool, and she has a feeling that someone is her.

"Drop it, Jill," Tucker snaps, a crack in his composed facade revealing a glimpse of the turmoil beneath. "It's not our business. It doesn't . . . concern us."

She laughs. "Doesn't concern us? Who are you kidding?" Her voice rises, incredulous. "Bodies, Tucker. Bodies on our property."

"Keep your voice down," he warns, glancing toward the staircase, his expression darkening. "Ethan—"

"Ethan always falls asleep as soon as you're done reading to him, and you know that. I've followed, trusted, and restarted my life for you. I think I deserve the truth, all things considering." She takes a breath, steadying herself. "The man we bought this house from, I have a right to know why he is involved with our lives. Why you've kept this from me."

Tucker's jaw clenches, a muscle ticking in his cheek. He looks away, his hands balling into fists at his sides. "You don't understand, Jill. There are things better left alone. For everyone's sake."

"Better left alone?" A bitter laugh escapes her, filled with disbelief and betrayal. "You think ignorance will protect us? Protect our family? You've done great on that so far, haven't you?" The moment she says the words and sees the hurt in her husband's eyes, she regrets them.

"Sometimes, yes." Tucker can't look at her, and his voice is barely audible. He pushes past her and heads back into the kitchen, where he goes to grab a bottle of beer from the fridge.

She follows, furious he'd walk away from her. "Is that what you've been doing? Protecting us?" Her gaze searches his, pleading for a sliver of truth. "Or protecting yourself?"

"Enough!" Tucker's outburst slices through the air, sharp and sudden. "Just stop, Jillian. Please."

She reels back as if struck, the unspoken words hanging heavy between them. A gulf opens up between them, one that seems as vast and insurmountable as the dark sky outside.

Jillian's pulse thrums in her temples, a relentless beat that echoes the frustration mounting within her. She takes a step to cover the distance between them. "Tucker, for once, just — just talk to me without the secrets. If there's danger, I need to know. We can't hide from this."

He retreats, his gaze skirting past her, finding interest in anything but the earnest plea in her eyes. "You don't understand. You can't." His voice is low and strained.

"I can't if you don't explain it. Let me carry this burden with you." Jillian's hands tremble, but she clasps them tightly together to still them. "That man . . . the trailer, the bodies — why? Why us?"

"I owe him." She almost doesn't hear him say the words.

"You owe him? For what? Why? Is this because of what happened in Parishville? Or even in Iowa?"

"It's because of him that we could even leave Iowa with our lives. Don't you get that?" His haunting gaze pierces her heart with the sharpness of a blade. There's so much he's not telling her, so much he's kept secret from her.

"Get that? Are you kidding me? Do you not think I see what's happening? Do you not think I've been aware of the danger we've been in and it's all because of a decision you made while keeping me in the dark."

Tucker remains silent, which only makes her more frustrated. "And here we are, a new town with the same old secrets. Tell me I'm wrong?" She demands an answer.

Tucker's eyes flicker with something unreadable — a swirl of fear, guilt, perhaps regret — and for a moment, Jillian thinks she sees a barrier crack. Then, as quickly as it's there, it vanishes, replaced by a stoic mask she's grown to hate over the years.

"Jillian," he says, an edge of warning lacing his tone. "Drop it."

"Drop it? How can I drop it when—" She breaks off, her throat tight with emotion. Before she can gather her thoughts, Tucker is moving, a swift and deliberate retreat.

"Tucker!"

But he doesn't turn back. His hand finds the doorknob to his study. He twists it and slips inside. The click of the lock is soft, barely audible, yet it reverberates through the silence.

Jillian stands alone in the kitchen, her breath coming in shallow gasps, a futile attempt to stifle the hurt threatening to overflow and overwhelm her. She wraps her arms around herself, seeking comfort in the emptiness.

Questions swirl in her mind, each one a sharp jab at the life she's built with the man who just walked away from her. The silence of the house presses in on her, suffocating, as she stares at the closed door of the study, knowing that behind it lie answers she's both desperate and terrified to uncover.

The low murmur of conversation bleeds through the study door, a teasing whisper of secrets just beyond Jillian's reach. She strains to listen, but the words remain elusive, tangled, and indecipherable. Her fists clench, the urge to demand answers at war with knowing the harder she pushes, the further her husband retreats. Ignoring all the warnings and doubts, she raises her fist to knock at the door when she hears Tucker's voice rise. The words she hears him say, in the tone he speaks, has ice filling her veins.

"Andy, they found it."

CHAPTER NINE

Becky Gardiner

Becky's fingers tremble as she reaches for the delicate porcelain cup, a hairline crack running down its side. She should have thrown it out ages ago, but it reminds her of the set belonging to her mother, and so she keeps it. The past isn't something she likes to dwell on, but after today . . . this one little tether to the life she once lived . . . it's what she needs.

That woman at the grocery store — it was only a split second that she saw her; she'd been in such a rush to grab Jamie and pay for their snacks before the game, but she recognized her.

She hopes she never sees her again. She can't. One whiff of any attachments, of familiarity with another person, and Colin will make her regret it somehow.

The last woman she'd been friendly with, someone she thought she might be able to call a friend, Colin killed, and made her help dig the grave.

Holding the cup up close, the warmth of the chamomile tea seeps into her bones, the steam fogging up her glasses. A temporary veil from the tension thickens the air in the small farmhouse kitchen in Fort Belton.

"The past isn't important. The here and now is," she murmurs to herself, setting the cup back down with deliberate care. It's a saying she's repeated over and over, a lifeline to get her through the horror of all that she's lived.

It's a saying her house mother had told her in the dead of night, while she lay on the thin mattress, crying from the pain her body was in from her latest training session with her Romeo. That man had been the meanest SOB she'd ever known, which was his goal. He would hold her close, stroke her hair, and whisper that no one after him would ever hurt her as much as he would . . . so if she could survive him, she could survive anything.

He was right.

Her gaze flickers to the open kitchen window, listening for the gravel crunch under tires, for the crazy barking of the dogs, alerting her that he's home. The only thing she hears is blissful silence. Glancing at the time, she sees there's only a few more minutes before she needs to become someone else. So, in this moment, she takes another sip of tea and lets herself just be.

Be herself. Be the girl she created from the darkness. Be the mother she always needed. Be the woman she hides to stay safe.

Leaving her seat, she heads to the window, one hand playing with the long braid in her hair, and she looks for her son. He's crouched by the chicken coop, scattering handfuls of feed to the hens gathered around him, his curly red hair blowing in the breeze. A soft smile plays on her lips as she watches the only reason she has for living.

It hasn't been easy, but it's the only life she has now — the only life she's worthy of. She should be grateful she has a home to live in on a permanent basis, with a son she gets to raise.

"Mom? When will Dad be home?" Jamie calls out, seeing her standing there.

"Pretty soon, bug." She raises her voice just enough to carry through the wind. "Why don't you come inside to wash up for bed? You can tell Dad all about the game today."

Jamie wipes his hands on his pants and leaves the coop.

"Catch the gate, love." She can't help but shake her head at his forgetfulness. He stops, dust swirling as he turns and throws the rope over the gate to keep it closed. She watches as he runs to the house, making sure the dogs stay on their side of the fence. One of the dogs runs along the chain link, his strides matching her son's.

While the dogs have the whole property to run and play in, Becky and Jamie only have a small fenced-in area where they can roam without fear of being attacked. The chicken coop, her vegetable garden, a small play section for Jamie, and a picnic table are within that area.

It's better than the small room she used to live in, which had only an eight-by-ten window that barely opened to see the outside.

He races into the kitchen, cheeks smudged with dirt, and his jeans streaked from the fun he's had outside. "Can we—"

"Go wash up first," she reminds him. He heads to the bathroom just down the hall, and she hears the taps running. "Can we go look for arrowheads tomorrow?" he yells out. "By the creek?"

Becky hesitates, her mind calculating the risks of such an excursion. "We'll see, honey." She aches to grant him this simple joy, but everything hinges on Colin and what he says she can do.

She catches a glimpse of a frown before he masks it with a grin. "I'll go put my finds in the chest, then."

"Good idea, bug." He's always finding something he considers treasure. "Don't be long though, all right? Dad will be home any minute." Her gentle words carry the weight of an unspoken warning.

He nods before rushing off, his footsteps pounding on the stairs as he races against time to hide his treasures.

She allows herself one last deep breath moments before Colin's truck pulls up. The German shepherds go crazy, their barks piercing as they wait for him to acknowledge them.

Every night, the first thing he does is give his dogs some love and food. He's the only one who feeds them, pets them, or gives them any type of command. He is the only one they will obey. He then leaves the gate open, giving the dogs free rein of the land.

He's raised them to protect his property, which includes her. He doesn't need cameras or another type of surveillance to keep her in line — all he needs is the dogs. She's scared of them and won't go outside if they are loose. She has the scars on her body to prove just how dangerous they are. On the days she's allowed to leave the property, Colin will park the truck in the garage, where the dogs don't have access, so she can leave safely.

Becky returns to the stove, stirring the stew with practiced motions as the front door slams shut.

"Becks?" Colin's voice booms from the entryway, the false joviality doing nothing to ease the knot in her stomach.

"Kitchen!" she calls back, tucking a loose strand from her braid behind her ear, bracing herself. By the time he walks into the kitchen, she's forced her shoulders to relax and has planted a smile on her face.

When she turns to face him, she catches the twinkle in his eyes and the ease of his smile. Today was a good day, then, which means it's a good day for her. He's dusty, covered in it from head to toe, the hem of his jeans caked in mud. He's still wearing his boots, which leave a trail as he walks toward her.

"It smells good," he says, though his eyes scan for faults, for any excuse. He won't find any, though. Not today. Today of all days, it's important that he sees no faults; otherwise, it won't be her who pays the price, but Jamie. Colin will ground her from attending the next game if she can't keep up with her duties. So far, that's only happened once.

"Thank you." Becky keeps her tone even. "Dinner is almost ready."

"I've been thinking about this stew all day," he grumbles, his heavy boots thudding against the floorboards as he approaches. "I'm sorry." He looks down at the mud on the floor. "I should have taken them off."

"It's okay. I'll clean it up." His kindness isn't lost on her, but she knows it's not accidental either.

She turns and continues stirring the stew, then turns the burner off. "If you place your clothes in the basket, I'll wash them while you eat."

"I'd like you to eat with me." His presence looms behind her, and his hand snakes across her waist. "Send the boy to bed early."

"He wants to tell you about his baseball game," she argues without any real power behind her words.

"And the boy determines what I want? Since when does he come before me?" His threat whispers in her ear, his breath coiling around her neck like a noose.

"No, of course not. I'm sorry. I wasn't thinking." She slowly closes her eyes and relaxes her body, forcing every muscle, every limb to relax.

As his fingers settle on her skin, crawling up beneath her shirt, she focuses on her breathing, on not showing any reaction to what she knows is about to come. He loves to leave marks on her skin, to see his bruises, to know his power over her is constant and never-ending.

She continues to stir the stew, the movement an anchor in the roiling sea of her anxiety. For Jamie, she reminds herself, for her son. She will endure, protect, and survive — for him.

CHAPTER TEN

Jillian

When they say news travels fast in small towns, they aren't kidding.

Everyone's gaze turns her way as Jillian pushes through the glass door of Shelby's main coffee shop. Most mornings, as long as she's not running late, she stops in at Sarah's Brews and Bakes for a steaming cup of coffee and either a freshly baked croissant or a muffin. Usually, she's greeted with smiles and friendly chit-chat, but not today.

"Did you hear about what's happening at the Harpers' place?" An elderly man mutters to his companion, just loud enough that Jillian can hear almost every word. "They found bodies out there."

"Shhh, Frank, that's her." The woman beside him meets Jillian's gaze, but only for a moment before she turns away, her cheeks flaring red for being caught gossiping. She gives the man a sharp nudge in his arm, causing the hot coffee he's holding to slop over its side.

"What the hell? Watch what you're doing," he grumbles, grabbing napkins from the holder. "And you think I don't know that's her? It's not like I'm saying anything she doesn't know."

"Hi, Frank." Jillian smiles at the old man. Most days, when she sees him in here, he gives her a brief nod before he goes back to reading the paper.

Hoping to be forgotten, Jillian waits in line to place her order, giving the racks of freshly baked goods an extra glance. If it's like this here, what will the office be like? More weird looks? More whispered gossip?

"Morning, Jillian. Rough morning so far, huh?" The pregnant owner, Sarah, offers a sympathetic grimace beneath her red cap.

"Well, I've had better." Jillian appreciates Sarah not beating around the bush with the obvious.

"No doubt." Sarah rubs her round belly, almost like it's a subconscious gesture. "What's happening at your place is all anyone can gossip about. Don't take it personal."

Before she can order, the door swings open again, and Martha Jenkins, wrapped in a loud floral dress and a scarf that wages a war of colors against her dress, steps in.

"Jillian, dear, there you are! As soon as I saw your truck outside, I just knew I had to come in. Normally, I like to go down to Lucy's diner for my morning coffee, but . . ." Martha marches over, her words slicing through the tense atmosphere. "I heard about what happened. Terrible, just terrible."

Martha's glasses slide down the bridge of her nose as she stands beside Jillian, ignoring any need for personal space. Her voice dips to a conspiratorial whisper. "You know, I knew something was off when we heard Old Man Cummings just up and left one day, selling his property to two easterners. That man was a mystery himself, disappearing for weeks at a time, sometimes even for months. Did you know he hired some out-of-towners to take care of things whenever he was away? A little suspicious, don't you think?" She tsks. "I'm going to tell Sheriff Mato, although she probably already knows all this."

Jillian takes one step back, eyes blinking rapidly, trying to follow Martha's fast talk.

Martha steps forward to close the gap Jillian created. "I can't imagine what—"

"Martha, please," Jillian interjects in a hissed whisper. Of all the people for her to run into this morning, why did it have to be this woman?

"Have you ever met him? Cummings, I mean? He was a mean SOB, if you know what I mean." Martha's gaze is solid, actively seeking secrets for her own personal treasure trove.

Jillian hesitates for the briefest second before answering, weighing each word, knowing anything she says and doesn't say will be repeated over and over throughout town. "Can't say I have, Martha. We bought the place without coming out here to check it out. Sight unseen, I guess you'd say."

"I remember you saying that when we first met. You saw that big wraparound porch in the photo and fell in love, or something like that. Am I remembering right?" Martha probes.

Her smile is weak, and her voice distorted, but Jillian manages to nod. "Yep, that's what I said."

Martha eyes her closely, the gleam shining bright in her gaze, suggesting she wants to prod more into everything Jillian isn't saying. "Just be careful, honey. People like that . . . well, you never know what they're capable of."

"Thanks for the warning," Jillian says, maintaining her facade of ignorance. Is it really a facade, though? Tucker has kept her in the dark about so many things, and even after last night, she still has no idea what happened, why it happened, or how they're going to deal with it.

Two trailers full of dead bodies isn't something you can ignore.

"You're one of us now, dear" — Martha pats her arm — "and we protect our own. That's something you'll quickly learn here. We may be a small community, but don't let that fool you." Martha glances around the small café with a stern look. "Isn't that right?"

Jillian drops her head, unease coiling within her stomach at each passing second the café remains silent. Finally, she hears the murmurs, and when she looks up, she notices all eyes are still on her, but their glances are warmer, the smiles more relaxed.

"Thank you," Jillian whispers to Martha.

"You've done nothing wrong, so why should you carry the burden of this town's gossip? Someone needs to find Cummings and make him accountable." Martha moves on, heading to a table, where she pulls out a chair that fills the room with its loud squeak.

Sarah hands Jillian her coffee and then slides a small box toward her. "Here," she says. "On the house. Figured you might need some extra sugar to get you through the day."

Driving down the street, there's a compulsion to turn around and head home, to stick her head in the sand and disappear until all of this is over, except she knows from past experience that never works. No matter what is happening, she's not going to run. She told Tucker that this morning before heading into the shower. She's not uprooting their life once again because of his secrets.

The office buzzes as Jillian walks in and settles into her chair. Everyone's curiosity clings to her skin, weighing her down. She counts how long it takes Trina to march down the hall toward her, wanting to know all the details. Five . . . six . . . seven . . . eight . . . and there's the footsteps, the *clack-clack-clack* of her heels against the tile floor. Jillian takes a moment to breathe before pasting on a smile and turning in her chair.

"Jillian, talk about crazy! Are you okay? I mean . . . it's all anyone can talk about right now—" Her voice rings loud as everyone else in the office stops talking, all needing to listen in with the thrill of the morbid.

Jillian cuts her off. "I'm fine. It's horrible and a night-mare for all the families involved, but those trailers have been out there for a long time." She raises her voice to make sure everyone hears her. "I only know what you all know, and that's barely anything, okay?" She tries to make eye contact with everyone in the room.

Trina lays a hand on her shoulder. "Of course, no one assumes you're involved. You just moved here. I wouldn't even worry about it." Trina retreats to her office when Jake appears in his doorway, arms crossed over his chest.

"Let's get back to work, people. No one leaves today until all those invoices are taken care of. Is that understood?" Jake's stress-filled voice sounds rough. "That includes you, Jillian." He gives her a pointed look. "Gossiping hours are on your time, not mine." He directs this to the rest of the room before giving Jillian a surprisingly sympathetic glance.

Jillian turns in her seat and faces her computer screen. A solid day of mind-numbing work is precisely the distraction she needs.

Trina returns just before lunch. "Come on, let's go." She hits a button on the keyboard to turn Jillian's monitor off. "You might have to stay late, but we're still allowed to take our lunch, and the last thing you need is to be eating at your desk."

Lunch is at their usual spot — the Fox Hole — a cozy diner where the scent of grilled cheese and tomato soup mingles with the low hum of conversation. Like before, the second she walks into the restaurant, all eyes are focused on her. A few women smile, but, for some strange reason, most men lower their gazes.

They place their usual order, and while they wait, Trina glances around the room. "Damn, being the fodder for town gossip has to suck," she mutters as she gives a few tables a healthy scowl.

"I'm just ignoring everyone," Jillian admits, wringing her hands together in her lap.

"Did you know him?" Trina asks, her curiosity a live wire.

"Who?" Jillian feigns nonchalance, focusing on the pale swirl of cream in her iced coffee that has just arrived.

"Come on, Jillian. Don't play dumb with me. Cummings — the man who sold you your place? Did you have any idea?" Trina leans forward, her gaze intense.

"Did *you* know him?" Jillian turns the question back around.

Trina shrugs. "I met him a few times. He was a miserable old coot, but no different from any other miserable old man around these parts, you know? Neil had drinks with him a few times, though."

"Really?" That news surprises Jillian.

Trina nibbles on her lip. "Yeah, I never liked it, but Neil said he reminded him of his own dad. Lonely, harmless . . . well, I guess we know now he's not so harmless. I wonder where he's at? Do you guys know? Rumor is he moved to Florida, of all places."

Jillian frowns, her heartbeat glitching for a moment. "Why would you think we'd know? If anyone does, it's the realtor who sold us the property."

"True. Kyle Travis knows everything about everybody in town. He's almost as bad as Martha."

"He gave us a really nice welcome basket," Jillian says. "It included gift cards from almost every place in town, snacks for Ethan, and a bathroom set of soaps and hand towels."

Trina snickers. "He prides himself on his welcome baskets. Personally, I'd prefer a fridge and freezer filled with stock items and casseroles. I mean . . . especially for a family like yours when you move across states."

"Yeah, that would have been nice. With the price of groceries, nowadays, anything helps." She appreciates the change in the subject. She'd love to talk about anything other than the previous owner and those trailers.

"Jake said you're staying late tonight?" Trina switches tracks, concern knitting her brow.

"Yeah, sorry about last night. I know you wanted to be at the game too. Tucker wasn't answering my texts and . . ." Jillian sighs, pushing her half-eaten sandwich aside.

"I wasn't particularly thrilled when I returned with your coffee and saw you were gone. There was a lot of grumbling, by the way, from everyone else who had to stay behind."

About to apologize, Jillian stops herself. She will never apologize for placing her son first — the sooner people realize that, the better. "It's important that at least one of us be at Ethan's games. He's had to deal with so much unrest in the last few years with our moves and . . ." She trails off, not wanting to say too much.

"I guess. That's one thing Jake often doesn't take into account, the fact that he hires parents. It is what it is — hopefully, you won't have to stay too late tonight."

The afternoon drags on despite the amount of work Jake keeps adding to her pile. By the time people start leaving, she's barely made a dent in the stack of paperwork on her desk.

With a quick tap of her fingers, she sends Tucker a text. *Have to work late — I can grab pizza when I leave.*

Tucker's response is swift, the direct opposite of yesterday. *No problem. Ethan and I can meet you in town for dinner?*

Jillian hesitates, her thumbs hovering over her phone. She pictures the scene: their family, the subject of whispered speculation, dissected by prying eyes over greasy plates and vinyl booths. That's not fair to Ethan, who probably got enough of it at school today.

The town's buzzing with gossip, and we're at the center. If you order the pizza, I'll pick it up. I'll give you a thirty-minute heads-up.

She waves as another group of co-workers leave through the front doors. She glances around the room to see who is left and it appears to be just her and Jake, who's watching her from his desk. She gives him a tense smile. With no other distractions, hopefully, she can plow through these invoices and won't have to stay any longer than needed.

61

CHAPTER ELEVEN

Lola

Lola's breaths are shallow as she navigates the narrow hallways, her steps almost silent against the creaky wooden floorboards of the Red House. She knows every creak, every crack, where to step, and where to avoid. It's a dance she's perfected over the years. She knows every inch of this place by heart, could walk around in a blindfold and still manage to move from room to room without being noticed.

The shadows cling to the corners, stretching in the waning afternoon light that filters through the dirty windows. She is a ghost here, unseen and unheard, slipping through the cracks just as she has learned to do since she was a child.

A sudden laugh echoes from the end of the corridor, a sound so out of place, it makes Lola's heart stutter. Her eyes dart, searching for an alcove, a door — anything to blend into — but there is nothing. There is no place to hide. There is no place to feel safe. The voice grows closer, accompanied by the soft jingle of jewelry and the rustle of expensive fabric.

"Goodness, who do we have here?" The voice is syrupy and sweet yet edged with steel.

Lola freezes. The owner's wife stands before her, a vision of opulence with perfectly coiffed platinum-gold hair, her gaze sliding over Lola's form with a practiced eye. The woman's fingers twitch like a predator sizing up her prey.

"Lola, isn't it? My, I didn't realize just how much you've grown." Her smile reminds Lola of a snake. "She's been keeping you to herself, hasn't she? Naughty Mother she is. Where is she, by the way? She didn't answer the door when I arrived." The woman steps closer, her perfume suffocating. "My, my, all this time under our noses."

Lola's pulse hammers against her temples. She tries to make herself smaller, to disappear into the wall, but there's nowhere to hide. "I'm sorry, I didn't mean to—" Lola's voice is a whisper, barely escaping her lips.

"Quiet now," the woman interrupts, her smile chilling. "You've got that look. Rare . . . exotic." She grabs Lola's face with her fingers, her hold strong and unyielding. Turning her head one way and then the other, her gaze is penetrating and powerful. "The scar is an issue, but some prefer the imperfections. Done right, you'll fetch a high price at the auction block." Her words slither through the air like a snake ready to strike.

Lola's disfigurement, once her shield, now marks her as something else — a rarity. Her observant eyes take in every detail: the glint of greed in the woman's gaze, the calculating tilt of her head. Fear twists inside her, but Lola clamps down on it, forcing calm into her veins.

"Would you like me to find Mother for you?" Lola swallows all the fear that burrows into her skin and blankets her facial features so the woman can't read her. Mother will fix this. Mother has always protected her, and even though she's warned her never to be in this situation, Mother will find a way.

"Yes, go fetch, will you?" The woman's laugh is hollow. "Be the good girl I'm sure you are. Tell her I'll wait in the showing room. Oh, and bring coffee. It's time Mother and I had a little . . . chat."

Lola walks away as calmly as she can. The need to escape is strong, but she knows she can't show any weakness. Once out of sight, she flies down the stairs and out the back door to the back shed, where Mother often goes for her afternoon tea. The shed itself isn't anything special, a one-room building with a small porch on the front, a door, and a single window covered by a curtain. Stepping up to the door, Lola hears the soft cadence of laughter and wishes she could retreat, hide, be anywhere but here. But she can't, so she lifts a hand and lightly knocks on the door.

Immediately, there's silence.

Lola steps back, so she's a good distance from the door, and keeps her head bowed.

"What is it?" Mother opens the door, her voice low and impatient.

"I'm sorry, Mother. I know I'm never to disturb you in here, but . . ." Lola slowly lifts her head and glances over her shoulder, half expecting to see the woman standing at the back door.

"Yes? Well, what is it?"

"The Lady is here." She knows Mother doesn't need any clarification. The Lady is always called the Lady, the only one with that title in Lola's life.

Mother swears.

"She wants coffee." Lola manages to utter, somehow finding the strength in the face of Mother's wrath.

"Then go make it. I'll be there shortly." Mother slams the door, and before Lola steps away, she hears angry whispers, a harsh slap, and then a cry. Knowing it wouldn't be prudent to be found waiting, Lola rushes back to the house and proceeds to make coffee. By the time Mother arrives, she has a tray waiting, with cups, a bowl for cream and sugar, and a few cookies Lola made that morning.

"She saw you, didn't she? The one thing I told you was never to happen and here we are. Well . . ." Mother pauses as she eyes the tray, her narrow gaze missing nothing. "Where are the spoons, girl?"

"I'm sorry, Mother." Lola pulls out a drawer and hands her two small spoons.

"Whatever happens now is on you. I've tried to protect you. God knows I've done my best and kept my promise, but this . . ." She stops, shaking her head. There's obvious sadness in her gaze, and the tray in Mother's hands trembles for a split second. "The past doesn't matter now. We've got to accept the here and now and figure out how to navigate it. I hope you're ready."

As Mother leaves the kitchen, a coldness settles in Lola's chest. Whatever happens now is everything she's had to prepare for while praying none of it would come true.

If there's one thing she's learned in her cold, harsh life, it's that fairy tales only happen in storybooks, real life is the hell you make it, and survival is never guaranteed.

CHAPTER TWELVE

Agent Meri Amber

The door to the Shelby realty office opens with a soft push and a loud *ding-a-ling*. Meri glances up in surprise at the bell and shakes her head. It's an actual cow-shaped bell.

"Did I warn you about KT?" Sheriff Mato cracks a smile. "He's a wise-ass chameleon. Born and bred right here, which he'll remind you when it suits him, a know-it-all who probably does, indeed, know it all when it comes to everyone's secrets, and he likes to straddle the line between cowboy and suit jockey."

Meri tries to picture him based on that description alone. She's seen a lot of cowboys and suits in her days but isn't sure what a combination of the two would look like, not in a town like this.

Mato snaps her fingers at her dog, Tala, and she sits beside the door, on duty.

"Sheriff Mato, what an unexpected surprise." Kyle Travis pushes through a door from the back, and it takes a lot for Meri to retain a neutral expression. The man is wearing navy suit pants, tan cowboy boots, a blue plaid work shirt, and a cowboy hat. "Good timing, too. I just got back from visiting a client and was about to pour myself a fresh cup of coffee. Can I grab one for you both?" Before they can answer, he disappears behind the swinging door, whistling.

"Are you even finished with that one yet?" Sheriff Mato glances at the cup Meri's holding in her hand.

Meri takes a long gulp of the lukewarm coffee and dumps it in a bin next to a desk. "I never turn down fresh coffee."

When Kyle returns, his smile is broad, but his gaze flickers with curiosity, or perhaps caution. He hands them both mugs, then looks toward Tala at the front. "Would your dog like a treat?" He points to a large glass jar sitting on the corner of his desk. "Only the best for our friends. They're all natural."

Sheriff Mato snaps her fingers and gives a hand signal. Tala beats it across the room and sits beside the chair, her head almost able to rest on the desk itself.

Meri still doesn't feel totally comfortable around the dog.

"I hope you enjoy the brew. I have it shipped straight from Hawaii," Kyle says, his gaze sharp. "I hope you're not a cream or sugar type of drinker. The best way to enjoy real Hawaiian coffee is straight."

Meri waits for Sheriff Mato to take a sip before she tastes hers. Mato takes another sip before setting the cup down on the table.

"I always enjoy a cup of your coffee, KT, you know that," Sheriff Mato says, a smile fixed on her face.

Meri has to stop herself from sighing. There's something about this man that smells off to her. The stank of manure lingers about him, which is probably normal if he has ranchers as clients. But the smell goes beyond that, something she can't pinpoint. She knows one thing: she never forgets a smell, and her nose has never let her down. There's something off about this guy.

"So, what can I do for you fine ladies today?" He casually gathers various papers, placing them in a folder, giving the impression that they aren't important, but Meri notices they all focus on the Harper farm.

He's playing dumb. Why?

"KT, this is Special Agent Meri Amber, and you know why we're here. The buzz is all around town, so don't play coy." Sheriff Mato arches a brow over her mug of coffee as she takes another sip.

She asked Meri earlier to let her handle Kyle Travis, and handling him, she definitely is.

"Those trailers out there on the edge of town. It's horrific. How can something like this happen here in Shelby?" Kyle leans back against his chair, the casualness of his posture at odds with the moment's intensity.

"Those trailers were on the Harpers' property," Sheriff Mato interjects, her voice gravelly and resonant in the quiet room. Meri watches the realtor, gauging his reaction.

Kyle's brows lift slightly, a gesture betraying his surprise. "The old Cummings place? That was quite a piece of work, let me tell ya. I couldn't believe Old Man Cummings actually sold it. Do you know I've been after him for years, years mind you, to sell? The countless buyers I've had lined up, where he would have made out like a pig in a cornfield, but he always turned me down. Craziest thing. And then what, three or so months ago, he calls me out of the blue and says he's selling the place and needs me to handle the paperwork."

"Everything," Mato insists, the word hanging between them like a loaded gun. "We want to know everything about that sale."

For a beat, the only sound is the clock ticking on the wall, marking time as if it underscores the urgency of Sheriff Mato's request. Kyle's eyes narrow, and he runs a hand through his thick hair before setting his hat back on his head.

"Well, all right then. Typically, these are confidential, as you're aware, but . . ." He opens up the folder on his desk, going through the paperwork. "It wasn't your usual sale, I'll give you that. But then again, nothing 'bout that property ever was usual."

Sheriff Mato leans forward, resting her arms on the edge of the desk. "I don't have time for this, KT. You know what we found out there, yes? Then you know how important this is. So do me a favor, start from the beginning, will you? Leave nothing out."

Kyle's fingers tap a staccato rhythm on the oak desk, his boots propped up beside an array of scattered papers. The room feels too small for his larger-than-life presence, the scent of leather and dust mingling in the stagnant air. He chuckles, a sound that doesn't quite reach his eyes. "Old Man Cummings, now there's a character straight out of a ghost story — I swear, the man was more shadow than flesh."

Agent Meri watches him like a hawk, her mind a cauldron of simmering questions, her senses sharp as she decodes the realtor's every gesture. How much is story, and how much is truth? How much of the truth is hidden in lies?

"Shadow, how?" Sheriff Mato asks, her voice low and even, playing the good cop to Meri's silent intensity.

"Well, you should know," Kyle says, giving Sheriff Mato a look. "Didn't you arrange patrols to go by his property every so often? Of all people, you would know the guy was hardly ever here." Kyle drops his feet to the floor with a thud.

Meri snatches a look at the sheriff. This was a piece of info she had failed to share. Perhaps this town is full of more secrets than she'd anticipated.

"The man paid in cash, always in advance, and always provided enough to cover while he was away. He wanted someone to look after the acreage, but—" He pauses, leaning forward, lowering his voice to a conspiratorial whisper. "There were parts of that land he kept off-limits. Told us to steer clear, or we'd regret it. Gave me the creeps, honestly."

Meri's eyes narrow, thoughts racing.

"Parts of the land, like where the trailers were located?" Sheriff Mato asks.

Kyle Travis nods. "That and others."

Meri makes a mental note to find out those other areas and do a search.

"Did he say why?" Sheriff Mato presses, her tone edging toward impatience. From the glance she gave Meri, she's on the same page.

"Never did, and I never asked." Kyle shrugs, the gesture too casual, too rehearsed. "That man had secrets, and I figured I'm better off not knowing."

Mato exchanges another glance with Meri. They both know that what lies unspoken often holds the key. "And the documents?" Mato prompts, her gaze not leaving Travis.

"Ah, right." Kyle Travis's fingers do another little tap dance on his desk before he hands over a few sheets from the folder in front of him. "Everything is through a shell company, so I don't quite know what you're looking for unless you're needing to figure out who owns that company, but... I figured you'd show up eventually, so I put together everything you'd need." He says it without any shame.

He hands over the deed, unmistakably official, revealing the name she has been chasing — a phantom no longer.

Meri's heart stops for a few beats. "Andrew Rawlings," she reads aloud, the syllables heavy with implication. Adrenaline surges through her as she repeats his name again. She found him. She finally found him.

"And she speaks. Nice to meet you." Kyle lifts a shoulder in a shrug.

"Who is Andrew Rawlings, and why isn't Cummings's name on this document?" Sheriff Mato asks.

Kyle stays silent longer than he should, but long enough to answer the question.

"Cummings is Rawlings," Meri says. These three words open more doors in Meri's soul than she thought possible. Could this be happening? "He's also a man I've been searching for."

"Did you know this?" Mato gives Kyle Travis a severe look.

Again, with the shrug. "Everyone is welcome to have their privacy; it's not my business to ask. As long as he had the documents to prove he was who he said he was, then legally, there's no issues. Right?"

"Privacy or secrecy?" Meri counters, her brain already dissecting this new information, the gears turning as she maps out the next move in this deadly chess game she seems to be playing with Rawlings. He's always been several moves ahead of her, but . . . this could be the key to changing everything.

"Guess that depends on who you ask," Kyle replies with a sardonic lift of his eyebrow.

Sheriff Mato taps the document, a silent acknowledgment of the gravity of their find.

Meri looks over the other sheets, memorizing all the details she needs.

"Listen." Kyle clears his throat. "These are all copies. Technically you should be giving me a warrant, but we take care of our own out here, don't we, Sheriff? Take them. I hope it helps."

Meri pulls out her phone. Her boss, Lindsay, needs to know this. Her fingers dance across the screen. The message is brief but explosive: *I found him. Andy Rawlings. Sending address, possible lead.*

She hits 'Send,' feeling the thrum of intense excitement in her veins. This could be it — the break she's been waiting for.

She snaps a photo of the sheet with Rawlings' address and sends it.

Lindsay responds immediately: *Sit tight. We check it out.*

Sit tight. Being so close to a breakthrough and told to sit tight is like telling a sugar-high child it's time for bed. Everything within her screams for action, the opposite of what she needs to do.

If Lindsay were here, he'd talk to her about how patience solves cases and how they need information before action. He'd probably tell her something like: 'Don't ruin everything by rushing now.'

And he'd be right.

"Is there anything else I can help you with today, ladies?" Kyle Travis pushes back his seat and stands.

Sheriff Mato's phone rings, the tone jarring in the quiet office. "Hey, Pete, give me some good news . . ." She stands and walks away, her voice growing softer the further she's from Meri.

Meri stands and stares down Kyle Travis, who seems somewhat uncomfortable. He leans over his desk, gathers all the papers together, and hands them over.

"Is that everything?" Meri asks.

He nods.

"There's nothing else we need to know about that property or its previous owner? I'd hate to come back and charge you with obstruction." She lets the threat hang between them and watches as the man's huge Adam's apple bobs.

"Everything is in there. Everything I know, you'll know once you go through it. Listen, Shelby may be a small town, but we're tight. People respect privacy."

"Privacy is one thing. Keeping secrets that result in murder is another." She steps away from his desk and sees Sheriff Mato waiting for her at the door.

Her phone rings just then. She's half a mind to ignore it but then notices it's her mom.

She answers, heading out the door and into the bright sun. "This is a surprise. Everything okay?"

"Hey, sweetie. I know we have a call scheduled for tonight, but I wanted to give you a heads-up before then."

There's something in her mom's voice that has Meri concerned. Once a week, she video calls with her parents. A few years ago, they complained that they never saw her anymore and that she was more focused on her work than life. She couldn't argue with them, but instead of feeling guilty and knowing nothing would change, she set up weekly calls with her parents, where she barely shared anything about her work, and they shared everything else, including all their neighbor's gossip. It was probably the one thing she looked forward to the most every week.

"Is something wrong?" To have her mom call like this is very rare.

"It's your dad. I don't want to worry you, but he hasn't been feeling all that well lately. He's had a few doctor's appointments and we're still waiting on tests, but when you see him tonight, don't comment on how he looks, okay?"

"Why, how does he look?"

Her mom sighs. "Tired. He's a grumpy old man, with some really bad heartburn. It's nothing serious, but you know how he gets. He doesn't want any fussing, from you especially."

"No fussing, got it. We'll chat tonight, okay? I can't wait to tell you about this wolf-dog I've met. I'll send some photos later. Love you." Her parents are huge dog lovers, with their own little Pomeranian-Shih tzu called Jasper that they spoil rotten.

"Everything okay?" Mato asks.

"Just my mom being all motherly. You don't mind if I send them some photos of your dog, do you?"

Mato opens the car door for her dog to jump in and smiles. "Go for it. And listen, I've got some news," she says as they get in the car and she turns on the air conditioning. "The coroner can confirm that" — she places a hand on Meri's arm — "none of the victims are your sister."

Not her sister. Relief crashes over her like a wave, cold and unexpected. "Thank you for telling me that," she manages, voice barely above a whisper. The words hang between them, laden with implications both grim and hopeful. There's still hope then, hope that her sister could still be alive.

"Thank you for providing her records." Mato's face softens, a mixture of sympathy and shared reprieve passing through her features. "The coroner's team is slowly identifying the victims, quite a few of them were listed missing, which helps the process. Since there are so many, they had to call in extra help from the state medical examiner's office."

"That's good news for those families." Meri knows personally what it's like to always be wondering, waiting for word about a family member who has gone missing.

Mato turns toward her, the furrow of her brow deepening with each word. "Crazy thing is, none of them local. They're all from different states."

"None from Montana," Meri repeats, the reality settling like sediment in her mind. It doesn't make sense to her — this small town, remote and unassuming, becoming a graveyard for souls that don't belong here. Since the victims are from different states, this now makes it an official federal investigation. She'll need to tell Lindsay.

"Which begs the question," Mato says, almost to herself, "why here? Did they arrive in Shelby breathing, or were they brought here already deceased?"

There is a brief silence.

"Transporting bodies across state lines . . . It's risky and attracts attention," Meri muses, her mind piecing together a macabre puzzle. "Unless it's someone who knows how to move unseen. Someone who understands the darkness."

"Or someone who's part of it," Mato adds.

"Either way," Meri says, her voice steady despite the turmoil inside her, "this is bigger than anticipated. And whoever is behind this . . . they chose Shelby for a reason."

CHAPTER THIRTEEN

Meri turns off the main road. The Harpers' farmhouse is up ahead, looming large against the backdrop of Montana's vast, azure sky.

There's a beauty out here that she's coming to appreciate.

She glances at the time. She's here later than she wanted to be. She'd hoped to come earlier when she knew it would only be Tucker Harper around, but after the news of Andy Rawlings, she needed a bit of time to do some more digging.

Lindsay's team hasn't yet received any new information on Rawlings. Still, one of her background searches came up with some fascinating tidbits of information on the Harper family.

Up ahead, Tucker Harper is stepping out of his truck. He turns as she drives down his driveway, his hands shielding his eyes.

She pulls up beside him and gets out. His eyes are covered by sunglasses, but there's a wariness tightening his jaw that she doesn't miss.

She smiles at him. He doesn't smile back.

"Special Agent Amber," he greets, his voice guarded. "What brings you out here again? I thought we answered all your questions already." His hands find refuge in the pockets of his work-stained jeans.

"Not quite," Meri states, her tone even, but her eyes search for cracks in his composure. She notes how he shifts his weight, the subtle clench of his fingers, and the tenseness of his shoulders.

"We told you all we know," Tucker says, his attempt at casual conversation betrayed by his demeanor.

"Did you now? I kind of doubt that," Meri says. At their initial meeting, it didn't take long for her to realize that Tucker isn't the kind of man who breaks under pressure. Nor is he the kind of man to volunteer information unless he's specifically asked.

So, it's up to her to ask the right questions.

"Are you suggesting I lied?" There's a defensiveness in his voice she's pretty familiar with. He's hiding something.

"Lied? I hope not. Sometimes things aren't what they seem," Meri replies, stepping closer, her gaze never leaving his. "Sometimes people hide things."

Tucker's face hardens. "We've got nothing to hide," he asserts, but the flicker of uncertainty that twerks with his lips tells Meri otherwise.

"Everybody has something to hide, Mr. Harper," she counters softly, watching as a muscle ticks in Tucker's cheek. She knows the pressure points and knows how to push without shoving. "It's just a matter of finding it."

A gust of wind ruffles the nearby grass, carrying with it an unspoken standoff. Tucker looks past her, toward the main road, and then back at Meri, his expression unreadable.

"The best we can do is live our lives, Agent," he says after a moment, his drawl thicker and clinging to the air between them. "Past is past."

Past is past. Why does that sound familiar?

"Unless it bleeds into the present," Meri suggests quietly, her words a challenge.

Tucker's silence speaks volumes and adds to the tension between them. She takes a few steps back, giving him some breathing room, and lets her gaze rove around the farm. There are secrets here, secrets that lie dormant beneath the soil, taunting her to come find them.

"Tell me about the previous owner," she says, her tone even, a scalpel cutting to the heart of the matter.

"Previous owner?" Tucker parrots, his gaze drifting. "We don't know anything about them. I saw the listing online, with pictures of the land. Jillian fell in love with the house and that porch" — he points behind him — "and the price was too good to ask any questions."

"Didn't ask or didn't want to know?" Meri's question is soft but laden with implications, her eyes sharpening on him like talons. It's strange that a person would buy property like this in northern Montana only based on photographs. Does it happen? Sure. But this sale occurred within a matter of days. The property hadn't even been listed.

"Sometimes a deal is just a deal." Tucker's defense is a flimsy barricade, betrayed by the tightness in his voice.

"Is that right?" Meri asks, folding her arms, her stance mirroring the unyielding nature of her inquiry.

That muscle she's been keeping an eye on jerks in Tucker's jaw, and he hesitates before replying, his words measured. "We've got nothing to do with whatever history this place has."

"Speaking of history," Meri says her mind a chessboard, pieces moving into place. "I've been digging into yours. You and Jillian changed your last name not long ago. Left protective custody, I hear. Care to share why?"

Tucker's face pales, a canvas washed of color, his facade cracking like drought-stricken earth. He locks eyes with Meri, and for a fleeting moment, she's sure he's about to share everything with her. Then he looks away and she knows that moment is gone.

"It's what I do, Tucker," she warns him. "I dig up secrets."

"Look, what happened before . . . it's got no bearing on now," he says, but there's an edge of desperation in his tone, a fortress besieged.

"Everything has a bearing." Meri presses on, stepping forward, her presence an encroaching tide. "Especially when lives are at stake."

"Lives? What lives? I thought you only found dead bodies?" His throat works over words left unsaid, the silence punctuated by the distant caw of a crow.

Meri waits, her stillness a vise, constricting around the truth she is determined to unearth. If there's one thing she's learned over the years, if you give a guilty man a rope, he'll eventually hang himself with the truth.

"Agent," he says, voice raw like gravel churned up by a passing tractor, "you're not hearing me. Our past — it's dead and buried. You digging it up doesn't change a damn thing about who we are now or even what you found, and you know it."

The wind picks up, carrying the scent of freshly tilled earth and a chill that has nothing to do with the weather. A shiver dances along her spine, but she stands her ground, her gaze never wavering from Tucker's agitated form.

"Dead and buried things have a way of resurfacing, Tucker," she replies, her tone steady despite the adrenaline coursing through her veins. "And I'm not in the habit of leaving stones unturned. If there's one thing you'll soon realize about me, it's that. Besides, last I heard, your past is getting closer to your present . . ." She pauses to gauge his reaction to her news, except there's nothing. Not a twitch. Not a stammer. Nothing. "Which," she continues, "I can see isn't news to you. Interesting."

His nostrils flare, and he steps closer, his presence imposing, an unspoken threat lingering between them. The tension coils tighter, a python squeezing the air from their shared space.

"We know nothing about those trailers and what they've been hiding. And regarding the previous owner, you can get more information from the realtor in town, than from me."

"So you're telling me there is no undisclosed relationship between you and the previous owner?"

His head jerks in a decisive nod. She doesn't believe him.

"Oh, I've already spoken with Mr. Kyle Travis, and he gave me the whole lowdown on Old Man Cummings. Except, we both know that isn't his real name, now don't we? What's with the owners of this property changing their last names, I wonder?"

"Get off my land. Unless you've got a warrant, which I doubt," he seethes, each word a barb meant to wound. "I've told you all we know. There's nothing else."

As if on cue, a van honks at the driveway's edge, and a child gets out.

"My son is here, which means it's time for you to go," Tucker says, his voice dropping to a low, dangerous timbre. He tilts his head toward the departing bus, a silent command to heed his words. "I won't say it again."

Meri takes a deliberate step back. Her mind races over the puzzle pieces she has yet to fit together. She can feel Tucker's eyes boring into her behind the shadows of his glasses. His stare promises this isn't over — not by a long shot.

"Like I said before, Mr. Harper, I have a feeling you know more than you're telling me. If it means I dig deeper into your past, then so be it." She half turns as if she's done with the conversation, except it's the exact opposite. "I promise you, I've got a lot of patience and determination."

"Word of advice, Agent Amber," Tucker says, "use that determination to hunt some real criminals and leave my family alone."

Meri's gaze lingers on the man as he walks toward his son, placing an arm around his shoulders and then heading up the porch and into the house. Her mind churns with thoughts, each more suspicious than the last.

Tucker might think he's good at hiding his secrets, but when playing this game, he's still at the beginner level. His face paled when she mentioned the past, and her comment about the previous owner and what she knows . . . a web of fear crisscrossed his face.

A cool wind whips across the farm, carrying the scent of damp earth and unease. There's more happening beneath the surface here and she needs to dig deeper, go harder. The boxes in those trailers were left there for a reason, and she knows she's getting closer to the truth.

She slowly turns and takes in her surroundings. There's something about this farm, something that feels off. The air is oppressive, and it's like the land is holding its breath, complicit in whatever lie the dirt is hiding.

Her eyes narrow as she pulls out a small notebook from her pocket, the pages filled with neat, methodical script. The pen in her hand is steady as she adds a new note, underlining twice for emphasis, before heading back to her vehicle. These secrets Tucker Harper seems to be guarding — they won't stay secret for long.

CHAPTER FOURTEEN

Jillian

By the time Saturday rolls around, Jillian can't wait to be away from the prying eyes and gossip. While Tucker loads the last of Ethan's baseball gear into the back of the truck, she stares out at the road, her arms wrapped tight around herself. Another police cruiser crawls past their driveway, their constant presence a heavyweight in her chest.

"Jillian, you okay?" Tucker's voice breaks through her reverie.

Is she okay? Not in the slightest. If she stays here alone all day, she will lose her mind.

"Hey, why don't we make a weekend of it? I mean, the game is two hours away — instead of rushing home, why don't we book a night at a hotel, one with a pool?" She keeps her voice light, upbeat.

Tucker's gaze searches hers for a little too long before nodding. "Sure, that sounds like fun and something Ethan would love."

"And I think we should get a dog. Not a small cuddly dog, a big one that barks and scares people." She blurts this out without thought, the words tumbling over each other in her haste.

"So, like . . . a guard dog?" Tucker shakes his head. "What happened to no dogs because you're allergic."

"Well, it wouldn't be a pet, right? Sleep outside, kind of thing." She shrugs, realizing how lame her words really are. "Or . . . we can just put in more security lights and maybe a few extra cameras?"

"Yeah, let's go with Plan B," Tucker says. "I've already put a call out for pricing. If we're going to stay, then we need to do everything we can to stay safe." His shoulders drop as he says the words, and he looks out over the driveway rather than at her.

It took a while before Tucker agreed to stop running from their past, to finally settle here, in Shelby. She still doesn't have all the answers she wants about Rawlings, with Tucker being tight-lipped about that man, and she doesn't understand why.

A thousand different scenarios have played out in her head the past few nights, trying to pinpoint the exact moment Andy came into their lives and why, but nothing she imagines will be close to the truth.

Things will probably get messy, but it's time they face things head-on. Maybe the next time she sees Sheriff Mato, she should come clean about their past.

Ethan's laughter echoes from the kitchen as he rummages through the cupboard, the plastic bags rustling like whispers. "Got the snacks!" he announces, holding up a triumphant array of chips and cookies as he stands in front of the screen door.

"Great choice, buddy." Jillian forces a smile. "Hey, listen, go pack your bathing suit, pajamas, and your toothbrush, okay?"

Ethan's eyes go wide as saucers. "Are we spending the night somewhere that has a pool?" Excitement lights up his voice. "Cool." He drops the snacks on the floor and races up the stairs. She should have known he'd be excited — he's been begging for a pool ever since they moved here. It's not like they don't have the space for one.

It doesn't take long for Jillian to pack a to-go bag for herself and Tucker. Within an hour, she's booked their hotel, and they're on the road.

Miles unfold like a spool of thread, with Tucker's hands gripping the steering wheel, steady and sure, and Ethan's soft snores filling the backseat. Beside her, the landscape blurs into a watercolor wash of green and gold, when Jillian sits up straight, gasping.

"What?" Tucker says, looking at her with fear in his eyes.

"Oh, my goodness," she says, breaking the silence in the car. "I totally forgot to tell you about who I saw at Ethan's last game."

"Jill, don't do that." Tucker holds a palm tight to his chest. "You almost gave me a heart attack."

"Oops, sorry." She winces. "But seriously, there was this woman at the last game — I actually bumped into her at the grocery store when I had to grab the after-game treats."

He glances over, one eyebrow raised. "What about her?"

"You won't believe this," Jillian says. "I mean, after all this time, the likelihood is crazy that it would be, but . . ." Uncertainty threads her voice as she thinks about the many times she thought she'd seen Becky in the past and was mistaken.

"Who do you think it was?"

"Becky." She knows how crazy that sounds.

"Your best friend from school who went missing?"

Jillian nods. "I know it can't be her, but . . ."

Tucker rubs his chin like he's thinking about how to reply.

"You don't need to say anything. I know it's not her. I've accepted that, but with her body never being found . . . I've kind of always hoped, you know?"

He takes her hand and lightly rubs his thumb over her skin. "There's nothing wrong with hoping. But if she were still alive, I think you, of all people, would know, don't you? I mean, and her parents, of course, but you two were insep-arable, right?"

Just hearing him say it is all she needs right now.

When they arrive at the baseball field, the chatter of families and the crack of bats against balls immerses them in the world of Little League. Coach Neil spots Tucker, a grin splitting his face. "It's about time! Care to lend an extra hand?"

"Sure thing, Neil," Tucker replies, clapping the coach on the shoulder as he heads to the dugout.

Jillian adjusts her sunglasses, the late morning sun blazing bright over the small baseball field. She can't help but smile as Ethan jogs onto the dusty diamond with the other eleven-year-olds, his oversized cap nearly swallowing his head. A proud smile tugs at her lips as she sees him take his position at shortstop, his favorite spot. Tucker stands near third base, wearing the same cap as the boys, coaching them with a mix of encouragement and instruction.

Is there anything better than spending a day on a ball field? This is everything she pictured country living to be like, and it fills her heart with joy.

As the game begins, the familiar sounds of a little league baseball game fill the air — the crack of the bat, the thud of the ball into a mitt, the shouts from the dugout, and the constant cheering from parents on the bleachers. Jillian settles into her spot on the worn wooden bench, her hands wrapped around the mug of coffee they'd stopped to grab on the way to the game. She loves watching her boys play and have fun.

Her gaze drifts across the bleachers. She smiles at some, nods at others. She does a double take when she finds the Becky-lookalike.

Unlike the last time, the woman isn't alone. A large man sits next to her. Something about the way the woman holds herself — the tilt of her head, the nervous flicker of her eyes — echoes a familiarity that sends a shiver down Jillian's spine.

Elina Bortax. They'd been good friends back in Parishville until Elina's husband had decided Jillian's influence in his wife's life was too negative, and he forced her to move back to Croatia without any notice. Jillian had been devastated at the instant loss of her friend. She has worried about her nonstop, but she has no way of contacting her to make sure she's okay. Jillian lost track of all the times she'd find new bruises, marks, and cuts on her friend. Elina never denied her husband's temper, but she also never sought help either. Nothing Jillian ever said or did seemed to make a difference. She only hopes Elina is okay.

This woman holds herself in the same way.

Even now, she's protecting one of her arms as if she's in pain. Has that man hurt her? The woman stares straight ahead, her smile non-existent, until her son leaves a group of other boys huddled on the grass and climbs the stands to sit beside her. Then her smile appears wide and genuine, her body relaxing as she focuses on her son.

Someone whistles. Jillian turns her attention back to the field and notices Ethan slightly crouched, his eyes sharp as he watches the pitcher wind up. Determination is etched on his young face, so focused, so eager. Her heart swells with a mixture of pride and nerves, the way it always does during these games. Ethan loves baseball, but he hasn't been on a team since they left New York State. This here, watching him, is a reminder of why they are not running again. Her son needs this in his life.

The first pitch is a ball, low and outside. The batter lets it go, and Ethan glances over at Tucker, who gives a slight nod and a thumbs-up. Jillian's gaze lingers on her husband for a moment. Tucker looks so at ease out there, like he belongs. Baseball has always been his thing, too.

"Come on, Ethan!" she calls out, her voice blending with the other parents' cheers.

The next pitch comes, and the batter swings. A solid crack echoes across the field as the ball shoots toward the gap between shortstop and third base. Jillian holds her breath. Ethan springs into action, diving to his left, his glove outstretched. Time slows as he hits the dirt, his tiny body fully extended. For a second, it looks like the ball might slip past him, but then — miraculously — he snags it in the tip of his glove.

"Yes!" Jillian shouts, standing up from the bleachers as adrenaline surges through her. The crowd erupts in applause when Ethan scrambles to his feet and fires the ball to first base; the throw is a little off but still good enough that it's caught. Ethan's teammates clap him on the back as he jogs back to his spot, a wide grin on his face.

Tucker gives Ethan a quick, approving nod, but Jillian can see the pride in his eyes. She loves these moments, seeing her two boys — one big, one small — lost in the game they both love. For a second, nothing else matters; this little bubble of baseball is the only world that exists.

When the game finally ends, Ethan's team loses by only two points, and while the kids are all sad they've lost, there's still a spark of excitement, too. As the teams shake hands, she catches Tucker's gaze. When he winks, she smiles all over again.

Lingering behind to help pack up and say goodbye to everyone, Jillian casually scans the crowd. She does a double take as she spots the Becky-lookalike off in the distance. The woman struggles to shoulder a bag while the man she's with walks ahead of her. Her son helps her sling the bag across her body, distributing the weight so her one arm isn't affected.

Something definitely happened to her.

"Look, Tucker," Jillian whispers to her husband, her finger subtly pointing out the pair. "That's her."

Tucker's eyes follow Jillian's gesture, studying the couple for a long moment. "She doesn't look like Becky," he says, a frown creasing his brow.

"You don't think so?" Her forehead scrunches as she stares at the woman off in the distance.

"I'll admit, it's been a while since you've shown me photos, but . . ." He shrugs, like it's a non-issue.

Jillian studies the woman again, questioning herself. Maybe she's projecting, maybe she's wrong, but either way, an unsettling sensation coils in her gut.

CHAPTER FIFTEEN

"Best day ever!" Ethan's voice rings out as he slides down the hotel pool's slide for the umpteenth time. Tucker's laughter mingles with the shriek and splash as Ethan launches himself into the water. Jillian lounges on the edge, her feet dipped in, watching her family with a contented smile. Yep, coming here was a smart decision.

The moment is shattered when Tucker's phone buzzes against the metal side table, an invasive vibration that draws a frown from Jillian. Tucker hoists himself up out of the pool and grabs his phone, the lines around his eyes deepening as he stares at the screen. With a hesitant glance at Jillian, he answers, stepping away so he can talk in private.

Jillian's gaze narrows, tracking his stiff posture with the phone held tight to his ear, the way his hand runs through his hair — a tell-tale sign of his anxiety.

He's not gone long. "Is everything okay?" she asks while he drops the phone on a towel and sighs.

"Everything's fine, just . . ." He pauses.

"Don't lie to me," she warns him.

His lips thin. "I wasn't going to lie to you," he says, his words clipped.

Jillian rises, water dripping from her legs, and walks closer. "Then who was it? And please don't tell me it was work." Skepticism colors her tone, the shadows of doubt creeping into her normally trusting nature.

Tucker forces a smile that doesn't quite reach his eyes. "I said I wasn't going to lie. It wasn't work, but it's also not something we need to worry about, right now, all right? We are here, as a family, having fun. That's all that matters."

She studies him, the man she thought she knew so well. Unease coils tighter in her stomach, but she nods, letting it go for the moment.

"Okay," she concedes, though her voice betrays her concern. Her smile is brittle, and the mask of normalcy they both wear now shows its cracks.

"Come on, will you get in the water or just dangle your feet and pretend you're having fun? Ethan's been dying to show me how he can hold his breath underwater, isn't that right?" Tucker says, reaching for her hand, attempting to bridge the gap his secrets have created.

"Come on, Mom. Let's have some fun," Ethan calls out.

She wipes all traces of her anxiety away and pushes back her shoulders. "Get in the water, of course," she says, raising her voice loud enough for Ethan to smile. "Besides, I didn't buy a new bathing suit for it to stay dry, now did I?" She jumps in before Tucker has a chance to move, making sure to splash as much as she can to get him wet.

"Oh, that's how it is, is it?" Tucker wiggles his brows as he gets into a pounce stance, which has Ethan giggling. Jillian does her best to move as fast as she can in the water, but Tucker launches himself beside her, grabbing her around the waist and pulling her under the water with him, all in one fell swoop.

After about an hour of playtime, Ethan finally mentions he's hungry, to which Jillian whispers a quiet "*Thank you, Jesus.*" She can only handle the chlorine smell of a pool for so long. It's late by the time they leave the hotel and head to a burger place Jillian saw on a Food Network television show.

"The burgers here are apparently amazing," she tells the boys as they pull into the parking lot. "I want to try their Hawaiian Sizzler with grilled pineapple and hot honey sauce."

"Pineapple and honey don't belong on a burger, Mom." Ethan's disgust makes her chuckle.

"Well, they do on mine," she says, sticking her tongue out.

The neon glow of the burger joint's sign casts a cheerful light over their faces as they walk toward the restaurant. She's looking forward to getting inside when vehicle lights flash, illuminating the restaurant door. She casually glances back, shielding her gaze from the bright beams.

Tucker opens the door for them, his hand tightening momentarily on Ethan's shoulder. "Go ahead and order for me," he says, a forced casualness in his voice. "I'll have a beer. Just need a minute."

She glances back toward the truck with the bright lights and nods, her stomach tightening, the sense of unease from earlier creeping back. She ushers Ethan inside, the aroma of grilled meat filling their noses and loud eighties rock blaring from the speakers.

"Can we get fries, Mom?" Ethan's voice is full of youthful anticipation, his eyes wide and hopeful.

"Of course, sweetie," Jillian replies, her gaze flickering to the door every few seconds.

Minutes tick by. Five. Ten. Ethan's chatter about school projects and baseball fills the void, but Jillian's responses are automatic and distant. The clink of glasses and the murmur of conversation from other diners swell around them, and she has to keep reminding herself to stay here, in the present, and not let herself be pulled into the scary unknown.

"Where's Dad?" Ethan finally asks, his brow furrowed, his gaze scanning the entrance.

"He should be here soon, I hope. Any second now," Jillian assures him, the lie bitter on her tongue.

When Tucker eventually slips into the booth beside her, twenty minutes have stretched into an eternity. His apology is swift, his eyes avoiding hers.

"Everything okay?" she presses, her voice low, insistent.

"Fine, just fine," he answers too quickly, plastering on a smile as he sips the beer she ordered, the froth leaving a temporary mustache above his lip.

Jillian watches him, the man who's supposed to be her rock, now more like shifting sand beneath her feet. She bites back the urge to question further, instead focusing on the appetizers that have just arrived. The garlic scent of breadsticks twists her stomach, and her appetite disappears.

"Dig in, guys," she says, mustering enthusiasm she doesn't feel while Tucker's silence looms between them.

"Who was that?" she asks when Ethan heads to the bathroom. She notices how Tucker scans the restaurant and remains laser focused on their son as he heads into the one-person stall. His shoulders haven't relaxed since he sat down, leaving her worried.

"Not now, okay?" He still won't look at her. "We'll talk about it later, back at the hotel."

Dismissed, Jillian bites her tongue the rest of the evening, forcing herself to nibble on her burger and fries, laugh at Ethan's jokes, and pretend she's not seething inside, wanting to lash out at her husband for keeping secrets from her.

When Ethan begs for more swim time before bed, Jillian doesn't have the heart to say no. With the indoor pool full, they make their way to the outdoor one.

"It's all ours," Ethan says as he runs and jumps into the water.

The water shimmers under the hotel's outdoor lights as Ethan's gleeful shout cuts through the cool Montana air. He bursts from the slide, a spray of droplets catching the light like fleeting diamonds. Jillian watches from a poolside plastic chair, her arms wrapped tightly around herself despite the sweater guarding against the evening chill.

She still isn't used to the cool evenings out here.

"Are you coming in, Mom?" Ethan calls out.

"Not this time, bud." She smiles, the tension in her jaw betraying the effort behind it. "You've got the whole pool to yourself."

She hears the slam of the metal gate and glances over her shoulder to see Tucker walking toward her. He sits beside her, his gaze unfocused, the ripples reflecting in his blue eyes that seem to hold a storm within. Jillian reaches across the space between them and rests her hand on his arm, a gentle reminder that he isn't alone, even if he feels that way.

"Tuck?" Her voice is barely above a whisper, but he turns, an immediate alertness to his posture.

"Everything okay?"

He exhales slowly. "We're in a mess, Jill, and I'm trying to get us out of it while respecting your need to settle here."

She nods, forcing herself to remain mum, giving him room to speak.

"I knew," he finally says.

She waits for him to continue, and when he doesn't, she puts two and two together.

"You knew about the bodies?" She swallows hard, keeping her voice low. Her grip on his arm tightens.

He shakes his head, then gives a halfhearted shrug. "Well, I knew about the trailers, but not what was inside, if that makes any difference."

And he's only telling her this now? Why not admit that in the very beginning? "It doesn't."

He drops his head. "Yeah, I figured."

"Care to elaborate?" She wraps her arms across her stomach.

"Andy just said to keep an eye on the trailers and make sure no dumb kids use that section of the property as a party stop. He told me he'd lost the keys years ago but that the trailers were so full of rot that it'd be best to stay out of them. He promised the next time he was out our way, he'd take care of them."

"And you believed him." It's not a question.

He nods. "I mean, if he wanted to be responsible for hauling them out and paying the dump fees, then I was good with that."

"So why not just say that to Sheriff Mato?"

"I froze."

Her brows raise at the simple answer. "You froze? Tucker, no matter what's been thrown at us, you've never froze. Not to me, not to the police, not even to those ugly SOBs who made us leave our home in the first place."

"Yeah, but I didn't know enough then to know any better. Now I do. I know what's at stake, and we're on our own now."

"Then let's tell Sheriff Mato the truth. Maybe we can get the marshals to help us again."

He shakes his head. "It's too late for that now."

Her heart sinks. "How deep are you in this?" She thought they were past all of this, that they were in the clear, safe. "Who was on the phone?"

"Rawlings." One word, but the low rumble in his voice doesn't quite mask the underlying tremor in his hands.

Jillian's heart claws its way up her throat. Rawlings — a name that carries a weight they both feel: the harbinger of things unspoken, of fears not yet faced. She hates that name. Hates the man she's never met but has her family within his grip. Hates that he's a part of their life, ruining their life, and for what? Why?

Tucker extends his hand, warmth radiating from his palm and into hers, serving as a lifeline amid the uncertainty that surrounds them.

"Was he . . ." She pauses, searching her husband's gaze for the truth she's not sure he'll tell her. "Was that him at the restaurant?"

Tucker shakes his head, a shadow passing over his features. "No, just one of his . . . friends." He pauses, the words seeming to weigh heavily on his tongue. "He's worried about us, Jill. Since we refuse to leave, he's arranged for someone to keep an eye on the place and on us."

His revelation hangs between them, a new phantom to contend with. The hum of the hotel's fluorescent lights above them grows louder in Jillian's ears, amplifying her fear.

"Someone's been snooping around, asking questions," Tucker adds, his eyes meeting hers, a silent plea for understanding — or perhaps forgiveness.

Jillian shivers. "Maybe we should've left," she whispers, the words tasting of defeat.

But Tucker steadies her with a firmness she doesn't expect, his hand warm and grounding on her shoulder. "We'll be okay, Jill. I promise."

She wants to believe him, to lean into the certainty that resonates in his voice. Instead, she looks past him to where Ethan splashes joyfully, the water glistening like stars in his hair.

"Watch this, Dad!" Ethan's voice carves through her hesitation, pulling at a smile she thought she'd lost in the maze of their troubles.

"Coming, buddy," Tucker calls out, before turning back to Jillian. His lips brush against hers, a kiss that speaks volumes, sealing his vow.

And then he's off, charging toward the pool with a boyish grin, taking a running leap. His body curls into a ball, and he plunges into the depths with a splash that sends waves crashing over the edge.

"Whoa, cannonball!" Ethan's laughter dances across the water, mingling with the sound of the splash, a brief but welcome melody of carefree abandon.

Jillian heads to the gate, staring out over the yard and parking lot. She doesn't feel safe. Someone is out there watching them, watching her. Are they there for their protection or worse?

"Jill, come here," Tucker calls out. There's something in his voice, a warning she catches, which she hopes Ethan is oblivious to. She casts one last look out at the parked vehicles and shivers.

No, she definitely doesn't feel safe.

CHAPTER SIXTEEN

Jillian folds a pair of Ethan's jeans as sunlight filters through the gauzy kitchen curtains, casting a hazy glow over the wooden floorboards. The quiet of the Sunday afternoon hangs heavy in the air, wrapping around her like a blanket — too still, too silent.

Tucker leans against the doorframe, his gaze distant. "I'm gonna drive around for a bit," he says, voice even. "Check what's going on out there and see if the cops are still just poking around the trailers or if they're spreading out."

Her hands pause, a tingle of apprehension creeping up her spine. "Should I be worried?" she asks, folding another shirt.

He shakes his head, the corners of his mouth pulling down in an attempt at reassurance. "No, I don't think so. Andy — he said he's taking care of it." Tucker's eyes meet hers, but they're like mirrors reflecting a stormy sky, impossible to read.

"Taking care of it," she repeats under her breath, not quite a question, not quite a statement.

Tucker pushes off from the doorframe, his movements deliberate. "Yeah."

94

"Okay," Jillian murmurs, more to herself than to him. The hum of the washing machine in the mudroom fills the silence. There's more she wants to say, to ask, but everything from her husband's posture to his hooded gaze tells her he won't answer, so why bother? All he'll give her are more half-answers and half-truths.

With one last look at Jillian, Tucker leaves. The sound of his truck engine starts up, soon fading into the distance. Alone again, Jillian lets out a long sigh. It's happening again: their past becoming their present, despite Tucker's promises.

Her cell phone rings. Jillian's hands pause over the laundry basket as she reaches for it. "Mom?" Her voice betrays none of her turmoil as she answers the phone, propped between shoulder and ear.

"Hi, sweetheart. How's my little man doing?" Kathy's voice is generally a familiar balm, but today, it grates on Jillian's frazzled nerves.

"He's good. Busy with baseball and loving it." Jillian bites back the restlessness that urges her to pace the kitchen.

"Oh, good. Listen, I've been thinking. I should come out for a visit soon," Kathy suggests, the words wrapped in the velvet of maternal concern.

It's on the tip of Jillian's tongue to say yes, that she'd love to see her and spend time with her, but then she thinks about everything going on.

"Actually, now's not the best time," she says, folding another shirt into a perfect square. "Work's been hectic, and with his baseball schedule, we're hardly home." Lies. Lies. Lies.

"Jillian, summer's almost here. Ethan will need someone to keep him busy while Tucker's working." Kathy presses on, her intuition piercing through Jillian's thin pretext. "Do you even have him booked into any summer camps?"

Jillian snorts. "I haven't even thought of that, and honestly, I'm not sure if they have programs like that out here, but I'll figure something out. Don't worry." The lie tastes bitter on her tongue, the truth a splinter lodged beneath her skin.

Kathy's silence is heavy, and Jillian knows her mother won't take her hedging for an answer.

"What's going on?" Her mother asks a simple question that is way too complicated to answer over the phone. "Are you guys okay?

"We're . . . fine."

"Is that husband of yours behaving?"

"Of course he is."

Her mother harumphs. "I find that highly unlikely. You can't get away from the mob you know, no matter how far you run."

"It wasn't the mob, Mom." She'd confided in her mother about what happened and why they had to leave for Iowa. Thanks to being in the witness protection program, it had been hard to say goodbye, not knowing when she'd ever see or hear from her mother again.

"Well, whatever they call themselves, they sound like a mob to me. They don't know where you are, right? You're keeping a low profile? When I fly out, I'll be sure to fly out somewhere far and rent a car to drive the rest of the way."

Jillian laughs. "You don't need to be so cloak and dagger, Mom, but I appreciate it. See if you can get a flight to Helena. We can shop while there, and it'll be a good excuse to stock up at Costco." Telling her mom not to come after she's already made her mind up is like telling a mouse not to go for the cheese left on the trap.

"Let me chat with Ethan, okay?" Kathy doesn't wait for an answer, her decision made.

"Sure, Mom," Jillian concedes, her voice the epitome of restraint. As soon as Ethan heard that it was her mom on the phone, he's been at her side, waiting. The two have a special connection, and she knows he'll be excited to have her mom come out.

"Hey, buddy," Jillian says, offering Ethan the phone with a smile. "Grandma wants to talk to you."

Ethan's face lights up as he grabs the phone. She ruffles his hair affectionately before turning to the task of making dinner, seeking solace in the routine of chopping vegetables and boiling pasta.

As she moves about the kitchen, the knife slicing through carrots with rhythmic precision, her thoughts drift to Tucker, out there somewhere, checking their property, searching for signs of prying eyes or police tape. Why is he so concerned? Are there more bodies? Are they caretakers of Andy Rawlings' personal cemetery? Her stomach tightens, but she forces herself to focus on the hum of the refrigerator, the bubbling of the pot, the domestic sounds that anchor her to the moment.

Through the gauzy curtain, she sees the outline of a police car, creeping along the road to the side of their property. Her breath catches in her chest, and she stands frozen, the knife forgotten on the cutting board.

"Mom?" Ethan's voice pulls her back. "Everything okay?" he asks, his blue eyes searching hers for reassurance.

"Everything's fine, sweetheart," she replies, her voice steady despite the tremor she feels inside. She turns away from the window, hoping her son doesn't catch the glint of fear in her gaze.

"Grandma says she'll forward her flight info once she's got it all booked. Her oven timer went off, so she hung up real quick. Said she had a cake in the oven and didn't want it to burn."

"Well, it wouldn't be the first time," Jillian mutters, but there's a smile in her voice. Growing up, her mother never had the skills for making meals or even baking, but she sure did try. "Do you know how many cakes we had to cut the burnt bottom pieces off when I was little?"

"We should make a cake." Ethan skips into the pantry for a boxed cake mix. Ethan loves baking, and they look for new recipes to try each week. Last week, they made cowboy cookies, which turned out delicious. This week, apparently, they are making a cherry-chip cake.

Jillian hovers while Ethan pulls out the mixing bowl and puts on an apron her mom bought him a few years ago. It's getting a little small, but he loves wearing it. When it comes to boxed cakes, Jillian lets Ethan take the lead. He cracks each egg into a small bowl and, with a fork, whisks it together before adding it to the dry mix. She helps him pour the oil into the measuring cup and then lets him use the hand mixer to mix it all. He hands her one of the beaters while he licks the other.

"Grandma told me to start making a list of all the things we can do this summer," Ethan tells her, his face covered in the chocolate batter.

"Well, that sounds like fun," Jillian says, glancing out the kitchen window as another police car drives past.

"Are the police going to put Daddy in jail?" Ethan's innocent question comes out of the blue, forcing Jillian's pulse to skitter. "Because of the dead people in the trailers?"

Jillian slowly drops the beaters into the sink and turns on the tap. "Why would you think that?" she stammers. They haven't brought up this topic with him yet, not because they didn't want to but because the time never seemed right. Tucker suggested they wait until Ethan brought it up himself, but she's been hoping he'd do it with Tucker around.

"Kids at school say it's Daddy's fault, but I know it isn't because we just moved here, and Lucas's dad said the bodies have been there a really long time." He looks at her, his eyes wide with concern, but she hears how he's trying to downplay it in his voice.

"You've been thinking about this for a while, haven't you?"

Ethan nods.

"Was Lucas the one who told you about what's going on with the trailers?"

He nods again.

She pulls him in for a quick and secure hug, knowing they both need it right now. "You're right. It's not Daddy's fault. I think it's sad that the . . . bodies have been there for so long, and no one knew."

"There are a lot of mommies and daddies who will be sad once they find out, huh?" Ethan struggles hard not to let the emotion in his voice take over, but she knows it's there.

"Oh, baby, I'm sorry. We should have talked about this before now, and that's on me. Yes, a lot of parents are going to be getting sad news, but at least now they'll know what's happened instead of still wondering, right?" Jillian tries hard to keep her voice steady and soft, emotional but not losing control.

"But Daddy didn't do anything wrong, right?"

"No, honey." She hugs him tight. "Daddy didn't do anything wrong. The police are just doing their job, trying to figure out what happened."

Ethan nods slowly, still unsure. "But why do they keep coming here? Why do they always want to talk to Daddy?"

This surprises her. "What do you mean? They've only been to the house once."

He shakes his head and won't look her in the eye.

"Ethan, can you please explain?"

He gives a slight shrug. "They were here this week when I got off the bus." His voice is very low and soft, like he's worried about getting in trouble, or getting his father in trouble.

It takes everything in her not to scream in frustration. The police were here, and Tucker didn't say anything? Why? She swallows back everything she wants to ask and instead reminds herself to remain calm.

Calm, like a gentle breeze. Calm, like a rose petal resting in the summer sun. Calm, like . . . nope, it's not working.

"Well, I wasn't aware of that, but I think they come because someone might have hurt those people, and they're trying to find out who," Jillian replies, choosing her words carefully. "And they're probably looking for some documents we have from when we bought this property."

Ethan's gaze seems to search hers for any hint of fear, so she makes sure he doesn't find any.

"Hey, how about you head outside to play while the cake bakes? I think I saw Dad out by the barn. He might be willing to throw some balls with you." If there's one thing that can distract her son, it's the offer to play ball.

Ethan's face lights up at the idea. "Can we have sloppy joes?" he asks, wrinkling his nose at the carrots, celery, and peppers in the strainer.

She eyes the produce and nods. Hiding these vegetables in the meat sauce won't be a problem.

As she watches Ethan run outside, she can't help but heave a heavy sigh. She knows the police investigation isn't over yet, and their family will be caught in the crosshairs — but how much is the question.

What else is Tucker not telling her?

CHAPTER SEVENTEEN

The bell above the rustic door chimes as Jillian pushes into Brews and Bakes. The scent of freshly ground beans and baked pastries envelops her, a comforting embrace that has her smiling for just a moment. Her gaze sweeps across the small, cozy interior before she heads to the counter.

After the morning she's had, she needs coffee, stat. Tucker left yesterday for a business trip, and of course, that's when Ethan's nightmares had to start up again. The poor boy has done so well for the past few months, but all of this craziness with the trailers and the police driving by all the time hasn't helped.

"Your regular?" Sarah rests her hands on the back of her hips and groans. "Have a baby, they say. It's the best feeling in the world, they boast. No one tells you about the pain and aches you feel while you have a peanut growing inside of you."

"Most of us wipe those memories the moment we hold our little peanuts for the first time." Jillian gives her a sympathetic glance. "And make it the tallest size you have, please," she says seconds before yawning.

"Make it two," a familiar voice adds from behind her. Agent Meri Amber steps up, offering an easy smile that crinkles the corners of her piercing eyes.

"Agent." Jillian half turns, a flicker of surprise in her tone. She is the last person Jillian wants to run into today. To hide her anxiety, she tucks a stray lock of brown hair back into her unruly ponytail, only to realize the gesture gives away how she's feeling, anyway.

"Call me Meri, please," the agent insists, her tone friendly, but Jillian is still on guard. She has yet to meet a cop without an ulterior motive.

"Meri, then." Jillian nods, allowing a tentative smile to curve her lips. "I didn't expect to see you here."

"Small town, smaller coincidences," Meri quips, accepting her cup with a nod of gratitude toward Sarah.

Jillian moves away from the counter, the agent following.

"Seems like you're a regular," Meri observes, taking a sip.

"Guilty as charged. It's the little rituals, you know? They keep things . . . normal." Jillian's words float between them, hinting at the chaos beneath her calm exterior.

"Normal is good. Especially with everything that's been going on," Meri acknowledges, her voice softening as she looks Jillian straight on. "I imagine the first thing you must do every time you move is find a good coffee shop. I know I do, whenever I go anywhere for a case."

Jillian tightens her grip on the cup, the cardboard sleeve creasing under her fingers. "Yes, well, a good coffee shop is important, don't you think?" She's not sure what the federal agent is hinting at, but whatever it is, she doesn't like it.

"You've been married quite a while, haven't you?"

Jillian nods. "We have." She doesn't give how many years, mainly because she has a feeling the agent already knows.

"And in all those years, you've moved what . . . five times? Or was it six? I mean . . . can you really count that safe house to different safe house move in Iowa? Probably not." Meri locks her gaze onto Jillian's with what Jillian can only take to be a challenge.

"What are you getting at, Agent Amber?" Jillian asks. "Sounds like you already know the answers, so why ask the questions? If you've got something to say, say it, please. I'm too tired to do this dance today." Jillian traces the rim of her coffee cup, the steam curling like whispers through the small lid opening. When she glances upward, she notices there are no questions on the agent's face, just a friendly smile.

"There's no dance, not right now. I guess, in a bad way, I was trying to tell you that I know what it's like to live with secrets."

Jillian's head cocks to the side while her gaze narrows slightly. "Just because someone lives with a secret doesn't mean it's bad. I understand in your line of work every secret probably is, but in real, everyday life . . . sometimes a secret is just a hushed-up truth others don't need to know." She glances at her watch and sighs. She's going to be late.

"Can I walk you to work?" Meri asks.

Jillian nods. "Do you do this often?" she asks once they are outside. "Go from town to town on cases? Must feel lonely."

"It can be. I've learned over the years that finding connections is important, though. It makes a world of difference, truth be told. Sometimes, those connections can lead to real friendships, which I know sounds . . . odd."

Jillian ponders this as they slowly walk down the main street. "Friendships. That relationship can be hard to come by, especially when one has to move so much in a short time period." She glances at Meri, who nods.

"I can see that. But, if the friendship is true, it won't matter where you move, or how far it is, right?"

"I'd like to think so. I had a friend move to the other side of the world, and we've lost touch. Well . . . no, that's not true. Her husband forced her to move back to Croatia. They left in the middle of the night, and there was no trace of her. It makes me worried, you know? It also makes me question just how safe a friendship with me is," she muses, talking more to herself than to Meri. "I mean, everyone I've called a best friend, and that's not many, end up disappearing."

"I'm sorry. Did you say your friends have a habit of dis-appearing?" Meri stops in the middle of the sidewalk, forcing Jillian to do the same.

"Yeah. Crazy, right? The first one was Becky. That was like what . . . twenty years ago," Jillian says, the weight of the decades pressing down on each syllable. "Goodness, it feels like forever, you know? We were just kids, walking home from a party, and then . . . she was gone."

Meri leans in slightly, her posture open, inviting Jillian to continue.

"We stopped at my house first. I waved at her as she kept on toward her house, which was only a few doors down. Once she'd passed our neighbor's tall green shrubs and I couldn't see her, I went in the house. I mean . . . we lived in a small town like this one. Everyone knew everybody, no one locked their front doors, and it wasn't like either of us hadn't walked the few steps between our houses alone, in the middle of the night, before." Jillian's voice falters, a crack in her composed facade. "That night was different, though. That night, she never made it home."

"Survivor's guilt is a heavy burden," Meri says gently, acknowledging the gravity of Jillian's confession.

Jillian doesn't reply at first, feeling the ghost of the past hover over her shoulder. "And the strangest thing happened recently. I saw someone who . . . who looked just like her." Her fingers tighten around the cup, knuckles whitening. "I know it's not. I mean, what are the odds, right? Twenty years later? But what if, right?"

"Memory can be a tricky thing," Meri responds, voice measured yet laced with concern. "If there's one thing I've learned over the years, trust your instincts. They've led you here for a reason."

The agent's empathy is a salve to Jillian's frayed nerves. "Thank you," she murmurs, the simple words infused with two decades' worth of hope and fear.

"It's what I do," Meri says. "I'm not sure if you know it, but my job is to find those missing for one reason or another."

"Like solving cold cases?"

Meri's shoulders do a little shrug dance. "Kind of. I work for a task force that brings down cells revolving around sex trafficking."

Jillian blanches. "Is that . . . is that what you think those trailers were used for?"

"What I think and what I know are two different things. What I know is that there are a lot of families who will soon get answers about their missing son or daughter. It won't be the answers they've been praying for, but at least now they will know."

"Do you . . . do you think that's what could have happened to my friend?" Jillian's voice breaks as she finds the courage to ask the question that's always sat there unanswered.

"I don't know. Do you happen to have any photos of Becky?" Meri's voice is soft, careful, as if she's navigating a minefield of memories.

A flicker of guilt crosses Jillian's face. She bites her lip, hesitating.

"I can't help you if you aren't honest with me," Meri reminds her.

"I . . . I took a picture," Jillian confesses, the words spilling out in a rush. "Not of Becky, exactly, rather, of the woman I thought was Becky, but I mean, it can't be her. It's from a distance, and kind of hard to see, and I feel horrid because I took it without her knowing but . . ." Her fingers twitch, itching to retrieve her phone but dreading the exposure of her covert act.

"Does it show the woman you believe to be your friend?" Meri's expression is unreadable, professional yet tinged with something softer, an understanding of the lines crossed by desperation.

"It does. But . . ." Jillian's heart hammers in her chest. "My family's in it too. I wasn't thinking — just acted on instinct."

"Jillian, you're trying to piece together a puzzle left unsolved for far too long," Meri reassures her, her tone firm yet not condemning. "Let's take a look, shall we?"

With trembling hands, Jillian fishes out her phone from the depths of her purse. Her hands shake as she unlocks her phone and pulls up the photo. She turns the screen toward Meri, who leans in to study it closely.

"And do you happen to have one from twenty years ago?"

Jillian nods, swiping through her phone again until she finds what she wants. She turns the screen back toward Meri. "Here." Jillian points to the tall girl standing beside her in the photo. "That's Becky."

"I know it's a long shot," she continues. "Tucker . . . he doesn't think it's her, but there's something about her that . . . I don't know. I just thought she looked like Becky when I saw her at the park. But seeing them side by side now . . ." She trails off, unable to finish the thought.

Meri's brow furrows as she scrutinizes the photo. "The resemblance is uncanny," she murmurs. "It's not unheard of either — for someone to go missing that long ago and still be alive. There could be any number of reasons she's never contacted her family . . ."

"Like she's been brainwashed or something."

"Or something. Sometimes it's out of guilt and shame. Or maybe she's not in a safe relationship, and saying anything could place her in danger. Listen, would you mind dropping me those photos?" Meri holds her phone out. "I can't promise anything, but I can look into it."

Jillian nods, a sense of relief and dread mingling inside her. The possibility that Becky might still be alive is both thrilling and terrifying. It doesn't take long for the agent's phone to ping with the sent files.

A flicker of hope sparks in Jillian's chest, warming the cold dread that has taken up residence there since Becky vanished. The agent's promise, unofficial as it may be, stitches a fragile lifeline to the part of Jillian that refuses to let go.

"Thank you, Meri," she breathes out, her voice barely above a whisper, thick with gratitude. "You have no idea what this means."

"I do. I, too, have someone I lost. I know what it's like always to wonder, to see her in the shadows of each person you see off in the distance. I get it." Meri gives her a firm nod. "It's why I do what I do — not just to find my person, but to help others find theirs."

They reach Jillian's workplace. "Listen, I know I already gave you my card, but here's another one. If you see her again, or think of anything . . . or if there's anything you feel I need to know about those trailers, please don't hesitate to reach out." Meri holds her hand out, the card between her fingers.

Jillian nods, clutching it.

"Again, no promises, but I work with the best, so if she's out there, we will find her."

CHAPTER EIGHTEEN

Lola

Lola's hands tremble ever so slightly as she arranges her meager possessions on the worn wooden dresser. The day she never thought she'd see is finally here.

A day reserved for her nightmares.

When Mother sent her up here to get dressed, she reminded her that everything that happens from this moment forth is of her own doing, that Mother has done all she can to protect her, to shield her, and now it's up to her.

She's never been without Mother's protection before. She feels exposed now.

A faded dress, a pair of scuffed shoes, and a single, delicate bracelet lie before her — the sum of her world. She carefully picks up the dress, knowing that, even with its plain fabric and frumpish look, there's no promise of invisibility. At every auction, every person has been bought.

No one ever goes unnoticed.

Slipping the dress over her head, the weight of the thin fabric settles on her shoulders like a heavy wool blanket. There's a chill in the room that clings and settles into her bones and never leaves. As a child, she used to believe the Red House was haunted with ghosts.

Now she knows the truth.

There's no mirror in her room, so she has no idea how she looks, but then, it doesn't matter. Her reflection in the small window is enough most days. Today, as she turns, her long dark hair falls like a curtain over the jagged marring of her face. The scars, once a living nightmare, have become a blessing over the years.

Until now. Now, even those scars can't save her.

Taking a deep breath, her chest tightens with an anxiety that coils around her heart. The air holds the scent of dust and decay, yet beneath it all lingers the faintest trace of defiance. A defiance Mother thought she'd beaten out of her years ago.

A sound pierces the silence, a sharp note rippling through the Red House. Lola's breath catches as raised voices slice into her sanctuary. She stills, every muscle taut, eyes wide with sudden alertness. The voices sound close. Too close.

"Unacceptable! I was promised exclusivity!" The first voice is a guttural growl, thick with entitlement and anger.

"Your demands are always changing," retorts the second, laced with a slick veneer of calm, barely concealing their irritation. "You can't expect—"

"Expect?" Mother's voice is haughty and full of rage. "You know exactly what is expected and who expects it."

Lola's heart jumps a beat as the voices grow louder and closer. Mother's not bringing them to her room, is she? Why would she do that? She's never done that before. Never.

She presses an ear against the door and listens. The *clack-clack-clack* of shoes echoes through the hallway, and she holds her breath, counting the steps as they get closer. Then they stop. She hears a grunt. A cough. The steps start up again, but this time, walking away from her.

It takes a moment before she can step away from the door. Her hands are shaking, and her heart is pounding heavy drumbeats through her chest.

She waits until she can't hear anything before her hand finds the doorknob. Easing the door open, a sliver of dim hallway light cuts into the room like a blade. She slips through the gap, like a ghost flitting through the shadows, into the empty hallway.

Why was anyone in this part of the house? It's usually off-limits to everyone but Mother and herself. It's an area without attention, with wallpaper peeling like old scars at the edge of the ceiling and knicks and dents in the drywall. Even a few of the lights are burned out.

It doesn't make sense, but nothing has made sense to her since meeting The Woman. Since then, everything in her life has fallen apart.

Moving down the hallway, she's careful to avoid the creaking floorboards. Her breaths come in shallow bursts as she heads to a room she'd forgotten about.

The Red House is a living, breathing character in the brief story of her life. Its creaks and groans are a language she was raised to understand — a necessity for survival. In the distance, she hears the murmur of raised voices, but they are far enough away now that the threat of being found has diminished.

A draft whispers against her skin as she slowly approaches the end of the hallway. With deft fingers, she searches for the faint outline of a door, one that is hard to see in the darkness. Years ago, the light in this area burned out and has never been replaced.

Lola glances behind her to make sure she's still alone. Using the key Mother dropped in her apron this morning, she opens the door and steps into a room forgotten by most, remembered by just a few. A room full of discarded memories, mothballs, and dust.

Lola scans the cramped space: the stacked boxes teetering, furniture shrouded in cobwebs and dust.

Slivers of light shine through a boarded-up window, just enough that, as Lola's fingertips graze over surfaces coated in the grime, she can see the streaks she leaves behind. She'd forgotten how cramped the space was, but then, she'd been smaller, too. Back then, she could hide beneath the tables, curl up on a blanket behind a shelving unit, read her books, lean against some musty pillows covered in even mustier blankets, and look through photo albums. Back then, all she'd had to do was hide away where no one but Mother could find her.

This room was her hiding space. *Is* her hiding space.

Mother once told her that this house was her life and that if she were lucky, she'd replace Mother in running things. She's been raised in Mother's shadow, watching undetected as she ran the house, helping her take care of the girls who arrived in the dead of night, and taking note of how she handled herself with the Lady. Surviving meant replacing Mother, which was her only future, until the Lady saw her and decided otherwise.

Lola slides a box off a chair and curls up on it, her legs tucked beneath her. She finds an old book sitting on a stool beside her, but her fingers pause midair as she hears a sound. The sound is unmistakable — the low creak of floorboards. She barely dares to breathe as the footsteps draw near, each thud against the old wood echoing like a drumbeat in her chest.

She thought she was safe. Mother told her she'd be safe in here, if she got here in time and unnoticed.

As quietly as she can, Lola climbs off the chair and wedges herself behind a teetering stack of boxes, her back scraping against the wall behind her as she tries not to hit them. The storage room's stale air clings to her throat, and Lola presses her hand against her mouth, stifling the panic that comes out in ragged breaths. She draws her knees tighter to her chest, willing her compact frame to become smaller, invisible. Her chest aches, her heart a wild thing clawing for escape.

"Mother," a gruff voice calls out, its tone suspicious. "The girl, Lola — she's not in her room."

The blood in Lola's veins turns into ice, a cold sweat breaking out across her brow.

"Impossible," Mother's calm and unyielding voice responds. "The girl would never disobey me." There's a rhythm to her words, a practiced ease that portrays power, perseverance, and a dare to defy.

But Lola hears the subtle shift — the way Mother's breathing tightens just so, the faintest quiver that speaks of danger. They know. They're searching for her; she's run out of time, and soon, this very room, the room meant as her salvation, will become a trap.

She bites down on her knuckle, tasting salt and skin, her eyes fixed on the thin line of light from the window. Her mind races, plotting, planning. If they find her here, she can only imagine the consequences she'll face. Mother will deny helping her, that much she already knows.

In the silence that stretches, Lola makes a vow. She won't be found — not here, not now. She doesn't know how or what she will do, but no one knows about this room, and with the door locked, the only way in is if she opens it.

Her ears strain to catch every nuance of the conversation outside. Mother's voice, calm and unwavering, weaves through the crack beneath the door.

"I was just there." The voice is tinged with irritation. "She's not in her room."

Lola squeezes her eyes shut, willing herself to become smaller, invisible, not daring to move, barely allowing herself to breathe, each inhalation shallow and measured.

The muttering is now inaudible, but Mother's response is immediate, the assurance in her voice wrapping around Lola like a protective cloak.

"Your incompetence is not my issue. I'll find her. Don't you have other charges to take care of?" Mother's declaration carries the weight of finality, leaving no room for further questions.

Relief, swift and profound, floods Lola's veins, washing over her in waves, loosening the tight bands of panic constricted around her chest. Mother just bought her some time.

CHAPTER NINETEEN

Agent Meri Amber

Hundreds, if not thousands, of people drive by this field daily on their way to Shelby or the Canadian border. She's driven by it too many times to count since she's been here.

Not once did she ever think to stop. To investigate. Maybe she should have.

This morning, while getting her coffee, she found a note left on the windshield of her rental car containing coordinates — nothing else. Curious, she showed the note to Sheriff Mato, who'd told her she'd check with her source while Meri checked out the location.

What she'd like to know is who left the note but Mato seems mum on the subject. Why? Who called in the tip on the trailers? For every answer she seeks, more questions arise and it's getting frustrating.

The rusted hulks of abandoned cars, trucks, and even military vehicles rise from the overgrown field like tombstones. With her coffee in hand, Meri walks through the maze of weeds, thinking about the number of ticks and other bugs clawing their way up her socks. It's a good thing she bought some heavy-duty bug spray. She's alone out here; there are no other running vehicles or people that she can see, and yet, her free hand hovers near the gun on her hip out of habit.

She has no idea why she's been sent to this location, but her instincts tell her there's something here.

A flicker of movement catches her eye. Meri freezes, listening, but only the wind rustles through the long grass. Not knowing what to look for, she heads to the closest dilapidated pickup truck. It's a Ford and rusted beyond repair. There's no fender, holes throughout the body, and spiderwebbed cracks in the glass.

That's when the smell hits her. Unmistakably sweet and sickly. Her stomach turns.

Preparing herself, she peers inside, but there's nothing in there besides dirt, rust, and animal droppings — nothing that would create that smell. She heads to the bed and yanks open the tailgate, immediately regretting it. Her hand flies to her mouth, bile rising in her throat.

Bodies fill the inside of the trunk. Victims who have been obviously brutalized before their bodies were dumped to rot.

Backing away, she leans on her knees and takes a few deep breaths. It's not like she hasn't seen this before, but it always hits her hard. The brutality. The lost lives. The horror of being left, forgotten. She looks around, wishing Mato was here already.

She sends Mato and Lindsay the same text: *Found another dump site.*

She returns to the truck and starts documenting the scene. It takes everything to distance herself from what she's seeing, her hands shaking with anger and revulsion. What kind of monster does this?

Her phone pings with a message from Lindsay: *Do you recognize what's hanging from one wrist?* He includes a copy of one of the photos she sent him, but with a large red circle around the wrist in question.

She gets as close as she can to see, but it only takes a moment to hit her.

Years ago, she'd come upon a similar scene. Her team had found a locked trailer with forgotten inventory. At the back of the truck bed, hiding behind boxes, were the remains of six women, all with a similar chain hanging from their wrists. On the chain was the image of a house outlined in red. That was it. No words. No other features. Just a red house.

That case is still unsolved.

It wasn't the first time she'd seen that bracelet, though. She has one with her at all times. It's back in her hotel room. Years ago, she'd received a package in the mail to her home address, and the only thing in that envelope was a bracelet with that symbol on it. She's always assumed that it was her sister reaching out.

She's never told anyone that she has that bracelet. She probably should.

Her phone pings with another message: *Look familiar?* Lindsay sends her an image of a photograph she's never seen, but it's a burned body wearing a similar chain on their wrist.

Her phone pings again, this time with a message from Sheriff Mato: *Fifteen minutes out. Bringing backup.*

Heading back to her vehicle, she dials Lindsay and waits for him to pick up.

"What's with the Red House?" she asks.

"I'm pulling up the files now." He sounds tired. "A few years ago, a house burned to the ground overnight, and inside, we found the bodies. Over the years, we've rescued a few girls who all wore the bracelet, but no one says much. They say they came from the Red House. No idea where it is or who runs it."

"I've come across the bracelet in the past, too. I wonder how it's all connected?" Off in the distance, she sees a puff of dust. It's too early for Mato to arrive, so who is it?

"Good question. We'll see what we can find here." She hears some muffled words in the background. "We may have found something. I'll be in touch if it's relevant. You'll keep me posted?"

"You know it, boss." Meri hangs up and searches her car for her cough drop. She needs something, anything, to get rid of the stench that lingers in her nostrils.

Keeping an eye on the dust cloud, she can hear a faint sound carried in the wind — a recognizable diesel engine sound. Besides Mato and whoever left the note, no one else local knows she's here. She presses herself flat against her rental car, willing her pounding heart to quiet, her hand on her holster.

The engine noise grows louder until it stops on the other side of her vehicle. A door opens and closes. Footsteps crunch on the gravelly dirt. Whoever it is, they are heading right for her. She silently draws her weapon, senses heightened. The footsteps round the corner of the vehicle where Meri stands, gun aimed steadily.

"Whoa! Easy there!" A middle-aged man throws his hands up in surprise. He wears a grimy jumpsuit and has an air of innocence about him.

Her instincts say he's not a killer, but she's been known to be wrong.

Meri lowers her weapon slightly. "Who are you and what are you doing here?" she demands.

"I work here. I was just checking on the cars before the salvage crew comes." His eyes flick to the open door of the pickup beside her. "What happened here?" His face pales.

Meri weighs how much to reveal. "Do you own this property?"

The man shakes his head. "Nah, I just keep an eye on it for the owner."

"And who's that?"

He swivels around and reaches for the phone in his pocket. "I should probably call him." He glances toward her and then at his phone.

"You can, or you can answer a few questions for me first." She mellows her tone, hoping to come across as more pleasing and less in-your-face.

116

His eyes narrow slightly. "Who did you say you were again?"

She didn't, but she doesn't need to remind him. She also hasn't failed to notice he has yet to give her his name. "I'm Special Agent Meri Amber. What do you mean about being here to check on the property before the salvage crew shows up?"

He points in the distance, an empty space in the field. "Another vehicle to add to the graveyard is on its way. The boss man told me where he wants it set, so I came out early to make sure it's an easy placement." He gives her a shrug. "He's pretty particular with how he wants things to look. Says the people who drive by need something to gawk at." He sighs. "Guess that ain't happening now, is it? Should I call the truck and tell them to turn around?"

Meri shakes her head. "No, it can come," she tells him. If there are bodies inside, she wants to be the first to know.

In the distance, sirens wail. Her backup is closer than expected. She gives him a hard look. "Who's the boss man?"

The man glances nervously around, scratching the top of his balding head. "Well, now, I'm not sure if I'm allowed to say, you know?"

"Allowed?" Surely Meri didn't hear him correctly.

"Well, that is . . ." He tries not to look at the bodies lying in plain view.

"If you know something that can help, I need to know." Meri softens her tone again.

"I'm thinking I should wait for Sheriff Mato." The man shuffles his feet and hangs his head, not looking at her.

Meri lets out a resigned sigh. "Good thing she's almost here, then, isn't it?"

He hesitates, a grim look on his face. "Listen, I don't know nothing about . . . this." He gestures helplessly to the horrific sight behind them. "I just do my job. Come check on the property, make sure there's no graffiti or nothing on the vehicles, and arrange new drop-offs . . . I don't look in them trucks." He swallows hard.

She nods. "I believe you. So why don't you share the boss's name with me?"

The crunch of tires announces Sheriff Mato's arrival. The man looks nervous as her dog jumps out of the back seat and runs over, sniffing his pants.

Mato marches over, giving her dog a look but not calling her off.

"Johnny, what are you doing here?" She glares at the man with one hand on her holster and the other on her hip.

"Just doing my job, that's all. I swear. Can you . . . can you call your . . . thing off, please?" From the catch in his voice, Johnny sounds like he's about to urinate himself.

Mato snaps her fingers and taps her leg. That's all it takes for Tala to sit at her side.

"Let's be a bit clearer on that, shall we?" Mato says. "Is your job to hide dead bodies inside pickup trucks or . . ."

Johnny's head shakes from one side to the other. "No, nononono. I was just telling the agent here. I take care of the property. Come by every so often, make sure the kids haven't spray-painted anything on the trucks, and situate new drop-offs when they arrive."

"One is on its way," Meri says quietly.

Sheriff Mato gives her a look. Meri nods. They're on the same wavelength because she can see the same question in Mato's eyes.

"You won't believe who owns the land." Mato stands with her back to Johnny, her voice full of exhaustion.

"Let me guess." Meri looks over at Johnny. "Old Man Cummings is your boss?" A low burn settles into Meri's veins. All this time. All the years of searching, never getting close enough . . . and he's been here in Montana all along.

Johnny hesitates, then lets out a resigned sigh. "Cummings is going to have my head. He's not a man to piss off. You know that." He points to Sheriff Mato, who only stares him down. "I didn't know nothing about . . . this. You've got to believe me." He gestures helplessly to the horror behind them.

"How long have you been working for Cummings, Johnny?" Sheriff Mato pushes back her shoulders and widens her stance, preparing for a long talk. Meri knows that stance well.

Meri also knows that Mato is holding back on her. This isn't the first time someone has indicated something to Mato that 'she should already know.'

"Years."

"And how often do you come out to this field?"

He shrugs, sticking his hands in his jeans and then taking them out. He's clearly uncomfortable. "I'm supposed to come out twice a month, just to check on things, you know? No graffiti, no vehicular damage . . . that kind of stuff. And when the boss has a new piece to add to the graveyard."

"Graveyard?" Mato's brows rise, and the dog beside her growls.

Johnny swallows hard. "That's what he's always called it, you know? A graveyard full of old shit." He waves his hands around to the trucks, military vehicles, and old cars.

Graveyard. Meri can't get that word out of her head. What else will they find once they start going through the vehicles? Or should she say who else will they find?

"Ever notice anyone come out when they shouldn't be here? Any fresh tire tracks or garbage lying round? Disturbance in the fields, that sort of thing?" Sheriff Mato asks, her tone conversational, yet Johnny would be a fool if he didn't hear the edge of steel.

Johnny shakes his head. "Nah. Who would come out to a place like this?"

"Well, you just said you come out to make sure there's no graffiti, so . . . has that happened in the past?"

Johnny glances up to the sky and rubs at his chin. "I mean, years ago, maybe. See that car down there?" He points to a gray Cadillac with weeds almost covering the windows. "Some kids came out one summer night and went to town with their spray paint. Had to turn the car around to hide it. Then I tried to clean it off before the boss found out."

"Did he?"

Johnny snorts. "Oh yeah, he did. And he was mad as hell. Stupid kids tagged themselves, so Johnny knew who to blame. You can bet they never touched his stuff again."

"What kids?"

Johnny's eyes widen with what Meri thinks is fear.

Sheriff Mato sighs. "Was Sheriff Low here then?"

He nods.

Mato looks to Meri. "I heard stories of a couple of teenage boys who'd been beaten up within an inch of their lives, but no one did anything about it. I also heard Cummings was responsible, but I didn't believe it at the time. That mean streak everyone talks about, I never saw it."

"Yeah, right." Johnny chuckles with disbelief. "Don't tell me you didn't know, everyone did."

Mato shrugs. "The Old Man Cummings I know and who you know are two completely different men."

Meri wonders how much of what is being said is for her benefit. From the way Johnny looks between the two of them, he's probably wondering the same thing.

In the distance Meri notices flashing lights. "Your team is here." Mato gives her a nod and heads to the driveway to direct the vehicles.

"Think I can go now?" Johnny takes a step backward.

"Yeah, no. I don't think so," Sheriff Mato says over her shoulder. "Tala, babysit." One simple command is all it takes for her huge dog to stand guard in front of Johnny and let out a low growl.

Johnny holds up his hands in surrender. "Okay, okay, no need to stick the beast on me."

Knowing the scene has been contaminated enough, Meri stands by her vehicle and watches Mato's team move in with surprisingly swift precision. The scene is carefully photographed, and Meri notes that the technicians capture every angle and detail.

"Thanks for waiting," a tech says to Meri, indicating she can approach now. She's handed a small jar of menthol cream.

"Put it beneath your nose; it'll help." Placing a dab beneath her nostrils, Meri crouches and scrutinizes the bodies. Though in various states of decomposition, she notes the victims share certain similarities — young, female, slight builds, all wearing the Red House bracelet. Her instincts tingle as puzzle pieces click into place.

Meri diligently scribbles her observations in a small notepad, keeping her hand steady despite the adrenaline coursing through her. She has to document everything while it's still fresh. This could be the break she's been waiting for.

The other officers spread out through the area, securing the perimeter with crime scene tape. But Meri barely registers their presence. She's mentally cataloging every detail to memory. There are clues here to Rawlings she's never seen before, and she needs to figure out how to make it all make sense.

Meri's mind races as the implications of this body dump sink in. The location is just off the highway on the outskirts of Shelby. Why? Why here? Why in plain sight . . . unless that's the answer. Who would think to look here?

Regardless of the answer, she knows it's not a coincidence. The calculating, meticulous Andy she's been searching for, he would never be so careless. This dump site has his fingerprints all over it.

She has to move quickly to assemble a timeline before any evidence disappears. Based on decomposition, she estimates the first bodies were dumped here at least six months ago.

The first site, those victims had been there for years. This site, months. So there must be others. How many other properties does Rawlings own that they don't know about? And why don't they know about them yet?

Meri's train of thought is interrupted by the crunch of more tires on gravel. The county coroner and evidence techs have arrived.

She watches their reactions carefully, curious about how they'll react to this latest body dump scene. She can't imagine they get too many of these out here. Most are shocked, but a few betray hints of unease, which she immediately notices.

Someone knows about this site. Someone here has allowed the dumping to continue unimpeded.

Is Sheriff Mato in on it, too?

Just then, a truck pulling a flatbed with an old Chevrolet truck rolls up. "That's my delivery," Johnny calls out.

Standing at the perimeter, Meri surveys the controlled chaos unfolding before her. While Sheriff Mato has the driver out of the truck and goes over his paperwork, she heads to the team, which is looking over the vehicle on the bed. Photographs are being taken before they open the trunk.

No bodies.

The tension that's been building within Meri lets go, and she reaches for the truck bed for support. The knots in her stomach untangle, the pain in her chest relaxes its grip, and she's able to take a long, clear breath. When Mato glances her way, she's able to smile at her.

"I'm going to let this guy go, since the truck is clear," Sheriff Mato says once they're standing side by side.

Meri nods. "No sense keeping him. What about Johnny?"

"Oh, Johnny and I will be having a nice heart-to-heart back at the station. You want to sit in?"

Meri thinks about it but decides not to. Whatever Johnny has to say, he's probably already said it. She needs to know if there are more bodies in the remaining vehicles out in that field and how Rawlings ties into the Red House.

"How many more properties does Rawlings own around here?"

Mato holds up two fingers. "These are the only titles we could pull for Rawlings under both aliases. If he uses another name, I haven't found it yet."

Meri doesn't say anything but knows her team will find out if he's going by any other personas.

"So, what's the deal between the two of you?"

Sheriff Mato steps back, a look of shock on her face. "Whatever the hell do you mean? You better not be thinking I'm tied into this."

Meri shrugs but keeps her face blank of any thought or emotion. The less she tells Mato, the better.

"He's a leftover from the last sheriff. I was given a low-down on him . . . the guy pays well to have people take care of his lands, but he doesn't like questions, and only ever comes around a few times a year. He comes, stays for a few days, sometimes a week or two, once even a month, before he gets on everyone's nerves and then disappears."

Meri stands there. No words need to be said. If the sheriff is guilty in any way, she'll find out.

Her phone rings. She turns her back on Mato. "What do you have?" she says, knowing it's Lindsay.

"Not much, but we did find out more about the Red House. You're not going to like it."

CHAPTER TWENTY

Jillian

The house is peaceful, save for the occasional creak of settling wood and the distant murmur of Tucker's voice from his office. With her hands wrapped tightly around the 'World's Best Father' mug, Jillian pads softly across the kitchen tiles, her slippers barely making a sound.

A sliver of light spills onto the hallway carpet — a golden thread in the darkness — as she approaches the office door. He said he had a call tonight, so she doesn't want to interrupt, but all she hears is his fingers tap-tap-tapping on the keyboard. He'll probably appreciate the coffee.

About to nudge the door open with her elbow, a name slices through the silence.

"Rawlings," Tucker breathes out, the word heavy with an unspoken history, "it's too much, man."

Jillian's heart thrums wildly. Her fingers tighten unconsciously around the mug, the heat seeping into her skin as she leans closer to the crack in the door. She peers through, catching a glimpse of Tucker's hunched silhouette. The blue glow of his computer casts ghostly shadows across his furrowed brow.

"Yeah, sorry about that. You're in too deep now." The voice on the other end of the speaker, Rawlings' voice, is like ice, devoid of warmth. "Nothing more I can do to shield you. You need to hide."

Tucker's hand sweeps through his thinning hair, a gesture of stress that doesn't go unnoticed by Jillian's watchful eyes. A thick strand of his white hair sticks up straight before he smooths it down. His voice, typically steady and reassuring, now trembles with a note of desperation.

"Jillian doesn't want to run."

There's a brusque tsk on the other end of the phone. "Jillian doesn't know the whole truth then, does she?"

"You know I can't tell her. She'll never forgive me."

"Better to have her hate you than dead, don't you think?"

She steps back at Rawlings' words, the hot coffee spilling over her hand. Dead? Is her life on the line? What isn't Tucker telling her?

"Why? Why me? I've never been involved in that shit. You know that."

"Doesn't matter what I know. It's all about what they believe, and you only have your father to blame for that. I'm just a cog in a wheel. You, of all people, know that."

"But if you tell them, they'll listen."

There's harsh laughter that feels like sharp daggers along Jillian's skin. "They don't listen to me, kid. It's a new generation taking care of things. Like I said, I'm just a cog, too old for their plans."

"But all I did was protect my family."

"That was enough."

"Shit." Tucker slams his hand down on the desk.

"Listen, kid, they just want you. They'll leave the wifey and kid alone, if you come in."

There's nothing but silence.

"Are you telling me to give up?" Tucker asks.

"What I'm telling you is there's still a way to protect your family, but only if you do it my way."

"I've been doing it your way, Rawlings. Look where it's got me?"

"Once you're in, there's no getting out. When you're ready, meet me at the old Franklin farm. You know where it is. It's abandoned. They won't think to look for you there."

Franklin farm? Why does that sound familiar? Jillian struggles to remember where she's heard the name, and that's when it comes to her. On their drive from Utah, they had to take a detour, and Tucker slowed down as they drove past an old farmstead a few hours southeast of here. He'd pointed it out as a place he'd visited as a kid, running through the cornfield, climbing the barn rafters. He called it the summer of heaven.

But why go there now? What is going on?

"From there, we'll head to the Red House," Rawlings continues, the name dropping like a weight into the stillness. "We can disappear from there. But Tucker, don't wait too long — there's only so much I can do before it's too late."

Jillian's grip on the mug slips, the glass falling to the floor, the hot liquid splashing her feet as the words sink in. Disappear.

He's going to leave her. He's going to disappear. Leave them behind.

She backs away from the door, her back pressing against the cold wall, the mug forgotten on the floor at her feet. Her mind races, stitching together the fragments of truth scattered before her. Tucker, her rock, her constant, her . . .

He's carrying so many secrets, the weight of them has changed him.

Jillian swallows the lump in her throat, steadying her breath. She's tired of it all. Tired of all the running. What good has it done them in the past? None. Those secrets keep following them, destroying whatever semblance of normal they struggle to create . . . and she's done with it.

Tucker's chair pushes back, and his heavy steps approach the door. The house walls close in on her as she draws deep breaths. She's not running. Not from him. Not from his secrets. Not from whatever danger is at their doorstep that he won't tell her about.

When Tucker opens his office door a frown creases his brow as he takes in the sight of her — the tension in her frame, the mug abandoned on the wood floor.

"Jill?" His voice is soft, almost tentative, betraying none of the urgency that just laced his conversation moments before.

She holds her head up high despite feeling like she's holding the weight of their future on her shoulders. "Who were you talking to?" Considering the storm raging inside her, she's surprised at how steady her voice is.

"What?" He shakes his head, looks back into the room, and then sighs. "You heard that, didn't you?" He steps closer, hesitating, as if unsure whether to bridge the gap between them with words or touch. "It's not what you think it is."

"Really? Because it seems like what I heard was pretty clear." Her brows lift as she waits for him to deny the truth. "I don't like the secrets, Tuck, you know that. It's tearing us apart." Her gaze locks onto Tucker's, searching for signs of the man she knows, the man she loves.

His face pales, the worry lines growing around his eyes becoming more pronounced. He takes a step back, a defensive move that betrays his surprise. "I . . . It's not what you think, Jillian."

"You keep saying that, and yet, I don't believe you." Her sharp words are forged from a blade years in the making. The girl who once lost her best friend to a mystery refuses to lose another person she loves because of secrets he won't share.

She lets out an exasperated sigh at his silence. "I heard you, Tucker. He told you to meet him at that farm. And that you can disappear at the Red House, whatever the hell that is." Throwing her hands up in the air, she goes to leave, hoping he'll stop her, but he doesn't.

She grabs a handful of paper towels from the kitchen to clean up the spilled coffee while Tucker stands there, holding the cracked cup in his hands. The cup, hand painted by their son, is now garbage, much like their marriage, unless something changes.

"Jillian, please." Tucker runs a hand through his hair, a gesture of frustration and fear. "Let me explain—"

"Explain?" The word is sharp, a crack in her voice revealing the strain beneath her composed exterior. "I need the truth, Tucker. I need to understand why you're tangled up with a man like Rawlings."

He looks at her, then really looks at her, and in his eyes, she sees the reflection of her own — same disillusionment, same determination. But where hers burn with the need to protect, his are clouded with regret.

"Okay," he says finally, the resignation in his tone mirroring the slump of his shoulders. "Okay, let's talk."

There, in the stillness of that hallway, Jillian braces herself, ready to peel back the layers of lies and deceit, her heart pounding a fierce rhythm against her ribs. This is it, the precipice of whatever shaky ground they're standing on, and she knows that whatever comes next could change everything.

CHAPTER TWENTY-ONE

Jillian's fingers trace the rim of her coffee mug. Despite the size of their kitchen, tonight it feels small and claustrophobic as Tucker sits across from her.

It's taking everything for her not to start the conversation or throw accusations at the man sitting beside her. After years of practice, she's realized her husband sometimes needs the quiet, the silence before facing the hard truth.

Tucker's gaze is anchored to the fresh cup of coffee she's poured him. At his side is a bottle of whiskey. With a heavy sigh, he pours a generous amount into his cup. The amber liquid swirls with the dark coffee, two worlds colliding. He takes a sip, then pushes the bottle toward her, but she doesn't take it.

She wants a clear head for this conversation.

"Andy Rawlings . . ." His voice is strained, but he doesn't say anything more.

Jillian stares at the kitchen, taking in everything they've built here. This house, this life . . . they are supposed to be safe here, far away from everything else that can hurt them.

"I've known him my whole life. He's been like a . . . second father, or favorite uncle or whatever," Tucker says, not looking at her. "He and Dad grew up together. Thick as thieves, my grandma always used to say." There's a slight smile on his lips as he mentions his grandmother. "Dad brought him into the family business, not as an owner or anything, but he got him hired as a driver." He shrugs, like the news isn't all that important, except it is.

He's known Rawlings his whole life? And she's only finding out about this now?

Harper Transport is a family-run business that dates back to Tucker's great-great-grandfather. Despite his family's insistence that Tucker help run the company, for one reason or another, Tucker walked away from the hands-on daily running of the company and instead handles the sales side of things: finding new contracts and keeping clients from turning to other transport companies offering cheaper rates.

"So he's . . . like an uncle?" Jillian tries to wrap her head around it. "An uncle I've never met, who never came to our wedding or drops by to visit."

"He's on the road a lot."

She absorbs this, nodding slowly. "Because he's a truck driver. And that's how you're tied to him?"

"Yeah," Tucker confirms, his hand resting on the table, tapping an uneven rhythm that betrays his inner turmoil. "Him and Dad, their friendship . . . it's old and goes way back. Like his dad and my grandfather were friends, once upon a time."

"What happened to them?" From the way he says it, it sounds like that friendship ended.

He shrugs. "Difference of opinion, I guess you could say. From what I heard, his dad wasn't too pleased when Andy started driving for the company."

"Why?"

He winces like the idea is hard for him to say or even admit.

"What aren't you telling me?"

He shakes his head. "It's . . . complicated."

"So uncomplicate it." When he looks away, she reaches out and takes his hand. "Does it involve the Red House?" Jillian's question drops like a stone into still water, ripples of implication spreading outwards.

"Jillian . . ." Tucker begins, his eyes reflecting a storm of emotions. "There's so much you don't know."

That much is obvious. "Then tell me, Tucker," she insists, her tone gentle yet unyielding.

Tucker stares at her, and she wonders what he sees — the mother of his child? His partner? His lover? Someone who has always supported him and weathered everything that comes their way? Or does he see something else in her? Something that makes him hesitate when it comes to trusting her with the truth?

"Okay." Tucker exhales, bracing himself to unravel threads of truth wound too tight for too long. His fingers stop their nervous dance on the table and he reaches for his mug, taking an extra-long sip.

"Rawlings . . ." Tucker starts, the whiskey on his breath mingling with the bitter scent of coffee. "He's more than my father's best friend; he was there for me when I couldn't turn to anyone else."

Jillian studies him, her brow furrowing as she sifts through the layers of what he isn't saying. Tucker has always been the rock she's been able to cling to, but even rocks can fracture under enough pressure.

"Dad was never there, you know? The company was always first, and he became distant when I said I never wanted a part of the transport business," Tucker confesses, a shadow crossing his features. "That's probably why I agreed to work remotely. All I've ever wanted was a relationship with him." His gaze meets hers, pleading for understanding. It's a silent testament that blood ties, however strained, are not so easily severed.

"I know. You never say no, and that's okay. It's not like he's the only company you contract out to."

Something crosses his gaze just then, and he turns away from her. "Don't," she says. "Don't push me out, okay?" She leans forward, resting her elbows on the table, her eyes holding his gaze captive. "If Rawlings is important to you, why have I never met him?"

Tucker shifts in his seat, and she can see he's trying to weigh how much to admit and what to hold back.

"He's not someone I want in our lives, to be honest, especially with Ethan. He . . . I don't want a repeat of my childhood for our son. He deserves the right to remain innocent and grow up to be anything and everything he wants to be without the tether of . . ." He pauses, clearing his throat.

"So you're protecting our son from him?" She struggles to read between the lines, to hear what he's not saying.

"I didn't realize he wasn't a good man until it was too late." He swallows hard. "He's involved in something dangerous," he admits quietly, the words sounding like ash.

"And so now you're involved in something dangerous, too? Damn it, Tucker, I thought we left all that behind?" It's hard to keep the frustration from mounting, from pushing him back into silence.

"We did. Or . . . I thought we had. Rawlings said it was over, that he'd protect us but . . ."

"But he can't, can he? Once you're in, there's no getting out. Isn't that what he said on the phone?"

Tucker sighs, like the world's weight rests on his shoulders, and he knows there's no escape. "I was never in. That's the problem. I was eighteen, it was spring break, and I wanted to go to the beach, you know? Rawlings had a load run down to Florida, so he offered to take me and drop me off. We were halfway there when we had to detour and pick up a . . . well, something." Tucker rubs his face with the palm of his hand. "I eventually got to the beach and then back home, but in between, Rawlings had me help him with a side job, and that side job has followed me wherever I go."

Jillian glances out the darkened windows and she thinks about the trailers and what was found in them. "How does this

132

tie to the bodies they found on our property?" If he's going to tell her everything, she wants to know everything.

He shrugs. "I swear, Jill, I had no idea about that."

"I don't get it, though. We were fine, weren't we? For three months, we had freedom, we were safe, and no one was after us from all that crap back in New York, but now . . . how are the bodies tied to you? Because they have to be, Tucker. Otherwise, none of this makes any sense."

Tucker looks at her, a maelstrom of fear and determination in his eyes.

"Jillian," he says, barely above a whisper, "I don't know. I swear." His words are heavy with a truth she can't quite grasp.

"There's still something you're not telling me," she says.

"They think I'm . . . part of something." His eyes flicker to hers, willing her to understand without saying more.

She can't give him that luxury. There's danger in half-truths. "Part of what, Tucker?" Jillian leans forward, her gaze sharp as flint.

"That group from New York, the one I got caught up in . . . they were only a small fraction of a larger . . . problem."

"What is the Red House? Rawlings mentioned you can disappear from there. What did he mean?"

Tucker drops his head. "A myth, at least I thought it was. I heard about it as a young kid, talked about in whispers. I haven't heard that name for years, not until tonight, to be honest."

"That doesn't tell me what it is, though. Or where, for that matter."

"The Red House . . . it's complicated, and my father is caught up in it too." He pauses, the shadow of fear passing over his features. "I don't know the details, I swear to you, Jillian. But it's dangerous, and it's why I need to meet Rawlings alone."

"Your father," she whispers, the pieces aligning in her mind like a puzzle nearing completion. "And you're caught in the middle."

"Caught or dragged." Tucker gives a dry laugh. "Either way, according to Rawlings, I'm in too deep to back out now."

Jillian's hand tightens over his, and her resolve anchors the chaos. "We'll find a way out of this, together."

"Together? Why would you want that? It would be safer without me in your life right now, don't you think?"

She pulls back, shocked at his words. "How can you say that? I love you, Tucker. We're partners, or have you forgotten that? Whatever is going on, we're in this together."

He leans back in his chair, and in that moment, she sees the man she fell in love with, who swept her off her feet, has taken care of her, protected her, and loved her.

"Okay, then. How do you suggest we get out of this mess? Because I'm at a loss."

Jillian leans forward and grasps her husband's hands within her own. "Well, that's easy," she says. "First, we stop trusting Rawlings to keep us safe, and we take back control over our own lives."

CHAPTER TWENTY-TWO

It's the end of the day and Jillian is locking up the office doors when her phone blows up with text messages from Tucker. She ignores it at first. He's probably just sending her a list of items to pick up from the store on her way home after having drinks with the girls from work. It's a monthly thing all the women do in the office, heading to the Blooming Cactus for drinks and appetizers and this is the first time she's been able to join.

Her phone goes off again. She heads down the sidewalk and pulls it out, but the messages from Tucker have nothing to do with grocery items. He sends her five messages in a row, all containing three simple words — a code for when all hell breaks loose and they need to run for their lives. A code they've had to use too many times in the last few years.

Lucy says hello.

Jillian backtracks to her truck and jumps inside. She guns it out of the parking lot, not caring about her speed as she zips down the main street and out of town. Her heart drums within her ribcage, and she pushes the accelerator down. She sends Trina a quick 'sorry, had to rush home' text, then tries calling Tucker, but there's no answer.

Shit and double shit.

Lucy says hello. They're just three simple words, words that if anyone else were to see, they'd think nothing of, but to them, it's their signal to drop everything and run. It was Tucker's idea, a cryptic safeguard against the threats that seem to circle closer to the life they've built together, but she thought after moving here she'd never have to see those words again.

As her truck skids to a halt in front of their farmhouse, Jillian's gaze locks onto the scene unfolding in the driveway. Tucker is there, his broad-shouldered silhouette moving with an efficiency that belies the chaos of the situation. Suitcases — far too many for a simple trip — are being loaded into the back of his truck, each thud of luggage another echo of her racing pulse.

"What's going on?" Jillian, slamming the truck door behind her as she races toward him.

"Jill, we gotta go. Now," Tucker says, not meeting her eyes as he heaves another suitcase into the bed of the truck.

"Why? What's happened?" She searches the property for Ethan but doesn't see him anywhere.

"It doesn't matter. We have to go. I packed most of what I thought we'd need — clothes, bathroom stuff, there's some food in here, too." He points to the full truck bed, his movements jerky, his voice teetering on panic.

"No." The word is sharp, a blade forged in the fires of too many sleepless nights. "I'm not going anywhere, Tucker. Not again. I don't care why." She's surprised at how strong of a stance she's taking, but the whole drive home, the only thing drumming through her head was '*not again. Not again. Not again.*'

She, they, can't keep living like this. She sees how it's affecting Ethan, and for that reason alone, she will cement her feet on this driveway and not move, no matter what Tucker says or how convincing he tries to be.

His eyes finally find hers, the usual calm within them now replaced by a storm of emotions he struggles to suppress. "You don't understand," he starts, but she cuts him off.

"I'm done running from shadows. I'm done tearing our lives apart every time someone whispers danger." Jillian's voice is a mixture of steel and desperation, a mother lioness defending her den.

"Jill—" He reaches for her, but she steps back, out of reach.

"Tell me why, Tucker. Tell me, what's so damn important that we have to leave everything behind?" Her words hang between them, unanswerable, the silence stretching like a thin wire.

The world around them pauses, holding its breath, waiting for the words that will define their fates.

"They know where we are, Jill. They know, and word is they're coming to take care of us, once and for all." His low voice is laced with urgency. "Rawlings . . ." He swallows hard. "This is how they take care of problems, Jill, and I promised you I'd keep you safe."

"How?" Jillian's question comes fast, sharp, the word slicing through the tension as she steps closer, her sneakers crunching on the gravel driveway.

He shrugs before reaching for another packed bag. "The wrong person saw the wrong report, I don't know. That part doesn't matter. What matters is that we're not safe anymore."

Jillian stands her ground. This is a small town. Sure, there's a prison close by, and Shelby is a way station for a lot of inmates who are done serving their time, but who would know them well enough to rat them out? "Who sent the tip, Tucker?"

His jaw clenches, a muscle ticking in his cheek as he avoids her probing gaze. "I don't know. It was anonymous."

"Anonymous." Her repetition of the word is skeptical. She searches his face for any sign of deceit. The last anonymous tip that forced them to run was from someone who saw them in a grocery store, so this time . . . it could be anyone. "And Rawlings, how is he involved? What has he done?"

Tucker's eyes dart away, his silence stretching into the space between them. He swallows hard, the truth — or the omission of it — seems to stick in his throat.

137

"Talk to me."

In his silence, the unspoken threats wind tight around Jillian's heart, squeezing until each breath becomes a battle. She can't do this again, and she won't do this again.

"Where is Ethan?" Jillian's hands ball into fists at her sides, but she focuses on the one thing that matters the most to her. Her son.

"He's inside." Tucker gestures a dismissive hand toward the house. "In his room playing on his gaming device."

"Good, then you have no reason not to tell me the truth. Why are our lives in danger and don't give me that crap from the other night, okay? What have you done?"

Tucker glances away. She can see he's trying to find the words, so she gives him the space to do so. "I didn't do anything, Jill, and that's the problem. That's always been the problem, don't you get it? Rawlings . . . he's trying to protect us, that's all. Sure, this whole thing with the trailers caught me off guard, too, but . . ."

"There's no but," Jillian says.

He shrugs. "You'd like the answer to be clear, straightforward, something you can understand without having to ask too many questions, but life just isn't that way, sweetheart."

"Don't you dare talk down to me, Tucker Harper." She grinds the words out, her jaw barely moving as she speaks.

He blanches. *Good.*

Swallowing hard, Tucker steps closer, but she won't have it. She holds up her hand, stopping him. "Just tell me the truth for once."

His lips thin. "Jill, Andy has another place," he says, his voice a strained whisper as if the trees themselves might be eavesdropping. "We can lay low there, just until all of this blows over."

Jillian bites her lip. The idea of fleeing to yet another one of Andy Rawlings' safe houses is like swallowing shards of glass.

"And what skeletons will we find in that place? No." The word is a bullet shot from a gun, final and deadly. "I won't do it. I'm done running, Tucker."

Tucker's gaze meets hers, searching for yield in her resolve. But between the furrow of her brow and the set line of her lips, he won't find what he's looking for.

"Jill, please—" His plea hangs between them, tenuous and trembling.

"Enough is enough." Her voice is steady despite the racing *thump-thump-thump* of her heartbeat. "We can't keep doing this . . . to ourselves, to—"

"Jillian." Tucker's voice breaks. He takes a step forward, reaching out, but she steps back, the gulf between them more than mere physical distance.

"Jill." He tries again, but she shakes her head, refusing to budge.

"Tucker," she says, her voice a low thrum of certainty. "I'm not leaving. Not again. We stand our ground. We face what comes. The trailers on this property are a horrendous, vile thing, but we've got nothing to do with all that. Let Rawlings clean up his own mess and keep us out of it."

The slam of the front door stops Jillian from saying anything more.

"Mom?" Ethan's voice is small, a whisper barely traveling the distance between them, but it strikes her with the force of a thunderclap.

She steps around Tucker, terror licking at her heart as she approaches their son. The fear etched into Ethan's youthful face is bright as day. His blue eyes are wide, reflecting the turmoil that's become their life — a constant upheaval no child should ever have to navigate. This is on her. On them. This is their fault, and they need to stop it and fix it before it gets any worse.

"Ethan," she says, closing the space between them and kneeling to meet his gaze at eye level. "It's going to be okay."

"Dad says we have to leave. Do we?" His voice hitches with the effort to remain brave. The question hangs in the air, a ghost of all the times they've packed up before.

Jillian tucks a stray lock of his sandy hair behind his ear, her fingers trembling against his warm skin. She swallows

139

hard, her resolve hardening like ice. "No, baby. We're staying put this time."

"Really?" There's a hopeful lilt to his words, a fragile wish on the verge of shattering.

"Really," she says, though her own fears claw at her insides. She pulls him in tight. "We're done running, kiddo."

"Promise?" His voice is muffled against her shoulder, seeking the security only a mother's vow can offer.

"Promise." The word is a blade in her chest, a painful oath that she will keep no matter the cost.

CHAPTER TWENTY-THREE

Jillian's hands tremble as she unpacks the stuff Tucker hastily threw together. She unloads the crumpled clothes, refolding them before she replaces them in the drawers.

Through the window, she catches glimpses of her husband pacing the front yard, cell phone pressed to his ear. His agitated gestures are a mirror to the angst and turmoil raging through their home right now. While she's forcefully putting clothes away, Ethan is in his room, his toy cars and action figures having the ultimate throwdown scene.

She's not sure what she's upset about the most: Tucker wanting them to leave, Andy Rawlings offering them safe passage again, or how all of this is affecting their son.

No, that's a lie. She knows what she's mad about the most — none of this is fair to Ethan. Maybe it's time to look for a therapist for him. Even with him being in baseball, his grades aren't doing well, he's withdrawing, and what friends he is making, he rarely wants to play with.

Standing at the window, looking down as Tucker paces between her truck and his, she hears the desperation and fear that carries with the wind. She can't hear the words, but she doesn't need to. He's still on edge. Her mind races — who is he talking to? Has he always kept these secrets, and she's only now realizing it?

That's on her if that's the case. She once could read him like a book, from cover to cover, never missing a line, but lately, all the pages in that book are blank. What is going on with him?

A muffled thud from down the hall snaps her attention back to the present. Ethan.

Jillian finds her son in his room, action figures and toy cars all in a pile on the floor, his lanky frame curled up on the bed.

"Hey, buddy," she says softly, perching on the edge of his mattress. "Everything okay?"

Ethan shrugs, picking at a loose thread on his comforter. "Why did Dad say we have to leave? Did I do something wrong?"

Jillian's heart clunks down to her stomach. She forces a smile, reaching out to ruffle his hair, her finger playing with the wide white streak that's growing back. She loves this streak, loves that it's in the same spot as Tucker's. When she first met Tucker, he'd let it grow out long enough to almost pull it back behind his ear. "No, sweetie. Your dad was just . . . being prepared. You know how he is."

But the lie tastes bitter on her tongue. She doesn't know anything anymore.

She can tell from how Ethan turns his face that he doesn't believe her. "Why would you think it was anything you did? Has something happened?"

It takes a bit, but eventually, there's a shrug of his tiny shoulders. "Mrs. Lamb says I need a lot of extra help in school." He sighs as if all of this is his responsibility. "I used to get good grades when we lived back home . . . so I thought maybe Dad wanted me to go to a different school."

She frowns. Sure, he's struggling, but that's to be expected since this is the third school he's attended this year. Again, that's on her, on them as parents, and not on Ethan.

"Ethan Tucker Harper, I want you to hear me and hear me good . . . how you do in school has no bearing on what happens to us as a family, okay? Pass or fail, or need extra help, it doesn't matter to me." She pauses and then gives him a goofy grin. "Well, okay, that's a lie. It does matter to me — of course, I want you to be passing. If Mrs. Lamb says you need some extra help, then I will go in and chat with her and see what we can do to make sure you get that help, okay?" She taps the underside of his chin with her finger. "But we are not moving from this house because of how you are doing in school. I promise you that."

He slowly nods, taking in her words. "Then why did Dad say we have to leave? I like it here."

"I like it here, too," she tells him. "Dad . . . Dad just got scared for a minute, I think."

"Cause of all the dead bodies they keep finding?"

She gives him a half nod, half wiggle of her head. "Wait," she says. "What do you mean they keep finding?"

Ethan nods enthusiastically. "It's all anyone talks about in school, Mom. You haven't heard? They found bodies in those trucks on the side of the highway. Billy, in my class, said his dad almost puked when he saw them."

Time stills. There's no thought, no words to say, just a blank black box of nothing as she stares at Ethan's bedroom wall.

"Earth to Mom, you okay? You don't get squeamish about this stuff, do you?" There's a note of disgust in his voice and she can't help but laugh.

"By stuff, do you mean hearing about more dead bodies? Yes, I get kind of squeamish." She nudges him in the side.

"Well, you are a girl," he says, giving her an epic eye roll.

She wants to tease back but then realizes what they're actually discussing. "Ethan, when did you hear this?" And most importantly, how did he hear about it before she did? The kids shouldn't know this stuff. If Billy's father is in the police force, he should know better than bringing work home like that.

Ethan breathes in deep through his nose and shrugs before sitting up in bed, hugging his knees tight to his chest. "Yesterday," he says.

"And you're just telling me now?"

He looks away. "Some of the kids said Dad's going to get arrested. That the dead people didn't start showing up until we moved here. Is that true?"

Hesitating, Jillian ponders how much to say and how much she needs to protect him. "Daddy isn't going to get arrested because he's done nothing wrong. But someone has, and I hope Sheriff Mato can figure that out." She pushes herself from the bed and holds out her hand. "Now, how about we do something fun to take our minds off things?" she suggests, desperately grasping for normalcy. "Want to help me make dinner?"

Ethan's eyes light up a fraction. "Can we have mac and cheese? The real kind, not from a box? And with hamburger in it?"

Jillian nods, relief flooding through her at this small victory. "Absolutely. Extra cheesy, just how you like it."

As they head to the kitchen, Jillian glances out the window again, watching Tucker's tense form in the fading light. He's still on the phone, still quite animated with his hands, despite his shoulders rounding like a boulder. Who is he talking to?

The kitchen fills with the comforting aroma of melting butter and browning meat as Jillian stirs the hamburger in the pan. Ethan, perched on a stool at the counter, meticulously shreds cheddar cheese, his tongue poking out in concentration.

"Mom?" Ethan's voice breaks the rhythmic sound of sizzling. "Is it true that we live on a cemetery?"

Jillian's hand stills on the wooden spoon. "A what now? Who told you something crazy like that?"

Ethan's eyes dart to the window, where Tucker's silhouette still paces. "Just kids at practice."

A chill runs through Jillian despite the warm kitchen. She turns to the stove, focusing on stirring the roux for the cheese sauce. "Ethan, you know how rumors can get out of hand."

"Yeah, but Coach Neil was talking to a few of the other parents. They stopped when they saw me, but I heard them say something about 'Harper land' and 'graveyard.'"

Jillian's mind races. She wants to protect Ethan, but she also knows her curious son won't be satisfied with platitudes, especially since he keeps bringing the subject up. She takes a deep breath.

"Sweetheart, sometimes grown-ups have to deal with complicated things. Whatever happened in this town and on our property happened before we moved here, okay? It has nothing to do with us. What's important is that we're safe, and that we stick together as a family. Can you trust me on that?"

Ethan nods slowly, but his brow remains furrowed. "I guess. But why does everyone keep whispering?"

Jillian moves to the counter, placing her hands on Ethan's shoulders. "People often gossip when they don't have all the facts. The best thing we can do is focus on what we know is true, and not spread stories we're not sure about. Okay?"

"Okay," Ethan agrees, but his eyes are full of questions Jillian isn't ready to answer.

Jillian slides the dish into the oven, setting the timer. Her gaze drifts to the window where Tucker's silhouette continues pacing back and forth, phone pressed to his ear. His agitated movements make her shudder.

Jillian's mind races. She doesn't like that someone from their past knows they are here. "Who is it?" she whispers to herself. Could it be someone recently released from prison with ties to the group from back home? Could it be someone inside the prison with enough influence to get someone else to do their dirty deeds? When will they ever really be free from the past?

Jillian's mind flashes back to hushed conversations, Tucker's haunted expression as he spoke of men who'd been 'sent away.' Could any of them be serving their time here?

A sharp knock at the window makes her jump. Tucker stands there, gesturing for her to come outside.

Tucker's face is a mask of grim determination. Jillian's heart gears up into high speed, ready for him to drop more bad news.

"We're fine," Tucker announces, his voice low and tight. "I spoke with Rawlings. He's going to make sure we're okay."

Jillian's eyes narrow, her fingers curling into a fist. "How?" she asks, unable to keep the edge from her voice.

Tucker runs a hand through his hair, his gaze darting to their backyard. "Andy's got extra eyes on the place," he explains, his voice low. "He'll hire security to drive around the fields and the house. Someone will be watching us when we're out and about."

The thought of being under constant surveillance makes her skin crawl. "I don't like this, Tucker," she whispers fiercely. "What about Ethan? How do you think he'll feel?"

She pictures her son's face, his innocent eyes clouding with fear and confusion. The idea of shadowy figures lurking at the edges of his baseball games turns her stomach.

"He doesn't need to know," Tucker insists, reaching for her hand. "It's for our protection, Jill."

Jillian pulls away, her mind racing. "Our protection?" she says, bitterness rising in her throat.

Tucker leans in closer, his gaze intense as he grips Jillian's shoulders. "He won't even know anyone's watching him," he says. "It'll be completely invisible."

Jillian stares into her husband's face, searching for a flicker of doubt, a hint of the truth she knows he's hiding.

"How can you be so sure?" she asks, her voice trembling slightly. She thinks of Ethan's perceptive nature, how attuned he is to changes in their routine. "Our son notices everything, Tucker. He'll pick up on it."

Tucker's grip loosens, and he takes a step back. "We don't have a choice," he says, his tone edged with frustration. "This is the best way to keep us safe."

Jillian turns away, her gaze drifting to the window, to the cozy kitchen inside, and then out to the yard, where the landscape stretches beyond the shelter of tall trees surrounding their home. She imagines hidden eyes in every shadow, every rustling bush.

There's more. She can tell from the look on her husband's face. "What is it?" she asks, her voice barely above a whisper.

Tucker runs a hand through his graying hair, his eyes stormy. "We need to talk about who might have found us," he says, his tone strained. "Someone from our past could be here in Shelby."

CHAPTER TWENTY-FOUR

The bitter aroma of freshly brewed coffee fills the kitchen, mingling with the lingering scent of burnt cheese from dinner. Jillian's hands tremble slightly as she sets two steaming mugs on the worn wooden table. Tucker slides into the chair across from her, his face etched with exhaustion.

Jillian takes a deep breath, steadying herself. "We can't keep living like this, always looking over our shoulder."

"I know." He wraps his hands around the mug.

The tick of the old clock on the wall seems to grow louder in the silence. Jillian's mind races, searching for the right words. She thinks of Ethan, finally asleep upstairs after an hour of excited chatter about his upcoming baseball game. How can she protect him from the darkness creeping into their lives?

Not if Tucker continues keeping secrets.

"You said that someone from our past is here in Shelby. How do you know?" she asks, her voice barely above a whisper. "Is that what Andy Rawlings said on the phone earlier?"

Tucker's jaw tightens. He looks away, focusing on the fields outside their kitchen window, now shrouded in darkness. "Jill, I—"

"And where have you been going?" The words tumble out before she can stop them. "You're gone so much lately, and I can never reach you. What's going on, Tucker?"

His eyes snap back to hers, a mixture of guilt and defensiveness flashing across his face. "It's complicated, Jill. I'm trying to protect you and Ethan."

Jillian leans forward, her coffee forgotten. "Protect us from what? Or who? Who from our past is here?" She doesn't understand why this simple question is so hard to answer.

Tucker runs a hand through his hair, a gesture he's struggling. "I think someone from that mess in New York was sent to prison here and they recently got out. I . . ." He stops and sighs. "The less you know, the better," he says. "Trust me on that."

Anytime someone says *trust me*, it means you shouldn't. That's a lesson she's had to learn over and over. "Tucker, I've been trusting you and look where it's landed us. We've moved across the country way too many times, our son is struggling in school because we keep running, and now we're here on a farm where dead bodies were discovered. I want to trust you, and God knows I have when I probably shouldn't have, but . . . if you want trust, then you need to earn it."

"Earn it? What do you think—" He pauses, twisting in his seat, staring out across their yard lit up by solar lights along the back porch and walkway. "Okay," he finally says, "I deserved that."

She only nods and pushes back the words hovering over the tip of her tongue, waiting for him to deny that truth.

"Our lives have been a mess since Parishville, I know that, and I know it's on me."

"Why?" She interrupts him, leaning forward to grab hold of his hand.

"Why what?"

"Why have our lives been a mess since Parishville?"

He looks like he's going to choke on his words as he tries to answer. Finally, he shakes his head and pulls his hand from her grasp, leaving her feeling more alone than she has in a long time.

"I don't want to make you complicit, Jill. I wish you could just . . . trust, or at least, respect that decision."

She folds her arms, not giving him an inch of what he's asking for.

"I'm doing everything I can to keep our family safe," Tucker says, his voice low and urgent. "That group I snitched on, they hold grudges and don't like being betrayed. That's why we've had to run so often, change our identities, go into witness protection."

"So why did we leave it then, if they're so dangerous? Why did you insist that we'd be safer on our own, that living a life without our roots, without our family, was slowly killing us?"

His shoulders slump and he rolls his neck in a semicircle before releasing a long sigh. "Jill . . . it doesn't matter where we go, or what we do to protect ourselves, they are always going to find us. They found us even with the marshals protecting us."

For a slow minute, she lets herself remember the craziness during that time. She'd been out, having just dropped Ethan off at his school and she'd come home to loud arguing in her kitchen. Tucker was arguing with two marshals, telling them they were worthless and had no idea what they were up against. When he saw her standing there in the doorway, he told her to go pack their things, that they needed to be on the road within an hour if they had any hope of staying alive.

She'd trusted him then. She packed suitcases full of items, leaving the suitcases at the door for Tucker to pack into their truck. The marshals were gone, Tucker was grim-faced, and within the hour, they were at Ethan's school, where they pulled him from class and headed for the main highway.

"Less than an hour after we left, that house was peppered with bullets and then set on fire." His voice is chock-full of regret, despair, and anger as she gasps. He releases the cup he's been holding and fists his hands. "I never told you that, and I probably should have."

"Set on fire?" Her heart hurts, pounding away in her chest. "Bullets? How could you not tell me this?" The full reality of what they'd run from hits her, and she wants to scream. "I deserve to know this stuff, Tucker. You can't keep secrets like this." A thick ball of worry grows as she imagines a similar scenario happening here. "Is that . . ." she struggles to find the right words. "Am I going to wake up one day and find someone standing over us with a gun to our heads?"

He reaches for her, but she steps back, needing the distance, angry with him for putting them in this situation. "I won't let that happen."

She snorts with derision. "Sounds to me like you can't stop it if it does."

He shakes his head. "I swear, Jill. It won't happen. I promise."

She exhales until her chest feels like it's about to cave in for the weight of the secrets encircling them as a family. "You should have told me." She can't shake the image of how close they were last time, and she never knew.

"You're right. I should have told you, but I was too focused on getting us to safety," he tells her, his voice laced with apologies. "Andy gave me directions to a safe house. He said to only stop when absolutely necessary and he set us up with someone willing to switch vehicles with us."

That explains so much now. At the time, she didn't understand why Tucker refused to stop for food, why they did drive-thrus and eventually got off the main highway, took a lot of backroads, and drove through so many small towns. They slept in various hotels and rentals. She never understood how he set them up since he was doing most of the driving, but it all makes sense now, knowing just how involved Rawlings is.

Rawlings set up everything for them. He has been their fairy godfather, and all this time, she's been viewing him as a monster.

Except he is one. She can't let a few good deeds negate the truth. For whatever reason, dead bodies were found on property that once belonged to him and he's trying to get her husband to run and disappear — without her. He is a monster. The good doesn't negate the bad.

"When did he offer this place to you? You showed it to me when we stopped in Kansas. Was it then, or did you know it from the beginning?"

"Andy offered it around then, yeah. And it's been good, safe . . ." He pauses, looks away, a shadow covering his face as he realizes what he's just said.

"It's not safe, Tucker, not now at least. So, who is here from our old life? From that group you were part of?" Jillian's heart races, waiting for him to answer.

"It doesn't really matter who, what matters is they are here. Andy knows we're not running, so he's set up security for us." He reaches for her hand and gives it a squeeze, an action she doesn't find reassuring. "People watching our backs."

She pulls her hand away. "We should have the police watch our backs," she says.

He meets her gaze, and for a moment, she sees a flicker of the man she married — open, honest, kind. But then his eyes shutter, and instead, she sees a stranger sitting across from her.

"That's the last thing we need," he says. "The police are only going to—"

A sharp knock at the front door breaks into their conversation. Jillian's head snaps up, her heart leaping into her throat. She glances at the clock — it's almost ten o'clock at night. Who could be calling at this hour? She rises, her legs unsteady beneath her. Tucker is behind her, his hand on her back. She gives him a look and almost wishes she hadn't. She tiptoes to the door while he opens the closet, pulls out a gun from the top shelf and stands ready.

Fear crawls over her skin, slithering its way across her chest until she catches a glimpse of a familiar silhouette through the frosted glass. Jake? What's her boss doing here?

Jillian opens the door, forcing a smile. "Jake, this is unexpected."

Jake shifts uncomfortably on the porch, his usual confident demeanor absent. "Evening, Jillian. Sorry to drop by so late. Is Tucker home?"

Her smile falters. "Tucker?" She glances behind her where her husband stands, gun now dropped to his side. He steps up, one hand gripping the doorway, the other holding the gun hidden behind her.

"Hey, man, sorry to drop by like this, but . . ." Jake says, stepping back and lifting his hands in a 'what can you do' manner.

"Jake," Tucker says, his voice tight. "Let's take this outside."

Confusion and fear mingle in Jillian's chest. Before she can say anything, Tucker brushes past her, his hand briefly squeezing her shoulder — a gesture meant to reassure her, but it only heightens her anxiety. He hands her the gun, which she unwillingly takes, then closes the door. She stands nearby, straining to hear, but she barely makes out what they're saying, other than — "Andy," "deal," "consequences" — each word stoking the fire of her suspicions.

Minutes stretch like hours before Tucker abruptly turns back to the house. Jake's face is pale in the porch light as he nods a curt goodbye.

The door slams shut behind Tucker, the sound reverberating through the quiet house. His jaw is clenched, eyes wild with an emotion Jillian can't place.

"Tucker, what's—"

"Not now," he growls, brushing past her. "I just . . . I need some time."

He strides toward his office, leaving Jillian frozen in the entryway. Just before he disappears inside, he pauses, his shoulders sagging.

"I'm sorry, Jill," he murmurs, not meeting her eyes. "You deserve an answer, and I promise to give it to you soon. But I need to . . ." He shakes his head. "I need to deal with this before it's too late. Let me fix this, okay? Just give me a little more time."

The office door closes with a soft click, leaving Jillian alone with her racing thoughts. Her mind is going in a million directions, none of them good. With her heart pounding, she tiptoes to Tucker's office door, pressing her ear against the cool wood. Her breath catches as she hears his muffled voice, tense and urgent.

"Andy, we need to meet sooner than later. This is spiraling out of control."

Tucker's voice drops lower. "No, not there. It's too risky. The usual place. What? No, I want to meet now, I don't care if you are . . . I swear to God, if anything happens between now and then, I'll kill you myself, and that's not an idle threat this time, old man. Enough is enough."

Jillian's mind pieces together the fragments of overheard conversations and unexplained absences. She backs away from the door, her legs unsteady.

In the living room, she sinks onto the couch and reaches for a notebook. She adds names of people who could be anonymous sources, who give her a wide berth or look at her weirdly at the grocery store. She adds Jake's name to her list and circles it. She then opens the text messages between herself and her husband, thinking about all the times Tucker went silent, and she adds dates to her list. Names, dates, suspicious occurrences — anything that might point to the danger toward her family. Living life with blinders on isn't an option anymore, nor is blind trust.

The man she married is not the man she thought he was. He can't be, not if he's linked with Andy Rawlings, a man who hid dead bodies on his property for who knows how long. Her fingers trace over Andy's name and underline it. There comes a point when trust doesn't deserve secrecy. She thinks of Sheriff Mato — a strong and steady woman.

"I should tell her everything," she whispers, the weight of the decision settling on her shoulders. "But what if I'm wrong? What if Tucker . . ."

She can't finish the thought. The ticking of the grandfather clock in the corner grows louder, each second urging her toward a choice that will change everything.

CHAPTER TWENTY-FIVE

Agent Meri Amber

Meri's eyes burn as she squints at the flickering hotel room lamp. Papers litter every surface in her room — the bed, the desk, even the floor. Her fingers, stained with ink, tremble as she reaches for another document.

She thinks better with paper and pen, she always has, and right now, she really needs her brain to work. It's all here — everything she's been searching for, except it feels like she's working on a puzzle with missing pieces.

What isn't she seeing?

The Red House. It's here, in all this mess, she knows it. But what is it exactly? Where is it? Who runs it? How has it stayed under the radar for so long? She has so many questions and very few answers.

"Look at it as a long game, Amber," she tells herself. "A shadow organization that's been running behind the scenes . . . someone knows something, they're either paid off to stay mum, or they are part of it."

Her phone buzzes and Lindsay's name flashes on the screen.

"Amber," she answers, her voice hoarse from hours of silence. She's been anticipating his phone call but hoped she'd have some sort of breakthrough or brilliant idea for when he called. She has none.

"How's it going?" Lindsay's gruff tone carries a hint of concern. "And how many carafes of coffee have you drunk?"

"Too many," Meri sighs, rubbing her temples. "I'm drowning in paper, but I've got nothing to show for it. Might have to raid the hotel's business center soon."

"Should've printed all that at the station," Lindsay chides.

"No." The word comes out sharper than intended. Meri takes a breath, softening her tone. "This is personal, Lindsay. There's something off about this town, and it's more than just the prison," she says before he can say anything. "I can't risk more eyes on it."

She can almost hear Lindsay's frown through the phone. "Fair enough. On all accounts, the sheriff has a tight grip on what happens there, but I trust your judgment; you know that. Besides, this is your show, we've got jurisdiction."

"I know."

He pauses. "Listen, Meri, about the Red House—"

Her pulse quickens. "What did you find?"

"More than I expected, and to be honest, I'm shocked no one has put two and two together until now." Lindsay's words hang heavy in the air. "Someone high up owns it, but we haven't cracked who yet."

Meri's mind races. "Political or cartel?"

"Maybe both," he sighs. "The level of shell corporations is ridiculous. They're hiding something big."

Meri's gaze falls on the tarnished bracelet sitting on her nightstand. She still has no idea why it was sent to her in the mail so long ago. She's always held on to it, believing it was from her sister. Twenty years of searching, and now they're so close. "But we're getting there?"

"We're close," Lindsay confirms. "Close to finding out who owns it and where it is. As to be expected, there's a lot of bureaucracy and red tape."

Meri nods, even though Lindsay can't see her. Her throat tightens as she thinks of all those who've passed through the Red House. All the families left wondering, like her.

Meri's brow furrows as she scans the documents, her eyes darting from page to page. "Connecting these together is . . ." She doesn't finish, but the fact her voice is tinged with frustration and disbelief says everything.

Lindsay's sigh crackles through the phone. "This is probably one of the most complicated setups I've ever seen, Meri. These people know how to cover their tracks."

She leans back in her chair, her fingers tugging at the elastic of her ponytail. She's getting a headache. "What else did you find out about the Red House?"

"Not much. Looks like it's used as a waylay station. No one stays there long," Lindsay explains, his tone grim. "They get cleaned up, drugged up, dolled up, and then sold to the highest bidder."

Meri's stomach churns. She closes her eyes, trying to block out the images her mind conjures. "And when they leave?"

"The only thing connecting them is their bracelet."

She looks at the bracelet, imagining her sister wearing it. What happened to her?

"There's more," Lindsay says, interrupting her thoughts. "I'm sending over one last file. A photograph of someone who may match your sister's description."

Meri's heart leaps into her throat. "Are you sure?"

"There's a resemblance, but it could be anyone, Meri. I don't want you to get your hopes up."

She swallows hard, her voice barely above a whisper. "Lindsay, after twenty years of searching for her, you don't have to spare my feelings. As much as I want to believe she's alive, the likelihood is . . ."

She trails off, unable to finish the sentence. Suddenly, Jillian's face flashes in her mind. "Wait. I need to tell you something. I've been looking into the Harpers more, and I don't like what I see, but I may have some good news for a change. Rebecca — Becky — Gardiner, she's that missing teenager case I asked you to pull for me, may be alive and living in this area."

"What?" Lindsay's surprise is evident. "What are you doing about it?"

Meri straightens in her chair, a spark of determination igniting within her. "I've put in a request for an age progression. It's a long shot, but . . ."

"But it's something," Lindsay finishes for her. "Bringing one home is always something."

She hears the hope in his voice. In Lindsay's opinion, every missing case he can close is worth celebrating.

As Meri hangs up, she stares at her computer screen, waiting for the file to arrive. Her fingers hover over the mousepad, trembling slightly. After all this time, any clue, any news, anything that leads her closer to knowing what happened to her sister is a good thing. Dead or alive, she just needs closure. Her family needs closure. She whispers a small prayer that whatever Lindsay sends will be the truth she's been searching for and not another dead end in a sea of disappointment.

The email notification chimes, piercing the tense silence of Meri's hotel room. She clicks on the file, her breath catching as it opens. A grainy photograph fills the screen, showing a woman with haunted eyes and hollow cheeks. Meri's heart stops.

"River," she whispers, her voice cracking.

The resemblance is undeniable. The shape of the eyes, the curve of the jaw — it's her sister, but a version ravaged by time and unimaginable horrors. Meri's vision blurs as tears well up, her hand trembling as she touches the screen.

The woman in the photo stares back, lifeless. There's no mistaking the vacant look in those once-vibrant eyes. Meri knows, with a certainty that chills her to her core, that she's looking at a dead woman.

Her mind races, connecting the dots. The Red House. The bracelet. The auctions. All leading to this moment of devastating clarity.

"I'm so sorry," Meri whispers to the image. "I should have found you sooner."

Anger surges through her grief, her fists clenching. Whoever did this — whoever ran the Red House, whoever bought and sold girls like commodities — they would pay. She'd make sure of it.

CHAPTER TWENTY-SIX

Jillian

The late afternoon sun beats down on Jillian's back as she kneels in the vegetable garden, her fingers buried in the warm soil. She plucks another weed, adding it to the growing pile beside her. The repetitive motion is soothing, her mind wandering with the mindless actions. For one reason or another, Jake had been on her all day and her nerves are shot.

Jake was different today. His voice was curt, like he couldn't stand to be in her presence, yet at the same time, he couldn't let her be out of it either. Every time she left her desk he stood at his office door, watching her. He'd even trailed her to lunch where he sat with someone she didn't recognize. Whatever is going on in Shelby, Jake is a part of it, and she now sees him differently.

Is he one of those who will be looking after her? Will she always be looking over her shoulder and wondering who's in Rawlings' pocket?

A car engine rumbles in the distance. Jillian looks up, shielding her eyes. Sheriff Mato's vehicle pulls into the driveway, kicking up a small cloud of dust.

Ethan, who was helping her pull weeds, darts to Jillian and grips her hand. "Mom, why is the police here?" His scared little voice doesn't go unnoticed. Jillian hates that there's fear within her son when he sees the police now.

"It's okay." She looks down and smiles at him. "Sheriff Mato is nice, remember?"

Ethan neither nods nor returns her smile. Jillian's stomach tightens as she forces an expectant smile on her face, one she prays Ethan can't see past. She's just as nervous as her son is. So far, anytime the police have shown up, it's never been good.

The car door opens, and Sheriff Mato's large wolf-dog bounds out, tail wagging furiously.

"I promised Tala she could play with her ball once we got here," Sheriff Mato says, smiling, her dark eyes crinkling at the corners. "Would you mind throwing it a bit while I chat with your mom?" Sheriff Mato asks Ethan as she bounces a ball in her hand.

"Wow! Can I, Mom?" Ethan stares up at her, eyes wide with excitement.

"Of course," Jillian says, ruffling his hair before dropping her arms to her sides. Jillian's fixed smile doesn't falter as Ethan tosses the ball and the dog races after it. Despite her son's infectious laughter, anxiety gnaws at her insides. Why is the sheriff here?

"How are you doing, Jillian?" Sheriff Mato asks, her tone casual but her eyes eagle sharp.

She wipes her soil-stained hands on her jeans. "I'm fine, Sheriff. Thank you for asking." She pauses, rapid fire heartbeats pulsing in her chest. At work, every time she reached for the phone, ready to tell the sheriff everything, she'd feel Jake's gaze and she'd stop herself. Now is her chance if she decides to take it.

She doesn't. "Please tell me you're not here with more bad news?"

The sheriff's gaze flickers briefly to the vegetable garden behind Jillian. "Just some more questions, if you don't mind."

Jillian's fingers twitch, itching to return to the familiar task of weeding. Anything to distract from the unease creeping up her spine. "Of course," she says, her voice steadier than she feels. "If I can answer, I will."

Sheriff Mato glances at Ethan, still engrossed in his game with the dog. She lowers her voice slightly. "Is there somewhere we can talk privately?"

Jillian's stomach drops. Private questions are never good. She gestures toward the porch. "We can sit over there if you'd like." Her mind races with a whole slew of possible questions she's about to be asked. Will Mato believe her when she says she doesn't know anything? Does Jillian even think that herself? From the little Tucker has said, she's been able to piece together enough information to know this is a place they never should have moved to.

Sheriff Mato settles onto the porch swing, her eyes scanning the property. "I've been looking over the documents for this place," she begins, her tone casual but her gaze piercing. "I couldn't help but notice your name isn't on any of them."

Jillian's hands clench in her lap. She forces them to relax, hoping the sheriff hasn't noticed. "Oh, that's because Tucker handled everything," she explains, aiming for nonchalance. "He's always been better with the paperwork side of things."

The sheriff nods slowly, her expression unreadable. "I see. And do you happen to know how much you and Tucker paid for the house?"

A chill runs down Jillian's spine despite the warm afternoon sun. Why is she asking about this? "I'm not sure I understand," Jillian says carefully. "Why is that important?"

Sheriff Mato leans forward, her voice lowering. "Because according to the records, you only paid $50,000 for this place. That's highly unusual, Jillian. A property like this — the house, the land — it should go for at least a couple million, probably more." She pauses, her eyes boring into Jillian's. "Don't you find that strange?"

Jillian's mind reels. Fifty thousand dollars? That can't be right. Tucker never mentioned anything about the price, other than it was a steal of a deal . . . and she just believed him. Knowing what she knows now . . . she wishes she'd dug into his comment more.

"I-I'm not sure what to say," Jillian stammers, her thoughts a chaotic whirl. "There must be some mistake." Her hands tremble as she brushes a loose strand of hair behind her ear. She can feel Sheriff Mato's eyes on her, searching for something — a tell, a crack in her composure.

"A mistake?" Sheriff Mato echoes, her tone skeptical. "That's certainly possible. But it's quite a significant discrepancy, don't you think?"

Jillian's throat tightens. "I-I suppose it is," she manages, her voice barely above a whisper.

Sheriff Mato leans toward her, her voice dropping. "Mrs. Harper, I have to ask, is it possible there was some kind of personal connection between Tucker and the previous owner? Something that might explain such an unusual arrangement?"

The question hits Jillian like a punch to the gut. She knows. She has to, otherwise, why ask? Maybe she's trying to connect the dots, put together the puzzle hoping Jillian will hand her the pieces, one at a time.

That's not going to happen. She doesn't even have all the pieces put together herself. She needs to know more before she knows how much or how little to say.

"That's a question you'll need to ask my husband, Sheriff Mato," Jillian says, hating how unconfident she sounds. "He handled all the details of the purchase."

She can feel her carefully constructed world starting to crumble around her.

"Of course." Sheriff Mato nods, her expression unreadable. "Is he around?"

Jillian shakes her head. "He had to run some errands, but I can let him know you stopped by."

"I would appreciate that, thank you." Sheriff Mato's gaze sweeps across the property, her eyes narrowing as she focuses on the driveway. "There's something else I've been meaning to ask you," she says, turning back to Jillian. "Have you noticed an increase in traffic lately? More vehicles driving by, perhaps?"

Jillian forces her hands to remain still in her lap and swallows hard, buying time to compose her thoughts.

"I . . . I suppose there has been some extra traffic," Jillian admits, her voice wavering slightly. "But we're still getting settled in. I hadn't really given it much thought. I assumed it was normal for the season, maybe?" That's a total lie, and she knows Sheriff Mato hears it. She has noticed. She's noticed and it bothers her.

Sheriff Mato's eyebrows raise. "You haven't found it bothersome? Unusual for such a remote property?"

Jillian's mind races while she forces a casual shrug, hoping her unease doesn't show. "Well, I figured people are just curious about the trailers and . . . and what was found there. It was in the news, after all."

The words feel hollow as soon as they leave her mouth. "Otherwise, I . . . I don't know," she adds lamely. Jillian hesitates, then asks the burning question: "Should I be concerned, Sheriff?"

Her heart pounds as Sheriff Mato considers her question. The silence stretches, thick with tension. She can't take it anymore.

"Ethan, honey," Jillian calls out, her voice a bit too cheerful. "Time to head inside and wash up, okay?"

Ethan looks up from where he's been tossing the ball for the sheriff's dog, his face flushed with exertion and joy. "Aw, Mom, can't I play just a little longer?"

"Now, please," Jillian says, her tone brooking no argument. She turns back to Sheriff Mato, forcing a smile. "Is there anything else I can help you with, Sheriff?"

Sheriff Mato studies Jillian's face, as if searching for something hidden beneath the surface. "Not at the moment,

Mrs. Harper," she says finally. "But I may have more questions later. You'll be around?"

The question feels loaded, and Jillian's throat tightens. "Of course," she manages. "We're not going anywhere."

"Good to know," Sheriff Mato says, turning to leave. "Running seems to be a specialty of yours, so I'll hold you to that." She whistles for her dog, who runs right to her side. "Have a nice night and please let your husband know I need to speak with him."

Jillian lifts her hand in a brief wave, her stomach churning until she swears she's about to be sick.

CHAPTER TWENTY-SEVEN

Saturday morning is her quiet time. While Tucker takes Ethan out to his practice, she likes to spend a leisurely morning sipping coffee, making muffins, and enjoying the only quiet time she gets during the week.

This morning, she intends to check off one of her to-do list items: go through the attic. One of the things she finds fascinating about this house is that the attic access is a door within their walk-in closet.

Armed with garbage bags, kitchen cleaning gloves, and her coffee thermos, she unlocks the attic door and makes her way up the stairs. Dust motes dance in the slanted sunbeams piercing through the small windows, one on each side of the attic, filling the space with a brightness she needs since Tucker still hasn't changed out the burnt lightbulb. Lightbulbs are a small thing on their ever-growing list of to-do's since buying this property.

Standing at the top of the stairs, she glances around the room with one simple question in mind: does she tackle the suitcases, which she hopes are empty, or the boxes, first?

The suitcases, left from the previous owner, are old and extremely dusty. She reaches for the handle of the first one.

It's large, and surprisingly heavy. Her heart thuds as her imagination runs wild — she's read a thriller about suitcases full of bones, and considering what has been found in those trailers on their property . . . she's a little hesitant in opening these.

That doesn't stop her, though.

There're only old clothes, pants, button shirts, and sweaters full of holes in the first suitcase. Nothing donation-worthy, so she throws everything into a garbage bag. The next suitcase is no different.

She puts those to the side and then focuses on the boxes. One box has faded photographs of a man and a child. She holds the image up close, her breath catching — is that Tucker as a child? The face is blurry, and the image is unclear.

She notices another box off in a corner. The word *PERSONAL*, done with a thick black marker, almost looks like Tucker's handwriting but not quite. She opens it to find some random items, including a small beautiful cedar box. She pulls that out and rests it on her legs. She can't stop looking at that photograph. She snaps a shot of it and sends it to Tucker: *Is this you?*

When her phone rings, she doesn't even look at the display, just answers. "Hey, weird that I'd find that photo, don't you think? Is that you or someone else?"

"What photo are you talking about?" Her mother's voice is not the voice she expected to hear.

"Mom, hey, sorry. I'm up in the attic cleaning and found some old photographs." She sets the photo off to the side, regretting her words. She's opened up a can of worms she is not interested in sharing with her mother.

"But why would you have found one of Tucker in there?"

"Oh, I doubt it's Tucker," Jillian says, backtracking. "It's hard to see, and I just thought it would be cute to send it to him."

"Speaking of photographs, you'll never believe what I found." Her mom's voice lights up, and Jillian pictures her mom with a huge smile. "An old photo album of you and Becky. I'm going to bring it out with me." she says.

"When are you coming out?"

"Tomorrow. I forwarded you my flight info. You will be there to pick me up, right?"

"Tomorrow? What? No, I didn't get anything from you, Mom." She pulls the phone from her ear and opens her emails. "Hang on, I'm looking." She scrolls through her inbox, spam, and deleted folders. "Mom, I've got nothing. When did you send it?"

"Oh, I don't know, Jillian. The day I booked it. I swear I sent it to you. Either way, I'll be there tomorrow afternoon, okay?"

Jillian closes her eyes. Why doesn't this surprise her? Her mother can be a bit flaky at the best of times — she lives in the moment, doesn't worry too much about anything, and trusts that everything will work out, and it does because everyone else around her takes care of all the little details for her.

"Anyway, aren't you excited about the album I found? It was tucked away in your old keepsake chest, along with some journals and letters. They're from old boyfriends, so I just threw those out, I hope you don't mind."

Old letters? Journals? "Did you read them?"

"Oh goodness, no, why would I do that? Why live in the past when we should put all our focus and energy into the present?" Her mother tsks. "But I will bring the album. There are some photographs in there I've never seen."

"Send me your flight details, Mom, so I can be there on time, okay? It'll be great to see you." She mentally rearranges her schedule and pushes her frustration down.

"Remember, I'm coming out for the whole summer. I want to spend time with that grandson of mine."

The whole summer? "What about Dad?"

"Oh . . . he'll probably come out later to get me. He wants to drive out and do the whole RV experience."

That doesn't surprise her. Her father had been a truck driver for most of her life, rarely ever around, always on the road. He once told her the road owned his soul. What does surprise her is that he'd rather drive out than fly? "But you don't have an RV."

"Well, not yet we don't."

Jillian shakes her head again before she hangs up. She can't believe her mom will be out here tomorrow or that her father is buying an RV. She's also not surprised. Just like she isn't surprised her mom forgot to send her the flight details, or that she's coming for the whole summer.

She glances down at the box in her lap, and without thinking, she opens it. The lid falls to the ground as she stares in horror at what she's holding.

Inside the box are pinkie fingers with painted nails. She cries out in shock. She drops the box, her stomach twisting and churning as she stares at those fingers.

All the thoughts rushing in torrents through her brain become chaotic as she struggles to work through who they could belong to, who could have done something like that and whose box did they come from?

Please, God, let it belong to Andy Rawlings. The pressure of this discovery threatens to crush her and everything she's worked so hard to build.

She hears a car horn, something Tucker has started to do lately to let her know he's home and somehow manages to push herself to her feet despite the disco beat of discord pounding in her chest. She heads to the closest window and wipes grime away from the glass.

Tucker's truck, the familiar beast, pulls up close to their front porch, the engine idling as she watches Tucker turn in his seat and say something to Ethan. Ethan's door doesn't take long to open, his sandy hair a wild halo as he jumps out, glove in hand, and rushes toward the house.

In the distance, a vehicle drives down the road and pulls into their driveway. She doesn't recognize it and has no idea who it is. A figure emerges, a man in a ridiculous cowboy hat and boots, and the longer he stands there, the more tension there seems to be between the two men.

She can't hear a word being said, but she notices her husband's reaction to the words being spoken: his hands flex at his sides, his shoulders are pushed back. He clearly doesn't like whatever he's hearing.

The man gestures, aggressive and demanding, his movements painting the air with desperation. Tucker responds with a shake of his head, measured and resolute, and she wishes she could see his face.

"Mom?" Ethan's voice from her bedroom, a distant echo of laughter and questions, has her leaving the window and rushing to the stairs. With one last look toward that box, she takes in a shuddering breath and makes her way down.

"Hey, that's cool. You've got your own secret staircase," Ethan says, standing at the bottom of the stairs, one hand on the railing. "Can I come up and look?"

"Hey little man, how was practice?" Jillian hides her shaking hands by jamming them into her pockets. "Oh, guess what? Grandma is coming tomorrow."

"What? No way, that's so cool." Ethan gives an air fist pump at the news.

"Right? So cool." Jillian nudges him out of the way and then closes the attic door, locking it and placing the key in her pocket. Ethan can never go up there, not until she's got rid of that box.

That box. What the hell is she going to do with it? The right thing would be to contact Sheriff Mato, but the right thing and the thing that is right for her family are two very different things right now — she's torn.

CHAPTER TWENTY-EIGHT

Jillian's chest is tight with tension, her heart beating to a bass drum, urging her to run, to race toward safety, and yet she does nothing. In fact, her feet won't move as she lingers in Ethan's doorway watching him sleep.

Everything she's done with her life since she knew she was pregnant has been for him.

Everything.

Everything she'd wanted, everything she'd been determined to do . . . her whole life purpose changed in one moment. Finding Becky, fixing mistakes she had no control over, figuring out what happened that night — none of it mattered as much as keeping her son safe. She's done everything since then to protect the life she's built, even if it goes against what she thought was important.

She's happy her mom is coming. She can help her protect Ethan while she figures out what is going on with Tucker and untangling all his lies and secrets.

With a deep sigh, she heads to her room, unlocking the attic door with shaking hands. Making her way up the creaking staircase, each groan of the old wood beneath her feet whispers a warning she knows she can't ignore.

Moonlight spills across the dusty floor, casting long shadows that dance with her every movement. She's alone — yet not. The past clings to the air, thick as cobwebs, and she can't shake off the chill that has nothing to do with the night air.

She turns on the flashlight app on her phone and moves it, illuminating the space around her.

"Jill?" Tucker's voice is a low rumble, slicing through the silence.

She spins, pulse leaping, to find him standing behind her.

Hands to her chest, she lets out a short puff of air. "I didn't hear you come up."

"What are you doing up here?"

"I ah . . ." She thought he'd lock himself in his office like he has most nights. "I was up here today and . . ." She points to the garbage bag she left earlier, her voice no more than a whisper, betraying the tension knot tight in her stomach.

"Why is it so dark in here? Where's the light switch?" He looks around.

"You haven't changed the bulb yet," she reminds him.

He nods, a simple gesture. He joins her in the cramped space, his frame dwarfing her.

"Is this where you found that photograph?" His question is cautious, a tentative step into the minefield.

"Among other things." Jillian's answer is equally guarded.

Tucker's gaze holds hers, a silent conversation passing between them.

"What else did you find?"

She bites her lip, forcing herself not to look at the box on the floor behind her. Her hand trembles as she pulls out the folded photograph from her pocket.

"Recognize him?" Her voice is barely audible, a shroud of apprehension draped over each syllable as she shines the light from her phone.

"I told you I didn't," Tucker says, taking the photo, his forehead creasing as he studies it. "I think it's Andy's son." There's a hardness in his tone that wasn't there before. "I only ever met him a few times, but I never really liked him."

172

"Andy has a son?"

"Had. He's dead now. Died in prison, last I heard."

"He what?" Jillian's eyes are locked onto Tucker's profile, searching for clues in the set of his jaw, the subtle twitch by his temple. "Why was he in prison?"

Tucker worries his lips seconds before his face hardens. "Heard he kept a woman prisoner in his home for years. Bought her from a sex trafficking ring, or so the news said."

Jillian sucks in a breath through her teeth. "Are you kidding me?"

"I wish. And, he was a preacher or something," he says.

"Who kept a woman captive."

"Yep. Always knew something was off about him, and I guess I was right." Tucker hands back the photograph, and his indifference speaks volumes.

Jillian places the photograph on a nearby suitcase and bends down. She reaches for the wooden box, barely wanting to touch it, barely sure of what she's doing.

"Here," she says, handing it to him.

His movements are mechanical, detached, already bracing for the worst yet refusing to acknowledge it. She watches him closely — does he know what's inside the box? Has he seen it before?

Is it his?

That's the one question she's not ready to ask. Not ready and doesn't want it answered, if she's being honest.

Tucker peers into the box, his expression unreadable, then quietly closes the lid without a word. He sets it down with deliberate care, distancing himself from its contents as if they were nothing more than everyday curiosities.

Jillian doesn't like what she sees. His lack of reaction is a riddle wrapped in the enigma of a man she thought she knew. She wants to ask, to pry open the vault of his thoughts, but something holds her back — the fear of unraveling truths that can't be woven back together.

The silence stretches between them until Tucker's voice slices through the stifling attic air. "Where'd you find this?"

Jillian's arm extends, her finger quivering as it points toward an open box. Her gaze lingers on his face, searching for something familiar, but there's nothing. The briefest flicker — a shadow passing over his features — his eyes darken, and he pivots away from her, his hands balled into fists.

She doesn't recognize this man. This stranger.

"Tell me that this belongs to Rawlings," she whispers, her voice fracturing. She wraps her trembling arms around herself while waiting for him to tell her what she needs to hear.

The words hang suspended between them.

Tucker turns away, his back a barrier between her and the answers he's not giving.

"Do we share this with Sheriff Mato?"

Tucker turns, his eyes locking onto hers with an intensity that pins her in place. "No," he says sharply, a crack of thunder in the silence. "I still need some time. This" — he glances at the box in his hands and swallows hard — "doesn't change that."

Jillian's heart stutters, and with a sudden burst of courage, she reaches out, her fingers grasping the fabric of Tucker's shirt. "This changes everything. Why don't you see that?" Her voice is steady despite the tremor threatening to betray her. "I wish you'd just tell me instead of thinking you must do this all alone."

Tucker pauses, the briefest hesitation, and in his eyes she sees a flicker of the man she needs as her partner.

His breath comes out in a ragged sigh, his silhouette framed by the light from her phone.

"Then what do you suggest we do?" he asks, the weight of his gaze settling on her.

Jillian's pulse thrums in her ears, a staccato rhythm that matches the racing thoughts in her mind as he finally leans on her, trusting her as a partner. She doesn't miss the way his voice wavers, the crack of a man teetering on the edge, waiting for a lifeline to save him.

"Are these yours or Rawlings?" She needs to know that first and foremost.

He shudders. "God, Jill, like I would keep something like that around."

Jillian breathes in slowly, forcing the air in through her nose and praying she won't throw up as she struggles with his response. That wasn't the answer she expected to hear.

His brow furrows as he stares down at the box. "If you tell the sheriff, she's going to toss this house apart, you know that, right? Every area of our lives will be in the spotlight. Is that what you want? That safety you're seeking — we'll never get it, not if you tell the police right now."

Right now. She hears the emphasis on those two words.

"But if I give you some time . . ." She doesn't finish, letting the sentence play out on its own.

He looks away, off into the distance where, for her, there are more questions than answers. "Everything will get resolved, and everyone involved will get what they deserve. I promise."

She steps close enough that her shadow merges with his. "I can't handle any more secrets, Tuck. I'll give you a little more time, but eventually we'll have no choice." Her words slice through the tension like a blade. Her hands tremble as she reaches for their Pandora's box of horrors, tucking it under her arm with more assurance than she feels.

"I know." Two simple words but there's a depth to them that weighs her husband down in ways she doesn't understand.

"Our lockbox over there." She points toward the other end of the attic. "I'll lock it inside and hide the key."

"Where?"

"Then the key wouldn't be hidden, would it?"

Tucker's expression is unreadable, but the hard set of his jaw stresses just how serious this situation is. She can't believe she's hiding evidence of an obvious crime, a crime her husband says isn't his, and she's choosing to believe him.

That's how it's always been though, hasn't it? Her choosing to believe him, all for the sake of the son they share. She hopes she's still doing the right thing.

CHAPTER TWENTY-NINE

It's been almost three hours since she picked up her mom from the Helena airport. Three hours of shopping, eating Costco hotdogs, listening to Ethan prattle on about everything and nothing to his grandma.

The whole time, Jillian couldn't stop thinking about how to warn her about the chaos in their life. She knows her mother's reaction. She knows what she'll say, and what she'll suggest.

Back when everything happened in Parishville, her parents had tried to get her and Ethan to move in with them, to leave Tucker and let him go to prison.

Once upon a time, before she'd gotten pregnant, she might have done that. Things are different now. She won't be the one to tear her son from his father.

She glances in the rearview mirror, and sees Ethan's eyes locked on the screen, headphones clamped over his ears, his world narrowed to the game he holds in his hands.

"Mom," Jillian starts, her voice almost lost to the road's whisper, "something's happened that you need to be aware of."

A loud exhale is the only sound her mother gives her.

"It's not what you think," Jillian says.

"Sweetheart, you have no idea what I think." Her mom turns and gives her a bright smile, but Jillian isn't fooled. She knows her mother. Knows the smiles. Knows the words behind the words.

"They found something on the farm. Bodies."

Kathy's hand pauses mid-reach for the car's air vent, her gaze flicking from the passing fields to her daughter's profile. "Bodies?" Her voice is a soft, disbelieving echo.

"Yeah," Jillian confirms, swallowing hard against the weight in her chest. "In two trailers in one of our back fields."

"Trailers? When did you get trailers?"

"We didn't. They were left here, from the previous owner."

"Well, I hope whomever that sick ba . . ." she stops herself and glances at the back, ". . . stard is, gets caught."

Jillian bites her lip. "Tucker considers the man family."

Kathy lifts her hands in the air and drops them with a thud on her lap. "And this just keeps getting better, doesn't it! Are you telling me you know the man?"

"No, of course not. Well . . ." She realizes she needs to amend that sentence. "I don't, but Tucker does."

"Of course he does." Kathy's chest expands with a large breath of air. "Why am I not surprised?"

"Mom, that's not fair." Jillian feels the question like a hook, tugging at the seam of all her decisions, both good and bad. "You know he wouldn't . . ." But the sentence hangs, unfinished and heavy.

"No, honey, I don't. I don't know what he wouldn't do because, at every turn, it seems like he's done it, hasn't he?" Kathy's voice is laced with skepticism. "Tucker's never been good news, Jillian. Surely you haven't forgotten that much."

Jillian's gaze flits to Ethan again. "I haven't forgotten," she says quietly, her mind racing through memories better left buried. "But people change, Mom. They do."

"Change," Kathy repeats, the word dripping with doubt. "Or just get better at hiding who they really are?"

"Dad changed, didn't he? That's why you let him come back home, isn't that what you've always said?"

The silence that follows is full of tension, the words unsaid carving the air between them into jagged shards. Jillian regrets saying anything.

"Tucker is nothing like your father." Kathy's whisper-soft voice almost wasn't heard.

Jillian's hands grip the steering wheel, her knuckles showing her tension. The silence in the car is thick. "I know. But life . . . life is complicated," Jillian says.

"Only because we make it that way. Sometimes the decisions you've made—"

"Stop," Jillian interrupts. She inhales deeply, the scent of stale airport coffee lingering in the car. "I wouldn't have Ethan if I hadn't stayed with Tucker."

Kathy shifts in her seat, turning to catch her daughter's gaze, eyes searching. "Oh, honey, I know, and for that, I'm so thankful, but that was all before . . ."

Jillian feels the unfinished question dangle between them, its implications sharp as thorns. She knows what her mother is asking without needing to hear it voiced. The ghosts of their past are always present between them, whispering from the dusty corners of their past.

"Okay, enough," Kathy says, shaking her head. "This really isn't the time for this," she glances in the back toward Ethan, again. "I'm excited to be here all summer with you guys." She reaches over and squeezes Jillian's hand. "I've missed you."

"I've missed you too. I'm glad you're here, even if it is last minute."

"Last minute, what are you talking about? I told you I was coming and even sent you the info."

"You told me yesterday, Mom, and I never got that forward." She gives her mom a look that leaves Kathy shrugging. "But it's all worked out, and I know Ethan is really excited to have you here. He stayed up late last night making all sorts of plans for you two. I'm a little jealous." She looks back at her son with a smile.

"I'm excited to see this place of yours, even if it does feel like it's in the middle of nowhere. How can you stand just looking at all these fields?" Kathy is wide-eyed as she stares out the windows.

"You get used to it. But it sure isn't like home, is it?" She's not going to admit just how hard it's been to get used to the change in scenery because that wouldn't be fair to Ethan, especially when she's tried so hard to help him adjust.

"Well, it has its own beauty, I guess." Kathy sighs then points straight ahead. "Is that your place?"

They pull into the driveway and park. Tucker is sitting on the porch and rushes down.

"Hey, Mom." Tucker greets Kathy, a smile creasing his face, lines of warmth in his sun-kissed skin. His voice carries the timbre of innocence — or practiced deception — Jillian isn't sure which. Her husband and her mother have a . . . different . . . relationship, one born out of mistrust on both sides.

"Hello, Tucker." Kathy steps out of the vehicle, her tone surprisingly tender as she approaches him. There's a grace in her movements, a deliberate softness that belies the tension of their earlier conversation. She brushes a strand of hair from her face, tucking it behind her ear.

Jillian watches them. Her mother's ability to switch gears — to present one thing and feel another — never ceases to amaze her. It's a survival skill, honed to perfection over years of protecting and nurturing amid uncertainty.

"Whoa, you ladies did some shopping," Tucker says as he drops the tailgate and whistles. "Ethan, I'll need some help, buddy."

Between the four of them, it only takes a few trips to lug in all the bags. With her mother's luggage sitting at the foot of the stairs, the rest of the things they bought sit on the kitchen table, the island, and the floor.

"I did warn you I'd be stocking up," Jillian reminds Tucker as he stands beside her, frowning.

"Yeah, but where are you going to put it all? Our pantry doesn't have that much room . . ." He shakes his head. "Or

179

is this your way of nudging me to hurry up and remodel the kitchen like you've been asking?"

The smile on her face should say it all. They have enough room in their kitchen and dining area to build the kitchen of her dreams, including a separate butler's pantry area that would make most home cooks weep with joy.

"Oh . . . a kitchen remodel? You should wait till your father comes out. He'd love to help you with that," Kathy says as she walks into the room, her arm slung around Ethan's shoulders. "Truth be told, your dad could use a project. He's been a little aimless lately. Did you know he bought an old Ford Mustang convertible and rebuilt it? I've shown you photos, haven't I? It's cherry red."

"A convertible? What made him do that?" Jillian doesn't mention her mother hasn't sent her any photos; she's never mentioned it at all until now.

"Here." Kathy holds out her phone for Tucker to take. He looks through the images, nodding his head ever so slightly. "You can't beat a good Ford, and that's one sweet ride. Does he drive it much?"

"Gosh, no. It sits in the garage ninety-five percent of the time. One weekend a month, during the summer months, we'll go for a ride, stop somewhere for a good steak dinner and ice cream, but that's about it," Kathy says.

Tucker shows Jillian the photos. The first is of her dad posing beside an old beater tucked away in a corner of an old barn. You can see the handprints left behind as someone swiped at the dust. The car looks a little beaten, the leather top ripped in places, cobweb-covered items hanging from the rearview mirror, and bags of something sitting on the front seats. The following few photos show the rebuild, and by the last picture, Jillian can see why the smile on her dad's face has grown an extra mile or two — the car looks amazing.

"Too bad Grandpa won't be driving it out here," Ethan says.

"Oh, who knows what that grandfather of yours will do. He might hook it up to the RV he plans on buying and just leave it here for you to drive." Kathy tussles the top of Ethan's hair. "But don't quote me on that. It's Grandpa's toy, so you might be waiting a while to drive it."

By the time they finish putting everything away, Jillian's stomach is rumbling, and she glances at the time. "So . . . what's everyone in the mood for tonight?"

Kathy leans her elbows on the counter. "Ethan and I have got this, don't we?" she says to the boy standing beside her. "Ethan specifically requested chicken alfredo with garlic bread for dinner, so that's what we'll make. Why don't you scoot outside and spend some time relaxing on your big porch? I'll call you if we need help," Kathy insists, her gentle features set in a determined smile. Jillian hesitates, torn between the urge to help and the need for a moment's respite.

"Honestly, if it means I don't have to cook tonight, I'm good with that," she concedes, her voice edged with relief. Cooking is not her number one favorite thing to do, and she hopes that's something her mom will take on while she's here. As she leaves, the screen door slams behind her, cutting off the chatter between grandmother and grandson.

Instead of sitting on the porch, Jillian heads toward where they want to plant a fall garden. Their summer garden is already growing on the other side of the house where it gets lots of sunlight.

"I've been researching, and root vegetables will do well for your fall garden. Garlic especially. Need to have that planted by September at the latest. Have you decided where you want it?" Tucker's voice breaks through her reverie. He stands beside her, hands buried deep in his jeans' pockets, his presence comforting.

"By the oak tree, maybe," Jillian replies, pointing to a spot where the ground swells gently. "Enough sunlight, shelter from the wind."

"Yeah, that would work." He nods, then shifts uneasily. "Guess this and our summer garden will be good projects for your mom and Ethan this summer."

"Mom does love a good project. She's like Dad that way." Jillian leans her head on Tucker's shoulder.

"Still kind of surprised she's here, to be honest," Tucker says, his voice rumbling. "Seems last minute, don't you think? Any guesses why?"

Jillian sighs and pulls away, wrapping her arms around herself. "No and I'm a little hesitant to ask, you know? With Mom, it can be anything. She needed a break from Dad, she's fighting with her best friends, she's missing Ethan . . . it could be anything or nothing."

"Have you told her about . . ." His head nudges toward the north field, where the trailers and bodies were found.

"On the way here."

"She blames me, doesn't she?" Tucker's voice is low, full of hurt with a flicker of resentment. "She'll never forgive me, will she?"

"Forgive but never forget, and always be prepared. That's Mom's motto," Jillian adds dryly. There's no sense beating around the bush because Tucker knows exactly how her mom feels about him. And yet, to his face, she's always kind, thoughtful, friendly, and even loving. You'd never know her true feelings if you didn't know their history.

"You didn't . . . tell her about the box, did you?"

Her heart skips at the mention, a jolt of anxiety coursing through her. "What? God no. Why would I do that? I just hope there's no more surprises," she says quickly, her tone clipped.

"Good." Tucker's eyes hold hers. "There's nothing else, Jillian, I swear. There's nothing else for them to find."

"Isn't there?" She stares at the shadowy edges of the farm where secrets seem to loom as large as the mountains themselves. "What about the attic? There are more boxes of his and those suitcases . . . one was full of old clothes, but what if they're evidence? God knows what Rawlings could've hidden up there."

"Jillian—" Tucker starts, but she cuts him off with a raised hand.

"Did you call him and tell him what we found?" she asks, her voice strained with the effort of maintaining a semblance of calm.

Tucker's gaze lingers on her a moment longer before he nods. "He knows. He's going to come out and take care of the rest of his things. I'll make sure it's when no one is around, though."

"I don't want to meet him or see him or even know when he's been here." She barely gets the words out, her stomach tightening into knots.

"He's not a monster," Tucker says quietly. He sounds hurt — but is he hurt with her or with Rawlings?

"What world do you live in, Tucker? What do you see in him that I don't — because I can tell you what I see. I see a monster. I see an evil man who has done some horrific things, and all he's brought us is pain and heartache." She holds up her hand as he attempts to interrupt. "No, don't even bother arguing. What you call helping us, I say has harmed us more than anything else, and now we're tossed into a world full of danger — a world you don't seem too interested in escaping from." Rage flows through her the more she thinks about how intertwined that man has become in her life, in her family, and it's no surprise her body shakes with that anger.

"I swear to God, Tucker, if you don't figure out how to disassociate us from him, I'll go to the police and tell them everything, and I don't care about the consequences."

She lets the threat hang there between them. She sees the truth and resignation in his eyes, and a flicker of hatred for the man she married, the man she gave up everything for, takes seed in her heart.

CHAPTER THIRTY

Jillian balances her notepad precariously on her knee, pen poised as she glances around the cramped office. "Okay, coffee run. What's everyone want?"

A chorus of orders follows — "Latte! Americano! Green tea, please!" Jillian scribbles frantically, her brow furrowing in concentration. Trina walks out of Jake's office and leans over with a conspiratorial wink. "I'll cover the phones while you're gone. Take your time — it's dead in here anyway, and Jake just gave me a task I'm not ready to tackle yet."

"Anything I can help with?" Jillian asks. What she really wants is to leave this desk and this phone, but she can't do that until Jake realizes her skills are better suited elsewhere, and it's going to take longer than the few months she's been here for him to see that. Plus, she'll need to prove herself first, but that's hard to do in a small office where everyone is very territorial about their clients, files, and projects.

"Actually, yes, and I even got permission from Jake to have you help, but we'll discuss that after lunch. First . . . coffee."

Excited about the idea of taking on a new project that doesn't involve billing, Jillian grabs her purse and the list. As she steps out onto Main Street, a rush of hot air bulldozes her. The news host warned it would be a hot summer, with gusts of hot wind, but she almost didn't believe them.

The cheerful jingle of the bell above the door of Brews and Bakes greets her as she enters. The rich aroma of freshly ground coffee beans envelops her, and she breathes it in, but as she approaches the counter, a familiar voice distracts her, stopping her dead in her tracks.

"... and then I said to Graham, 'Well, if you're going to be that way about it ...'"

Jillian whirls around, her eyes scanning the room until they land on a familiar figure seated at a corner table. Mom? What is she doing here?

Her mother, Kathy, sits with her back to Jillian, gesturing wildly as she speaks. But it's the woman across from her that has Jillian sighing with regret. Martha Jenkins, the town's gossip, leans in eagerly, her eyes gleaming behind her thick-rimmed glasses.

Jillian's mind races. Why is Mom here? And with Martha, of all people? She freezes as she remembers the bodies recently discovered on their property. What if Martha is fishing for information? What if Mom lets something slip about their past?

She takes a hesitant step toward their table, her heart pounding in her ears. Should she interrupt? Warn her mother? Or pretend she hasn't seen them at all?

Sarah's voice cuts through her internal panic. "Hey, Jillian, coffee run time, huh? Is there a list or is it the usual?"

Jillian turns back to the counter. She hands over the office's coffee orders, her mind whirling with possibilities of what's being discussed over in that corner booth. What secrets is her mother sharing without even knowing she's doing it?

"Jillian? Is that you? Kathy, look, it's your daughter."

Jillian turns and sees Martha waving at her while Kathy twists in her seat, her smile warm but tinged with surprise. Jillian gives her mom a smile, watching as Kathy excuses herself from the table and approaches, her footsteps light on the worn wooden floor.

"Jillian, honey! What a coincidence," Kathy says, reaching out to squeeze her daughter's arm.

"Tell me about it, I didn't expect to see you in town today. I thought you were going to spend the day in the garden?"

Kathy's eyes twinkle. "Oh, I did, after seeing Ethan off on the bus. But then I started thinking about dinner, and I decided to pop into town for some supplies. Tucker said I could use his truck. When I saw this place, I remembered you said you loved their baked goods, so I thought I'd treat myself to a coffee. I ran into the sweetest lady. Martha, her name is."

Jillian's stomach churns. She leans in close, lowering her voice. "Mom, be careful. Martha's the town gossip. She'll spread anything you tell her faster than wildfire."

A knowing smile plays on Kathy's lips. "Oh, I picked up on that pretty quick. But don't worry, I'm not spilling any family secrets." She pauses, glancing back at Martha's table. "Actually, I'm the one getting the juicy details, especially when it comes to the previous owner of your property."

Jillian's eyebrows shoot up. "Really? What kind of details?"

"Nothing concrete yet, but Martha seems to know a lot about his . . . shall we say, colorful past?"

Jillian bites her lip, conflicted. "Mom, please be careful. We don't want to draw too much attention, especially with everything that's happened. But . . ." She hesitates, her curiosity warring with caution. "If you can find out more about him without revealing too much about us, it could be helpful."

Kathy nods, her expression growing serious. "I understand, sweetheart. I'll tread lightly, I promise. Sometimes it pays to let others do the talking."

Jillian watches Kathy return to the table with almost a sense of regret. She trusts her mother, but in a town this small, with secrets this big, even the tiniest slip could have devastating consequences.

"Jillian, dear!" Martha's voice carries across the coffee shop, her arm waving enthusiastically. "Come join us while your order's brewing!"

Jillian hesitates, her fingers drumming against the countertop, but curiosity tugs at her, so with a deep breath, she plasters on a smile and approaches the table.

Martha's eyes glimmer with excitement as Jillian slides into a chair. "You know, I was just telling your mom here what a shame it would be if you and your husband decided to move, after everything that's happened. I mean, it's understandable, but it would be a shame."

"Move? Why would we?"

Martha leans in, her floral scarf brushing the tabletop. "Who wouldn't? Bodies on properties you own? Late-night meetings happening in your fields? Ex-cons keeping watch over your house? Pick one, that would be enough for most people." The concern in Martha's voice seems genuine, but everything she's saying is ridiculous.

"I'm sorry, late-night meetings and people watching our house? What are you talking about?" Jillian leans in, arms out on the table. She thinks about all the vehicles she's been seeing at night and turns to Kathy.

"Mom, have you seen—"

"Cars drive by during the day? Yes, but isn't that normal around here? I mean . . . there are other houses on your road, right?"

"Well, there's the Jacks, but they're a few miles away. Old Man Cummings — well, now you, owned a lot of the land around here. He rents it out, of course, to local farmers and businesses, but . . . a lot of that land out by you is well . . . you," Martha says.

Jillian forces a weak smile. "Right, I knew that. Sometimes it amazes me just how much property we own. I mean . . . back at home, it would equal a small town, right, Mom?" Her laugh falls flat.

Kathy clears her throat, smoothly changing the subject. "Martha, you mentioned earlier that there's a prison nearby?"

"Oh yes." Martha nods vigorously, her glasses slipping down her nose. "You can't miss it, it's right off the highway. My Harold works security there, you know."

Jillian's ears perk up at this, her mind racing. Could there be a connection between the prison and the bodies on their land?

Martha continues, oblivious to Jillian's sudden interest. "There's this wonderful organization in town called Second Chance Beginnings that helps the men when they're released. It gives them a place to stay, and helps them find work. It's all about second chances, you see."

Jillian nods. "I've heard about them. Trina's mother works for them, I believe."

"Oh, she does. She has for years," Martha says.

Kathy leans back in her chair, holding her coffee cup. "Doesn't that scare you?"

"Scare me? Why? Sheriff Mato is here. She keeps a good eye on things, she and her team watch out for us. The prison might be right outside the town, but we've never been in danger."

"Never?"

"Go ask her yourself, if you don't believe me," Martha says. "We do our best to help out those folks. Including Old Man Cummings. Why, he'd hire them from time to time."

Jillian's head snaps up. "What?"

Martha beams, clearly thrilled to have such an attentive audience. "Oh yes, he'd bring them on to help maintain his properties when he was away. Said everyone deserves a fair shake." Her eyes widen as she gives a sharp inhale. "In fact, I bet that's who's driving by your place."

"Is it safe?" Kathy asks, hand to her chest.

"Of course. I wouldn't be worried in the slightest."

As Martha prattles on, Jillian's mind whirls. Martha might not be worried, but she certainly is. She catches her mother's eye, seeing her concern mirrored there.

"Jillian, your order is ready." Sarah's voice cuts through the hum of the coffee shop.

Jillian jumps, her reverie broken. "I should get those," she says, pushing back her chair.

"Why don't I help you, honey," Kathy offers, rising to her feet. "Martha, it was so lovely to sit down with you over coffee. I'll be here for the summer, we'll need to do this again."

"Jake called and asked for some pastries," Sarah says as she hands over a box as well. Jillian's hands tremble slightly as she reaches for the cardboard tray. The weight of the information Martha has shared settles heavily on her shoulders.

"Here, let me carry some of that," Kathy says, taking the tray.

They push through the door, the bell chiming as they step outside. Jillian inhales deeply, trying to clear her head.

"You okay?" Kathy asks, her voice low and concerned.

"Why are you here, Mom? Not that I'm upset. I've missed you, and I know Ethan loves that you're here for the summer, but why? Has something happened? Is everything okay between you and Dad?"

Kathy's steps falter for just a moment before she laughs. "Well, that came out of the blue. Does there have to be a reason for me to come visit, other than I miss my daughter and grandson?" She sniffs. "Your father and I are fine, don't you concern yourself about that. I just wanted to come out and see you, sweetheart. That was all. Seems like I came at the right time, too."

Jillian nods, not trusting her voice. They walk in silence for a moment, their footsteps echoing on the quiet small-town sidewalk.

Finally, Kathy speaks. "I don't like it, Jilly. I don't like any of it. It's a good thing I came out when I did. The idea that those men from the prison know your property better than you do, that they're driving by, keeping an eye on you . . . it doesn't sit right with me."

Jillian swallows hard. "I know, Mom. I know. I need to talk to Tucker about this." She thinks of Ethan, who loves

189

to play out in the yard. She thinks of Tucker, who spends countless hours checking on their property. He'd mentioned Andy had people looking after them, is that what this is? Does Tucker know them? Has he met with them? Talked with them?

"There's something not right about all of this," Jillian says, her voice barely above a whisper.

Kathy nods, her eyes scanning the street as if looking for hidden dangers. "Maybe you need to talk to the local sheriff? Should you maybe consider coming back home and—"

Jillian cuts her off. "I'm not running, Mom. Not again. Something needs to change. There are too many secrets and I'm done with being kept in the dark. Done with others knowing more about what's happening in my life than I do."

"There's my girl," her mom says softly.

Her mom is right. For too long she's let someone else dictate the actions of her life, and enough is enough. Enough running. Enough being a sheep and following along. When did she give up and just follow blindly all because someone said they knew better?

CHAPTER THIRTY-ONE

"What the . . ." Jillian leans forward in the seat of her vehicle. It's been a long day, an even longer night with Ethan's baseball practice running late, and the last thing she wants is to deal with more surprises in her life.

An unfamiliar pickup hitched to a trailer sits in front of their porch.

"Mom, whose truck is that?" Ethan's voice cuts through her thoughts. In his baseball uniform, dirt from the diamond still clinging to his pants, he peers out the window with wide, curious eyes.

"Are you expecting company?" Kathy asks. Her brows are knitted as much as Jillian's are.

"No . . ." Then she remembers what Tucker said about Rawlings coming out. But he's supposed to come when they aren't around . . .

Before Jillian can formulate a proper response, the front door of their house is thrown open, revealing two figures outlined against the warm glow.

"Well, I'll be . . ." Kathy says softly. "I think you know who they are, don't you, bud?"

Jillian glances in the rearview mirror, just in time to see the spark of excitement light her son's eyes. He's unbuckled and out the door before Jillian has the chance to say a single word.

"Grandpa! Grandma!" Ethan's excitement is a palpable force, charging toward them like an unleashed current. His arms wrap around his grandparents in an embrace that bridges over a year of absence.

Jillian watches from the vehicle, her hand still resting on the key she's just pulled from the ignition. Why didn't she know they were coming out?

"Looks like we've got surprise guests," Kathy remarks, her tone light but not without a hint of the same puzzlement Jillian feels.

"Just what we need." Jillian pushes open her door and steps out of the truck.

"Logan, Lucille, this is a surprise." Jillian gives her in-laws hugs of welcome, mustering all the hospitality she was raised with while her mind tries to figure out why they're here.

Tucker emerges from the doorway, the entry light casting his shadow long across the porch. His brows are knit together, a clear testament to his surprise as he watches Ethan in his grandfather's arms.

"What is this, grandparents' week?" The words slip through clenched teeth before she releases a sigh.

"Didn't know they were coming," Tucker says almost to himself as he steps off the porch, his voice low enough that only Jillian catches it over Ethan's excited chatter.

"Mom, Dad, this is awesome!" Ethan's voice rings out, pulling Jillian's attention back to the boy, who bounces between his grandparents with an energy she envies.

"It's pretty cool, that's for sure." Jillian's tone carries a weight that doesn't reach the surface.

"Dad, why don't we move that trailer while Ethan gets cleaned up?" Tucker motions toward the trailer as if to shepherd them away from further awkwardness. "The previous owner had hookups for a trailer just over here, which is convenient, don't you think?"

Jillian catches how he says it like he's trying too hard to make an off-handed comment. Did his father already know about the hookups, which is why they brought the trailer? It's not unrealistic that Tucker would have mentioned it to either his mom or dad in passing when they bought the house, but it still seems too on the nose.

Tucker's father, a stoic shadow beside his chatty wife, merely nods, his gaze scanning the stretch of the yard as if he's measuring it, calculating. It's Tucker who steps in, guiding him away with a hand on his shoulder. "Come on, I'll show you where to park," he says, and they walk off, leaving a trail of dust and unsaid words.

"What great timing," Lucille says, snapping Jillian's attention back. "I told your grandpa that we shouldn't have stopped for so long to eat today — otherwise, we would have been there to see your game." She beams a disappointed look at Ethan.

"It wasn't a game, Grandma, just a practice. And Coach Neil was grumpy because Dad didn't come tonight, so it was good you weren't there. Right, Mom?" Ethan kicks off his shoes into the corner and brushes his dirty hands on his already dirty pants.

"Hey, bud, you know where your shoes go," Jillian reminds him. "Head on up to change, too."

"Why wasn't Tucker there tonight?" Tucker's mom snaps her finger at Jillian, something she does when she wants someone's attention and something that annoys Jillian to no end.

At the beginning of their marriage, Tucker used to snap his fingers at her too. That quickly stopped.

"He had a work thing come up for one of his clients." Jillian gives her mother-in-law a pointed look.

"Kathy, I didn't realize you would be here too. It's so good to see you. It's been too long," Lucille says, filling the silence hanging between the three of them. "Although, I guess if we had called beforehand, I'm sure you would have told us, Jillian, isn't that right? So really, the fault is on us." Her hands

193

weave through the air, sketching out their journey in invisible lines as she speaks.

"Why didn't you call or even email?" Jillian asks as she leads the way into the kitchen and fills up a glass of water.

"Well . . . honestly, we thought we'd surprise you. And Logan has always talked about doing a cross-country trek — we live in a beautiful country, and we've always wanted to do more traveling," she says, her voice carrying the lilt of adventure. "And what better way than with our home hitched to the back of the truck, right?" She gestures toward their trailer, where Tucker and Logan appear to be having a heated discussion.

"Oh, those boys . . ." Lucille tsks before shaking her head with dismay. "Why can't they just get along for once?" She looks away.

Jillian notices the frown before Lucille gives a broad smile. She knows more than she's letting on, but if there's one thing Jillian has learned, it's that Lucille never shares unless she's ready to.

"So, Kathy, how long are you here for?" Lucille asks as she leans against the kitchen counter, looking around.

"The summer. I figured Ethan would enjoy the company," Kathy says. "How about you?"

"Oh, isn't that nice, I'm sure he loves having you here. And what help that will be for our kids, don't you think? Tucker can focus on work, and Jillian won't have to take time off or find some ridiculously overpriced group event so he doesn't get bored at home." Lucille glances out the window, a frown marring her face as she does so. "I think I should go out there and see if I can help." She pushes the back screen door open and walks out onto the back porch, never answering Kathy's question.

Jillian glances at her mom. "That was weird, right?"

Kathy sucks in air through her front teeth. "I'm not sure weird is the right word for it. And what's going on out there?"

Jillian shakes her head. "Things haven't been easy between Tuck and his dad, you know that."

"Right, with work and stuff. But that . . . have you looked out the window, hon? That seems like more than work issues, don't you think? Tucker isn't mad that they showed up without warning, is he? Do you think they know about . . ." She glances around. "The bodies?" Her voice is lowered into a whisper.

Jillian pushes a curtain to the side and shakes her head. She doesn't like what she sees. "I think I'll join them," she tells her mom.

"I'll wait here for Ethan," Kathy says, filling a kettle and turning on the stove.

Jillian opens the back door, making her way toward the others. Whatever argument the men seem to be in the middle of stops as she approaches.

"So, did you figure out where to set up the trailer?" Jillian adds a forced casualness to her voice.

"Yep. Dad is going to get it in place right now, aren't you, Dad?" Tucker says, seemingly calm and nonchalant. Jillian sees right through him, though, with the way he shoves his hands in his jeans' pockets.

Logan leaves, with Lucille following. Jillian stands beside Tucker, not saying a word until her father-in-law climbs into his pickup.

"Tucker," she hisses under her breath, half turning toward her husband. "Be honest with me, did you know they were coming?"

He shakes his head, his eyes darkening. "I swear, Jill, they just pulled up not even ten minutes before you got home." His voice is low and earnest, a slight tremor betraying his surprise — or is it anxiety?

"How lucky are we that you have this all hooked up." Lucille's cheerful voice slices through the tension in the air. "I'll be honest, I was a little worried about having to walk outside in the dark just to use your washroom, you know? But now that we can hook up to the septic — it's perfect. I promise we won't be a bother either. We'll have our meals out here, too."

195

"Oh, don't be ridiculous," Jillian says. "Our home is yours, you know that."

"That's so sweet of you." Lucille gives her a sly smile. "You know, I was thinking maybe we could do s'mores out on the fire-pit tonight before Ethan heads off to bed. What do you think?"

Jillian checks the time and winces at how late it is. Night practices are always tough on Ethan the next day and tonight will be no different, especially if he's up later. He's already hyped up because of their unexpected visitors, but to add a sugar high? That just means trouble.

"Oh, I know it's late, but we only just got here and would love to spend some time with him . . ." Lucille continues.

"Yeah, I think that will be okay," Jillian replies through a lump in her throat. She forces a smile.

"What will be okay?" Tucker asks as he joins them.

"Your mom wants to toast some marshmallows and make s'mores with Ethan before he goes to bed," Jillian tells him, keeping her tone neutral.

"Are you kidding me? That kid will be hyped up on sugar all night and then a bear in the morning," Tucker says, laughing. "Come on, Mom . . . that's not fair."

"Oh, posh, he'll be fine. It's just one late night. If it helps, your father and I can drive him to school in the morning, so if he's grumpy, we'll deal with it."

Ethan's laughter fills the air as he runs out of the house toward them, bright and carefree. Jillian swallows her concerns. These are the memories that will stick, the kind that Ethan will bring up over and over again. This is what she has always said is important to her — family, family that is there, consistent, always showing up, no matter what. How can they say no to such a simple request?

"Why don't you go get that firepit started," she says to Tucker, "and I'll go find us some marshmallows and choco-late." She turns away from Tucker and drops her smile.

"What's going on?" her mom asks as she waits on the porch, a cup of tea in her hands.

"We're making s'mores," Jillian says, walking past into the house. She knows it'll take some time for Tucker to build up the fire, so she pours herself some hot water, adds a spoon of honey and a few drops of lemon juice and sits at the table, enjoying the silence, for as long as it lasts.

The windows are open, and she hears the excitement coming from everyone outside. Some of it is forced, but some is genuine, and she doesn't want to let her questions and concerns ruin Ethan's night.

Ethan is what matters, and through all the craziness that seems to be surrounding her and Tucker, if her son can get through it all unscathed, and if that means having both her in-laws and her mother here . . . well, suck it up, buttercup, she tells herself.

Pushing herself up from the table, she pulls out the s'mores bin from the pantry. It's full of crackers, marshmallows, and different kinds of chocolate. With her mom here, they've been reorganizing, and it takes no time to get all the ingredients she needs.

Hearing Lucille's voice outside, Jillian can't help but wonder why they are here. Why now? Tucker's parents are not the spontaneous kind — everything is structured, put in their calendar, color coded and planned out in advance. Them showing up, out of the blue with absolutely no warning . . . something's up.

A log snaps loudly from the firepit outside, and she catches Ethan's small frame silhouetted against the fire's glow, his laughter mingling with the night air.

Kathy's voice floats in from the open window, questioning and bright, but the answers are vague, brushed aside with anecdotes of roadside attractions and diner recommendations.

Tucker heads across the yard and joins her inside. "Need any help carrying things out?"

Jillian points to the basket of goodies he can carry.

"Listen, they're just excited to be here," he murmurs, close enough for his breath to fan her neck. His reassurance aims to be soothing but lands on hollow ground, doing little to stifle the unease that seems to swirl around her.

"But to just show up? That's what I can't figure out."

He stares at the floor, not looking at her.

"What were you and your dad arguing about earlier?"

He shrugs, turning his attention out to the window. "Just . . . things. Basically, that very question: Why show up unannounced? He wouldn't give me a reason, just said it was a last-minute decision, and they wanted to surprise us."

"Surprise us? Your mom and dad? Has something happened to them? Is one of them dying? Because that's the only thing I can think of . . . unless . . ." Her voice trails as an idea worms its way into her brain and sinks its claws in deep.

"Rawlings? No. I asked. He said things blew up between them when we went into protective custody."

Jillian thinks about that for a minute. "But I thought you said they were best friends? And he still works for your dad's company, right?"

Another shrug. "Guess I'm out of the loop. Come on, let's get out there so we can get our son to bed before it gets too late. You can give my mom the gears later and see if she tells you any more."

"Your mom spilling secrets? That will be the day." Jillian follows Tucker down the porch steps and into the backyard where the rest of their family waits. She can't help but notice the glances between her in-laws, the worried brow, the tilt of a head when they think no one is looking.

Something is up, and she needs to figure out what.

CHAPTER THIRTY-TWO

The drive to Great Falls, where they are meeting everyone for Ethan's game, is a quiet one. While Jillian's fingers tap nervously on the steering wheel, her mother stares out the passenger window, her gray-streaked hair pulled back in a tight ponytail, lines of worry etched on her face.

For some reason, her mother isn't talking to her, and she's not sure why.

"Ethan's excited for the game," Jillian says, trying to fill the heavy silence. "His first one where both his grandparents, minus Dad, of course, are there to see him play. I think he's hoping to get a home run, and if that happens, you'll forever be his good luck charms."

Kathy nods absently, her gaze remaining fixed on the passing fields.

"I received an email today," her mom eventually says. "I've debated telling you about it, considering . . ." She heaves a heavy sigh before leaning back against the headrest. "It's only fair that you know, I suppose."

Jillian glances over and sees her mom playing with her phone. Kathy clears her throat, and Jillian almost asks her not to tell her any more. She has a feeling whatever her mother is about to say, it's not going to sit well.

"We are invited to attend the memorial service, twenty years in the making, for Rebecca Gardiner." Her mom clears her throat once more and sets her phone down with a slight grunt.

"I'm . . . I'm sorry? Did you say a memorial service?" For Becky? That can't be right. Becky's parents would never do that. They'd never give up on their daughter, no matter how long she's been missing. They would never . . .

Oh, God. The gut punch of grief and devastation, of fear and betrayal, roll over her in one fell swoop, and the truck swerves into the neighboring lane, where she's met with severe honks.

"Crap." Jillian rights the vehicle and waves an apology to the driver giving her the finger. "I deserve that, my bad."

"Jillian Kathleen Harper," her mother yells, one hand clasped tight to her chest. "Would you please be careful! You almost gave me a heart attack." She grips the 'oh no' handle above her while giving her a stern look.

"Sorry, Mom," Jillian says, pulling her foot off the gas and slowing down a little on the highway. "I'm just . . . surprised. And why wouldn't you tell me about this?"

Her mother shrugs and stares out her side window.

"I kind of need an answer, Mom." Frustration laces her tone, and she doesn't bother to hide it.

"I figured you said goodbye to her long ago," Kathy says softly.

"What the . . ." Shocked doesn't even begin to describe the wave of emotions that hit Jillian. "Why would you say that? No, wait, don't bother answering that. I already know."

The air between them is filled with regret, remorse, and resentment.

"Well, you did marry him."

There. She's said it. After years of silence, her mother finally speaks the one thing she's probably always wanted to say but never has.

"That doesn't mean I gave up on her, Mom. It means I realized he had nothing to do with her disappearance. I've told you this." Her grip on the steering wheel tightens, her knuckles whitening as she struggles not to explode.

This is not the right time or place to be having this conversation.

Twenty years ago, when Becky went missing, Jillian swore that she would never stop looking for her friend, believing she was alive, and praying for the day she would return. For twenty years, she's tried to keep that promise.

When the police came back with no leads, choosing to believe she was a typical teenage runaway, Jillian stepped up and took action on her own. There wasn't much she could do, especially at her age, but that didn't mean there was nothing she could do. She and Becky shared a love of photography, and they had countless rolls undeveloped when she'd gone missing.

The first thing Jillian did was process those rolls. She spent hours, days, weeks poring over each photograph, taking them apart — one party at a time, one group of people at a time, figuring out who was who from the different parties they'd attended.

That's where she first saw Tucker.

He ended up in several photographs she and Becky had taken on their cameras. He was usually in the background, and no one knew who he was until an ex-boyfriend from the football team recognized him as a 'friend of a friend from out of town.'

It took her almost eight months before she was able to meet him in person, but when she did, she had a plan.

After eight months, the police still had no leads to Becky's disappearance. She'd disappeared in the space of three houses, and no one knew why . . . except for Tucker, or so Jillian believed at the time.

She knew in her heart of hearts that he was somehow involved. Stranger danger, teenage kidnappings, sex rings . . . It was all over the news, and it was all anyone talked about at school. Assemblies were held, warning about the dangers of online chat groups and how to stay safe at parties, and Jillian took all those warnings seriously.

Becky wasn't the only girl in their county who had gone missing.

Jillian believed Tucker was part of a group that scouted out girls from parties, but she needed concrete proof for the police to believe her.

So she returned to party life, attending every party she'd been told about. Her only goal was to find Tucker and get close to him.

In a rare moment of vulnerability, she confessed to her mom what she was doing. If it had been any other mother, in any other town, Jillian would have been grounded and forbidden to attend another party for the foreseeable future.

But, it turned out her mother was more open-minded than Jillian had expected. Or maybe it was because Kathy knew her daughter and knew Jillian would have found a way to attend the parties, grounded or not. Rather than allow her to walk to the parties by herself, Kathy drove her there and picked her up. She'd ask about every new person Jillian had met and whether that 'Tucker boy' had been there.

It took a few months, but she finally found him. He was tucked in a back corner, with a red cup in hand, talking with a bunch of guys. All she did was smile at him, and he left that group and headed straight toward her. It wasn't love at first sight, at least not for her. He claimed he knew she was the one for him the moment they met.

She still rolls her eyes at that.

The first thing she said when her mother picked her up that night was: I found him.

Her next steps had been carefully planned. Her main goal was to find out if he knew or recognized Becky. When she showed him photos of her, there'd been no glances of recognition on his face. When she talked about her, he never once looked like he had a secret to hide.

That didn't mean she completely believed him, though.

She got close to him. Close enough that he invited her to meet his parents. Close enough to realize he'd been a college frat who liked to go to parties and just happened to be at ones she and Becky had also been at.

She never found any evidence linking him to Becky's disappearance.

That never stopped her mother from reminding her of her initial hesitation and belief about him.

It didn't help when he got caught up in that business back in Parishville, either. Any trust her mother had begun to give Tucker disappeared when they found out what and who he'd been mixed up with.

"When is the memorial?" Jillian asks, forcing herself to focus on the here and now, not the accusations her mother flung her way. Twenty years may have passed, but the absence of closure is always there for Jillian. The memorial service will only be a new wound on top of old scars.

"End of the summer. They're hoping you'll come." Her mom's voice rings with resignation. "I'm . . . I'm hoping you'll go with me and your father."

"You know, I thought I saw her a few weeks ago," Jillian says, her voice somewhat muffled from holding back tears of hurt.

"You what?" Her mom turns in her seat, pulling at her seatbelt to look at her.

"Yeah." Jillian nods. "At one of Ethan's baseball games. Well, first, actually, it was in a store. But I could have sworn it was her." She leaves one hand on the steering wheel while the other rubs at her thigh. "I'm always looking for her, Mom. I've never given up on her. In fact, an agent from the FBI is going to look for her." She says this last bit with some hesitation.

"A what? The FBI? And you just telling me this now?"

Jillian shakes her head. "There's an agent who's investigating the bodies found in those trailers, and surprisingly enough, finding lost people is what she does for a living. She offered to help."

Kathy grabs on to Jillian's hand and holds it tight. "I-I don't know what to say, Jill. Other than I'm sorry I said what I did." She swipes at the tears trailing down her cheeks. "It was cruel and came from a place of fear."

"Fear of what?" Jillian's brows knit as she glances at her mom.

Kathy shrugs. "That should be obvious, don't you think? After everything that's happened in your lives the past few years . . ." Her voice trails off, like she's afraid to finish it.

So Jillian does it for her. "You're afraid of what the future will hold for us."

"Aren't you? I know you love Tucker, but, honey, what he's done to your family, that's not someone stepping up to be the best father he can be, or the best husband either, for that matter."

"You only see things from the perspective I give you, Mom." Which, in all likelihood, is unfair. She shouldn't always use her mom as a shoulder when she's mad at Tucker.

"Don't start doubting yourself. You've always had an instinct about things like this." Kathy pats her hand.

That doesn't make sense to Jillian. "But you doubt me," she says. "Specifically, my instincts about Tucker and his non-involvement in what happened with Becky."

Kathy sighs. "Are we talking about Becky, or are we discussing Tucker? I'm confused."

Jillian stretches her arms out, pushing her back against her seat. She tries to smother a yawn but loses. "Moving out here is challenging at the best of times, like all the driving. Nothing is close," she says with a hint of complaint, but her main goal is to change the subject.

Kathy covers her own yawn. "I've noticed that. Your gas bill on these trucks must be stupid. It's a good thing that husband of yours makes a lot of money. There's also no privacy, have you noticed that? Sure, trees surround most of the houses I've seen so far, but beyond that, it's all fields. You can see someone driving up to your place for miles."

Jillian thinks about the police lights that were endless when the trailers were first discovered. "Tell me about it."

"Do you miss home?"

Jillian nods. "Of course I do."

"So why didn't you move back when you had the chance? After . . . everything. You could have, right?" Kathy asks. "I mean, whatever happened to that place close to us? I thought you were about to put in a bid?"

"This place just jumped into our laps, I guess you could say. Tucker found it, showed me the video of the house, and I was sold. You know I've always wanted a wraparound deck on an old farmhouse."

"But in nowhere Montana close to a prison? Do you want to raise Ethan close to a bunch of criminals?" Kathy's lips thin into a straight line, and her brows burrow tight together.

"Criminals who are housed in a private prison." This is a conversation they've had on repeat now. First, when she'd told her mom about the place, right before they moved in and even after. When they drove past the prison today, all her mom did was stare out the window at it, like she was taking it all in, memorizing every detail she could see.

"Private or state-run, doesn't matter. What if one escapes? Can you imagine how many of them live around you after they get released?"

"Come on, Mom, for an argument, that's pretty lame. We're perfectly safe, and Tucker wouldn't have moved us out here if he thought otherwise." She tries to laugh like the exact thought hadn't occurred to her as well, but it falls flat.

"Hmmm." There's so much more Kathy could say and from the stiff line of her upper lip, she's doing her best not to say it.

Her mom is right, though, in more ways than Jillian wants to admit.

CHAPTER THIRTY-THREE

Pulling into the grocery store in Great Falls, Jillian glances at her mom and finds tears pooling in her eyes.

"What's wrong?" she asks, killing the engine.

"Jilly . . . about this woman you saw, the one you think looks like Becky." Kathy's voice is hesitant, probing. "Are you sure?"

Jillian meets her mother's gaze, eyes flashing with barely contained emotion. "I know it sounds crazy, Mom. But I can't shake this feeling . . . I think it's her."

Inside the store, Jillian grabs a basket and heads down the snack aisle, her mother trailing behind. She throws juice boxes, pumpkin seeds, and granola bars in haphazardly, her mind a million miles away.

"Our brain can play tricks on us, honey. Especially if you're always looking for her, like you say you are. Maybe you saw what you wanted to see?"

Jillian shakes her head, a box of fruit snacks suspended in midair. Her chest tightens, a dull ache blooming behind her ribs. "Maybe, but it was uncanny. All the other times, I knew after a second it wasn't her, but this time . . ." She swallows hard. "Her parents, I never thought they would give up."

Kathy shakes her head sadly. "It's not that they've given up. You know how involved her father is with that organization back home. I think this is them finding closure. Molly Gardiner especially needs it. She's become a bit of a recluse. I try to visit as much as I can, invite myself over for coffee, and bring something to snack on, but . . . it's hard. She's not the same woman she used to be. Accepting that her daughter is dead . . . it's the hardest thing a parent can do."

"Would you have?" Jillian asks once they're back in the truck and navigating Great Falls' roads.

"Would I have what?"

"Accepted I was dead, if it had been me and not Becky?" She hates that she's even asking, hates that she needs to hear the words she knows her mom will say.

"Oh, honey." Kathy looks horrified. "I would never give up on you, no matter what, but at the same time, I can't blame them either. They've been stuck in stasis for all these years, always waiting, never knowing, watching everyone else move on, live their lives . . . their friends having grandbabies . . ." She says this last part as tears form in her eyes.

"They must blame me. I know they've never said they did, but deep down, they have to. I was with her that night and I should have made sure she got home safe. Whether they blame me or not, they should. It's my fault she disappeared. Mine."

"You were a kid, honey. It wasn't your fault. It's never been your fault."

"Mom, I . . ." Jillian struggles to find the words. "The woman I saw. She didn't just look like Becky. She had the same birthmark by her eye . . ." She traces a fingertip along her own face, remembering. "Here, I'll show you, I have a photo . . ."

"You what?"

Jillian shrugs. "I even gave it to that federal agent I told you about." She fumbles with her phone and shows the image to her mom.

207

"Keep your eyes on the road, please. Besides, it could be a coincidence," Kathy says softly but without any confidence.

Jillian heaves a sigh. "It could." That's the same thing she's been telling herself too.

"Do you think she'll be here today?"

Jillian doesn't answer as she pulls in, following a line of pickups. The parking lot is full, vehicles jammed in beside each other. She parks in the far back lot, wedging between two other trucks.

"It's possible," she finally answers, "but there are a lot of ball diamonds here, and the team could be playing at any time."

"Well, I'll keep a lookout for a woman that looks like Becky," Kathy says.

"You do that, Mom." Dust from the parking lot swirls around Jillian's running shoes as she steps down from the pickup, the roar of the baseball crowd already filling the warm afternoon air with a sense of electric anticipation.

"You weren't kidding when you said it would be busy, were you?" Kathy follows, pulling the wagon filled with sunflower seeds, snacks, and bottled water. "Where will we find the others?"

"Tucker says they're in field two." She waves her phone so her mom can see. When she turns, she notices her mom is struggling with the wagon. "I can pull that."

"No need, I've got it. It's awkward with all these rocks, that's all." She gives a hard tug and hurries to catch up.

Jillian nods, her mind only half on where they are and why. The other half is lost to a visage haunting her every moment — a woman with deep-set eyes and scars that tell stories no one should own. Ever since her mom told her about Becky's memorial, something hasn't sat right with her. She thinks about that woman she saw. The resemblance to Becky, striking and unsettling, gnaws at her insides.

"Mom." She pauses as they leave the parking area and step onto the grass, hesitant, but needing to say the words she didn't say earlier. "About that memorial service for Becky . . ."

Kathy stops, mid-stride, and turns. The lines around her eyes deepen, etched by a familiar sorrow, a shared history of loss. "I'm sorry I told you like I did, that wasn't . . . fair of me."

Jillian nods, both accepting the apology and agreeing with her. "I don't know if I can go and say goodbye to Becky, especially when I don't believe she's gone."

Her mom rushes forward and gives her a tight hug. "Then don't. At least, don't say goodbye. But come to respect them and their wishes, share stories and memories of Becky. I think, deep down, that's what they want. To remember her."

Swallowing hard, Jillian steps back. "I'll think about that." She leads the way, taking the wagon from Kathy, and heads to the pitch where Tucker chats with Coach Neil. He doesn't notice her. His father is beside him, arms crossed over his chest, his face filled with a furious frown.

"That doesn't look good," Kathy mutters. "Where's Lucille? Oh . . . I see her in the bleachers. How about I go join her, and you can deal" — her hands move in a circular motion — "with whatever is happening over there."

Jillian glances over to see Lucille waving at them. She waves back and watches Kathy climb the steel steps to sit beside the woman.

"If I find out the son of a . . . bulldog," Coach Neil says, glancing around him and realizing his voice carries way too much, "who is responsible, I can promise you he won't be walking away unscathed."

"But who is the anonymous source? That's what I can't figure out," Tucker mutters, giving his father a veiled look. His father only shrugs, his posture saying he has nothing to do with anything, so leave him out of it.

"To be an anonymous source, you first have to know something. What kind of evil SOB could live with knowing about those" — he lowers his voice — "bodies, and not say anything."

"That's talk more for around a beer, than a ball diamond, don't you think, guys?" Jillian sets the wagon up close to the water jug, interrupting them. "Come on, little ears don't need to hear about this."

Coach Neil has the decency to hang his head in shame before he gives her a weak smile. "You're right. It's nice to meet your father-in-law here." He points toward Logan. "What a surprise, having them drop in like that, too, am I right? Seriously, if my family dropped in unannounced . . ."

Tucker claps his hands together. "So . . . the game, looks like it's going to be a tight one," he says, a blatant attempt to change the subject. "We're down a few players due to some stomach flu that's going around, I guess, which you already know since the Forresters called you this morning," Tucker clarifies as Jillian gives him a pointed look.

"Which is why we took separate vehicles, and I stopped to grab the snacks and juice boxes," Jillian says.

"Well, all I know is we appreciate your help," Neil says. "This is stuff my wife always had to take care of, you know, part of the whole coaching responsibility gig, thing."

"Happy to help. Trina also texted that she'd be late to the game." Jillian opens the granola bar boxes and heads to the dugout to hand all the players one. She winks at Ethan, knowing anything else would embarrass him.

She leaves the men and heads to the bleachers, climbing the steps until she finds a seat beside her mom. She folds up a blanket and covers the cold, steel bench with it.

"Glad you made it!" Lucille chirps. "Tucker's been pacing a hole in the dugout. You know how he gets."

Jillian forces a chuckle, but she doubts Tucker has been pacing. Ethan's team is up first, and it's Ethan's turn at the bat. She rubs her hands along her jeans, realizing she's more nervous than he is.

Beside her, Kathy leans in close, her voice low. "Have you told Tucker? About the woman?"

Jillian hesitates, giving Lucille a quick look. "Yeah. He thinks . . . he thinks I'm imagining things. That it can't possibly be her."

"What do you think?" Kathy presses gently.

The crack of the bat against the ball makes Jillian jump, her heart pounding.

Lucille leans closer, her brow furrowed with concern. "What are you two whispering about over there? Who can't possibly be who?"

Jillian worries her lips as she glances around, but she doesn't see the woman, which doesn't mean anything. With five ball fields, if that team was playing today, she could be anywhere.

Kathy offers a smile. "Oh, just someone Jillian thought she recognized at the store earlier. Probably nothing."

But Lucille isn't letting it go. She fixes Jillian with a probing stare, her head tilted. "Someone from your past? From . . . before?" She whispers that last word. "Are they dangerous?" She clasps her hand to her chest and half stands before sitting down again. "We need to tell Logan and Tucker. They need to know if we're in danger."

Jillian's stomach twists at what Lucille is implying. "No, no, nothing like that," she says, trying to calm the woman down before too many people notice her outburst.

"Jillian's best friend from high school went missing," Kathy says, "and the woman at the store looked like her."

"Ahh," Lucille says, her head nodding. "I think I remember that you lost a friend."

Jillian swallows hard, her voice barely above a whisper. "Becky. Her name was Becky."

Lucille nods slowly, her eyes distant. "That's right. I remember now. You used to talk about her all the time. Such a tragedy, what happened to that poor girl."

The crowd around them erupts in cheers as Ethan rounds third base, his face flushed with exertion. Jillian, Kathy, and Lucille all jump to their feet. Lucille, with her fingers in her mouth, lets out a shrill whistle while Kathy and Jillian clap and shout. Ethan keeps running, rushing onto the home plate and jumping high, his arms raised in triumph.

"That's our boy," Lucille shouts with excitement. "Tucker said he was good but, man, look at that kid go! You must love coming to his games," she says as they sit back down. "I can't wait to come to more."

"How long are you staying again?" Kathy asks.

Lucille doesn't answer. Jillian nudges her mom and shakes her head, indicating to let it go.

"What?" Kathy mouths, rolling her eyes. "It's just a question," she mumbles before leaning forward, resting her elbow on her knees, and watching the game.

"After the game, we thought we'd head to Fuddruckers," Jillian says, glancing toward Lucille. "It's Ethan's favorite . . ." Her voice fades as she catches sight of a young woman with hair the same shade as Becky's once was, laughing carelessly with friends. The resemblance is uncanny. She blinks hard, chasing away the mirage.

A heaviness settles deep within her heart over her friend. She misses her. She always has, and always will, but that feeling is more like an echo of a memory, rather than a present presence, and that's hard to accept.

CHAPTER THIRTY-FOUR

Walking out toward their vehicles as a group, Jillian shares smiles with both Kathy and Lucille as Ethan walks in between his father and grandfather, whooping it up with fist bumps and hop-skip-jumps as he twists around and walks backward. "This means I get to play in the games room, right, Dad, because we won?"

"What's this now? A games room?" Logan says, giving Tucker a look.

"Yeah, Fuddruckers has sweet games, Grandpa, and a bakery Grandma is going to love. Can we bring home a pie, too? I mean . . . I did score the first and last home runs of the game. That's pie-worthy, right, Mom?"

"What kind of place calls themselves Fuddruckers?" Logan grumbles.

"The place with the best burgers and shakes, that's who, Grandpa." A serious look covers Ethan's face before a smile whips across it. He races toward Tucker's truck.

Kathy tucks her arm through Jillian's as they walk across the parking lot. Jillian's eyes dart between her celebrating son and a beat-up pickup truck that drives past, her heart racing as she recognizes the silhouette behind the wheel.

"Crap, I ah . . . I forgot something in the bleachers," Jillian says, her voice wavering. "You guys go on ahead. I'll catch up."

Tucker raises an eyebrow. "You sure, hon? We can wait."

"No, no. It's fine. I'll just be a minute." Jillian forces a smile, willing her family to leave. "Mom, why don't you go with Tucker in his truck? No sense in you waiting on me."

Kathy gives her a surprised look but then shrugs. "Think you can squeeze one more in that back seat?" she asks Tucker.

"I'm tiny, Grandma Kathy, there's lots of room." Ethan takes her hand and pulls her toward the pickup.

As they walk away, Jillian fills her lungs with courage and twists on her heels, as if she's headed back to the bleachers, but the truth is, she's searching for the pickup that just drove past. Each step she takes feels heavier than the last, with the gravel crunching beneath her feet, matching the rhythm of her pounding heart.

That was Becky in that truck, wasn't it? Not just a figment of her imagination, not just someone she thinks could be her friend. Deep inside, she knows she's right. She knows it's her.

Jillian's mind races with a thousand questions as she approaches the vehicle. Her hands tremble slightly as she watches the woman jump out of the cab and open the back door. She starts to call out, then stops herself; why, she's not sure.

The woman casually glances her way and freezes. Jillian's breath catches in her throat. Those eyes — she'd recognize them anywhere, even after two decades. But now they're filled with a wariness that wasn't there before.

Becky raises her hand, palm out, signaling Jillian to stop. The gesture is firm but not unkind, leaving Jillian frozen in place, uncertainty coursing through her veins.

"Mom, can I go now?" A young boy's voice pipes up from inside the truck.

Becky's attention shifts to her son, her face softening. "Sure, kiddo. Head on over to field four. I'll meet you there in a bit."

The boy hops out, his cleats kicking up dust as he sprints away. Becky watches him go with a mix of love and worry while Jillian watches on. Her friend has been frozen in time for so long within her memory — to see her now, here, as a mother, an adult . . . it's almost unreal.

"Be careful, buddy!" Becky calls out, her voice carrying a protective edge that Jillian recognizes all too well.

As the boy disappears into the distance, the air between the two women grows thick. Jillian's mind reels, struggling to reconcile the girl she once knew with the woman standing before her now.

What happened to you, Becky? Where have you been all this time?

The questions burn on the tip of Jillian's tongue, but she remains silent, waiting; the words she's dreamed about saying all these years are suddenly gone.

Taking a deep breath, steeling herself for what comes next, Jillian finally utters the only word that matters. "Becky." Her voice is barely above a whisper, but loud enough for her old friend to take a step forward.

The name hangs between them, two decades of unanswered questions and unspoken grief. Jillian searches Becky's face, looking for traces of the carefree girl she once knew, but finds only weariness and caution etched into her features.

Becky's lips curve into a sad smile, her eyes reflecting a mix of resignation and something deeper — perhaps regret? "I suppose this was inevitable," she says softly, "even after all these years." She pauses, her gaze flickering over Jillian's face. "How are you, Jill?"

The simple question catches Jillian off guard. How can she possibly sum up twenty years of life, of wondering, of guilt? Her mind races, grasping for the right words.

I'm fine, she wants to say. *I've missed you every day. I've worried about you. I've blamed myself.*

Instead, she swallows hard and manages a shaky, "I'm . . . I'm okay. I—"

The words catch in her throat as she realizes that nothing about this moment feels how she thought it would. There's no relief, no peace, no excitement or joy at seeing one another again. Instead, there's an undercurrent of tension that shouldn't belong, and yet, it does.

Jillian's heart triple beats in a rhythm only she hears. The words, the right words, are a struggle to find. "I've thought about you every day. I never stopped hoping—"

"Stop." Becky cuts her off, her voice sharp and brittle. "This is so unreal, you know?" Her eyes soften for a moment, a flicker of the girl Jillian once knew. "I used to dream about this moment so many times. Not this moment, but what it would be like to find each other — or that you would find me, or that I'd be free and could come home and you'd be there waiting . . ." She shakes her head, her expression hardening. "That was your son you were walking with, wasn't it? Just like his father."

Jillian stumbles back a step, the ground shifting beneath her feet, the words hitting her like a physical blow. "I don't . . . Becky, please, I don't understand."

"He looks just like him, you know?" Becky's head cocks to the side. "Do you keep his hair cut short to hide the white streak? It's not working, in case you were wondering."

"What are you talking about?" Thrown by the sudden change in topic, Jillian places a hand on the back of the truck for some stability.

Becky's gaze shifts, focusing on something over Jillian's shoulder. "That was your husband you were walking with, wasn't it? And those were his parents? I recognized the dad. And your mom, too."

"My . . . his . . . Becky, I—" Jillian struggles with what she's hearing.

"Tucker, right?" Becky interrupts, her tone unnervingly flat.

A chill runs down Jillian's spine. "How did you know that?"

Becky's lips twist into a humorless smile. "Hard to forget that streak of white hair." She pauses, her eyes boring into

Jillian's. "If you want to know what happened to me," Becky continues, already turning away, "why don't you ask your husband?"

The world seems to tilt on its axis. Jillian feels dizzy, unmoored. "What? No, that's not—"

"Tucker was there that night, Jillian. The night I was kidnapped. So was his father. In fact, his father was there the day I was auctioned off, a sex toy to the highest bidder."

As she walks away, Becky calls over her shoulder, "Do me a favor and leave me the hell alone. I don't care why you're with him, maybe you were sold to him, maybe you love him, but I want nothing to do with him, thus, nothing to do with you. Do you understand me?"

Jillian stands rooted to the spot, her mind reeling. Tucker? There? How could that be possible? Why would Becky think she was sold to him? No. None of that can be true. She knows Tucker. She knows he wasn't part of any of that. And yet, the foundations of her world are crumbling, and she doesn't know which way to turn.

CHAPTER THIRTY-FIVE

The neon Fuddruckers sign flickers above as Jillian pushes open the heavy glass door. The familiar scent of grilled burgers and fries hits her, but instead of comforting her, it turns her stomach. Becky's words echo in her mind, a relentless drumbeat that won't be silenced.

She plasters on a smile as she approaches the table where her mom, Lucille, and Tucker wait. "Sorry I'm late," she says, taking the seat next to her husband. She hears an excited "Oh yeah" from Ethan, who's playing an arcade game with Logan.

Just looking at her son makes her want to cry.

Her husband's arm brushes against hers as he shifts his seat to give her more room, and she flinches involuntarily. Tucker's brow furrows, his blue eyes searching her face.

"Everything okay, honey?" Kathy asks, leaning across the table.

Jillian nods, perhaps too quickly. "Just a little headache. Nothing to worry about." She sees the questions in her mom's gaze, but she can't answer them. Not right now. Not until she's had some time to think about what Becky said.

"I already ordered your grilled chicken sandwich and chocolate Oreo milkshake," Tucker tells her. "I know

218

we usually split with Ethan since it's a lot of sugar, but he convinced Dad to let him have his own milkshake this time."

"He'll be fine. What's a little sugar going to do?" Lucille waves her hand like it's a non-issue.

"Keep him awake, that's what," Tucker says, casting Jillian a concerned glance.

"Well, maybe we'll just have a slumber party in our trailer tonight," Lucille offers. "If that's okay with you, Jill?"

"Sure, Ethan will love that," Jillian says, not paying too much attention to what's being said. All she can think about is that her best friend, the woman she's been searching for all these years, is alive.

She's been alive all this time.

"All he talks about is building another fort in that little bunk bed area in the trailer. He had so much fun doing that with Logan last time, and personally, I think Logan had just as much fun, too," Lucille announces, her cheerful voice cutting through the tension.

"Yeah, he'll love it," Jillian repeats, leaning back in her chair, fixated on her son as he looks up to Logan with a mixture of hero worship and love.

Becky recognized him. Logan. Tucker's father. How? From when? She refuses to meet Tucker's gaze even though she can feel it boring into her soul. When he looks at her, he'll see something, and he'll know . . . and she's not ready for him to know what she doesn't even know herself yet.

She's so confused.

An excited shout from Ethan catches her attention, followed by Logan's hearty laugh. The normalcy of it all clashes violently with the turmoil in her mind. Logan . . . the unease that has sat like a heavy fog ever since talking with Becky isn't dissipating; it's only growing heavier, larger, denser to the point of suffocating her.

Tucker's hand finds hers under the table, a gesture that she usually finds comforting, but now, it's dead weight.

". . . so are we getting that coconut pie to bring home? Do you know how long it's been since I last made one of those? It feels like forever." Lucille's voice filters through Jillian's thoughts.

She blinks, realizing she's missed part of the conversation. Tucker's grip on her hand tightens slightly, a silent question.

"Sounds great," Jillian manages, forcing a smile while inside all she can do is scream.

She doesn't say much once their food arrives. She barely enjoys the milkshake and says nothing when Ethan drinks hers after finishing his own. She tries to smile, to be engaging, to listen to the conversation, but all she can see is the white streak of hair passed down from grandfather to son to grandson. The same white streak of hair that Becky remembers from when she was kidnapped.

She pushes back her chair and rushes to the bathroom, her stomach rolling from the angst and disgust that's rooted so deep inside her soul she'll never be free from it. Becky is wrong. She has to be. She's remembering something else. Someone else. Not members of her own family.

She's splashing water on her face when the bathroom door opens, and her mother comes in. "Are you okay?"

Jillian can barely nod. "I don't feel so well," she says. "Do you think you can drive back tonight?"

Her mother's hand, warm and comforting on her shoulder, is everything she needs.

"Of course. Everyone else is waiting outside. What's going on?"

Jillian shakes her head. "I . . ." She's so tempted to tell her mom about Becky. The words are there, on the cusp of her tongue, but she swallows them. "Not here. I . . ." She glances around the bathroom with the two gray stalls, a small room with an odor that has her wanting to vomit again.

The air outside is almost no better, the hot air sticking to her skin like sandpaper. Tucker is in his truck with his parents, and her first instinct is to tell Ethan to come home with her, that he's not safe in that vehicle, but she's reacting before she can get the truth.

And she needs the full truth before she can make any decisions.

The drive home stretches like an endless ribbon of asphalt, each yellow line blurring into the next. The coconut cream pie sits in her lap, its sweetness cloying in the confined space.

"Honey, what is going on?" Kathy's voice breaks the tense silence as she drives, her knuckles white against the weathered leather. The whole drive, she's muttered under her breath how much she hates driving the giant monster of a truck, and the whole drive, Jillian has just ignored her. "You've been off all evening. What's going on?"

Jillian's throat constricts, tears threatening to spill. She swallows hard, her words coming out in a choked whisper. "I was right, Mom. I was right. Becky . . . she's alive."

The car swerves slightly before Kathy regains control. "What? How do you know?"

"I saw her. Talked with her. She's . . . she's been alive this whole time." Jillian's composure crumbles, tears streaming down her face.

Kathy pulls over. She turns to face her daughter, eyes wide. "Oh, Jilly . . . That's wonderful, isn't it?"

Jillian's body shakes with sobs. "I should be happy, shouldn't I? My childhood best friend is alive. But I . . . I feel like my whole world is falling apart. The things she said . . ." She shakes her head, trying to dislodge the words from her memory.

Jillian's mind races as her mother wraps her in a tight embrace. The search parties, the sleepless nights, the years of guilt and wondering — and all this time she's been alive, but never safe. Kidnapped. Sold. Auction. Sex slave. She can't get those words out of her head.

"I should have done more," she whispers against her mom's shoulder. "I should have looked harder, asked more questions, stopped listening to the lies. I . . ." She chokes on a soundless sob as it tears through her throat.

Her mom rubs her back, whispering words of comfort to Jillian until she pulls back and tries to pull herself together. She grabs a tissue from her purse and wipes her eyes.

"What did she say, hon? What did Becky say to you that has you so broken up?"

Jillian tells her mom, watching the horror grow in her eyes as she shares everything Becky told her — every horrific thing. She tells her about Tucker and Logan and watches the heartbreak unfold on her mother's face.

"What have I done, Mom?" she whispers. "What have I done to our family?"

CHAPTER THIRTY-SIX

"Everything's changed," Jillian says. She's sitting in the cab, frozen with emotion. Kathy is next to her, hands still stuck to the wheel.

"We'll need to go in, hon. Eventually." Kathy flexes her hands on the wheel. "Are you ready?"

"No, but Lucille's already peeked through the curtains twice to see why we haven't come in, so there's really no choice, is there?" Swallowing all her pain and betrayal, her hand trembles as she pushes open the door.

"Do you want me to carry the pie?" her mom asks, looking at the tilted coconut cream pie she's struggling to hold.

"No, I got it." She takes a moment to steel herself. The porch light casts long shadows across the white-painted wood, mirroring the darkness that's crept into her heart. She hesitates taking that first step, her mind a whirlwind of conflicting emotions.

What she says and does in the next few hours will determine the course of her life from that point forward. Will she be a coward and not confront her husband and father-in-law? Will she stand her ground and tell Tucker about Becky and the accusations she's made? Will she give her husband a chance to defend himself?

There's no defense for what he's done if Becky is telling the truth. There's also no reason for Becky to lie, unless she wants Jillian's life to be in ruins.

What if there's more to the story? That's what she can't let go of. There's always more than one side to every story; it's only a matter of wading through all the lies and misconceptions to find the nugget of truth.

What is the truth in this instance? First glance, it's easy: Becky was kidnapped. What's messy is Tucker's involvement and whether or not Jillian has been blind to that this whole time.

She doesn't want to believe he's guilty. For years, she's rested peacefully, thinking her husband knew nothing about Becky.

"Well, it's about time," Lucille calls out, holding the door open, hand outstretched, as she waits for Jillian to bring the pie. "We were wondering what was taking so long. Logan is hankering for dessert, so I put on a pot of decaf coffee, and we've just been waiting for you. Is everything okay? It looked like you two were having quite the conversation out there?"

When Jillian doesn't answer, Kathy gently places her hand on her back. "Everything is fine, Lucille. We were having one of our mother-daughter chats, that's all." She gives Jillian a light squeeze. "I'm sure you know how those go," she continues as they walk past Lucille. "Now, did you mention you'd made some decaf coffee? I didn't know Jillian had any of that in her cupboard."

"Oh, she doesn't, it's ours. The bag is almost done, so I'll need to run into town and grab some soon. Our doctor recommended we either switch to decaf after three in the afternoon or give it up entirely."

"Give up coffee? At our age, there's a lot we have to give up, but some we shouldn't, isn't that right?" Kathy gives Lucille a quick grin as they both head into the kitchen.

Feeling adrift, Jillian slowly removes her shoes and places them in the closet. She then shuffles her feet into her house sandals and tries to concentrate on what needs to be done. Ethan needs to have a bath. Tucker will read to him. She'll have to pretend there's nothing wrong until they are finally alone, which could still be hours from now.

Just thinking about that exhausts her. She sighs loudly.

"Jillian?" Tucker looks up from the couch, his brow furrowing at her expression. "Everything okay?"

Jillian's throat tightens. She wants to scream and demand answers. She wants to cry and request comfort. But all of that dies on her lips. "Fine," she manages instead. "Just tired. It's been . . . a long day."

She watches him, searching for a flicker of guilt, a telltale sign. But Tucker's face remains neutral, even concerned. It makes her sick.

All this time, he's pretended he's never seen Becky or even knew her. All this time, he's encouraged her never to give up hope, keep searching and believing, and all this time, he's known what happened to her.

She thinks back to when she told him she thought she'd seen Becky at that game. Had he been surprised? Genuinely surprised, or was it an act? Had there been a shadow of guilt trickling on his face, or . . . she actually can't remember what he'd been like or even said.

"Jillian, do you want some tea?" Kathy stands in the doorway separating the entryway from the kitchen.

"I'm thinking I need something a little stronger," Jillian says. She grabs a beer from the fridge and opens it, taking a long gulp.

"Ethan is getting ready for his bath," Lucille says. "He's so excited to have a sleepover in the trailer. Logan is out there right now, getting everything ready to build an epic fort."

Jillian shakes her head, about to tell Kathy that her son will never be alone with that man again, but Kathy stops her by laying a hand on her arm and giving it a tight squeeze. Jillian gives her a stern look, but there's something on her mom's face that she doesn't want to deal with right now.

Without saying a word, she takes the bottle and heads outside, her steps fast and heavy. The night air is cool against her flushed skin. She sinks into a rocking chair, its gentle creaking a soothing counterpoint to her racing thoughts.

The backyard stretches before her, a sea of shadows. Towering pines line the property, their silhouettes stark against the star-strewn sky. Beyond them, beyond her gaze, stands the gate leading to the field next to them.

A field they own but one she's never visited. On the front end of that field is where the trailers sit. The trailers that had been mausoleums.

Jillian's gaze fixes on that gate. In the short months that they've lived here, never once has she been interested enough to check out any of the fields they now own. Fields that farmers and corporations lease from them, according to Tucker.

But Tucker has. He's been out there a lot. For hours. Exploring, taking stock, to the point of even being unreachable sometimes. Why? What's out there that he's so interested in? Did he know about the trailers and the secrets they held within? He swears he didn't, but she's not sure if she believes him anymore.

A sudden, overwhelming urge to explore and find out for herself grips her.

The screen door creaks open, and Kathy appears, two steaming mugs in hand. "I figured you were done with the beer and could use this now," she says softly, offering one to Jillian. "I may have added some whiskey to it, though, heads-up."

Jillian wraps her hands around the warm ceramic, inhaling the comforting aroma. "Thanks, Mom," she murmurs. Then, almost impulsively, she asks, "Want to go for a walk?"

Kathy raises an eyebrow. "Now? It's pretty dark out there."

"A drive then. Just to the trailers," Jillian says, her voice on the edge of desperation. "I need . . . I need to see." Rising from her seat, she takes a step toward the stairs when the back door opens with a crack.

Tucker stands in the doorway, his broad shoulders filling the frame. "Where are you two headed?" he asks, his voice deceptively casual. But Jillian catches the tension in his jaw, the way his fingers grip the doorframe a little too tightly. He overheard her, didn't he?

"I'm feeling restless and . . ." She pauses, fully looking her husband in the face. "I need to see the trailers," Jillian says, keeping her voice steady.

Tucker's eyes widen, a flash of fear crossing his face before he schools his expression. "That's not a good idea, Jill," he says, his drawl more pronounced than usual. "It's not safe out there, especially at night."

"Why wouldn't it be safe?"

Tucker runs a hand through his hair, a nervous tell she's seen a thousand times. He fingers the shock of white for a moment before dropping his hand. "The police still have that area blocked off. And besides, there's nothing to see. They've taken all the trailers away for evidence."

A chill runs down Jillian's spine. "When did they do that? Shouldn't they have told us they were doing that?" she asks, her voice barely above a whisper.

The silence stretches between them. Tucker's gaze flicks to Kathy, then back to Jillian. She can almost see the gears turning in his head, weighing his words carefully.

"They did it a few days ago," he finally says, but the hesitation in his voice betrays him. "I was there when they took them."

"And you didn't think to tell me?"

He pushes his shoulders back. "I didn't think you wanted to know."

Jillian glances over at her mom, who is staring down at her cup of tea as if trying to minimize her presence.

"I didn't, but now I do."

"Why?" There's genuine concern in his gaze, and the anger bubbling up inside Jillian subsides for a moment.

"Those trailers, they're a stain on the past, Jilly. Not on us, not on our future. I wish we could get past all of this, you know?" He wipes his hands across his face. "I almost wish we'd never come here, that I'd never agreed . . ." His voice trails off, lips thin in a hard line of regret.

"Agreed to what, Tucker? What did you agree?"

He shakes his head, looking toward Kathy, then back to her. "It's not important. Listen, why don't you ladies come inside? Make some popcorn, watch that Bachelorette show you were talking about, and I'll hide in my office, okay? If you want to see where the trailers were, we'll head out in the morning, together. Okay? Just . . . don't go out there tonight."

Off in the distance, a splash of light appears through the trees, then quickly disappears. Jillian notices the way Tucker is laser focused, how his shoulders square back, chest puffed out, but most importantly, she notices the way his hands fist before, one by one, he pushes each finger out straight, something he does when he's trying not to explode with emotion.

She can push further, prod deeper, force him to answer her, but thanks to those lights, she knows she's not about to get any answers from him. Not right now, and certainly not with her mother listening.

"Is that something you need to deal with?" Kathy stands and faces Tucker head-on, with something in her voice Jillian hasn't heard in a very long time.

Tucker runs his fingers through his hair, wincing as he opens his mouth to say something, then closes it.

"Are there eyes on this property, Tucker?" Kathy asks, her voice firm. "Because if there are, that's not something I'm comfortable with, regardless of the reason, and neither should you be."

"It's for our protection," Tucker says. Jillian hears the pleading in his voice, and she can't help but wonder why it's there.

"Protection from what? From whom?" Jillian asks, her voice quiet but just as firm as her mother's.

"I just . . . listen, Jill, I need to go deal with that." He points toward the lights in the distance. "But later, we need to talk, okay?"

She half snorts. "So you can reassure me you have it all under control, that you're only doing this for me, for us, and that everything will be okay? Because if that's what you're going to say, I don't want to hear it, sorry. What I want is the truth. All of it. What's going on, why Jake came to see you, who we need protection from, all of it, Tucker. And if you can't give me that, I'll take the steps necessary to make sure someone else does."

Her body thrums with a tension that pulsates like a neon light. Tucker's eyes widen, and she can read him, the fear, the worry, the *crap-she-knows* thought that flashes through his brain.

Her frame remains stoic. Solid. She's not backing down, not giving in, not stepping back like a good wife and letting her husband handle things. Not anymore.

The truth of things is simple for her: whether she knows her husband has secrets doesn't matter. What matters is that she's made excuse after excuse to turn a blind eye, to give him the benefit of the doubt, to trust and support him because that's what a good wife does.

She's never been that kind of a *good wife*, and it's time they all know it.

CHAPTER THIRTY-SEVEN

Lola

The door to Lola's room bursts open, startling her from a fitful sleep. Mother's silhouette looms in the darkness, her urgent whisper piercing the night.

"Lola, wake up. You need to leave. Now."

Mother's hands shake her shoulders, her touch gentle yet insistent. With her heart pounding, she blinks away the haze of sleep, her mind racing to catch up with what Mother's saying.

"What's happening?" Lola's voice is rough, a whisper.

"Just do as I say, girl. Pack your things. Now hurry up, but be quiet about it."

Mother's eyes dart toward the hallway, her body tense with anxiety. Lola springs into action, her movements swift and practiced. She pulls on jeans and a sweater, her fingers fumbling with the buttons in the dim light.

As she grabs her small backpack, Lola's thoughts whirl. Is this the moment she's both dreaded and longed for? The chance to escape the Red House? Or is it another drill, another test like so many other times?

She stuffs a handful of clothes, her toothbrush, and the single book she owns into the bag. Her hairbrush clatters to the floor, and she freezes, listening for any signs of disturbance beyond her room.

"Quickly, Lola," Mother urges, her voice strained.

Lola nods, her long hair falling forward to shield her scarred face. She's about to zip up the bag when a thought strikes her, stopping her cold. The box. She can't leave without it.

Dropping to her knees, Lola reaches under the bed, her fingers searching until they close around the small container. She pulls it out, clutching it to her chest like it contains her soul.

"What are you doing?" Mother hisses, her patience wearing thin.

"Please," Lola whispers back, her eyes pleading. "It's all I have left of . . . her."

Mother's expression softens for a moment, understanding flickering across her features. She nods, and Lola carefully tucks the box into her bag.

Following Mother down the back stairs, her heart pounding with each creaking step, sends a jolt of fear through her body. The kitchen, eerily quiet in the early morning light.

Mother pauses at the door, her hand on the knob. Lola reads the fear in her eyes, which scares her more than anything. "Listen carefully," Mother whispers, pressing keys into Lola's trembling hand. "I made a promise to keep you safe, damn the consequences. You know where to go. Stay there until everyone leaves. Is that clear?"

Lola nods, her throat too tight to speak. She clutches the keys, feeling the cool metal bite into her palm.

"Stay low, keep to the shadows, and for all that's holy, do not make a sound," Mother adds, her voice barely audible. A tear trails down Mother's cheek.

In a surge of emotion, Lola throws her arms around her, hugging her awkwardly. It's brief and clumsy but conveys everything she can't say aloud.

"Go," Mother urges, gently pushing her toward the door.

Lola doesn't need to be told twice. She darts into the yard, her feet swiftly carrying her across the dew-covered grass. She knows where she's headed. Behind overgrown bushes is an old tool shed in the back corner of the yard: a place no one would think to look if they were searching for her.

Clutching her bag tight to her chest, she stays hunched over, scooting around trees and shrubs until she reaches the shed. Her fingers shake as she fumbles with the keys, finding the right one for the rusted padlock. There's not much room inside; the air is musty and thick with the scent of old wood and forgotten tools, but she finds a blanket on the floor, along with some bottled water, an apple, and some granola bars.

Mother has prepared this place for her.

The auction isn't until later this morning, so Lola settles onto the blanket and pulls the box out of the bag, holding it in her lap. Of all the things she owns, this is her most precious. Inside this box is her whole world, or what remains of it.

She slowly opens it, her fingers caressing the items inside with tenderness. There isn't much — a scarf, a necklace, a photograph, and a letter. She lifts out the scarf, wrapping it around her neck, burrowing her chin inside the soft fabric. Her mother's smell is no longer there, but that doesn't matter. This was her mother's, and it was hers as well. Mother told her that she'd been wrapped in this scarf as a baby, held in the arms of the woman who gave birth to her.

The photograph is of two teenagers, both so similar in looks yet so different. Mother didn't know who the other girl in the photo was, and so they would make up stories when she was younger about who it could be: a best friend, a cousin, maybe even a sister. Lola stares at the image of her mom. She would know her anywhere if she were still alive. If it weren't for the scar on her face, a scar given to her as a newborn, she could be her mom's identical twin.

Lola fingers the scar and feels its jagged edges. She's not sure how someone could scar a baby like she'd been, and yet, she's thankful for it. This scar has been the one thing that has saved her from the auction block.

She lets her eyes drift close and doesn't open them again until she hears the short blare of a car horn. She sits up and presses her eye against a small hole in the wall, her heart pounding.

She hadn't meant to fall asleep. What if someone had been out here, looking for her? She wouldn't have known.

One black SUV pulls up, then another follows. Lola's breath catches. Soon, the driveway is full with sleek black SUVs.

"It's starting," Lola whispers, her voice barely audible.

Men and women emerge, their attire a stark contrast to the Texan setting. She can't see them, but she doesn't need to know what will happen over the next hour: diamonds glitter, and silk shimmers, while they laugh and chat, sip their expensive champagne, and bid on people they consider objects.

Lola's fingers dig into the rough wood. She would have been one of those objects today, too, if it weren't for Mother.

Lola's muscles ache from holding still, but she doesn't move. She's too scared to. Time crawls by as she watches, waiting. Finally, people emerge from the house and climb into their vehicles.

Lola knows what will happen next. The buyers will leave, excited for their new purchases to arrive. Mother will hand the girls a glass of champagne, then wait for them all to fall asleep from being sedated. One at a time, she'll arrange for the girls to be taken to whatever location their buyer requested until there's no one left but the two of them.

Only one car remains, its sleek black exterior a blot against the pale gravel. She knows that vehicle.

The Lady's car.

Minutes stretch into an eternity before the front door finally opens. The Lady emerges first. Behind her, Mother follows.

Two burly men flank her, their hands resting on concealed weapons, a clear threat.

"Oh no," Lola whispers. She's too far away to hear anything that is being said, but she can imagine it. Every decision comes with a consequence, every promise made can be tested. Is Mother facing the consequence of protecting her?

A flash of movement. A deafening scream splits the air.

Mother crumples to the ground, her hand clutching her face.

"No!" Lola's scream tears from her throat, raw and primal. Tears streaming down her face, fingers digging into the wood, she waits for the Lady and her men to drive away. She watches as Mother slowly climbs to her feet and turns her way.

She waits for the signal that it's safe to come out.

CHAPTER THIRTY-EIGHT

Agent Meri Amber

Meri stares at the photo on her desk, her fingers tapping the edges of the paper. The face looking back at her is hauntingly familiar yet changed by time — older, wearier, but undeniably Becky Gardiner.

Moments like this don't come as often as Meri would like. Usually, these photos bring heartbreak, confirming the deceased body matches someone on their victim's list. It usually entails a phone call to a loved one, confirming something they never wanted to have confirmed. But Becky Gardiner is presumably alive, so this is different. A nice different. A welcome different.

There are specific steps that are taken when a missing person is found, especially when that person is an adult. The first thing Meri did was confirm that the person in the photo Jillian sent her was actually the same person, using photo age progression technology.

She reaches for her cell and sends Jillian Harper a text.

I have an update on Becky. Do you have time for a quick chat?

Meri tries to imagine how Jillian must feel with everything going on, then she stops. She doesn't need to imagine. She knows how it would feel to get that glimmer of hope that the person you've been searching for for so long could still be alive.

She also knows how it feels to have that hope dashed and destroyed. She knows how hard it is to pick yourself up and not lose hope.

How about twenty minutes at the park on the corner of Front and Fifth Street? Back area with the benches?

Meri sends her a quick reply and then gathers her purse, folding up the printout of the age progression and placing it within. A coffee shop just down the street makes a pretty good cold brew and is on the way to the park.

Twenty minutes later, Meri settles onto a weathered wooden bench beside Jillian, condensation from their iced coffees dampening their palms. The summer sun beats down on the park, the quiet buzz of small-town life a stark contrast to the weight of what Meri's about to share.

"I have something to show you," Meri says, her voice low, cautious but friendly. She pulls out the photo, holding it so Jillian can see. "I used age progression software on Becky's old picture. It's not perfect, but it's close enough. This is what she would look like now."

Jillian's breath catches. Her eyes widen, flickering between the photo and Meri's face. "It's surprisingly accurate."

"Surprisingly accurate?" Those are very precise words being used. "Have you seen her again?"

Jillian's hands shake as she takes the photo, her fingers ghosting over Becky's features. "This past weekend in Great Falls. Ethan had a ball game there," Jillian says, her voice barely audible. "I saw her drive in, and so I approached her." She takes a deep breath, steeling herself. "I almost wish I hadn't." The words were barely loud enough to be shared, but Meri caught it. Caught the regret, the disappointment, the guilt in her voice.

Something happened. Things were said. Hearts destroyed.

Some people don't want to be found, some hide away on purpose, and others don't believe they're worthy enough to return to the life they used to have.

In her research, Meri discovered some things she's not sure Jillian wants to hear. A very active sex trafficking cell operated within the area where Jillian and Becky grew up. Back in those days, there were a lot of runaways or missing person cases presented as runaways. Now, they know the signs, they see the patterns, and going through all the files, the first thing Meri noticed was those patterns.

A lot of teenagers, from the ages of fourteen to eighteen, went missing. They didn't come home from school or they snuck out to attend a party and never made it back home.

Meri leans in, filling the space between her and Jillian, wanting the woman to know she's here, she's listening, and there's no sense hiding anything from her. "Tell me everything."

Jillian recounts the confrontation, her words tumbling out in a rush with spurts, pauses, and tears.

With each detail, Meri's brow furrows deeper, her mind racing to connect the dots. Most everything about Jillian's story makes sense, especially with the knowledge that Becky had been kidnapped and sold for sex. Except there are large gaping holes. What is she hiding?

"I get the feeling she's not safe," Jillian finishes, her voice cracking.

"Did you set plans to meet up? To see each other? Did you exchange phone numbers or . . ."

As Meri speaks, Jillian shakes her head. "No, nothing. I-I don't think she wants me in her life. She blames . . . me for what happened to her."

Meri's hand rests on Jillian's arm, a gesture of comfort and shared determination. "You are not at fault," Meri reassures her.

There's more to this story than Jillian is sharing. She takes a different route, her eyes softening with empathy. "I can't even imagine how you feel right now, Jillian, to have found her after all these years . . ." She leans back, a small smile playing on her lips. "You must be so happy and relieved to know she's alive."

Jillian's lips curve upward, but the emotion doesn't quite reach her eyes. "I am, of course. It's just . . ." Her gaze drifts to the sprawling park around them.

The slight tremor in Jillian's hand as she lifts her iced coffee doesn't go unnoticed, and neither does the way her shoulders bow forward beneath her light shirt. There's more to this story, lurking just beneath the surface.

"Jillian?" Meri prompts gently, her tone inviting confidence.

Jillian turns back, meeting Meri's gaze. She opens her mouth to speak, but says nothing. The words are there; Meri can see them in the way Jillian's lips form and then relax, but for whatever reason, she can't voice them. Instead, the smile on her face is forced, leaving Meri on guard.

"Did something happen?" Meri finally asks.

"It's nothing," Jillian says, her voice barely above a whisper. "I'm just . . . processing, I guess."

Meri sees it all — the fear flickering behind Jillian's gaze, the way she nervously tucks a strand of hair behind her ear. Whatever Jillian's hiding, it's eating her up inside.

Jillian's fingers tighten around her coffee cup. "Meri, I-I was wondering about your work in the sex trafficking unit." The words tumble out, her voice a mix of curiosity and apprehension. "What made you get involved in something like that?"

Meri's gaze sharpens, her instincts on high alert. She leans forward slightly, her voice low and measured. "It's a tough field, but someone has to fight for those who can't fight for themselves." She pauses, studying Jillian's face. "Is there a particular reason you're asking?"

Jillian's gaze flickers away, focusing on a distant point beyond the park. "I was just curious," she says, her tone unconvincing. She hesitates, then adds, "How did you find out about the trailers?"

"An anonymous source, why?"

Jillian shakes her head. "I don't know. I guess it really doesn't matter in the end, right?"

Meri thinks about that for a moment and realizes she'd never followed up with the sheriff about that one key fact. Or who could have placed that note on her vehicle either.

"How would someone know if . . ." Jillian's voice breaks. "If a person they knew was involved in something like that?"

Meri's brow furrows, her mind turning over possibilities. "Are you asking about signs that someone might be involved in selling someone as a sex slave?" she clarifies, her voice carefully neutral. There are other ways to say it, but at the very core of what people are doing, slavery is still very real, very active within the United States.

Jillian visibly recoils at the question, her body tensing as if struck, which somewhat eases Meri. The plastic cup in her hand crinkles under her tightening grip. "No, not . . . not selling," she stammers, her voice barely above a whisper. She swallows hard. "Involved somehow. Maybe . . . maybe not by choice."

Meri's eyes soften, recognizing the struggle playing out across Jillian's face. She leans back slightly, giving Jillian space while maintaining their connection.

"I see," she says, her tone gentle but matter-of-fact. "These organizations, Jillian, they're complex. There are many roles, many layers." She thinks through some of the cases and frowns. "Not everyone involved is there willingly — they've been coerced, blackmailed, voluntold, or even sold into the organization themselves. There's really no clear answer unless I know more information. Do you have more information?" She lets the question hang between them.

A warm breeze rustles through the trees and off to the side a group of children are having fun in the playground. Jillian glances toward them and sighs.

"From scouting vulnerable individuals to the actual selling, there's a whole network involved," Meri continues, her words measured and clear. She pauses, gauging Jillian's reaction. "But I want you to understand something crucial: when these operations are uncovered, everyone involved faces arrest and trial. The law doesn't discriminate based on the level of involvement."

Jillian is an open book, all her thoughts and feelings playing along her face. Meri can read her, word for word, line by line, and what she's reading she doesn't like.

"Even if . . ." Jillian struggles to form the question. She takes a deep breath, steeling herself. "Even if someone was forced into it initially? What if they're no longer involved?"

"Jillian, what aren't you telling me?" Meri asks.

Jillian shakes her head. She stands abruptly, the bench creaking beneath her. "Thank you. This has been . . . informative." Her voice wavers slightly, showing her inner turmoil. She takes a step away, her iced coffee forgotten on the bench.

"Jillian, wait." Meri's voice cuts through the air, sharp and urgent. This is ending in all the wrong ways, and yet, she'll walk away from here with more information than she thinks Jillian intended to give.

"Your friend," Meri continues, her tone softer now but laced with concern. "Is she in trouble? Is she safe?"

"I . . . I'm not sure," Jillian admits, her voice quiet. "If she's not safe, what can I do? How can I help her? Should I tell her family? They're going to be holding a memorial for her . . ." She pauses, the palm of her hand covering her lips as she gasps.

A flicker of understanding passes across Meri's face. She takes a step closer, lowering her voice. "There are a few things we both can do, Jillian. For myself, I'll be in touch with the agency that first reported her missing, and they'll notify her family. Becky is an adult, though, so it's up to her if she wants to connect with her family. For yourself, you can try to establish trust. If you can, create a safe space for her to open up. Provide a way out if she needs one."

Jillian nods, clearly drinking in every word.

"Second," Meri continues, "document everything. Times, dates, locations of your interactions. It could be crucial later."

Jillian visibly starts at the implication of 'later.' She wraps her arms around herself, shivering despite the hot Montana sun.

"And most importantly," Meri says, placing a gentle hand on Jillian's arm, "if you believe she's in immediate danger, don't hesitate to call me. We have resources and connections with support organizations."

"Thank you," Jillian says, her voice stronger now. "I . . . I think I know what I need to do."

Meri studies her face, concerned. "Just be careful, Jillian. Whatever you're planning . . . don't put yourself in danger."

Jillian nods. "I'll be in touch," she calls over her shoulder, leaving Meri standing alone in the park, watching her go with a mixture of admiration and apprehension.

Meri checks the time. Sheriff Mato should be back soon, but before she talks to her about Becky, she needs to do some further digging into the Harpers. Jillian is hiding something, and she's determined to find out exactly what that is.

CHAPTER THIRTY-NINE

Becky

Becky stares at the house that's now her home whether she likes it or not, and kills the engine. She turns to Jamie, his face looking up at the dark clouds in the sky, and she manages a smile. "Go on and clean up, champ. I'll be right in to make dinner."

"Think it's going to rain?" Jamie asks as he unbuckles his seatbelt.

"Looks like a good storm is coming our way. Better make sure your bedroom window is closed, okay?" Jamie bounds out of the truck with youthful energy. Becky watches him disappear around the corner of the truck and head to the farmhouse. He rushes inside, closing the door behind him.

She takes a minute to steady her breath. Colin is home and even though he knew about the tournament and that she'd be late, that also means nothing. If he's in one of his moods . . . all hell can and will break loose.

She reaches for the grocery bags in the passenger seat. Hopefully, the fact she stopped at one of his favorite bakeries for cornbread to go with the chili, the meal he'd requested for today, will be enough to keep him sweet.

The plastic handles dig into her palms as she approaches the front door. It's dark inside, no lights left on for her — except, they'd been on when Jamie went into the house. Her heart sinks. She knows what this means.

She balances the bags on her hip, fumbling for her keys. The door doesn't budge. He changed the locks again, didn't he?

"Colin?" she calls out, her voice barely above a whisper. "I'm home." She tries the doorknob again then taps lightly on the door. She knows he's close. She can feel him there, staring at her.

"I know I'm late. Jamie's game went on longer than I thought it would, and I—"

The door swings open, and Becky's world narrows to a single point: the shotgun Colin cradles in his arms. Everything stops. She wants to run, to grab Jamie, and flee, but her feet are rooted to the worn wooden porch. This isn't the first time he's turned a gun on her. Hopefully, it's not the last, either.

Colin's eyes, hard as flint, shoot death glares into her. "Where've you been?" he asks, his voice deceptively calm.

Becky's mind races. She needs to defuse this, to slip back into the role of dutiful wife. "Jamie's game, remember?" she says, forcing a lightness into her tone that she doesn't feel. "I stopped for groceries on the way back. You said you wanted chili, and I know how much you love the cornbread from that bakery in town. I put in a special order and had to pick it up. Plus, I stopped for some groceries to go with dinner; we were out of sour cream and cheese. I thought I'd mentioned I would need to stop. I also grabbed some fresh apples, figured I could make you some apple crisp. I'm sorry if I didn't. I should have sent you a text." She's rambling. She knows it — he knows it. She also knows he likes it when she's panicked. It gives him more power, stealing her calm, her peace, her strength.

She holds up the bags as if they're an offering, a shield against the storm brewing in Colin's eyes. He remains motionless, his finger resting just outside the trigger guard. The silence stretches, taut as a wire.

"Can I come in? Please."

She wants to call out to Jamie, to make sure he's safe, but the words die in her throat. Any false move could set off Colin's temper.

His jaw clenches, a muscle twitching beneath his skin. His eyes never leave hers as he steps forward, the floorboards creaking beneath his boots. The rhythmic tap of the shotgun against his arm sends shivers down Becky's spine.

"No one was here when I got home," he says. "Heard the truck, but for all I knew, it was a stranger coming to rob me." His voice is low and controlled. The implied threat is clear.

Becky's heart pounds against her ribs. She thinks of Jamie, praying he's staying out of sight. "Colin, please," she whispers, her voice barely audible over the rustling of the plastic bags. "It's just me. I'm home now. I should have called or texted. I'm sorry."

Colin's grip on the shotgun loosens slightly, but his eyes remain hard. He takes a step back, his hand outstretched. She hands him the bag with the cornbread, hoping to appease him. He takes the box, his gaze flickering down to it for a brief second.

She exhales, relief flooding through her, but as she moves to enter, Colin's arm shoots out, shoving her backward. Becky stumbles, the grocery bags slipping from her grasp. An apple rolls into the yard. She catches herself against the railing, her pulse racing.

"Colin, what . . ." she starts, but the words die as she meets the cold fury in his gaze.

Colin's jaw clenches again, his knuckles white around the shotgun. "I came home to an empty house. No dinner. No wife."

Becky's mind races, fear clawing at her throat. She swallows hard, trying to keep her voice steady. "I-I was at Jamie's baseball tournament. Remember? We talked about it last week."

Colin's eyes narrow, a flicker of confusion crossing his face before the anger returns. "Like that's an excuse to be late. I'm tired of them. You seem to have forgotten how good you have it with me, haven't you?"

"It's not an excuse, Colin, I swear," Becky pleads, her words rushing out.

She watches Colin carefully, searching for any sign of recognition. Her heart sinks as his expression remains blank, then darkens further.

"You've always been a liar, haven't you?" he snarls, taking a menacing step forward.

Becky's hands tremble. It doesn't matter what she says right now. Nothing will be right. "I'm sorry." She bows her head, ready for the strike she knows is coming.

Colin's hand shoots out, but he doesn't hit her. Instead, he reaches inside her front pocket for her phone. "You're sorry?" he shouts, making Becky flinch. "All you ever think about is that boy and what he wants. How about what I want? Or what I need? I needed my woman home, taking care of things like she's supposed to!"

Tears prick at Becky's eyes, a mixture of fear and frustration. "Please," she whispers, her voice barely audible over the pounding in her ears. "Let's just go inside. We can talk about this. I'll make dinner right away."

Colin glares at the phone in his hand, his jaw clenching. "Why is your location turned off?" he demands, his voice low and dangerous.

Becky's mind races, confusion clouding her thoughts. "I-I don't know," she stammers. "I never turn it off. Maybe it's a glitch?"

Colin's eyes flash with a mixture of rage and suspicion. "You think I'm stupid?" he growls. "You're hiding something from me!"

His hand lashes out, the back of his palm connecting with her cheek, the force of the blow sending her stumbling backward. Pain explodes across her face, and she tastes blood.

The world spins. Becky blinks, trying to clear her vision. She wants to run, to scream, but she knows it will only make things worse. Instead, she straightens her spine, planting her feet firmly on the ground.

She's been through worse. She will survive this. She has to.

"I'm not hiding anything," she says, her voice trembling but determined. "I was at the tournament with our son. That's the truth."

Inside, Becky's heart hammers against her ribs. She wonders if Jamie can hear what's happening from wherever he is. God, she hopes not. She has to stay strong, for him. For herself.

Colin looms over her, his breath hot on her face. "You better not be lying to me," he hisses.

Becky meets his gaze, fighting the urge to look away. "I'm not," she insists, praying he'll believe her this time.

His eyes narrow. Without warning, his fist connects with Becky's stomach, driving the air from her lungs. She doubles over, gasping, the pain radiating through her core.

"Stop," she wheezes, struggling to catch her breath. "Please, Colin."

But her plea falls flat. Colin's face is a mask of cold fury, his eyes devoid of empathy. He reaches out, grabbing her arm roughly.

"Keys," he demands, his voice a low growl. "Give me the truck keys. Now."

Becky's heart sinks. She knows what this means. With shaking hands, she fumbles in her pocket, producing the keys. Colin snatches them, a cruel smirk playing on his lips. He holds them out toward the truck, locking it with a decisive click. Becky watches, her stomach churning with dread.

Backing toward the house, Colin's gaze never leaves her. "You don't need to come in," he says, his tone mockingly casual. "Enjoy the fresh air. Think about your choices. The dogs can keep you company."

Becky takes a tentative step toward the house, her voice trembling as she tries again to reason with him. "What about Jamie? He needs dinner. I should—"

His eyes contain a dangerous glint, reflecting in the porch light. "Jamie?" he scoffs, his tone dripping with disdain. "You think I can't take care of my own son?"

Becky flinches, her words dying in her throat. She wants to argue and fight for her place in her child's life, but fear keeps her rooted.

Colin's lip curls into a sneer. "I'll handle dinner. You . . ." He pauses, savoring the moment. "You can stay out here and think about what it feels like to be neglected. To come home to an empty house, wondering where your family is."

The words hit Becky like a physical blow. "Colin, please," she whispers, her voice barely audible. "I'm so sorry."

But Colin is already retreating, his face a mask of indifference. "Maybe next time you'll remember your priorities," he calls over his shoulder, the door slamming shut with finality.

Becky stands there, the cool night air biting at her skin. She wraps her arms around herself, fighting back tears.

CHAPTER FORTY

Jillian

Jillian forces her fingers to unclench from the steering wheel even while her foot presses down on the pedal, her eyes darting between the road and the clock on the dashboard.

She's late. Again.

Jake had given her a late assignment and insisted he needed it by end of day, while he, of course, left the office early to go play a few rounds of golf with his buddies. Trina patted her on the back and offered to bring Ethan home after the game, but thankfully, her mom and Lucille had everything taken care of.

She pulls into the dusty baseball field parking lot. Through the windshield, she spots Kathy and Lucille seated in the bleachers, Ethan's practice in full swing.

"Damn it," she mutters, fumbling with her seatbelt. As she steps out of the car, the familiar crack of a bat meeting ball echoes across the field. "If it's not one thing, it's another." Ever since her talk with Agent Meri, she keeps thinking about what she said, and the ramifications for Tucker if Becky's words ring true.

They were supposed to have had their chat last night, but she didn't hear him come home after leaving to check out the lights on the other side of their field. He must have at some point because Lucille had mentioned over coffee that he'd come to pick up Logan at some ungodly hour.

Despite her text messages throughout the day, Tucker has yet to respond to a single one. To say she's a little pissed is an understatement. She's also scared, too. Memories of the phone call she overheard when he made plans to meet with Andy won't leave her. What if he did it — what if he and his father left to meet Andy and something happened? Or what if Andy convinced them to run and disappear, and her husband is gone for good?

So many 'what ifs' run through her head. He would contact her to let her know, wouldn't he? He wouldn't just disappear.

Hefting her bag over her shoulder, she sees Lucille stand up from her seat and wave, her silver hair glinting in the warm summer sun. "Jill, over here! We saved you a seat."

Jillian climbs the metal steps, offering an apologetic smile. "Thanks. Work was—"

"Crazy, we know, Trina gave us a heads-up," Kathy finishes, patting the space between them. "You didn't miss much. Ethan's been practicing his curveball."

Settling onto the cool metal bench, Jillian lets out a long breath. Her gaze finds Ethan on the pitcher's mound, his face scrunched in concentration as he winds up for another throw.

"He's getting better," Lucille remarks, pride evident in her voice.

Jillian nods, but her mind wanders. Tucker should be here at the practice, especially considering he's one of the coaches. She can only imagine what Coach Neil is thinking . . . her husband can't live up to his commitments, which isn't a good look, especially since they're still new to the town.

When she catches Neil's eye, she sees the questions there, but she can only shrug. He shakes his head and turns away,

249

but not before she catches the flash of irritation on his face. She doesn't blame him.

"Earth to Jillian." Kathy's voice cuts through her thoughts. "You okay?"

Jillian blinks, forcing a smile. "Yeah, just . . . tired. Has anyone heard from Tucker or Logan? I've been texting him, but he hasn't responded."

Lucille shakes her head. "The boys have been quiet all day. I'd be worried, except you know how those two can get . . . see someone they know and talk the whole day about nothing."

Noting the lack of worry on her face, Jillian wonders if she's overthinking things. Lucille would know, wouldn't she, if something was up? Logan wouldn't just leave her behind without a word, would he?

"How was your day with Ethan?"

Kathy's eyes light up. "Oh, we had a blast! Ethan took us on a tour of Shelby. We were going to come by and see you, but Trina said you'd already left for lunch. We then ended the day with a tour of that train museum in town. You should've seen his face when—"

As Kathy launches into a detailed account of their day, Jillian's thoughts drift again. Whether Agent Meri Amber had said it or not, she heard the warning in her tone today, and something inside her says she said too much to the wrong person. Definitely to the wrong person. And yet . . . until she talks to Tucker and gets clarity—

"Mom! Did you see that?" Ethan's excited shout snaps Jillian back to the present. He's jumping up and down on the mound, grinning from ear to ear.

"Great job, sweetie!" she calls back, hoping her momentary distraction wasn't obvious.

As practice winds down, Jillian can't shake the feeling that something's off. Tucker's absence, the unspoken conversation hanging between them, adds up to a knot of unease in her stomach. She watches Ethan gather his gear, his enthusiasm infectious as always. Despite everything, he seems happy, and seeing that happiness within him is all she needs.

As families begin to disperse. Jillian stands, stretching her stiff muscles. "Thanks for bringing him," she says to Kathy and Lucille. "I don't know what I'd do without you two."

Lucille squeezes her arm. "That's what family's for, dear. If you lived closer, you'd never have to worry about this, you know that, right?"

"Jillian?" She turns to find Coach Neil behind her. "Do you have a few minutes?"

She casts her mom a questioning glance. "Go ahead, hon. We'll drive Ethan home and get dinner started. Does that work? Nothing fancy, we were thinking sausage on a bun and potato salad, if that works for you."

Jillian sighs with relief. "Anything I don't have to cook is okay with me, you know that," she reminds her mom before hugging her. "If Tucker is home when you get there, can you let me know?"

Her mom gives her a brief nod before she corrals Ethan to grab his bag and walk with them to their truck.

Jillian takes a deep breath of the warm evening air, steeling herself for whatever conversation Neil wants to have with her.

"Hey, Neil, what's up?"

"We've got another tournament coming up, and I need to know if Tucker is available. His schedule seems to have gotten a little away from him, and I need someone I can rely on."

Her first instinct is to apologize for Tucker, to play the good wife, and to smooth ruffled feathers, but she stops herself from uttering those words.

"Unfortunately, I'm not my husband's keeper," she tells him. "If you have issues with him, he's the one you need to be speaking to."

Neil shrugs. "That's fair and something I'd expect my own wife to say, but the thing is, getting hold of your husband isn't easy, you know?"

251

Jillian thinks about all her unanswered text messages and grimaces.

"Truth be told, I'm considering asking him to step down for the rest of the season," Neil says, leaning in close enough so only she can hear his words. "I don't want to assume or even judge, but I think he's getting mixed up with the wrong type of crowd, if you know what I mean."

Jillian shakes her head. "I have no idea what you mean, Neil." A flare of anger seeps in at his words, at his judgments. Who does he think he is?

"I've seen him hang with a few guys that . . . well." He runs his hands over the stubble on his jaw. "I don't know how to say this other than just saying it without any sugar coating."

"Please do," Jillian tells him, her tone frosty.

"Well, those men he's been hanging around were in prison for kidnapping, sexual assault against minors . . . that kind of stuff, and I need to think about these kids, first and foremost. You understand that, right?"

Jillian's brows furrow as she struggles to comprehend what Neil just said. "Sexual assault against minors? What are you talking about? Tucker wouldn't knowingly hang around people like that."

Neil shrugs. "I didn't think so either, but . . ." He sighs, then looks around. "You're right. This is something I need to tell Tucker personally. Just . . . be careful, okay? And keep an eye on Ethan? You can never be too careful around here."

Standing in shock, there are no words Jillian can speak to stop Neil from leaving. She casually lifts her hand in a wave toward Trina, who stands to the side. The smile she receives from her friend is gentle, as if she knows precisely the bomb her husband just dropped.

Her steps are heavy as she heads back to her truck, her thoughts muddled as what feels like a puzzle is dumped on a table, and she has to put it back together.

But what is she putting back together? She has no idea.

Becky Gardiner waits at her truck, arms crossed, her figure a silhouette against the fading light. Memories flood back, along with all the recent hurt and pain, as Jillian approaches her long-lost friend.

"Becky?" she calls, her voice wavering. "What are you doing here?"

Becky stiffens, her head down. "We need to talk, Jill."

Jillian's mind races, her heart in a vice grip. "Of course," she manages.

"Was that Kathy I saw leaving with your son?" There's a wistfulness in Becky's voice, an echo of a memory.

Jillian nods. "Mom was so excited when I told her you're okay—"

Becky snorts.

Jillian steps closer, trying to get a good look at her friend, but her face is angled away. "I am so happy to see you, even if you don't want to hear that." The words are ripped from her chest leaving jagged scars along her heart.

Becky half turns so she's not facing her directly. "Why wouldn't I want to hear that? That first time I saw you in that store, I swore I'd seen a ghost. Then I forced myself to believe it was your doppelganger, or that I'd forgotten what you look like and . . ." She blinks a few times and swipes a finger across a cheek. "I've missed you. I've missed . . . the memory of who I thought you were."

"I'm still that person."

The skepticism on Becky's face is like a rope twisting around her body, tightening until she can't move or even breathe.

"I know you think the worst of me, but the person you think I am and the friend I truly am are two different people, Beck, I swear it. I haven't given up looking for you. I've searched for your face in every crowd, and I've never stopped blaming myself . . . I could have walked you home, or even just stood there and waited till you got in your door. I've played the should have, could have game every single day since you've been gone, whether you believe that or not."

Becky's lips firm up. "I'm not here to talk about that . . ." she says, her gaze searching everywhere around them.

"What's going on, then? Is this about Tucker?"

Becky's eyes widen, a flicker of fear passing through them. "No, it's . . . it's not about Tucker. Oh, my God, you haven't told him about me, have you?" She worries her hands together. "Maybe this is a mistake after all." She wraps her arms around herself in a tight hug.

"No, no, I haven't. I tried to confront him last night, but . . . well, he's gone somewhere and . . ." Becky isn't here to hear about her problems or marriage issues.

She waits as Becky turns her back on her. Will she leave? She looks like she's about to bolt. "Please, if I can help . . ."

A whoosh of air leaves Becky's body, her shoulders sagging, her arms hanging at her sides. "That's why I'm here. I need your help in protecting my son."

Jillian's concern for Tucker momentarily takes a backseat to the urgency in Becky's voice.

"Of course," Jillian says, reaching out to touch Becky's arm. "Anything you need."

Becky nods, a ghost of a smile crossing her face. "I wish it were that simple. Can we go somewhere and talk?" A few cars pull up into the parking lot, another team, a different league, is here for practice.

Jillian leads the way down the road and pulls into a secluded spot overlooking Shelby's rolling fields, with Becky pulling in beside her.

"Becky, what's going on?" Jillian asks, her voice gentle but firm, their truck engines ticking as they cool while they stand between them.

Becky shifts, and for a moment, the fading evening light catches her face. Jillian's breath catches in her throat. The bruising around Becky's eye is a sickly purple, her jaw swollen and discolored.

"Oh, God," Jillian whispers, her hand instinctively reaching out.

Becky flinches, turning away again. "It's not as bad as it looks."

Jillian's mind races, concern and anger warring within her. "Who did this to you?"

"That's not why I'm here," Becky says, her voice barely audible.

"Then why?" Jillian asks, struggling to keep her emotions in check. "I thought you didn't want to see me again?"

Becky's shoulders slump, and she finally turns to face Jillian fully. The bruises look even worse head-on, and Jillian has to force herself not to recoil.

"I need your help, Jill," Becky says, her eyes glassy with unshed tears. "I don't know who else to turn to."

Jillian's heart pounds. "I'm here. Just tell me what you need."

Becky glances over her shoulder, acting like someone might overhear. "As I told you, it's not for me," she says, her voice low and urgent. "It's for my son. Jamie."

The pieces start to fall into place in Jillian's mind. The bruises, the secrecy, the desperation in Becky's eyes — it all paints a horrifying picture.

"Is he in danger?" Jillian asks, her maternal instincts kicking into overdrive.

Becky's lip trembles. "Not yet, but . . . I'm afraid he will be. Colin, he's . . . he's getting worse."

Jillian's fists clench at her sides. "Colin? Is that your . . . is he the one who did this to you?"

Becky nods, almost imperceptibly. "I can take it. I've been taking it for years. But Jamie . . . he's starting to notice. To ask questions. I'm scared, Jill. I'm so scared of what might happen if . . ."

She's unable to finish the thought. Jillian's mind races, trying to process everything.

"What can I do?" she asks, determination strengthening her resolve.

Becky fumbles in her pocket, pulling out her phone. "I need your number. If . . . if something happens, if Jamie needs help, I need to know there's someone I can reach out to, who can be there for him."

Jillian takes the phone, her fingers brushing against Becky's trembling hand and adds not just her phone number, but her work information and her home address. "Of course. Anything. But Becky, you don't have to stay. We can get you help, both of you—"

"No," Becky cuts her off, fear flashing in her eyes. "It's not that simple and Tucker . . . he can't be involved, okay?" Her fingers race across her phone screen and Jillian gets a ping. "Here's everything you might need. I'll even add you to the list of approved adults who can pick him up from school."

"We have a trailer," Jillian says, her thoughts speeding up as a plan emerges. "No one knows about it. It's parked at a trailer park close to Helena."

Becky swallows hard. "What about your husband? He can't know about me or my son. He's a dangerous man, and his father is even worse."

A brick drops in Jillian's stomach at her words but before she can ask any questions, she notices a glimmer of hope in Becky's eyes. It's quickly dashed when Becky's phone rings.

"Shit," she mutters. "I have to go. He watches me, and if I'm not home when he expects me to be . . . ." Despite not finishing her sentence, her meaning is clear.

"Can you call me tomorrow? Or text? Whatever is easier. We can make a plan to get you safe, okay?"

Becky nods, climbs into her truck, and leaves Jillian staring at the new information on her phone. The true weight of what Becky's asking hits her, along with the terrifying life her old friend has been living all these years and the people responsible for it.

CHAPTER FORTY-ONE

Jillian steps out of the shower, wrapping a towel around her body. She looks at her bed, untouched since yesterday. It's now four in the morning, and she hasn't slept a wink, sitting in the living room all night, unread book on her lap, as she watched the front door, waiting for the sweeping lights from Tucker's truck to shine through the windows.

There were lights, but never his.

The house is eerily quiet as she heads downstairs, the kitchen empty. Grabbing an ice pack from the freezer, she holds it against the back of her head to help with the migraine that is creeping forward, its tendrils entwining with her blood vessels. If she's not careful, she'll be stuck in bed in extreme pain for the day.

The last time she'd had a migraine like that was before they moved here. Her doctor blamed it on stress; honestly, Jillian couldn't disagree with her.

Tucker leaving with no word, including the accusations from Becky about him, equals a boatload of stress. Where is he? Lucille keeps trying to sell her on him being on a short business trip with Logan, but that doesn't sit right with her. He would have told her if it was work-related.

She pulls out her phone, checking for missed calls or texts. The screen is blank.

Something is wrong. It has to be. This isn't like Tucker. He wouldn't just disappear like this.

Jillian paces the kitchen, gnawing her lip. Should she call the police?

Maybe she's overreacting, but when she puts together all the pieces of his secret phone calls, what she's overheard, and the fact he won't tell her anything . . . there are too many red flags for her to ignore.

She does the one thing she should have done in the middle of the night but didn't: she heads to Tucker's office. She's never been one to go through his phone, look at his contacts, spy on his locations and who he follows on social media, but this situation might warrant it.

The office looks normal at first glance. But as Jillian scans the room, her breath catches. Tucker's laptop is missing from the desk. His phone charger dangles empty by the outlet and when she yanks open desk drawers, rifling through papers, she notices the leather-bound notebook Tucker carries everywhere is gone.

She heads to the safe located in the bottom cupboard of the bookshelf. The safe door is left open and other than her and Ethan's passport, the shelves are empty.

Tucker isn't away on a short trip. He's actually gone. Gone gone. He's left her. Left her son. Left the life they were building for Rawlings.

She's not sure she'll ever forgive him for that. Him or his father. If everything Becky said was true, she'll never forgive his father. Ever.

She takes a deep, shuddering breath as the early Montana sun streams through the windows. All right. Enough is enough. He's gone, and she needs answers, one way or another.

And there's one person who can give them to her.

258

CHAPTER FORTY-TWO

Agent Meri Amber

It's been a long day, and rather than go back to her tiny hotel room, Meri finds herself in the Tap Room, a small bar on Main Street. The faint twang of country music mingles with the clinking of glasses and low murmurs of conversation in the dimly lit bar.

Hunched over her laptop, tucked away in a corner booth, she lifts a hand to the bartender, indicating she's ready for another cold draft. Something has been bothering her all day, something she needs to get to the bottom of before she can progress any further in her quest to hunt down Andrew Rawlings. Her fingers fly across the keyboard as she digs deeper into the web of connections surrounding the Red House.

The door swings open with a creak, a gust of air rushing in. Meri's eyes dart up, and she recognizes the two men who enter. Tucker Harper, his broad shoulders tense beneath his flannel shirt, follows behind an older man with a weathered face and steely eyes. Logan, she realizes — Tucker's father.

Sheriff Mato said these two were supposed to be out of town.

Her fingers tap dance on the keyboard as she pulls up her messenger app.

Been meaning to ask, have you figured out the anonymous source yet?

Dots appear as Sheriff Mato writes back.

Security guard from the prison. Trusted source, always good tips. Why?

Meri doesn't respond as the Harpers slide into the booth beside hers. She keeps her head down, her research forgotten as she hears Andrew Rawlings' name. She knew they were tied to him.

"I wish you didn't come," Tucker says.

"If I hadn't, you'd be dead and in the ground. You know that."

"I've got it handled," Tucker growls.

Logan chuckles and Meri finds herself leaning forward, ever so slightly.

"Looking to our mutual friend has only . . . made things messier. I had no choice and the sooner you realize that, the better." Logan's voice drops even lower, forcing Meri to strain even more.

"I don't like this, Dad," Tucker mutters, his voice tight with anxiety. "We should go home. Jillian has left a lot of messages, and I'm going to have hell to pay for not touching base with her."

Logan leans in, his gravelly voice barely audible. "I told you already, we can't go back to the house, and you can't talk to your wife. Not yet. After all our running around today, do you still think it's safe to go home? We've done a lot, son, and not all of it legal. You realize that, don't you?" He lets out a long sigh. "Your mother will handle things with your wife; don't you worry none about that."

"You've cleaned it all up, not me. And yeah, since it's all taken care of, why can't we go home and act like nothing is wrong? If anyone comes knocking, we'll tell them the truth. I left some insurance back at the house, just in case."

Logan snorts. "How did I end up raising someone so naive? I told you to get rid of them. Are you seriously trying to get your family killed?" Logan leans close, elbows on the table, his voice so low it's hard for Meri to hear. "We're here picking up something, and then we're leaving. We're running out of time and choices, and there's no security here. The organization has too many people here, or haven't you noticed?"

"Why would I notice Dad, since I'm not part of any of that."

"Keep deluding yourself into thinking that, boy." Logan sighs and raises a hand toward the bartender.

"I'm trying to do the right thing and you being here . . ." Tucker runs his hands through his hair as he pauses.

"We're past that. The Red House is our only option now. We just need to get there."

Meri catalogs every word. The Red House. Rawlings. A mess that needs cleaning up. Her fingers dance along her keyboard as she takes notes of the conversation.

Tucker's voice is strained when he speaks again. "I can't. I promised Jillian no more running. We're building a life here."

"Don't be stupid." Logan's tone is harsh, unyielding. "You know what needs to be done."

Meri's heart pounds against her ribs. The implication in Logan's words is clear, and it chills her to the bone. She thinks of Jillian — determined, kind-hearted Jillian — blissfully unaware of the darkness surrounding her husband.

Or is she? She thinks back to their conversation at the park and the questions she asked just before they parted. Does Jillian know more than she's letting on?

Tucker's struggle is palpable in the heavy silence that follows. Meri imagines his expressive eyes, torn between loyalty to his father and love for his wife. When he finally speaks, his voice is barely a whisper. "There has to be another way."

The bartender comes over with Meri's beer. She keeps her head down, her computer screen angled away, as he slides it over.

He stops at the other table and sets two beers down. "Drink fast and leave. Here's the number you asked for," he says, his voice rushed as he keeps looking her way.

"Thanks," Logan says, dismissing the guy.

Tucker waits until they're alone again before he pushes his beer forward. "I'm not going." His voice cracks, revealing his torment.

Logan's tone is low and menacing. "You don't have a choice."

Meri's fingers continue their tap dance as she types their conversation as best she can. It's hard to hear most of what they're saying.

"What do you want from me, son?" Logan asks, his voice suddenly weary. "My hands are tied just as tight as yours are. More so, if you think about it."

"Then untie them."

"What do you think I'm trying to do? I was raised in this life, just like you were." Logan snorts.

A sharp ringtone cuts through the tense atmosphere. Meri's muscles tighten as she strains to listen, her fingers hovering over her keyboard, ready to take further notes.

Logan's voice drops to a near-whisper. "Yeah?"

Meri holds her breath, her heart pounding. She catches fragments of Logan's side of the conversation.

"Been a long time, old man," Logan says. "Time to end this, don't you think?" He pauses for a bit. "The old Franklin farm . . . Midnight . . . Got it."

Her mind races; she has no idea where the old Franklin farm is located, but if they're meeting at midnight, it's a good drive away. She sends Sheriff Mato another text: *Ever heard of the old Franklin farm?*

Meri stares at the three little dots that show Sheriff Mato in the middle of replying.

Funny you should mention it. It turns out 'Old Man Cummings' owns that one, too.

Meri shakes her head. So they're headed to another property owned by Rawlings. How many of these places are there?

262

Been abandoned for years, from what I can tell. Just had someone go do a drive-by today. Why?

Meri is contemplating how much to tell the sheriff when Logan hangs up and tells Tucker they need to leave.

Meri's thoughts whirl. There will be a midnight meeting at an abandoned farm, and she has a sneaky feeling Andy Rawlings will be involved, even though she can't prove it. Does she trust the local sheriff with this news and let her take the point, or does she tag her in after the fact?

Regardless, she needs to update Lindsay.

She reaches for her beer and takes a long pull as she watches the men leave. A glance toward the bar shows the bartender staring at her. Leaving now would only make things obvious, so instead, she texts Lindsay with an update.

Bring in the sheriff and go with backup. His tone is clear, and he won't listen to any arguments on her part.

She sends a thumbs-up emoji and then replies to the sheriff.

I've got some news — got time?

Sheriff Mato replies within seconds. *My door is open, and new case of beer in the fridge.*

Meri downs the rest of her beer, gathers her things, and heads to the bar to pay her tab. Her mind is already racing ahead to the Franklin farm, and not only what, but who they may find there.

CHAPTER FORTY-THREE

Jillian

Jillian's head throbs as she pushes herself to her feet and climbs the stairs to her ensuite bathroom. She stumbles to the medicine cabinet, fumbling for the bottle of prescription migraine pills she only uses for emergencies. Her hands shake as she swallows two with a gulp of tap water.

"Jillian? I saw your lights on and was concerned." Lucille's voice calls from the hallway. "Are you all right, honey?"

Jillian winces at her loud voice. "I'm fine," she lies, her voice hoarse. "Just a migraine."

Kathy appears in the doorway, robe wrapped tight around her body, her hair all over the place, concern etched on her face. "Oh, honey, you don't look okay. Why don't you try lying down?"

"I can't," Jillian mutters. "I'm too worried about Tucker and everything that's happening." Her mom takes her by the hand, ignoring her words, and helps her to the bed. The cool sheets offer little comfort as she sinks into the mattress. Dazzling lights play at the edges of her vision, and she knows it's too late to stop the migraine now.

"Where's that eye mask I bought you for Christmas? The one that's supposed to help? How many migraine pills did you take?" Kathy asks, her mothering tone brisk, decisive, and one hundred percent in control of the situation.

"In the freezer, and yes, I just took two of them. They're in the bathroom if you want to see them. I can't remember when I take the next dosage," Jillian mutters, her eyes closed but her stomach feeling like she's stuck on a life raft in the middle of a tumultuous ocean.

"I'll take a look. Don't you worry about a thing. Here, Lucille, why don't you sit with her while I grab that eye mask and an ice pack," Kathy says as Jillian hears Lucille shuffle in.

Lucille perches on the edge of the bed and grabs Jillian's hand. "I . . . I have some news," she says hesitantly. "I spoke with Logan."

Jillian's chest tightens at her words. "When? What did he say? When are they coming home?"

"Not for a few more days," Lucille explains, not quite meeting Jillian's gaze. "Tucker hasn't gotten a new phone yet, says he has an old one here at the house, which is why he hasn't called. But everything's okay. You shouldn't worry."

Jillian's first reaction is relief, but that's quickly replaced by a streak of doubt. Something about Lucille's tone doesn't ring true.

"Did Logan say where they went?" Jillian presses. "When they'll be back?"

Lucille shakes her head. "He didn't give details. Just said not to worry."

Jillian studies Lucille's face, searching for any sign of deception. The older woman's smile seems forced, her eyes shifty.

"Not worry?" She wants to laugh but it'll hurt too much. "He does know who he's talking to, right? With everything that's been going on, of course I'm going to worry. Tell me you aren't." She challenges Lucille, keeping her gaze on her face.

"I'm not." Lucille gives a quick little smile but there's no honesty behind it. "Logan doesn't always share about the business side of things with me, and honestly, it's better most of the time not to know. Sometimes being kept in the dark is the safest place to be," she says softly.

There's more behind her words than she's admitting, and Jillian doesn't like that she's not able to read her like she should. This headache is making everything foggy. "You're sure that's all he said?" Jillian asks, her voice low.

"Of course," Lucille replies, a touch too quickly. "Now, why don't you try to rest, you poor thing, those pills will kick in soon, I hope."

As Lucille leaves the room, Jillian's mind races. Why would Logan call Lucille but not have Tucker call her? He could easily use his father's phone. And why the vagueness about their whereabouts? And what kind of emergency is so important that they had to leave without saying goodbye?

She hates to say it, but she doesn't trust Lucille. Not one bit. But if she's lying, then what's the truth?

The house's silence presses in on Jillian as she lies in bed, her thoughts tumbling. The migraine medication dulls the edges of her anxiety, but can't erase it completely. She's drifting in and out of a fitful doze when her phone buzzes, startling her fully awake.

Unknown number. Her hand shakes as she answers.

"Hello?" Jillian's voice is thick with sleep and worry.

"Jill? It's me."

Jillian bolts upright, wide awake and definitely regretting the sudden movement. She gently lies back down. "Becky?"

"Yeah." There's a pause, filled with unspoken history. "Are you . . . are you still willing to help me?"

"Of course," Jillian says without hesitation. Her mind races, pushing aside her own troubles. "What do you need?"

"I need to get out." Becky's voice trembles slightly. "Colin's out of town, and our boys have a game together tomorrow."

"Okay, that's not a problem," Jillian says. "I have a place you can go and you'll be safe there."

She describes the trailer in Helena, painting a picture of safety and seclusion. As she speaks, Jillian can almost see Becky nodding on the other end of the line.

"There's even an old car there," Jillian adds. "It's nothing fancy, but it runs. You can have it."

"And you're sure it's safe. No one knows about it?" Becky asks, her tone insistent.

"No one. Well . . . Tucker, obviously. We stayed there for a bit before we moved into this house, we prepaid for the year to keep the trailer there and honestly, he's probably forgotten all about it." Jillian hopes she sounds convincing.

"You won't tell him, will you? Promise me you won't tell him," Becky pleads.

"I swear," Jillian says, meaning it with every fiber of her being. She still hasn't had the opportunity to talk about Becky and her accusations with Tucker, but until she does, she won't utter another word about her friend to him.

"Thank you," Becky breathes, her voice full of emotion. "I . . . You don't understand what this means."

Jillian notices her mom standing in the doorway, a concerned look on her face.

"What about my mom," Jillian asks softly. "Can I at least let her know you'll be okay and safe?"

There's no answer, not right away. But finally, Jillian hears a gentle sigh. "Yes, you can. Ask her not to say anything to my parents though. I'd rather do that in person, okay?"

Jillian smiles. "Okay," she says. As they hash out the details of tomorrow's plan, a spark of hope ignites in her chest. Maybe, just maybe, she can make things right after all these years.

CHAPTER FORTY-FOUR

The sun dips below the horizon, casting long shadows across the baseball diamond. Jillian's eyes dart anxiously between the parking lot and the empty bleachers, her heart racing with each passing minute. Where is Becky?

"Earth to my daughter . . . where are you?" Kathy snaps her fingers three times in front of Jillian's face. "Did you even hear a word that was just said?"

Casting one last glance toward the parking lot, Jillian sighs. "Sorry, Mom."

"She still hasn't shown, has she?" Kathy whispers, careful to keep her voice low enough for Lucille not to overhear.

Jillian shakes her head. She glances down for the millionth time at her phone, wondering why Becky hasn't at least called her. Has something happened? Is she okay?

"Did you try calling her?" Kathy asks.

"I thought about it, but what if she's not in a safe place, you know? I don't want to add to an already bad situation."

"What are you ladies whispering about over there? Aren't you watching Ethan? Look, he's made it to third base. If he makes it home, they'll win this game." Lucille lifts her fingers to her mouth and lets out a huge whistle. "Go Ethan!"

Properly chastised, Jillian forces a smile and claps as Ethan barrels toward the home plate, sliding in at the last minute. All three of them jump from their seats, whistling and yelling, along with the others in the stands as the team celebrates yet another win.

"She'll come," Kathy whispers into her ear, squeezing her arm.

"I hope so." Jillian casts another look over her shoulder.

For the next twenty minutes or so, she focuses on Ethan, celebrating with him about his winning run, listening to his excited chatter and agreeing that a stop for ice cream sounds absolutely perfect. And yet, even after loading everything into the truck, she's still watching, waiting for Becky to show.

They are the last to leave, partly on purpose, but partly because Coach Neil knocks on her truck window.

"Hey, Jill, sorry to bother you." He looks in and waves at Ethan. "Great slide there, bud," he says giving him a smile. "Your mom is going to have a heck of a time getting that dirt stain out."

"You know it was a good game by the number of stains, right Coach Neil?" Ethan says, parroting a saying Neil uses during each game.

"That's right, kiddo." He glances over at Jill. "Can you let Tucker know I need to talk to him? I've tried calling and texting but . . ."

"Oh, he lost his phone," Lucille says, leaning forward from the back. "The boys had to go on a business trip but should be home soon."

Jillian gives her head a little shake and sighs as Neil gives her a 'what the hell' type of look. "He knew he was supposed to be here today. I made it really clear I needed him. He's kind of burned a bridge here, Jill. I hope he realizes that."

There is absolutely nothing Jillian can do but nod. She doesn't blame Neil at all. "I'm sorry," Jillian says. "I'm not the one who should be apologizing, but since Tuck isn't here to do it himself . . ."

269

"I'll wait for that apology, don't worry. I don't hold this on you. I should have had you help me coach these kids, out of all the parents, you're the one who has never missed a practice or game."

"Yeah, Mom. How about next season?" Ethan interjects.

She gives him a smile through the rearview mirror, then notices a truck slowly pulling in from off the highway. Her pulse quickens and her hands get all clammy. "Funny, funny," she says, desperate to get out of the conversation. "We're headed into town for some ice cream," she tells Neil.

"Same here," he says. "Maybe we'll see you there." He says this to Ethan who gives him two thumbs-up.

Jillian pauses for a beat or two, waiting for Neil to climb into his truck and leave, before she gives her mom a look.

"Listen, guys, I'll be right back, okay?" She gets out of the truck, closing the door before anyone can ask her any questions.

By the time she makes it to Becky's truck, she's already out, her weary gaze full of tears. "I'm sorry I'm late," she says, her voice barely above a whisper.

Jillian pulls her into a fierce hug, feeling Becky stiffen before relaxing into the embrace. "I was so worried," Jillian murmurs, fighting back tears.

She pulls away, fumbling in her pocket. "Here," she says, pressing a set of keys and a folded paper into Becky's hand. "The trailer keys and directions. It's not much, but it's safe." She then pulls out an envelope from her back pocket. "This is to help tide you over for groceries and gas and whatever else you need."

Becky hesitates taking the envelope but then nods, her fingers closing around the lifeline Jillian's offering. "Thank you," she breathes.

Jillian blinks back tears, wishing she could do more, say more. "I wish—" she starts, but Becky cuts her off with a shake of her head.

"No wishes. I learned a long time ago they're not worth it," she says, her voice thick with emotion. "We'll be in touch though, I promise."

"Becky?" A tearful voice calls out, and Jillian turns to see her mom running toward them, her arms outstretched. "Oh, honey," she says as she pulls her in for a hug. "I couldn't let you leave without seeing you in person. I'm so glad you're okay, that you're not dead," she says with a hiccup full of tears.

Becky pulls away. "I'm not dead. But I'm not okay either. But my son" — she looks toward the truck — "he will be, and that's what is important."

Kathy riffles through the purse she's slung over her shoulder and pulls out a small zipped bag. "I wasn't sure what you would need the most, so there's some prepaid visa cards and other gift cards and a new phone for when you need one." She pushes the bag into Becky's hands. "And don't bother arguing with me. Your mother would do the same if the shoes were reversed. And if you ever need anything more — you call me or Jillian, you hear? You are not alone anymore, girl."

With tears streaming down her face, Becky takes the bag. "No one else knows, right?" she asks Jillian, wiping at her cheeks.

"No one knows," Jillian repeats back. "Be safe, please. And call me as soon as you can. If you run into any issues with the trailer, tell them to call my cell and I will confirm your stay there, but you shouldn't have any issues."

Becky nods, giving the printout of the map a glance. "I'll leave the truck there and take the car, if that's okay? We'll only stay a day or two, so that I can stock up on things, and then we'll head out east."

"To your parents?" Kathy asks, holding her hands tight to her chest.

Becky nods. "I'll take the long route just in case, but yes, that's the plan."

"Do me a favor, hon? Call them and tell them. Your father will meet you somewhere. He'll help to make sure you get home safe. You don't have to do this alone, okay?" She reaches out and grabs Becky's hand. "I think you'll be surprised at how resourceful your dad has become. He joined a group that helps victims of sex trafficking restore their lives, all for you."

Becky's face crumbles. "For me? He did that for me?"

Kathy nods. "He never knew what happened, but he never gave up hope. He never believed you ran away, and if you were kidnapped . . . well, if he couldn't help you, then he was going to help others. Call them, please?"

Becky nods. She gives Jillian one more hard hug. "Thank you," she whispers into her ear before she climbs back into her truck and leaves.

Jillian intertwines her arm with Kathy's as they walk back toward her truck. "That was nice of you, Mom," she says.

"Nice had nothing to do with it. She used to call me her second Mom, did you know that? What I just did was nothing compared to what I should have done. I should have tried harder, like you did, to find her."

Jillian swallows back the lump forming in her throat. "I didn't know that about Mr. Gardiner."

"It's been about ten years or so now that he's been involved with that group. He does a lot of fundraisers, and even bought a few townhouses that he lets those who are newly rescued live in. Gives them a place to stay, to start fresh, you know? In fact, he's gotten quite a few of us involved."

Jillian stops just short of the truck and gives her mother a strong look. "You and Dad?"

Kathy nods. "Gives us something to do since we both retired." She pats her on the hand. "I'll tell you all about it later, if you're interested."

"Who was that you were talking to?" Lucille asks the second they get back in the truck. There's a tone in her voice that's beyond mere curiosity.

Jillian gives her mom a look before she twists in her seat and looks at Lucille. "Just a friend, why?"

Lucille sits back in her seat, arms crossed. "She looked familiar, that's all. Maybe I saw her in town or something."

"Maybe," Jillian says casually, even though she knows that's not true. There's no way Lucille knows Becky, right? There's no way Lucille would be involved in something like that. Becky never said so but that doesn't mean . . . Her stomach twists and she reaches out and grabs hold of her mom's hand, squeezing hard as she struggles not to vomit.

"Hey, Mom, why is the sheriff here?" Ethan asks, pointing behind them.

Sheriff Mato's cruiser pulls up, and it's all Jillian can do not to cry. There's too much happening right now. Between her husband leaving without a word, to helping Becky escape, to realizing the man she married isn't the man she thought she knew . . . she can't take any more, she really can't.

She puts her hand out her window and waves at Sheriff Mato.

"Evening, Jillian," Sheriff Mato calls, striding over. "Tucker with you by chance? I need to ask him a few questions."

Jillian's protective instincts flare. "Well, he's not here with us," she says.

Sheriff Mato leans in and smiles at everyone. "I can see that. He's missed another game then? That's too bad."

Jillian glances at her with surprise. "Are you keeping track of my husband, Sheriff?"

"Just town gossip, that's all. But I do need to speak with him. Mind if I follow you home?"

"You can follow, but it'll do you no good. My husband had to leave town for business." Jillian keeps a smile on her face, hoping it's relaxed enough not to cause any red flags.

The sheriff's eyes narrow. "Did he now? That's too bad." She sighs and straightens, one hand still on the door. "He'll be home soon though?"

Jillian nods. "That's the plan. But then you know how things go."

"No, actually, I don't. How do things go?" Sheriff Mato places one hand on her holster, very casual, but it's enough to emphasize who is really in control here.

"Oh, my husband had some business come up and asked Tucker to join him. Nothing serious," Lucille pipes up from the back, a wide smile covering her face.

Sheriff Mato nods. "Do you know when he'll be home?"

"A few days probably," Lucille continues, not giving Jillian a chance to get in a word.

"Well, when he does, make sure you let him know I need to see him, will you?"

Jillian nods. "I have Detective Amber's number on my phone. Should I just let her know?"

Sheriff Mato shakes her head. "No, this doesn't concern her. Call me directly if you don't mind."

Doesn't concern her? What else is happening around this town that Tucker is involved in then? Jillian's heart skips a beat as the Sheriff looks off into the distance like she's weighing something and isn't sure if she'll like the outcome. Either way, Jillian has a feeling she doesn't want to be around when she makes that decision.

"Will do," Jillian says carefully. "Now, if you don't mind, it's getting late. I promised Ethan some ice cream before bed."

Watching the sheriff walk back to the car, Jillian's mind whirls with so many questions. What does the sheriff want with her husband?

CHAPTER FORTY-FIVE

Back at the house, Jillian heads to the living room, her laptop beside her on the couch.

Her mom suggested that she look through Tucker's emails, to see if she can find any answers there, if she could access his email account. That's a big if.

She has no idea if his account has a password lock, but if she knows her husband — and until lately, she thought she did — figuring out his password shouldn't be too hard. He had this dumb saying when they were first together and once let it slip that it's the only password he uses; he just changes the symbols and letters occasionally.

With trembling fingers, she types out *Y0u&M3=10v3*. You and me equals love. Her lips flirt with a smile as she remembers the little dance and twirl of his fingers when he'd say it at the oddest of times: like driving down the highway, or when he'd surprise her with her favorite milkshake or even when they sat on the couch, watching a movie. He always knows how to make her smile.

Bingo. It takes a few minutes for all his emails to be added to her computer, but as she goes through them, she doesn't find anything suspicious or different. Everything is work-related, baseball-related, or with family back home.

His sent and deleted boxes, though, are empty.

There is, however, one single email waiting in the drafts folder.

Jillian's fingers tremble as she opens the folder. Her breath catches when she sees a single unsent message. The subject line reads, "To Jill: The truth about everything."

She half closes the laptop lid, not ready for this. She wants to have found nothing. She wants to be able to say her husband is in the clear, that there's a reason for everything that has happened or what's being said about him. But that email erases all the things she wants and needs right now.

If she doesn't read it, then it won't be true. That's how that works, right?

Except that's just closing her eyes and being weak, and she's done with being weak. The truth has been her obsession for twenty years, and now that it's within reach, she won't turn a blind eye. Not again.

With a deep breath, she opens the lid and double-clicks. Tucker's words fill the screen:

Jillian,

I'm sorry for leaving like this. I don't know when you'll find this, but I hope it gives you some clarity before I can explain everything to you in person. You asked for honesty and said you wanted to do this together . . . but I don't think you fully understand what is happening, nor should you. My job as your husband is to protect you, protect our family, and that's what I'm trying to do, even if I've done a piss-poor job of it.

I'm not the bad guy. No matter what anyone says, I need you to believe that.

I'm also not innocent in any of this.

The honesty part: Dad isn't here for a simple visit, but you've already guessed that, haven't you? He's here to clean up for Andy Rawlings since I told Andy that I'm done. I'll explain what that means later. For now, all you need to know is that I am doing everything I can to make sure you and

*Ethan are protected. Unfortunately, that also means I have
to go away for a little bit.*

*The police are going to come back with some questions.
Take them to the barn. Behind the rafter — the one with
the old pitchfork hanging from it — there's a box with the
evidence they'll need. All my papers to support what I'm doing
and evidence to take down Andy are there.*

*I'm headed to Texas with Dad. I hope I'll come back
to you. I want to come back to you and explain everything in
person. I hope you'll forgive me when you find out the truth.*

Always and forever, Tucker

Jillian's mind reels as she struggles to read behind Tucker's
words. There's so much he's not telling her, and yet, at the same
time . . . She presses a hand to her mouth, fighting back nausea.
The pieces are falling into place, but the pictures they're forming are more horrifying than she could have imagined.

She stands, her legs unsteady. "I have to check the barn,"
she whispers to herself.

"Jillian? What are you doing still up?"

She glances up in surprise to see Lucille, her cell phone in
one hand, a book in the other. She tilts her head as she looks
at Jillian's face and then down to the laptop she left lying on
the couch.

"Have you heard from Tucker?" She asks, her voice gentle yet sharper than a carving knife.

Does Lucille know? Is she part of it all or an innocent
bystander blinded to the truth, like her?

"I was supposed to talk to Logan. He generally checks in
every night, but he hasn't yet. I'm all out of my decaf tea, but
I remember seeing some in your pantry, so I thought I'd come
in here and wait for his call, I hope that's okay."

He checks in every night? Yet Tucker doesn't call at all?

"Do you talk to Tucker?"

Lucille's face furrows into a frown. "Talk to Tucker? Of
course, dear. He always says to tell you hello."

"Where are they, Lucille?"

Lucille swipes her hand in the air. "Oh, honey, you already know the answer to that, I'm thinking, don't you? Logan is doing what he's always done, trying to keep Tucker safe. Other than that, I try to stay out of it. Best if you do, too. Before you know it, the boys will be back, and everything will be well. Now, I'll just go make my tea. You try to get some sleep, okay? You look positively ragged." Lucille gives her a little push on her arm as if trying to force her to head to the stairs.

Jillian digs in her feet and pulls back. "Keeping Tucker safe? What does that even mean?"

Lucille shakes her head. "Sweetie, that's a conversation best had between you and your husband."

"Well, I can't exactly have that, now can I?"

Lucille shrugs. "That's on him then." All the sweetness evaporates from the woman's voice, and instead, there's a steeliness that Jillian rarely ever hears. "The less you know, the better. Trust me on that. Now, honestly, go to bed. You're not doing Ethan any good being so sleep-deprived. Don't you think the poor boy is going through enough, what with Tucker not being here and the police — being around?" She tsks then turns away.

Jillian moves to follow her, unwilling to drop the conversation, but her phone buzzes in her pocket before she takes a step. She pulls it out, thinking it can only be Tucker at this time of night, but it's an unknown number.

Her thumb hovers over the screen.

"Hello?"

"Jillian?" The voice is hushed, frantic. "It's Becky."

Jillian's heart leaps into her throat. "Becky? Is everything okay?"

"I'm at your trailer." Becky's voice breaks. "There's someone outside. I'm scared, Jillian. I think they found us. You said no one knew we were here, right?"

"I swear it," Jillian says, adrenaline surging through her veins. Her mind swirls a mile a minute as she considers what

278

she can do. It's a two-hour drive to Helena, and there's nothing she can do at this moment to help her. Except . . .

"Jill, I think they're here looking for me. They keep talking about the woman and the kid, and they're peering into the truck now. I don't know what to do," Becky whispers.

"I'm going to call our sheriff. She'll be able to help."

"No, no police. God, no police, you don't understand . . ." Becky's voice breaks again as the panic rises.

"Okay, there's a back door from one of the bedrooms. Do you remember seeing it? You should be able to get out from there. Try to get someplace safe and then call me . . . I'll be there in two hours."

"I saw it when I was scoping things out before. Okay, I'll call you when we're safe. Please hurry."

Of course she's going to hurry. After twenty years of guilt and searching, if Becky needs her, she will be there for her, no matter what.

Rushing into the kitchen to grab her keys, she stops when she realizes Lucille is holding onto her purse.

"I need that," Jillian tells her. She reaches for it, expecting her mother-in-law to hand it over, except Lucille places the strap over her body and sits at the table.

"No, I don't think you do," she says.

"Lucille, I'm sorry. I don't understand what's going on, but I would like you to hand over my purse, please." She forces her voice to relax so that her words sound non-threatening.

"No, sweet love, you're the one who doesn't understand. You won't be going anywhere." She taps the table with her finger. "Why don't you sit down and join me." There's a sweet, serene smile on Lucille's face, but it doesn't match the challenge and decisiveness in her voice. "I must insist," she says when Jillian doesn't move.

With leaden feet, Jillian takes the necessary steps to reach the table. She slowly pulls out a seat and cautiously sits, perched on the edge, instinctively knowing something is wrong.

"Let me guess," Lucille says, her fingers twirling over an empty cup. "That was your long-lost friend, Rebecca, wasn't it? The one who disappeared when you were only teenagers. You wouldn't shut up about her for the longest time," she says, inhaling deeply. "It really was quite tiresome."

"I'm sorry?" Jillian doesn't know why she's apologizing, but her stomach sours as she watches a swath of emotions flow over her mother-in-law's features.

"That girl has been a pain in our side for a long time. I thought she'd finally disappeared, and life was . . . comfortable again with her out of the way and forgotten. Why Andrew thought having you move out here would be a good thing, I'll never know. That man likes to play with fire, and he's too old for it now." She pauses, tapping her finger on the table. "Unless, that's why." She huffs slightly. "You know, I told Logan that something fishy was going on with that man, but Logan wouldn't hear of it. He trusts Andrew, heaven knows why. That man has been a thorn in our side from day one, I tell you."

While Lucille drops truth bomb after truth bomb, Jillian sits there stunned into silence. All the things are being confirmed in one very long testimony, and while the woman doesn't hold a gun over her head, she feels like it's there.

"Oh, come now." Lucille tsks. "I would have thought you'd figured all this out by now, especially with that girl back in your life. She told you everything, I'm sure. Don't play dumb now, dear. Now isn't the time. We have other things we need to take care of first."

"She has a name," Jillian says. "Calling her *that girl* is degrading." She tries very hard to keep the anger out of her voice as she holds her phone beneath the table and discreetly tries to pull up Sheriff Mato's contact.

Lucille snorts. "She's just a girl to me. One of many. You have no idea . . ." She leans forward and shakes her head. "Phone on the table, Jillian. Come on now, let's play nice, shall we? After all, we are family."

Staring down at the table, Jillian nods. "Family, right. A messed up one, for sure. How did I never see it?" She says this part to herself. "I didn't want to see it, did I?"

"Don't be too hard on yourself, love. Tucker has always protected you and made sure you stayed in the dark. Truth be told, that boy of mine doesn't like this side of the family business much. We thought Andy would help with that, but he's done the opposite. That man coddled him more than he should have, and we let it happen."

Jillian stares at the woman she realizes she doesn't know with shock and disgust.

"You kidnap and sell young women, more like teenagers, for money. Why would you think he'd be okay with that?" Bile rushes up her throat, and she struggles to swallow it down so that she doesn't throw up.

"They're just commodities, love. It's only business, nothing personal."

Jillian can't believe what she's hearing. Especially from a woman like Lucille. A woman who would give you the shoes off her feet, the sweater off her shoulders, the purse she spent a fortune on if a stranger needed it. Jillian still remembers the time she cleaned out her wardrobe of clothes, designer shoes, and handbags for a women's shelter.

Where did that woman go? Who is this woman sitting at her table now?

"I'm calling the police." No longer hiding her phone, Jillian pulls it up and is about to call Sheriff Mato, when Lucille does the one unimaginable thing.

She pulls out a gun.

CHAPTER FORTY-SIX

Becky

Becky's heart pounds as she presses her ear against the thin trailer wall. The muffled voices outside grow louder, more insistent. She clutches Jamie tight, feeling his small body tremble against her.

"Mommy, I'm scared," he whispers, his voice barely audible.

"Shh, baby. It's okay," Becky murmurs, stroking his hair. But it's not okay. They've been found. The question is how? Jillian swears the only person who knows about her is her mother. Becky always trusted Kathy and seriously doubts she would have done this.

But then who? It can't be Colin, not unless he came home early. Maybe Jillian is playing her, deciding she needs to protect her precious husband and his reputation. She shakes her head. No, that's not Jill. She wouldn't do that.

Pulling slowly back from the wall, she scans the cramped space of the trailer. Her eyes dart frantically, making sure she hasn't left anything behind. She'd brought one backpack into the trailer, thankfully. The rest of the stuff is out in the truck.

The sound of heavy boots crunching on gravel outside has her flinching. They're getting closer.

"We know you're in there!" a gruff voice calls out. "Come out now, and we won't have to do this the hard way."

Becky's mind races with what their future holds if the men get them. She'll be killed and her son sold, much like she was. Colin might get his son back, but she highly doubts it. She tries to steady her breathing, to think clearly, but panic claws at her throat.

Her son whimpers, burying his face in her shirt. "I want to go home."

Home. The word stabs at Becky's heart. Home should be someplace safe to lay your head, and that's never been something she's had, not since the night she was stolen off the sidewalk right in front of her house.

She pulls her son closer. "Listen to me, baby. We're going to be okay. I promise. But I need you to be very quiet now. Can you do that for Mommy?"

He nods, his eyes wide with fear and trust.

Becky's mind whirls as she tries to remember everything Jillian told her about the trailer and where the back door is hidden.

"Screw this," she hears one of the men outside mutter. "Let's just break down the damn door."

Time's running out. Becky knows she has to act now, or it will be too late.

"Hold on tight, baby," she whispers to her son. "We're going to play a little game of hide and seek."

Becky's heart hammers as she scans the dimly lit trailer. Her eyes finally land on a small door near the back, partially obscured by a worn curtain.

She grabs her son's hand, her voice barely above a whisper. "Remember how we practiced being quiet as mice? It's time to play for real."

The boy nods solemnly, his small fingers tightening around hers.

Becky moves swiftly, every rustle of fabric as she grabs the backpack sounds deafening in the tense silence. She slings it over her shoulder, wincing at the weight.

"What if they hear us, Mommy?" her son asks, his voice trembling.

Becky kneels, meeting his eyes. "Then we run faster than we've ever run before. But they won't hear us, because we'll be so, so quiet. Okay?"

She eases the hidden door open, praying it won't creak. A gust of cool night air hits her face, carrying the scent of pine and distant woodsmoke. Freedom. And danger.

Becky takes a deep breath, then whispers, "Let's go."

They slip out into the darkness, the trailer park a maze of shadows and muted voices. Becky's eyes dart constantly, searching for movement, for the glint of headlights, for anything that might spell disaster.

Her son stumbles, and she scoops him up without breaking stride.

"Where are we going?" he whispers against her neck.

Becky swallows hard. "Somewhere safe," she lies, because the truth is, she has no idea where is safe anymore. All she knows is that it's not here, not with those men so close.

As they weave silently between trailers, each distant voice, each barking dog, sends a jolt of terror through her. She searches for landmarks Jillian mentioned in the darkness.

"Almost there," she murmurs, more to herself than to her son. "We're almost—"

A beam of light cuts through the night, sweeping across their path. Becky freezes, her breath catching in her throat.

She presses herself against the cold metal of a nearby trailer, her son clutched tightly to her. She can feel his rapid breaths, matching her own panicked rhythm. The light sweeps past, missing them by inches.

"Mommy," her son whimpers, his voice muffled against her shoulder.

"Shh," she soothes, stroking his hair. "We're okay. We're playing a game, remember? Like hide and seek."

But this is no game, and they both know it. Her mind races, desperate for a plan. They can't keep running aimlessly through the trailer park. Sooner or later, they'll be spotted.

She scans their surroundings, and sees a rusted pickup truck, its bed filled with junk. It's not ideal, but it might work.

"Sweetie," she whispers, kneeling down. "I need you to be very brave. Can you do that for me?"

He nods, his body shaking.

"I'm going to hide you in that truck. Stay very quiet, no matter what you hear. I'll come back for you soon."

"Don't leave me," he pleads, clinging to her arm.

Becky's heart breaks, but she forces a smile. "I'll never leave you. I promise. This is just part of our game." She inhales deeply, praying for strength to leave him behind. What if she doesn't come back?

"If you fall asleep, that's okay," she tells him. "It's no different from when we go camping in our truck, right? If I'm not here when you wake up, I want you to go to—" She looks around and sees a trailer with a bunch of bikes and other toys lying in the grass. "I want you to go there and tell them you're lost, okay?"

"But you'll come back, right?" Jamie whimpers.

"This is just Plan B, okay? It never hurts to have a Plan B, or even a C," she mutters to herself. She's always talking about a Plan B with Jamie, a necessity depending on Colin's mood swings.

Jamie gives her a deep nod before she helps him into the truck bed, tucking him beneath a tarp. She turns away with a final, lingering touch to his cheek, steeling herself for what comes next.

Creeping back toward Jillian's trailer, she prays the men have given up and left. Unfortunately, by the orange glow of cigarettes, that's not the case.

"I'm sick of this shit," a gruff voice complains. "Why's it always us getting called for these piddly jobs?"

"You know why," another bored voice responds. "We're the cleanup crew. It's what we do."

"Yeah, but why's it always gotta be chasing down broads? Can't we get some real action for once?"

Becky's blood runs cold. These men are professionals. She presses into the shadows, straining to hear more.

The second man's voice, sharp and authoritative, cuts through the night air. "Shut your trap and be grateful for the paycheck. When the bigwigs give an order, you don't question it. You just do it."

Becky recognizes the tone immediately. He's been out to their house a few times to talk to Colin. He oozed danger. Colin once threatened that he'd stick that guy on her if she got out of line, and she'd end up wishing for death if that ever happened.

She shivers.

The first man grunts, clearly cowed. "Yeah, yeah. I get it. But there's gonna be hell to pay when we come up empty-handed."

The response is clipped. "Maybe. Or maybe it was just a bad tip."

Becky's mind races. A bad tip? Who could have tipped them off about her whereabouts? Her heart pounds so loudly she's sure they must hear it.

"What if she was here and split?" the first man suggests.

"Then we find her," the other says, his voice low and menacing. "We always do."

Becky backs away slowly, her breath caught in her throat. She has to get back to her son, has to find a way out of this town before the net closes around them.

As she thinks about where to go and what to do, one thought echoes in her mind: they have to leave Helena tonight, no matter what it takes.

The first man reaches into his pocket, pulling out a sleek black phone. His movements are deliberate, almost casual, but there's an undercurrent of tension there. Becky's pulse quickens, her fingers digging into the rough bark of the tree she's using for cover.

The sound of buttons being pressed cuts through the night air. He holds the phone to his ear, his posture rigid. Becky strains to hear, her own breathing seeming thunderous in the silence.

"Ma'am," he says, his voice smooth as silk but with an edge of steel beneath. "There's no one here."

Becky's mind races. Who is he talking to?

The man listens for a moment, his face an impassive mask. "Understood," he says finally, ending the call with a sharp click.

Becky's legs tremble as she tries to stay still. She needs to move and run back to her son, but fear keeps her rooted.

"Pack it up," he orders, his voice carrying easily in the night air. "We're done here."

Relief floods Becky, but she doesn't dare relax — not yet, not until they're gone, and she and Jamie are far away from this place. The men climb into their truck, the engine roaring to life, headlights cutting through the darkness.

It takes time before she finally allows herself to breathe. But even as she turns to slip away, a chill runs down her spine. This isn't over. Not by a long shot.

Heading back to where Jamie hides, she calls Jillian's number. It rings twice before it goes to voicemail. She hangs up. Somehow, someone found out she's here and she is no longer safe.

So she does the one thing she never thought she would do.

She calls her father.

It's late and she's sure he's in bed, but he picks up on the third ring.

"Daddy?" Her voice shatters as she hears his sharp inhale — then a sob.

CHAPTER FORTY-SEVEN

Agent Meri Amber

The moonless night cloaks the old Franklin farm in an inky darkness that sets Meri's nerves on edge. She crouches behind a weathered fence post, her eyes straining to pierce the darkness. Sheriff Mato and two deputies flank her, one with a set of binoculars glued to his eyes as they watch from afar.

"Any movement?" Meri whispers, her hand hovering near her holstered weapon.

Sheriff Mato shakes her head. "Nothing yet. I think you're right. I think you were made and spooked them off."

Meri nods, but doubt gnaws at her. If she had somehow tipped her hand and scared them off, that's on her, and she knows it. After years of chasing shadows, she can't bear the thought of coming up empty-handed now.

"Give it another hour," she says, more to convince herself than the others.

Time crawls by, each minute stretching into an eternity. Meri's legs cramp from holding her position, but she doesn't dare move. Her mind races, replaying every step that led her here, searching for any misstep that could have alerted Rawlings.

At the hour, she stands. "I'm going to check the barn," she announces, her voice barely above a whisper.

"Meri, wait—" Sheriff Mato starts, but she's already moving.

She creeps toward the dilapidated structure, her footsteps silent on the ground. The barn looms ahead of her, a hulking silhouette against the star-studded Montana sky. Meri draws her gun and flashlight, taking a deep breath before easing through a cracked door.

The beam of her light cuts through the musty air, revealing rusted farm equipment and piles of hay. Meri's heart pounds as she sweeps the space, every shadow concealing a potential threat.

In the far corner, something catches her eye.

A set of shelves sagging beneath the weight of dozens of metal boxes. Meri's brow furrows as she examines them. These aren't what she expected — they're old, covered in thick dust and cobwebs. Rawlings Junior couldn't have brought these here.

"Damn it," she mutters, holstering her weapon to shine her flashlight on the boxes. She won't touch them, won't open them even though she already knows what's inside. If she wants to find Rawlings and put him away for the rest of his despicable life, the chain of evidence will be necessary.

She texts Sheriff Mato and waits. It feels as though that's all she's done this whole case. Find and wait. Hurry and wait. Discover and wait. She's tired of waiting, tired of Rawlings slipping through her fingers time and time again. It makes her stomach churn just how close she was to finally meeting him face to face tonight.

Meri's breath catches as her fingers trace the label on the nearest box. *Emily Winters, 1978*. Her heart pounds as she scans the shelf. The dates stretch back decades, a grim timeline of Rawlings' reign of terror.

"Amber?" Sheriff Mato's voice calls out.

"In here!" she says, her voice tight. "You need to see this."

"What've you got?"

Meri gestures to the boxes, her hand trembling slightly. "More boxes, some even dating back to the seventies."

The sheriff's sharp intake of breath echoes in the dusty barn. "These are like those boxes in the trailer, aren't they?"

Meri's mind races, piecing together the horrific puzzle. "We need to process these immediately, and yes, they'll be the same, at least I think so. Every serial killer has a signature, and these boxes are his — there'll be personal effects, clothes . . . and letters."

"Letters?"

"He makes them write to their loved ones," Meri explains, bile rising in her throat. "A final, twisted goodbye." And she's been waiting for twenty years to find River's box to read that letter she knows her sister must have written.

As Mato calls in the team, Meri stands rooted to the spot, staring at the names. Each box represents a life cut short, a family destroyed.

"We've got you now, you bastard," she whispers, her fingers curling into fists.

Meri steps out into the night, her breath forming small clouds in the air. She pulls out her phone, fingers trembling slightly as she types out a message to Lindsay: *No Rawlings, but found more boxes. Decades of victims. Local team is on site. What's next?*

The response comes quickly: *Stay put. Team enroute to Texas. Red House location probable.*

Meri's heart races. The Red House — the epicenter of this nightmare. She types back furiously: *I'm coming. Need to be there.*

Lindsay's reply deflates her: *Negative. Write your report. Process boxes. Connect tomorrow.*

She grits her teeth, frustration bubbling up. "Dammit, Lindsay," she mutters, shoving the phone in her pocket.

"This is going to be another all-nighter," Sheriff Mato says, stepping out of the barn. "You staying?"

Meri nods. "Since we missed Rawlings, those boxes are my priority after your team does what they need to do."

Sheriff Mato reaches down and sets her hand on the head of her dog. "I figured."

Meri heads back to her vehicle to grab her kit. It's going to take time for Mato's team to arrive and she's not in the mood to waste time. Something catches her eye as she stands on the side of the road.

Without thought, she climbs into her vehicle and heads down the dark country road, to where she'd seen headlights flicker on and off. There, nestled in a group of trees lining a dirt road are two vehicles.

She slows, curiosity piqued.

"What do we have here?" she whispers, killing her lights and circling back.

Meri eases her car off the road and carefully closes her door. Out here, any sudden noise will carry. She creeps through the field, staying low, and it doesn't take long for her to hear hushed and angry voices. As she gets closer, she recognizes them.

Tucker. Logan. And . . . Rawlings? Is he really here?

First, she pulls out her phone, shields the screen so the light can't be seen, and sends Mato a text message alerting her to where she is and what's happening. Next, she turns on a recorder, something a tech installed on her phone. If she's close enough, the recorder should pick up what's being said.

"You can't protect him," Rawlings hisses. "The Oil Man's cleaning house. The Lady, too."

Logan's voice is tense. "We're going to the Red House. Clear our names. It's the only way to do it, and you know it."

"You'll get yourselves killed," Rawlings spits back. "The first thing those two will do when you arrive is order your deaths. You understand that, right? I thought you wanted to protect your son, not put him within shooting range?"

Meri inches closer, straining to hear. Tucker's voice joins in, desperate.

"I'm done. Keeping my wife and son safe is all that matters."

Rawlings laughs, a chilling sound. "Safe? There's no 'safe' anymore, Tucker. You're in, or you're dead. Your whole family.

And it'll be on Logan's head." Stones skitter as if kicked by a boot. "Why do you think I've been sending you around the country to properties I own under aliases? If someone hadn't found those dang trailers, you guys would be safe right now."

"And who ratted you out about those trailers, huh? You don't think they don't have people set up in that prison that's close by? My boy will never be safe with you around." Logan's voice carries hints of distress and anger.

Meri's mind races. The Red House. The Oil Man. The Lady. How deep does this go?

"Sorry about this, Andy. But I got orders and it's either you or him."

A sudden movement catches Meri's eye. Logan's hand darts to his waistband, and before she can process what's happening, a gunshot shatters the night air. Rawlings crumples to the ground.

"No!" Tucker shouts, his voice raw with panic.

Logan grabs Tucker's arm, yanking him toward the truck. "Get in! Now!"

Meri's training kicks in. She reaches for her weapon but hesitates. She's outnumbered, outgunned. The truck's engine roars to life, tires spitting gravel as it peels away into the darkness.

Her heart pounds in her ears as she fumbles for her phone, fingers trembling as she dials.

"Shots fired at my location," she says, her voice steadier than she feels. "Rawlings is down. The Harper men just sped off in their truck. Send an ambulance."

She ends the call, her mind a whirlwind of thoughts. This is it. The moment she's been waiting for. The man who's haunted her career, her life, lying helpless before her.

Meri approaches cautiously, gun drawn. Rawlings is still breathing, shallow and ragged. He looks different from what she expected. An older version of his son, his face etched with years of sadistic torture. His piercing eyes lock onto hers, a mixture of pain and . . . is that amusement?

She kneels beside him, applying pressure to the wound. "Don't you dare die on me, Rawlings," she mutters. "You've got a lot to answer for."

The wail of sirens grows in the distance. Meri's mind races. Logan. Tucker. The Red House. How many more secrets will die with this man if she can't keep him alive?

Rawlings' lips curl into a pained smirk. "Well, hello, Detective or is it Agent now? Congrats on the promotion."

Meri's jaw clenches, her eyes narrowing as she maintains pressure on his wound. "Save your breath, Rawlings. You'll need it to explain yourself to the jury."

He coughs, a wet, rattling sound. "Oh, I doubt that very much. I won't survive the ride to the hospital, and we both know it."

Meri leans in closer, her voice low and intense. "Oh, you'll survive. I'm not letting you die now that I've finally found you. Where's the Red House? What's Tucker's involvement in all this?"

Rawlings' eyes dance with a perverse glee. "You're asking the wrong questions, girl. Always have been."

She feels her frustration mounting, years of pursuit crystallizing in this moment. "Then enlighten me," she hisses.

"The game's bigger than you know," he wheezes. "Didn't you get my little gifts? I knew there was a rat in that prison and figured I'd have some fun with it. Didn't you like my little gifts?" He coughs and blood lines his lips. "The boxes in those trailers? Thought I'd help you on your little treasure quest, courtesy of my son. And what about your sister's bracelet? I never got so much as a thank you card." The words, though hard to hear, are crystal clear.

The ambulance screeches to a halt nearby. Rawlings' eyes close.

"Stay with me," Meri demands, giving him a shake. "What about my sister? Where is she?"

His lips move, but she can't make out the words. She leans in closer, heart pausing mid-thump.

"Her box . . ." he whispers. "At the Red House along with her little girl. You want both? Follow the . . . oil . . ."

As the paramedics rush in, Meri sits back on her heels, her world tilted on its axis. Her sister had a daughter?

CHAPTER FORTY-EIGHT

As she watches the flashing ambulance lights drive away, Meri's phone vibrates in her hand. She glances down at the screen, her father's name flashing like a warning beacon. Her stomach drops as she answers.

"Meri, sweetheart, it's Mom. Dad is in the hospital. I know you're on a case, but . . . I think you need to come home." Her mother's voice is tinged with sadness and exhaustion and her words hit Meri with a physical blow.

"What happened? Is he okay?"

"He had a heart attack while letting Sugar out for the night. I would have called sooner, but . . ." She pauses, and Meri knows she's struggling not to cry. "Please, just come home."

"I'll be there as soon as I can, I promise. I love you," Meri says as she hangs up. She sees Sheriff Mato give her a questioning glance, but she ignores it as she dials Lindsay's number. Each ring feels like an eternity.

"Lindsay," he answers gruffly. "What's the update?"

"I found Rawlings. The senior Harper shot him, I saw it. He told me my sister was at the Red House and she has a daughter. But listen . . . My mom just called and Dad's had a heart attack and I don't think it's good. I need . . ." Her voice breaks, betraying her usual composure. She's a mess, her mind is all over the place, and her heart is being pulled in two different directions.

Family first. If there's anything Lindsay has tried to hammer into her, it's that family is always number one, no matter the circumstance. He's going to tell her to go home, but if she has a niece out there, a niece who could be in danger . . .

"Slow down, Amber. Take a breath, for Pete's sake. Tell me what's going on?"

She follows his advice and breathes in deeply. "Logan Harper shot Rawlings, who is on his way to the hospital now, but I don't expect him to make it. As for the Harpers, they're headed to the Red House. There was mention of an Oil Man and a Lady, whoever that is, and my sister's box is there, along with her child."

The words tumble out, each revelation feeling like a weight lifted from her shoulders. But the burden of her father's condition still presses down, threatening to crush her.

Lindsay's voice softens, concern evident. "That's a lot to process, Meri. What's the next move?"

She appreciates he's leaving this in her hands, her decision to make. "Home. Family first, right?" She swallows hard, fighting back tears.

"Family always comes first. You go be there for your mom, I've got things from here."

Meri hesitates, torn between her duty and her family. "Are you sure? This case—"

"Is important, yes. But so is your family. I'll get in touch with Sheriff Mato and we'll go from there. I already have a team in Texas, and we're pretty sure we know who the Oil Man and the Lady are. We'll manage. Keep me updated on your dad, okay?"

She nods, forgetting he can't see her. "Thank you, Lindsay. I will."

The northern Montana night stretches before her — rolling fields, weathered barns, and the looming presence of the mountains. It's all so foreign to her. Home awaits, a place of comfort and painful memories intertwined. Her dad has to be okay, he just has to be. And with Lindsay's team headed to Texas, maybe there will be a conclusion to their own family pain after twenty years.

And a niece. It's a lot to take in.

Meri straightens and notices Sheriff Mato on the phone, no doubt talking to Lindsay. Mato gives her a nod and a wave, and Meri heads down the road to the vehicle.

She'll go home, face the ghosts of her past, and pray that her father pulls through. But even as she turns to leave, her thoughts drift back to the Red House, to her sister's child, to the tangled web of secrets that has surrounded her life.

One secret, one mystery has finally been brought to light, at least. After all this time, she finally met Rawlings face to face, and instead of the monster she's made him out to be, he is just an old, ugly, evil man that has what's coming to him. She won't feel sorry for his death. She won't mourn him or whatever empty space he leaves behind.

A man like that . . . he deserves what's waiting for him on the other side.

CHAPTER FORTY-NINE

Jillian

The cold steel of the gun barrel glints in the dim kitchen light, steady in Lucille's hand as she aims it at Jillian.

She's been on the phone for a few minutes, her gaze steady on Jillian. By the time she ends her call and telling whoever was on the other line to leave wherever they were and to wait for her call, her face is a mask, and her eyes are chips of ice.

Jillian doesn't recognize the woman in front of her.

"You won't be calling the police, dear," Lucille says, her voice smooth as silk. "It's time you and I had a little chat. Logan doesn't think you're ready, but in my opinion, you should have been brought in a long time ago."

"Brought in?" Jillian's heart pounds, her palms slick with sweat against the worn wood of the kitchen chair.

"To our real family business. The transport side is just a front, a cover, if you will."

Jillian lifts her chin, refusing to show fear. "I already know all about that," she says, her voice stronger than she feels. "And I want nothing to do with it."

A flicker of surprise crosses Lucille's face, quickly replaced by a cruel smile. "That's a shame. Especially since Tucker is so heavily involved."

The words hit Jillian like a physical blow. *Heavily involved?* As in, still involved? No, that's not possible. She would know. Tucker would never . . . But doubt creeps in, its cold tendrils wrapping around her heart. All those late nights, the phone calls, the unexplained absences.

Jillian goes to stand, but the gun follows her movement with deadly precision.

"Sit down," Lucille orders, all pretense of politeness gone. "You might not think it, but I'm quite comfortable with a gun. Logan and I go out to the shooting range all the time, you know. You and Tucker should do that; it's quite therapeutic, you'd be surprised. And any time we have a little tiff, I just picture his face on the tin cans, and all is well. So no, love, I'm not afraid to pull the trigger. I'd hate to, though — poor Ethan would be so disappointed to lose his mother."

The threat hangs in the air, heavy and suffocating. Jillian slowly lowers herself back into the chair. How could she have been so blind?

Lucille's eyes narrow, her grip on the gun unwavering. "Now, hand over your phone," she demands, her voice cold and precise.

Jillian's fingers tighten instinctively around the device in her hand. Not only is it her lifeline, her only connection to help, but she's also been recording this whole conversation with Lucille.

Before she can respond, a sharp knock echoes through the house.

They both freeze. Jillian's heart pounds in her chest, hope rising within her. The knock comes again, more insistent this time.

From upstairs, Jillian hears her mother's worried voice. "Jillian? Is everything okay? I see the sheriff's car outside, what's going on?"

Swallowing hard, Jillian calls back, trying to keep her voice steady. "It's fine, Mom. I've got it. Go back to bed." She silently prays her mother will hear the hidden urgency in her words.

Turning back to Lucille, Jillian meets her mother-in-law's icy stare. "I need to answer that," she says, her voice barely above a whisper. She stands slowly, her legs trembling. "If you want to shoot me in the back, go right ahead."

With each step toward the door, Jillian expects to feel the searing pain of a bullet. She reaches for the doorknob, her hand shaking. Taking a deep breath, she pulls it open.

Sheriff Mato stands on the porch. "Evening, Jillian. Sorry to bother you so late at night, but I need to come inside. Is your mother-in-law here? I knocked on her trailer door but there was no answer."

Jillian's knees nearly buckle with relief. She fights to keep her voice steady. "Sheriff. I-I'm so glad you're here." Her voice drops to a whisper. "My mother-in-law . . . she's at the kitchen table. She has a gun."

Sheriff Mato's expression hardens, her hand moving instinctively to her holster. "Step to the side, Jillian," she instructs, drawing her weapon in one fluid motion.

As Jillian steps aside, Sheriff Mato snaps her fingers sharply. The sound of paws thundering up the porch steps fills the air, and her Tala appears at the sheriff's side, ears alert and eyes focused.

"Ethan is upstairs," she whispers. She doesn't want any bloodshed. Not tonight.

Sheriff Mato moves forward, her dog at her heels, gun held steady. Jillian follows, her steps tentative, as they approach the kitchen.

Lucille is still at the table, her posture relaxed, almost regal as if this were nothing more than an inconvenient and ill-timed social call. The gun rests on the table in front of her.

Lucille's eyes flick from the sheriff to Jillian, then back again. A small sigh escapes her lips, tinged with what sounds almost like boredom. "I assume I'm under arrest?" she asks, her voice eerily calm. "I haven't heard from my husband, so something must have gone wrong."

A chill runs down Jillian's spine at her mother-in-law's words. How can she be so composed? What kind of person treats a situation like this as if it were nothing more than a minor setback?

The reality of the situation crashes over Jillian like a wave, and she leans against the wall for support. This woman, who she's known for years, who's held her child . . . She's been involved in this whole thing from the beginning. Her, Logan . . . and even Tucker.

Sheriff Mato's voice cuts through the tense silence, firm and authoritative. "That's correct, Lucille. Stand up, please." She pulls out a pair of handcuffs, the metal glinting under the kitchen light. "I thought I'd let you know, we have Andrew Rawlings in custody."

Like a punch to the chest, Jillian's breath catches. Does this mean Andy Rawlings is out of their lives?

"He's been quite . . . informative about your involvement in the sex trafficking industry," the sheriff continues, her words dropping like bombs in the quiet kitchen.

Jillian's world tilts on its axis. She glances at Lucille, but her face is void of any type of emotion. Who is this woman?

"Tucker," Jillian whispers, her voice barely audible. She clears her throat, forcing the words out. "Is Tucker all right?"

Sheriff Mato doesn't take her attention from Lucille. "There's going to be a manhunt for both Harper men, Jillian. I am sorry about that."

Jillian finds herself nodding, like she's preparing herself for the worst to come.

"Logan shot Rawlings tonight," Sheriff Mato says.

Lucille snorts. "It's about time," she mutters. "That man has been nothing but trouble from the beginning. We even had to come out here to clean up his mess." For a moment, the woman looks old and exhausted.

"We know where they're headed, it's only a matter of time before we have them in custody."

The room spins. Jillian grips the back of a chair, steadying herself. Tucker, a fugitive. Her fear a reality. How can this be happening?

A chilling sound breaks through her shock — Lucille's laughter. It's not hysterical or unhinged but calm and confident. "You'll never catch them," she says, her eyes glittering with a mix of pride and defiance. The network is vast, and they'll get to safety. You don't need to worry about them," she says to Jillian. "Tucker will be home soon; just wait and see."

Jillian stares at her mother-in-law, seeing her truly for the first time. *She's evil. Pure evil.*

Sheriff Mato's firm, official voice cuts through the tension. "Lucille Harper, you have the right to remain silent. Anything you say can and will be used against you in a court of law."

Jillian's attention is drawn to a movement on the stairs as the sheriff continues reciting the Miranda rights. Her heart clenches as she sees her mother standing there. But the small figure behind her makes Jillian's breath hitch.

Ethan. Jillian wants to rush to him, to shield him from this nightmare, but she's rooted to the spot.

"Mom?" Ethan's voice quivers. "What's happening?"

Kathy presses Ethan further behind her, but Jillian still sees his messy hair and flushed cheeks. The commotion must have woken him.

Jillian lies but hopes he doesn't hear it in her voice. "It's okay, sweetie. Everything's going to be fine. Go back to bed, all right?"

Ethan shakes his head. "Why is Grandma Lucille in handcuffs? Is she in trouble?"

Lucille's cold and jarring laugh fills the room. "Oh, Ethan, just like your father at that age, always asking questions, always seeing more than others think you understand."

Jillian's blood runs cold at Lucille's words.

"Ethan," she says, her voice firmer now, "go to your room. Now."

She waits until her mother has him back upstairs. Her mind races with what their future will hold, with questions of how she's failed to protect her son. How will she ever be able to explain that the people he loves the most are monsters?

CHAPTER FIFTY

Agent Meri Amber

The heart monitor's rhythmic beep cuts through the hospital room's silence. Her father lies still, tubes snaking from his arms, his chest rising and falling. His eyes are closed, his skin is pale, and it takes everything for Meri not to collapse.

Meri's mother, Evelyn, sits in a chair on the other side, perched on the edge of her seat, her hands gently rubbing her father's. Her normally neat bun is a mess with wisps of gray hair framing her weary face. The lights in the room cast harsh shadows, emphasizing the lines of worry.

"You didn't have to come, but I'm glad you're here. I've missed you, sweetheart. We both have." Her mom's voice is soft, barely audible above the hum of medical equipment.

Meri hesitates, her throat tightening. None of that matters right now. Nothing matters other than the present and her frail father lying in that hospital bed.

"Now, tell me what I tore you away from. Ever since you joined the FBI, you've been so busy. What case are you working right now? I'm stronger than you think I am," her mom says.

Meri hears the reproach in her voice, but she's not sure she should tell her, no matter what her mom says. Burdening her mother with more pain, bringing up the past at a time when the future seems bleak, now isn't the time.

"Meridith Amber, I'm serious. Give me something to focus on other than this, please." She waves her hand tiredly toward the bed.

"I've been looking for River's kidnapper." The words are ripped from Meri like a thorn stuck deep in a thumb. "Following leads, chasing ghosts."

Evelyn's eyes meet hers, a flicker of understanding passing between them. "And what did you find?"

Meri's hands clench in her lap. "Evidence that she's . . . gone. That she's been gone for a long time."

The words are heavy and final. Meri watches her mother, bracing for a breakdown, but Evelyn simply nods, a sad smile tugging at her lips.

"I've always known, deep down. Both your father and I knew," Evelyn whispers. "But you needed to find out for yourself. It's who you are, Meri. You've always needed to uncover the truth, no matter how painful."

Meri feels a lump forming in her throat, tears threatening to spill. Her mother's quiet acceptance is unsettling and unexpected.

"There's more," Meri says, leaning forward. "River . . ." She pauses, not sure how to say these next words. "River might have had a child, a daughter, before she . . . before she died."

Evelyn's eyes widen, a spark of life returning to her tired features. "A child? River's child?"

Meri nods, her mind racing with possibilities. "It's not certain, but we're looking into it. Well, Agent Lindsay is."

"You've never given up. I can't tell you how proud of you we both are," Evelyn says, her voice suddenly strong and resolute. She reaches across the bed, grasping Meri's hand. "You found your sister and she's coming home, just like you always promised."

A surge of determination mixing with the grief and uncertainty swirls inside her. She squeezes her mother's hand, then looks over at her father's unconscious form.

She promised she'd bring her sister home alive, and that's a promise she has to come to grips with breaking. But she found her niece, and that has to matter. That does matter.

She lays a hand on her father's arm and gives it a squeeze. She needs her father to wake up, to be okay, to be able to see that all the years searching for River hasn't been in vain.

She needs to hear her father's voice telling her he's proud of her too.

CHAPTER FIFTY-ONE

Meri's fingers trace the unfamiliar contours of her childhood dresser, now stripped of its once-vibrant stickers and teenage mementos. What was once her childhood bedroom is now a cute but non-descriptive guest room that feels more like a stranger's space than her own.

Returning home is never easy — too many memories reside within the walls, the old shabby carpets, the chipped bowls, and scuffed floors.

Her mom is downstairs cooking. Cooking is her stress reliever, and today's menu includes beef stew, homemade rolls, and a cinnamon coffee cake for dessert. Her father is doing better, but it will still be a few days before he's home, and her mom isn't sure what to do with herself, other than to feed Meri all her favorite meals.

Her phone buzzes, and Lindsay's name flashes on the screen. This is the call she's been anxiously waiting for. It kills her that she can't be there, in the middle of the action, but she's needed here, more. As Lindsay keeps reminding her, he has the best team at his side and she needs to trust him.

Meri's heart races as she answers. "What's happening?"

"I'm sending you a live link," Lindsay says. "You need to watch this now." His voice crackles with urgency.

She fumbles with her laptop, perching on the edge of the bed. The video loads, revealing a scene that makes her breath catch.

"That's the Red House?" Nothing like hiding in plain sight. It's a large red two-story Texan-style ranch house with a large, wide front balcony that's swarming with law enforcement.

"Oh my God," Meri whispers, leaning closer to the screen. She watches as young women are led out, some crying, others looking shell-shocked. "They're saving them."

The scene is chaotic, but she appreciates that Lindsay is letting her in on the action, even from this distance. It looks tense, not that she finds that surprising in the least. In the distance there's a convoy of unmarked SUVs with tinted windows, and a swarm of agents, dressed in tactical vests emblazoned with FBI and Homeland Security, move with precision, their weapons drawn, their voices firm but calm as they give orders. Some agents move to and from the house while others secure the perimeter.

A group of about six girls, looking dazed and terrified, are led out by agents. They are wrapped in blankets, their fingers clutching the edges tightly. Their steps are slow, and they are joined by female agents who walk beside them, offering quiet support. They look like kids, but she knows their ages could range anywhere from teenagers to young adults.

Meri leans in close to the screen, studying the faces, memorizing every detail.

"Look who we found when we arrived," Lindsay says, his call on speaker.

Her trained eyes scan the chaos, searching for familiar faces. Then she sees them — Logan and Tucker Harper, being led away in handcuffs. Tucker's face is a mask of defeat, his shoulders slumped. Logan looks calm. What does he know that they don't?

"Wait," she says, her voice tight. "That girl." She points to a person on the screen, then remembers Lindsay can't see her. "She's young, with long, dark hair partially obscuring her face, is she . . ." She looks exactly like River.

The young woman is holding a box. A box Meri recognizes. As she hands the box to a waiting agent, Meri notices the way her hands shake. She's got to be so scared.

Lindsay's voice is soft, almost reverent. "That's Lola, Meri. Your niece."

The world tilts on its axis. Meri stares at the screen, drinking in every detail of Lola's face. She sees echoes of her sister in the set of her jaw, the curve of her cheek. "She's alive," Meri breathes, tears stinging her eyes.

"She's alive." Lindsay confirms.

"That box, it's River's, isn't it?" Meri's hand trembles as she reaches out, touching the screen where Lola's image flickers. "Her last letter will be in there, along with her clothes and a . . ." She inhales sharply as an image surfaces in her mind. "There should also be a butterfly necklace." The weight of unspoken words, of years of searching, crashes down on her. "Lindsay, I need to see her. I need to read that letter."

"You will, I promise," Lindsay says. "How is your father?"

"Well enough that I can leave. I need to see her, Lindsay, I'm serious."

"You'll have flight details within the hour."

"What about the Harpers?" She keeps an eye on the screen and sees both men being led to two different police cruisers.

There's a long sigh. "You're not going to believe this . . ."

CHAPTER FIFTY-TWO

Jillian

The steady rhythm of a baseball smacking against leather gloves is all Jillian hears as she sits on her front porch, her attention torn between the scene before her and the silent phone in her lap.

Her dad's jovial laugh carries with the wind as Ethan makes a particularly impressive catch, jumping higher than the last time. His hair flies up with the movement, his cheeks glowing with happiness. It's good to see him smile. It's been a rare sight this past month and she's not sure how they would have survived all of this without her parents' support. Her father arrived in his newly purchased RV a few days after Lucille was hauled away in handcuffs.

That alone was a nightmare. To have a gun pulled on her, by someone she calls family, is something she still can't wrap her head around.

"Did you see that, Mom?" Ethan calls out, his voice cracking with excitement. "Grandpa says I might make the school team this year!"

Jillian pushes down the constant knot of anxiety in her stomach and gives him a wave. "That's great, bud," she calls back, her voice sounding hollow even to her own ears.

She glances down again at her phone, clicking the 'Home' button to see if there are any missed messages or phone calls, but Tucker is doing what he's done in the past . . . he's staying silent. She never thought she'd accept getting ghosted by her own husband, and yet here she is, maybe not quite accepting it, but definitely expecting it.

He'd begged for tonight to spend time with his son, taking him out for dinner in Great Falls, but where is he? Not here, that's for sure. Once again, she's the one who will bear the brunt of their son's disappointment. Once again, she'll be the one trying to find a plausible excuse.

Truth be told, she's okay if he doesn't come. The idea of Ethan leaving her side, even for a few hours, makes her want to throw up.

"Everything okay, sweetie?" her father asks, walking up to the porch with Ethan in tow. His face is tight with concern as he studies her in the way a parent does. Ever since he arrived, he's been her strength, her rock, the stability for her and Ethan, giving her space to feel, collapse, and fold within herself when needed.

And she's needed to do that a lot. Thank God her parents have been here.

Jillian swallows hard. "Tucker's running late," she says, glancing at her phone again. "He was supposed to be here twenty minutes ago."

She doesn't realize Ethan is standing behind her dad. His face falls, his earlier excitement gone. "He promised," Ethan says, his voice full of disappointment.

Jillian's heart sinks. She hates that she can't shelter him from all of this; that this is one more stain on his childhood he will never forget.

"I'm sure he's just stuck in traffic or something," Jillian says, arms open wide for him to crawl onto her lap. She ruffles his hair and checks to see if he believes her or not.

He doesn't. They both know there's no such thing as traffic in Shelby, Montana.

"Sure, traffic," Ethan mumbles, his face burrowed into her arm.

Her stomach clenches, twisting and turning as she holds her son in her arms. She hates that this is their life right now. Ever since that night when the Sheriff showed up and arrested Lucille, things haven't been right, and she knows Ethan senses it, no matter the plethora of excuses she gives him.

She's scared, furious, uncertain, distrustful, and all those feelings are directed toward herself and no one else.

She knew. She knew from the very beginning but she allowed herself to be swayed, blinded, and even fell in love despite all the red flags that were flashing right in front of her face. The chaos in her marriage is on her. The scars on her son's soul, that's on her too.

"Why don't you head inside and wash up?" Jillian plasters on another fake smile that's become all too familiar. "I'm sure your dad will be here any minute."

"Come on, kiddo," her dad says, ushering in a reluctant Ethan. "Maybe that grandma of yours is finished making those cookies for tomorrow, huh? Maybe we can sneak a few past her, what do you think?"

Jillian stays where she is, watching the empty road ahead of her.

"Where are you, Tucker?" she whispers, her fingers tightening around her silent phone. Her mind drifts back to the conversation that shattered her world a few weeks ago. Tucker's words echoing in her head, each syllable a fresh wound.

"I grew up harboring a dark family secret, one that I didn't want clouding our lives, one that I didn't want Ethan a part of. I made mistakes, a lot of them, but I've also been trying very hard to right those mistakes, too." He said everything and nothing at the same time, but she held her silence, giving him the opportunity to finally share whatever burden he carried on his own. "My grandfather owed some debts, and those debts became a family burden. All our troubles, all . . .

my troubles, have been because of mistakes my grandfather made." He angled his body toward her, their knees almost touching. Her mind working overtime as she tried to read between the lines of his confession.

"I need you to be clear, Tucker. Stop talking in riddles and just tell me what's going on." Her voice was calm. "Your mother pulled a gun on me, with our son upstairs, do you have any idea how that felt?"

"I'm not going to excuse my mom for what she did, nor will I forgive her, either." His voice brokered honesty, and she believed him. "Jill, I've been working with Homeland Security," he'd said, his gaze clouded with guilt and fear. He looked her straight in the eyes when he said the words, as if trying to prove he wasn't lying to her. "They promised no jail time if both my father and I testified against a sex trafficking ring he was forced to be a part of."

Her legs had given out. She'd collapsed onto the worn sofa, her vision blurring with tears as all her fears collided into one big giant hole. She had so many questions, had so many things she wanted to say, to scream and yell at him, to pound her fists against his chest in anger and fear, but only one word came out.

"Why?"

The question was directed as much to herself as to him. Why hadn't she listened to herself all those years ago? Why hadn't she trusted her own intuition? Why had she let herself fall in love with a man she knew deep down wasn't good?

Those are questions she'll probably never be able to answer. She'll also never be able to forgive herself, either.

She flinched when Tucker's hand reached out. "I was trying to protect you, Jill. You and Ethan and . . . I made a lot of mistakes, mistakes from even before Becky. I . . . had no choice. I need you to believe that. I was just a kid and the threat of what could happen if I said no always hung over me." His fists tightened. "I swore I would make it up to you when I fell in love with you, and that's exactly what I've been trying to do."

Looking back, she realizes he's never apologized for what he did to her friend. For what he did to her by lying to her for all these years, first, when she asked him if he knew Becky, and lately, when she told him she thought she'd seen her at the beginning of summer.

Now, as she waits for him, the weight of all their secrets presses down on her. She manages to get to her feet and moves to the porch railing where she leans down, gripping the weathered wood with her palms.

Since that night, she's had a lot of silent conversations with her husband, imagined discussions of what their next steps should be, of things that she wished she'd said but hadn't.

"Going back would mean not just forgiving him. It would be saying that what he did didn't matter anymore. Forgive and forget, right? I can't do that. What kind of message would that give our son? To Becky and all the other girls and women like her?" she whispers. Their marriage, their already fragile marriage, broke apart that night and there is no fixing it.

She'd made her decision. Now, she just has to make sure she's strong enough to live with it. Family means everything to her.

"Mom?" Ethan's voice breaks through her reverie. "Is Dad coming soon?"

Jillian turns, forcing a smile, and sees him standing in the doorway, a cookie in hand. "Soon, honey. I see you got that cookie, huh? How does it taste? How about you grab me one, too, please?"

She turns back to face the road, her fingers drumming along the wood. How much time does she give him before it becomes too late?

The screen door creaks open behind her and she's half expecting to see her son with another cookie in hand. Instead, it's her mom, carrying two glasses of iced tea. The crushed ice clinks softly against the sides, a cheery sound at odds with the tension thrumming through Jillian's body.

"Thought you could use a cold drink, sweetie," Kathy says, her voice gentle. She sets the glasses down on the porch railing, the condensation from the glasses dripping downward.

Jillian manages a weak smile. "Thanks, Mom."

The rumble of an engine cuts through the evening. Jillian's hand freezes, the glass halfway to her lips as Tucker's pickup truck pulls in, kicking up a small cloud of dust.

While Tucker parks and kills the engine, Jillian grips the railing with a tension that comes straight from her heart.

"Why don't I give you a minute and grab Ethan." Kathy gestures vaguely toward the house.

Jillian smiles. "Thanks, Mom." The truth is, she'd prefer to have Mom stay, to be her support, but she takes a deep breath — she's strong enough to do this on her own.

Tucker moves slower than usual, walking toward her, as if carrying an invisible weight. When he meets her gaze, the distance between them feels both vast and suffocating.

This is it. This is the last time they'll be together on this property. Tomorrow, she and Ethan embark on a road trip with her parents back to New York State, while Tucker stays here to pack up their belongings with a moving company. He'll follow shortly after, trusting TK to sell the property. The family business has folded, and Tucker is in the middle of canceling contracts that his parents had set into place to support the Red House and its owners. Or so he says. She wants to believe him, but ultimately, it's up to the authorities to keep him in line.

Seeing him, it's like a sugar spoon chipping away at the walls she's slowly cementing around her heart. Will it ever get easier? She loves him, she's always loved him, but now that love is infected with feelings of disgust, revulsion, and contempt. There's no balancing the scales, not now.

"Hey," he calls out, his voice carrying a forced casualness that makes Jillian's heart clench.

"Hey," she echoes, wondering how a single word can hold so much unspoken pain.

THE END

314

THANK YOU

Reader groups are amazing and I feel honored to be part of them.

I have to give a huge shoutout to my own reader group — Steena's Secret Society — for all your support and help. I've said it before and I say it again — I could not keep writing these books without you in my corner! Thank you! Amy Coats, thank you for being there, encouraging me, listening to me, giving me your thoughts as I wrote such a complex topic. Also, a big thank you to the following people from Readers Coffeehouse, another awesome reader group, who helped to breathe life into this book with me: Eileen O'Bryne Keane, Barbara L. Waloven, Judy Erwell, Crystal Jones, Cara Cantrell and Lindsay Ess and so many others.

Kate Lyall Grant, I'd share my chocolates with you any day! Thank you for helping to shape this idea into a story worth reading, for seeing the promise and potential and most of all, for believing in me.

Most of all, I want to give a huge shoutout to my husband: you were the first to encourage me to follow my passion and you are always there, making sure I continue to pursue my passion and write my stories. I love you.

THE JOFFE BOOKS STORY

We began in 2014 when Jasper agreed to publish his mum's much-rejected romance novel and it became a bestseller.

Since then we've grown into the largest independent publisher in the UK. We're extremely proud to publish some of the very best writers in the world, including Joy Ellis, Faith Martin, Caro Ramsay, Helen Forrester, Simon Brett and Robert Goddard. Everyone at Joffe Books loves reading and we never forget that it all begins with the magic of an author telling a story.

We are proud to publish talented first-time authors, as well as established writers whose books we love introducing to a new generation of readers.

We won Trade Publisher of the Year at the Independent Publishing Awards in 2023 and Best Publisher Award in 2024 at the People's Book Prize. We have been shortlisted for Independent Publisher of the Year at the British Book Awards for the last five years, and were shortlisted for the Diversity and Inclusivity Award at the 2022 Independent Publishing Awards. In 2023 we were shortlisted for Publisher of the Year at the RNA Industry Awards, and in 2024 we were shortlisted at the CWA Daggers for the Best Crime and Mystery Publisher.

We built this company with your help, and we love to hear from you, so please email us about absolutely anything bookish at feedback@joffebooks.com.

If you want to receive free books every Friday and hear about all our new releases, join our mailing list here: www.joffebooks.com/freebooks.

And when you tell your friends about us, just remember: it's pronounced Joffe as in coffee or toffee!